THE QUIGLEY MISSION

A DANNY QUIGLEY ACTION NOVEL

E.J. RUSS MCDEVITT

The Quigley Mission:
A Danny Quigley Action Novel

ISBN-13: 978-0-9734902-3-7

DEDICATION

I am dedicating this book to my wife Marie for her ongoing support and encouragement, to my daughter Lynn Ouellette for her suggestions on plot strategy, Grandson Jon Carey for his massive time investment in editing, and Michele Rutland in France for her intuitive review.

www.russmcdevitt.com

CHAPTER 1.

30 MONTHS PREVIOUS.
BASRA, IRAQ.

The first puff of wind followed by some grains of sand from the street below flicked across his face. He swore.

A sniper's nightmare!

Danny Quigley inched back from the roof of the mud building and spoke into his attached throat mike.

"Cobra One, this is Striker One, did you catch that weather shift? Over"

"Roger that, Striker One. If they don't come soon you won't get that distance shot, and the bastards will be right on top of us. Want to abort? I can call it in, if you like. They can send the gun-ships in. Over."

"Negative, Cobra One. They want to make sure we take him out. Give it a bit longer. It's a one-time chance to get this guy. Think of all the lads he's killed with those roadside bombs he's put together, over."

"Roger that. I'll warn the extraction team to be ready, just in case. Over and out."

Danny eased back to the edge of the rooftop and cautiously peered over. Apart from some of the citizens of Basra, dashing around and closing windows against the incoming storm, the road out of town, stretching five hundred yards, was empty of vehicular traffic.

He checked the sights on his Heckler and Koch 7.62-mm, PSGI snipers rifle set for five hundred yards. Not a really difficult shot for a trained sniper, but throw in a rising wind with increasing sand density, a moving vehicle, and the odds start to ramp up. He began to wonder if he should have kept his spotter with him, rather than position him on the edge of town to alert him when the terrorists arrived.

It still looked possible.

All it needed now was for the convoy of terrorists from across the Iranian border to roll into Basra, and one cunning bomb maker would be playing with his 70 virgins that night.

Military intelligence had learned from an informer that the Iranian would be visiting Basra to attack the Iraqi army contingent, now that the Brits had turned the city over to them. In the ensuing change over, the British sniper's section had been moved to Afghanistan.

Danny Quigley, as part of a four man Special Air Service team (SAS), had been flown out from the U.K. via Turkey and Baghdad, to handle the mission. The operational briefing had taken place on the flight out.

Danny had completed the prestigious U.S. Marine Corps snipers' course during his first years transfer to the SAS regiment, and had been tapped for the mission. The unit had been transported down from Baghdad to Basra in a chopper, which landed in the street outside. In the deliberate confusion of the blowing sand and noise from the chopper blades, Danny and Scotty McGregor, call sign 'Cobra One', had disappeared into some pre-arranged safe houses belonging to relatives of the Iraqi military.

A third team member, call sign 'Watchman', normally the sniper's spotter, was posted on the edge of town. He was in possession of the most recent picture of the Iranian, Mohammed Al Sudabi. On identifying the target, Watchman would contact Danny and inform him of the vehicle and the target's position in the convoy.

That was the weakness in the plan.

The occupants could have their faces covered or be wearing masks. With the rising sand storm, that was more than likely. The short notice of the Iranian bomb maker's imminent arrival meant that the SAS team had to rely on the ready made assault plan, without the opportunity to thoroughly examine it and challenge it in the usual SAS fashion.

Scotty was positioned on a rooftop fifty yards back on the opposite side of the street from Danny's position. He was armed with a U.S. 5.56-M16A1 assault rifle fitted with a 40-mm M205 grenade launcher, to take out some of the terrorist vehicles. It was assumed that the terrorists would more than likely continue speeding down the street, seeking revenge after the attack.

The plan was for Danny to exit his position after the kill, and join the fourth member of the team, waiting in a jeep in a makeshift garage across from Scotty's position. Further out, two U.S. Apache helicopter gunships, each carrying eight Hellfire anti tank missiles, were on standby to strafe the terrorists' convoy as they tried to withdraw.

The Iraqi military would immediately throw up roadblocks around the city to net any escaping terrorists.

Like many an operation in the past, all they could do now was to wait, while the rising wind and sand started to make a mockery of their plans.

Danny's radio sputtered.

"Striker One, this is Watchman. Convey approaching. Six vehicles in all.

No visual on personnel as yet. Two hundred yards away. Approaching fast. Doing approximately sixty miles per hour. Wait One for ID. Over and out."

"Roger that, Watchman. Cobra One, did you get that, over?" he asked Scotty.

"Roger that, Striker One. Over and out."

Danny looked through the telescopic sight, tightening his hold on the wooden pistol grip as he rested his jaw against the adjustable cheek rest. It was already sighted for the five hundred yard shot, but he knew that he would have to compensate for the increased wind velocity. The swirling sand was already blurring the end of the street, where he expected the terrorist convoy to appear at any moment.

His radio burst into life.

"Striker One this is Watchman. Not sure on ID. Faces covered. Only clue, front passenger in vehicle number 2 waved to the vehicle behind which pulled into a side street. Could indicate that he's the top 'raghead'. Watch for the jeep that pulled off. May be approaching from a parallel street. Over."

"Roger that, Watchman. Striker One out."

At that moment the terrorist's convoy came tearing into view at the top of the street.

Danny sighted in on the first vehicles and groaned as he grappled with the rapidly decreasing vision. Difficult, but still worth a shot, he thought.

He lifted the rifle slightly and tried to steady the sights in on the passenger in the 2nd vehicle. He shifted his stance as he followed the target, feeling the sweat break out on his brow.

It was now or never. He had to take the shot.

He breathed in deeply, and as he let the air out, continued to track the target, and gently squeezed the trigger.

A hit!

The terrorist was thrown sideways, disappeared out the door of the vehicle, and thumped in a cloud of dust, into the street. Then all hell broke loose.

Danny quickly moved the rifle to the first vehicle and took a measured shot at its passenger.

Another hit.

He emptied the five shot magazine quickly but carefully across the other vehicles. In the swirling sand he wasn't sure if he had caught any of the other occupants. The remaining terrorist vehicles were now tearing down the center of the street, firing left and right at the top of the buildings. One of the vehicles exploded in front of Danny's position.

Scotty had the grenade launcher in operation.

Bullets raked across the rooftop in Danny's direction, tearing off scraps of mud, wood and metal.

Time to get out.

Slinging the sniper rifle over his shoulder, he reached into his pack for the U.S. Ingram 9-mm MAC 10 submachine gun, with its two taped 30 round magazines.

He sprang for the door leading to the stairs. Immediately a hail of fire greeted him from below and he flopped back away from the opening.

The ground floor was supposed to be held by three Iraqi army regulars.

Betrayal, or had they been taken out by some locals in league with the terrorists?

No time to speculate. He had to get out, and fast, or this could turn into a total disaster.

The SAS, like General Patton, believed in attack using awesome firepower where possible.

Danny reached into his pack and withdrew two hand grenades. Sitting on the roof of a mud brick building, meant what he planned to do was risky. It could bring the whole building down. He pulled the pins and tossed the grenades down the stairs. Shouts of alarm sounded below. There was an almighty thump and the building suddenly shook as they exploded. The stairs had disappeared and there was a huge swirl of dust and debris below. Danny swung his legs over the opening then jumped down into it, hoping for a firm landing. He hit the ground rolling. Bullets ripped sideways at him from a nearby room.

As he barely moved the Ingram, he fired a short burst in the direction of the shots. Screams greeted him.

He lunged to his feet, sprayed with the Ingram on both sides, and headed towards the back door. He was aware of a number of dead and injured people sprawled out on the floor, some wearing Iraqi army uniforms. Automatically, he kept pumping bullets to all corners of the room. Pausing briefly to flip to the second magazine taped to the empty one, he took stock of his situation. Sporadic fire was still coming at him and the back door had already been blown flat. Diving through, doing a forward roll and hosing the Ingram left and right, he came back onto his feet. He glimpsed fleeting shapes and savage turbaned faces, swinging weapons towards him. As if in a slow moving dream, he cut a swathe through them, firing left and right, and kept running. Bullets were flicking around him. How could they be missing him? he wondered.

He felt almost invulnerable, as if wrapped in a protective bubble …. probably the last thought most people had in that position, before they got killed!

At one point he threw two more grenades, but didn't wait for the results. He hared off down the side of some mud houses, firing at dark shadows and anything that moved. Coming close to where the extraction vehicle was supposed to be, he started shouting:

"Quigley coming through. Quigley coming through!"

There was a shout back.

"What the hell kept you Danny?"

Scotty had made it across the street as well. He clawed his way on board and sprawled inside. In seconds the driver tore straight off towards the open desert. They knew that their spotter would be doing the same. Danny and Scotty kept up a continuous fire on any movement to the left and right of the vehicle, as they raced away.

Their driver, Trooper Larkin, shouted back at them.

"Choppers are incoming. Best put some distance between us and them. They will hose down anything moving. Let's get back to our rendezvous point and wait for the result to come in."

CHAPTER 2.

It was a good result.

The Iranian bomb-maker had been taken down with a sniper's bullet.

The complete terrorist convoy had been eliminated. The house, whose roof Danny had been perched on, contained seven bodies, three of them Iraqi soldiers. The bodies of a further five terrorists were strewn around the building, killed by shrapnel and bullets. Scotty had taken out two vehicles with their occupants. The Apache choppers had shredded the rest of the terrorist group and their vehicles.

The SAS team were flown back the shorter route into Kuwait, where they were treated with a certain amount of awe and respect by the Americans who normally used their Seal and Delta teams for special operations. The Brits, of course, knew about the SAS and what they were capable of.

Military airports were even more chaotic than their civilian counterparts. That meant long waits, getting bumped by people with more urgent priorities and senior ranks.

They got back five days later to the U.K., to their base at Credenhill in Hereford, tired and wrung out from the mission. As they clambered wearily out of the vehicle, a Corporal Davidson from administration clapped Danny on the shoulder.

"Major Wainwright wants to see you."

"Yeah, yeah, the usual debrief bullshit" said Danny, starting to push past him.

Henderson gripped his arm.

"The debrief is later. The Major wants to see you right now Danny, in his office."

7

"Me alone? What about the team?"

"Just you mate, and he means right now."

Danny threw his pack to Scotty.

"Here take care of this. The Major wants to see me a.s.a.p. I'll catch up with you later."

Major Wainwright stood up when Danny came through his office door. Rank was rather casually observed in Special Forces where respect was earned out in the field. His CO fell into that category, having operated with Danny on various missions.

"Great work in Basra, Trooper Quigley. Intelligence are delighted, I'm told. That bomb-maker has constructed his last IED for starters, and the rest of his team are eliminated. Now, I know we usually give you a break after an op like this, and the other lads in the team will get one. However, something has come up that we believe could make use of some of your other talents."

"We?" Danny queried.

At that moment, the door behind Wainwright opened and a tall man dressed in U.S. military uniform stepped through. He wore the rank of a Lieutenant Colonel, with military police flashes.

Danny felt himself tense.

The Colonel noticed and grinned.

"I have that effect on soldiers. Usually with good reason."

Wainwright smiled too.

"Trooper Quigley I'd like you to meet Colonel Bob Kokaski. He's CO of the U.S. military police presence here in the U.K. Colonel, Trooper Danny Quigley. As I mentioned, he's just back from a hugely successful mission in Iraq."

They shook hands, studying each other.

The American was big, but fit and hard looking as well, his tight brush cut, giving him a prize-fighter's appearance. Probably around age 40, Danny thought, and a career soldier, from the ribbons he wore.

He also knew that he probably was showing the signs of someone who had just come off a stressful mission.

Danny was just under six feet tall, with a hard lean body and a piratical hawk-like face. He wore his black hair long and had a short beard which Special Forces in Afghanistan grew to blend in on missions up in the mountainous ranges leading into Pakistan. Danny's piercing blue eyes observed the American carefully.

Major Wainwright coughed, and sat forward.

"Danny, the Colonel knows that other ranks and Commissioned Officers relate on a pretty informal basis in our unit, so we'll proceed on that basis."

He pulled two chairs forward.

"Why don't we all sit down for this little chat. Now, you may know that the U.S. military have started bringing troops back from Iraq and Afghanistan to the U.K. for R&R. Most of them are American marines and their parachute regiments."

"Tough bastards" the Colonel interjected.

Wainwright continued.

"They are basing them mainly in the barracks at Aldershot. At least the ones who can't afford to fly their wives over from the States. Those guys just rent a cheap hotel up in London, and shack up for the duration, and cause no problems."

He glanced at Kokaski.

"It's some of the rest of them that are causing you problems, right Colonel?"

"Yeah, problems is probably a mild word for it" he sighed, pursing his lips, as he sat back, looking at Danny.

"Here's the thing. These guys have been on three, four and even more tours in Iraq and Afghanistan. A lot of them have had their marriages break up as a result. Some are kinda punch drunk and screwed up from their active duty. Post-traumatic stress, from seeing their buddies and civilians blown to pieces every day, and every time they step out on patrol, various factions are trying to kill them. I understand you've been there and know what I'm talking about."

Danny nodded.

"How does this involve me Colonel? Iraq is winding down anyway, so that should ease the pressure of having to fight two wars."

"Well yes, President Obama, as promised, pulled us back out of the major combat role, but we still have a training and protection role to fulfill. The President has taken up the Afghanistan war as one of his priorities, and is rolling more troops over there, a lot of them straight from Iraq."

Danny shook his head.

"Okay, there's some good things happening in Afghanistan, but it's not a winnable war, in the sense of how we view winning."

The Colonel grinned.

"I wish you'd speak to the Secretary of Defense. He thinks we can win it. I'd love to kick it around with you over a beer some time. However, right now, my problem is one of discipline. Some of our lads on R&R up in Aldershot, are becoming uncontrollable. They go out to local pubs and pick fights with anyone who looks sideways at them."

Danny looked puzzled.

"What about your military police? You guys have whole battalions of them, pretty hard men and specially trained in unarmed combat, from what I've seen and heard."

The American sighed.

"That was right five years ago, and then Abu Ghraib happened. The name Military Police became a dirty word. It used to be an automatic entre to any civilian police force back home. The smart ones saw the writing on the wall and got out the first chance they had, with no 're-ups', and unfortunately it was the good ones who left. Since Iraq and Afghanistan, we've become strictly prison guards. No real police work or time off for some of those criminal investigation courses that used to make us attractive to the civilian police market. We now have to rely more and more on reservists who don't have the training, or in many cases the attitude or temperament, to handle highly trained troops. Remember, our guys have been in action and have worked on their unarmed combat skills because their lives could depend on it. My MP's just can't handle them!"

Danny leaned forward impatiently, the accumulated stress and tiredness of the mission starting to creep up on him.

"Colonel, I still haven't the faintest clue why I'm here. Sure, it sounds like you have problems, but you'd be better having this conversation with the Chief Constable in Berkshire, or your own Provost Marshall, if you have such a figure. With respect, I need to get back and shut my eyes for about sixteen hours."

His voice showed his increasing impatience.

Wainwright cut in.

"Danny, we both appreciate how you feel, and if it was me, I'd be getting pretty pissed off right about now. Give the Colonel another five minutes and he'll have painted the whole picture for you and what he was hoping you could help with. Okay?"

Danny was unimpressed.

"Yeah, let's cut to the quick Colonel. I've run out of juice."

The Colonel stood up and started pacing as he talked.

"Okay, messaged received Danny. Now here's the thing, our MP's have been doing joint patrols with British MP's, the redcaps, around Aldershot, and policing the trouble spots. That's two U.S. MP's and two British redcaps. They recently responded to calls for assistance to some local pubs and had a second back up team with them. One of those pubs has become the watering hole of the marines, and another, the parachute brigade. In both of those establishments, the joint patrols were beaten up, manhandled, and tossed out into the street."

Danny looked startled.

"Eight MP's couldn't handle some trouble in a pub? I can't believe it! So what's happening now?"

"Believe it," the Colonel said, slapping the table in frustration. "Effectively the pubs have become no-go areas, and right now we don't respond to any calls for assistance."

"What about the civilian police? Surely they'd get involved, wouldn't they?" Danny asked.

"Ha, you'd think so wouldn't you? I've had it on good authority that unless someone's been murdered, the civilian cops just pull over to the side of the road for twenty minutes and then roll up when the ruckus is over and the assailants gone back to barracks. The Chief Constable says it's an American problem, and they don't want the hassle and expense of charging U.S. servicemen in British courts."

Wainwright jumped in.

"The good news is that the whole problem has been caused by virtually a small bunch of men. There's no doubt these guys are tough and well trained. Some are graduates of karate schools back home, judo or boxing, and of course have their unarmed combat training. This applies to both the marines and the parachute regiment. A few really hard men who now have a following, and who don't give a shit about military discipline. May even want to get kicked out of the Forces. We can supply you with names, backgrounds, and pictures of these people Danny."

"To do what exactly?" Danny asked, looking increasingly frustrated.

"Danny, I know your skills. When it comes to unarmed combat, it's like you have some sort of in-built computer. You anticipate an opponent's move even before he thinks about it. You have incredible upper body strength and when you strike with your hands, you either disable or break bones. On top of that, your judo, karate and akido training, gives you great variety in your fighting skills. To cut to the chase, we want you to head up a special MP patrol to take these ringleaders down. Not just to arrest them, but to humiliate them in front of their mates or buddies, as the Colonel would call them. That's the only way that we can see, to nip this in the bud before the British Government is asked by the locals in Aldershot, or the Chief Constable, to cancel all future R&R to the U.K. for U.S. Forces."

Danny stood up.

"Thanks gentlemen, but I'll pass. There's no way I'm going to go up against troops that have gone through hell over in Iraq and Afghanistan. I've been there. I know what they've come through. And now you want to unleash me on them like some sort of Doberman Pincer? Well, pardon me all to hell sirs, thanks but no thanks!"

As he turned to go, the American caught him lightly by the arm.

"Danny, I commend you for your views, and I agree totally with them. I tell my guys all the time to hold back and give the troops every bit of slack they can, bearing in mind that we still have to have discipline to run the military. Here's the brunt of it Danny. For 98% of the troops, R&R here in the U.K. has been a godsend. They can chill out in an English speaking country, where no one is trying to kill them on a daily basis. Quite a few marriages have been saved by guys flying their wives over for a short reunion. A number go up to London or over to Stratford for the plays, or even fly up to Scotland for a few days, not to mention your golf clubs, which have opened their doors to our boys. Now all this is being put at risk by, at the most, a dozen hard-asses: people who, quite frankly, have turned into bullies. Quite dangerous bullies as it happens, because of their skills in unarmed combat. We just want you to take those few trouble-makers down in front of their followers, and we believe that could nip the whole thing in the bud. We'll give you every support you need, and set it up any way you want. Will you at least give it some thought Danny?"

Danny looked from one to the other, then held both his hands up in front of them as if for their inspection.

"Just how far do you want me to go with these hard-asses Colonel?"

He looked startled.

"What do you mean?"

Danny held his hands up.

"These hands are trained to kill any individual I have to take on. Tell me, just how many body bags do you want before you nip this thing in the bud?"

"For Christ's sake Danny, we don't want you to kill any of them!"

Danny lowered his arms to his sides.

He nodded to Wainwright.

"Tell him Major."

"I think what Danny's saying Colonel, and this didn't occur to me earlier, but when he's in the thick of battle, he's focused on inflicting the maximum damage possible in the shortest time. It's a highly trained survival mode, and difficult for him to notch it down to your military police arrest procedure. You know, using as much force as is deemed necessary for the situation, and all that stuff."

Danny turned and left the room without a further word.

The two officers sat looking at each other. Finally, the Colonel stirred.

"Well that's that Major. I certainly didn't want any fatalities from this particular exercise. What a pity, he's one impressive guy. He might have pulled it off."

"If anyone could, it would be Quigley. It may not be a lost cause just yet. The guy's on his uppers right now. I'll give him a weekend pass and talk to him again. He's a chap who loves a challenge, and particularly martial arts. When on leave he goes off to dojos in Korea and Japan to train with the best."

"And presumably doesn't leave his opponents dead on the mat," the Colonel said thoughtfully. "Come on Major Wainwright, laying it on a bit thick back there, weren't we? Bodies of American service men strewn all around Aldershot? Let's get real!"

Wainwright chuckled.

"Where Quigley is concerned I never exaggerate. He's a walking killing machine, and no two ways about it. But could he tamp it down enough to achieve what you want, and take those hard asses down in front of their peers? Interesting thought. You know Colonel, it might be worth my while to have another word with Danny. I know him quite well and what makes him tick. If I present a clearly defined strategy to him, with boundaries on how far he should go with those troublemakers, he might buy into it. Of course he'd have to get a decent shave and haircut to be an army redcap. How does that sound Colonel?"

"As long as he doesn't ease back on those guys, because of his sympathy towards them, and end up getting himself hurt. Remember, they back each other up, and it's not a dojo exercise after all, where certain rules are established. Tell you what Major, just the way Quigley moves, I wouldn't want him coming after me, and I've taken down some hard men in my day...... but sure, why not? Have another go at Quigley and come back to me."

CHAPTER 3.

First Lieutenant Naomi Richards of the U.S. military police detachment, U.K. contingent, hated her red hair. How can a policewoman expect to be taken seriously, disciplining soldiers, when they keep glancing at her hair? Especially when it keeps bursting out from under her cap, regardless of how she crams it under. She had gorgeous hazel eyes, and the clearly defined features of a top model didn't help either. Okay, she was a fit five foot eight inches and looked the part in her military uniform, but she wished that she came across as tougher and meaner, rather than as an attractive female. Especially now, that she had been selected for some sort of 'shock' joint military police patrol, to tackle rising violence in the local pubs involving some tough U.S. military units.

Her, as part of some shock patrol!

She sat in the waiting room of her military police commander, shaking her head, sending a few more strands of hair tumbling down out of her cap. In frustration, she tried to shove them back under, just as the secretary looked across at her.

"You can go inside now Lieutenant."

Naomi smiled her thanks and, standing, straightened her uniform and strode to the door, knocked twice and stepped inside.

The first person she saw was her C.O., Colonel Bob Kokaski, who was already on his feet waiting to greet her. Beside him stood Bob Kilroy, a lean lanky Texan who she already knew as a U.S. military police captain. The third man was a tall, hard looking individual, wearing a U.K. military police redcap uniform.

The Colonel cleared his throat.

"Lieutenant, I'd like to introduce you to Sergeant Danny Quigley who is heading up this disciplinary joint military police patrol, to sort out the little problem we've been having in the local pubs."

She was starting to look at Sergeant Quigley, but her head shot back to her CO.

"Little problem sir? All our patrols are suspended at present. I wouldn't call that little!" She glanced around the room.

"Just the two of us? I mean who else is involved sir? Those guys out there are mean and tough, and with respect, our guys don't particularly like British redcaps telling them what to do."

Captain Kilroy cut in.

"I've been trying to tell the Colonel just that, but he insists that Sergeant Quigley here can handle it. Some sort of rambo, I'm told. If I had my way I'd…"

"Yes, yes Captain Kilroy. We've already been over that and you've made your feelings clear. If your guys had been up to the job in the first place, we wouldn't have this problem."

The Colonel looked apologetically at the Lieutenant.

"Slight difference of opinion here as you can see. Captain Kilroy's solution is to descend on the establishments with a massive force of MP's and literally tear the places apart. Unfortunately, the static from that kind of operation would blow up in the media, and questions would be raised in the British House of Commons about the wisdom of continuing the policy of using the U.K. for R&R purposes."

The Lieutenant flicked her eyes sideways at the Sergeant, who stood there observing her.

"So what is Sergeant Quigley proposing then?" she asked, eying him up and down.

She noticed a slight flicker of amusement cross his features.

"I'll fill you in later Lieutenant. Suffice to say that Captain Kilroy's role is to mop up after us. Make sure the ambulances are there in good time and so on."

She looked around helplessly.

"Mop up after us? Ambulances? Am I missing something here? And why me, a woman? I would have thought you would have a dozen big jocks on a so called 'shock patrol' sir."

The Colonel grinned.

"Sergeant Quigley requested a woman. You can ask him later as to why. Now, Captain Kilroy is taking you for a briefing to acquaint both of you with the troublemakers and some background on them. Oh, by the way, Sergeant Quigley is in total charge of this operation and is answerable to me directly. He will, of course, show you the proper respect due to your rank. Now, the operation starts tonight so you three have a lot to cover. Good luck."

CHAPTER 4.

Shadows were falling when Danny swung into the parking lot of the female quarters just outside Aldershot.

As he expected, Lieutenant Naomi Richards was already waiting and jumped quickly into the military police jeep. He glanced approvingly at her smart appearance then, saying nothing, swung the jeep around and sped back out onto the main road.

It was she who broke the silence.

"You never got around to telling me why you wanted a woman as a partner, Sergeant Quigley."

"No I didn't, did I? Well, it's partly psychology. These are tough, mean bastards who've seen action and will be expecting a really heavy reaction from military authorities. Imagine how disconcerted they'll be when we two stroll in, and afterwards, when we've sorted them out, how are they going to explain it to their mates, their buddies as you call them - being sorted out by a lone redcap and a U.S. policewoman? The Colonel wants them taken down a peg or two, humiliated, in his words."

"So, I'm sort of like a prop really. I just pirouette around the bar and the marines and para troops will turn into friendly lap dogs? Come on Sergeant, get real! Those guys will eat us alive! They've already chewed up a bundle of our MP's."

Danny chuckled.

"You could be right Lieutenant. Now I already explained what I want you to do, once we're inside."

She shook her head in exasperation.

"Stay out of your way, basically, is how you put it."

He glanced sideways at her.

"Look, in simple terms, I have a job to do and I'm good at it. I don't want to lose my focus by having to go to your rescue if some of those hairy assed troops start putting a beating on you. Your main value is the uncertainty and distraction our entry will create. Understood?"

"Yeah, understood Sergeant. Why am I carrying this military police billie then?"

"It's standard dress Lieutenant. We don't want them to start thinking things through too much."

She nodded morosely.

"I sure miss that 9 millimeter we carried around overseas. It's a great leveler when you're a woman."

"Not just when you're a woman Lieutenant.... shit!"

The mobile phone on the seat rang shrilly.

Danny grabbed it, hit the on button and put it up to his ear.

"Yeah?"

He could hear the voice clearly.

"We got trouble starting here. Can you come quick?"

"Where are you calling from?" he demanded.

"The Plumed Partridge…it's getting ugly."

Danny rang off and put his foot to the floor, sending the jeep flying forward.

"It's those damned marines! Nice idea giving the barman a direct link phone to us. Get on to Kilroy and have him get the backup in place. We're only a few minutes away, so let's rock and roll."

CHAPTER 5.

Corporal 'Buzz' Edwards had been a car mechanic in Charleston, North Carolina, when two things happened at once: his wife divorced him, and the garage he worked in closed down. His latest bad luck in his job made it a lucky day for the recruitment sergeant in the mall. He accosted 'Buzz' and his buddy 'Loop' Kelly as, glassy eyed, they weaved their way from a nearby drinking club.

Before they knew it, they were being shipped out to basic training in the Marine Corps and six months of hell.

Surprisingly, they both survived. More surprisingly, they adapted to military life and even came to regard the Marine Corps as their family.

Iraq was a shock and a baptism of fire, but the hardness layered up in them and they learned to survive mentally and physically. They became competent at their trade…. killing, but inside they were still small men, and they hated civilians.

'Buzz' particularly associated his lifetime of bad luck to the 'fucking civvies' and was involved in a number of questionable shootings of civilians in Iraq. After Abu Ghraib, the U.S. military were running scared of any further scandals and swept the rumors of unwarranted violence under the carpet.

In Aldershot, England, Corporal 'Buzz' Edwards, awaiting a transfer to Afghanistan, had gathered a small group of disenchanted troublemakers around him, including his buddy 'Loop' Kelly.

He still didn't like civilians and he particularly hated the English 'limeys' and their abrasive accents.

Now he towered over two men who had come in to the bar 15 minutes previously.

He was surrounded by six of his buddies including 'Loop' who stood grinning expectantly, at what they knew was about to happen.

The two civilians had swiveled around in their seats, looking nervously at the group of Americans who had closed in around them. 'Buzz' clamped a rough hand on one their shoulders.

"Well, well, looky here boys. A couple of queers have wandered into our pub. Someone should have told them this is strictly for U.S. marines, not limp-wristed faggots."

One of the civilians thrust his head forward.

"We're not queer, we're both married and have kids. Furthermore, myself and my family have been coming here for hundreds of years. You're just a bunch of blow-ins, as far as us locals are concerned."

'Buzz' crinkled up his face in amazement and turned to his crowd of supporters.

"Hear that lads? Blow-ins, he called us, and us out saving civilization while these limey bastards, sit here on their asses."

He turned and viciously slapped the man's face twice, sending him crashing back against the bar. At the same time four of the marines grabbed hold of the two men as "Buzz' and 'Loop' started beating them.

The first time 'Buzz' became aware that something was wrong was when the shouts of encouragement from the rest of the contingent of marines, suddenly stopped and he heard a loud English voice behind him.

"Well, so this is what the great American marines are reduced to in their time off, thumping untrained and helpless civvies who can't fight back. 'Buzz', why don't you pick on someone your own size."

'Buzz' turned and saw a tall British redcap standing, smiling and relaxed in front of him….. alone, apart from a female First Lieutenant, leaning back casually against the door.

He was still trying to compute the situation in his mind, hearing a redcap speaking his name, as he started to swing a punch. Danny caught hold of his arm and broke it, carrying on with a brutal side chop to his nose that sent a crimson torrent of blood down his clothing. 'Loop' started moving to his rescue, but a heavy boot crunched into his right knee, breaking it also and sending him collapsing onto the floor, howling in pain.

A fist skidded off Danny's shoulder as he turned slightly, thumping a clenched fist back into the crotch of the assailant. He heard him scream as he hooked his legs and sent him flying into the path of two marines, who launched themselves at him. A pair of arms wrapped around him from behind and someone started firing punches at him from the front. Danny swiveled sideways, wrapping his right arm around the man's back, and locked him into a high hip throw, slamming him to the ground. At the same time, he dropped straight down with his knee on the man's rib cage, hearing it crack. A boot came swinging at his face as he started to get back up. He blocked it with crossed arms, using it as a lever to get fully back on his feet, and kicked savagely at the man's crotch, following it with a jaw- breaking elbow strike. Another marine leapt from the bar swinging a bottle at him. Danny blocked it and spun the man around into the start of a strangle hold, hurling him backwards into the metal bar rail with a satisfying thud. In his peripheral vision he saw a figure swinging a pool cue at his head and managed to step backwards in time to avoid it. As the man overbalanced, Danny gave him a viscous head butt that made him collapse to the floor, spouting blood.

Suddenly aware of the sound of further blows, he turned and stared in astonishment at the First Lieutenant, who had used her club most effectively, de-mobilizing two further marines who had rushed forward to join the fray. All he could do was to give her a mini salute. She grinned and tilted her head.

Nine men lay groaning and screaming on the floor of the establishment. The rest of the marines stood back.

Just then the door of the pub burst open and Captain Kilroy and a group of MPs came charging into the room. He stopped in amazement and looked at the scene.

"Good God, Quigley! What did you do to these guys? It looks like you ran over them with a tank!"

Danny strolled across.

"I think they've picked on their last civilian for starters. Bullies eventually get their comeuppance. Oh, I had some help from the First Lieutenant there. She whacked those two who decided to join the fun."

He started moving towards the door.

"We have to get back on patrol. Let's go Lieutenant."

As Danny, followed by Naomi, pushed through the door, a number of medics arrived with stretchers.

She shook her head, running to keep up with him.

"When you laid on the ambulances Danny, I actually thought that you and I would be the first two people on them."

He threaded his way through the growing throng of military police and medics and jumped into the jeep. When Naomi climbed into the passenger side he tapped her shoulder.

"Hey, well done back there with the club. That was nice work. Where did you learn to do that?"

"My dad was a New York policeman. No one can match them for using a club to subdue a perp. He showed me how when I joined the military police. Speaking of which Danny, where did you learn to wreak such havoc on highly trained military personnel?"

He grinned.

"Danny is it already? Well I guess the Colonel warned you I wasn't much for acknowledging rank, so I'll just call you Naomi for the duration. Let's go and have a cup of tea and I may share a little of my background. Oh and by the way, I'm not a sergeant. I'm a lowly trooper. They just gave me a temporary rank for the operation."

"Yes, that cup of tea sounds great. I'm dying to find out just who and what you are."

She found out very little, but Danny learned some details of her life-married for four years to a career military person, now posted to Afghanistan. No children and little chance of having them as they had barely spent eighteen months together since their marriage, with cross postings for both of them.

Danny caught a sense of her vulnerability when she shared her situation, her lip quivering slightly, and the way she averted her eyes.

"I don't even know if we can ever be together again in the same way. I've changed, I know he's changed, and when he's away on operations, I barely hear from him and then it's a tight lipped message with very little intimacy."

Danny sipped his tea thoughtfully, looking at her. God, she was beautiful, he thought, with her burnished red hair and finely honed features.

He couldn't see how any man could go away and forget her for very long.

"Yeah, the military is tough on marriages Naomi. We have the same problem in the British army. By the way, what does your husband do in the military?"

She looked at him carefully.

"I'm not supposed to say this, but he's a Seal, and right now he's on a prolonged operation in Afghanistan. The only reason I mention it is that you're one of them, aren't you?"

He sat forward, startled.

"A Seal? Good God no. That is strictly a U.S. force. What made you say that?"

"Well, of course I know that the Seals are an American unit. I meant Special Forces. I can tell by the way you walk."

"The way I walk? You gotta fill me in on this Naomi."

"Well Colin, that's my husband, filled me in on their Seal training in Coronado in California and the 'week of hell' that's part of it. Also how many really tough guys drop out as the training ratchets up, and the few who complete it. He says that it's such an elite group of men that by the end of the training, they even have a distinctive walk, and he could pick a Seal out in a crowd anywhere. That's what I meant Danny. You have the walk. It's a bravado, a confidence, a really 'don't give a shit' attitude. And you've got all of that in spades. Am I right?"

He sat for a moment, thinking.

Finally he stirred.

"The Seals are warriors. Their training, as you say is brutal, but the finished product is an awesome fighter. I met some in Afghanistan when an operation went wrong. A team was cut off and the chopper that went in to rescue them got shot down. Big losses of personnel. You're right, I am in the U.K. Special Forces and we were called in at the tail end of the Seal team operation to provide some additional resource, so I did meet and talk to a number of their unit at that time. As to the perceived lack of communication from your husband, I have to say this. When you're operating in a hostile environment, you have to focus totally on where you are and what you're doing. None of us brooded on home, our marriage, kids and so on. To do so could undermine your focus, and you or your team buddy could end up dead. I would hazard a guess that Colin reacts the same way. There's no soldier Naomi who could forget what you look like, believe me. He'll be back before you know it, with bells on. Hey, things could be even better between you, after all you've both been through, so don't even start to entertain thoughts otherwise. Okay with that?"

Tears sprang into her eyes and impulsively she leaned forward and kissed his cheek.

He shook his head, pleased with her reaction.

"In deference to your warrior out there somewhere laying his life on the line for what he believes in, I would like to think that I'd acted honorably as a friend and I'm sure he would do the same for me. Who knows, I might even meet him some day. The world of the Special Forces is a small one today."

He stood up.

"I've got an idea and I think we should move on it tonight. So if you're game let's go. I'll explain on the way."

She looked uncertainly up at him, then without a word followed him outside.

A half hour later he pulled up in front of the Running Hare, a pub where the parachute brigade hung out during their off time.

She grabbed his arm as he was starting to get out of the jeep.

"Shouldn't we get Captain Kilroy's patrol to stand by? This could backfire big time, and things could be worse than ever around here, Danny. Let's enjoy tonight's victory. Who knows, the other may pull their horns in."

He shook his head.

"I've realized that when the word gets out to the other units as to what happened earlier tonight, we'll have lost the element of surprise. I can't afford to wait for Captain Kilroy to re-organize and get up here. I have something in mind, don't worry. I'm not just wandering in there looking for a fight. Okay?"

She nodded reluctantly and followed him to the door of the Running Hare and went inside.

Total silence descended on the pub as they stepped inside. Someone swore as they missed a cue ball and sent it spiraling off the pool table. The silence lasted as long as it took for Danny to stroll over to where a bunch of U.S. soldiers in civilian clothes were starting to put their cues down. They turned and looked at the approaching redcap, and the First Lieutenant.

Danny stopped in front of the group.

"I'd like a word with Bobby Lee Casson, if I may" he said loudly.

The men looked around at each other and across at the other pool table.

A large six foot two black man, still holding a pool cue, pushed through the crowd and came and stood beside him. There was a scowl on his face.

"What the fuck is this? A redcap busting into our off time and calling me out in front of my buddies. You got one minute to get your ass out of here and that Lootenant with you. You hear me boy?"

Danny smiled and stuck his hand out which the soldier automatically grasped without thinking.

"Danny Quigley... Now I'd appreciate a quiet word away from this lot, and then I'll be glad to get my ass, as you say, out of here and leave you and the boys to your fun. Can we do that, Bobby Lee?"

"Why the fuck should I?"

Danny smiled.

"A big macho guy like you - surely you're not scared of a lone redcap and a woman? Come on, a couple of minutes is all I want."

Danny nodded to a vacant spot near a window, and started walking over.

Bobby Lee looked around uncertainly at the group milling around, shrugged, and then put his cue down.

"Ah, what the fuck" he muttered, stalking over to where Danny was standing.

"This better be good," he growled.

Danny stood directly in front of him, and with his military boots, they were almost eye-to-eye. Casually, he adopted a defensive position, though he wasn't expecting to be attacked. He brought his hands out in front of him as he started speaking.

"I'm curious, Bobby Lee, a former Master Sergeant with twelve years in, busted down to a Pfc. And you on your way to being a Sergeant Major I'm told, suddenly becomes a troublemaker, racking up various misdemeanors. As I say I'm curious."

The big man stared at him.

"Just who the fuck are you man? A Brit meat-head in possession of my personal details. What is this?

"Someone who wants to help you Bobby Lee."

The man bristled and leaned forward, his face close to Danny's.

"Do you know who you're talking to buddy. We're airborne! There's not a man in here who hasn't got his wings, and that separates the men from the boys. You've got shit on the front of your uniform."

Danny grimaced.

"Yeah, I was shit scared the first time I had to jump off the tower. You get over it though."

The black man stared.

"You got your wings?" he asked.

"Yeah, HALO, HAHO, the whole bunch. You name it Bobby Lee."

"But where?….. shit you haven't even got one ribbon on your uniform, and you a sergeant, with two fucking wars on for the past several years."

Danny glanced quickly at his watch, leaned forward and whispered.

"Would you believe it if I told you that ten days ago I lay on top of a mud brick building in Basra, with a sniper rifle. Don't worry, the ribbons for my uniform will catch up with me."

Deep down in Bobby Lee's eyes, something started to flicker. It seemed to take forever to flow out into an awareness in his features.

"Basra… wasn't that….?"

A dawning look of comprehension suffused his features and a slight tremble came to one of his knees, which he immediately stiffened.

He took a short step backwards, still staring at Danny in fascination.

"I haven't seen you in a long time." he whispered.

"Seen me?" Danny asked, puzzled.

Bobby Lee nodded. "I was eleven years old, standing in the school yard, knowing I was going to get the shit kicked out of me."

He paused.

"You could take me couldn't you?" he whispered.

Danny nodded. "Yes, I could…… but I have too much respect for you to want to, or show you up in front of your men Bobby Lee."

The man nodded thoughtfully.

" I hear you. You say you want to help me. Okay here's the deal. I was a good soldier. I went here and I went there, and because of that everything fell apart at home. My thirteen year old daughter is pregnant, my nine year old son has been suspended from school for a drug misdemeanor and my wife is on tranquilizers. I asked for compassionate leave, and what do I get? Another fucking posting to Afghanistan to bolster what they're now calling 'Obama's war'. Well, I've had enough, and I intend to keep kicking the traces until they get rid of me. So how d'you like that?"

Danny shook his head.

"A dishonorable discharge, after all you have done for your country? We can do better than that. Now here's the thing. The powers that be are considering stopping all R&R trips to the U.K. because of the trouble you guys are causing. You know how it's been a Godsend for a number of your guys, having their wives come over, so I don't know if you're aware of the consequences of your men's actions over the last few weeks."

"Closing it down? Jesus, that would be a disaster. Just how real is this?"

"It's real Bobby Lee, believe me. Now here's the thing. Could you meet me at the military police detachment in Aldershot barracks tomorrow at twelve noon? I may just be able to help you in your situation. I won't promise you anything, but let me give it a shot. Will you do that?"

The soldier stood looking at him for what seemed a long time. Then as if coming to a decision, he reached forward and grasped his hand with both of his.

"Will I do that?" he whispered. " You better believe it."

With that he turned and strode across to the crowd of soldiers standing silently, expectantly, waiting for him.

Bobby Lee stood up on a chair and started shouting.

"Everyone back to barracks right now, and I mean everyone! We need to talk and sort something out. Let's go."

Outside the pub, Danny and the First Lieutenant sat in the jeep and watched them silently file out and start walking back towards the camp.

She let out a huge breath of air.

"Danny, you really believe in living on the edge! When I saw you walking up to that bunch of paras......"

She stopped and looked at his battledress.

"I just noticed myself. Just where the hell are your ribbons?"

He yawned.

"That's a long story Naomi. Perhaps after I finish up tomorrow I can fill you in."

The following day he was greeted by an ecstatic Bobby Lee, who found himself restored to his former rank and on a compassionate flight and posting home.

The Colonel was delighted with military discipline restored in the area.

Captain Kilroy stared in awe and vowed to have more respect for the redcaps in future.

By pre-arrangement, after Danny had changed into his civilian gear, he collected his car, drove over to the Officer's Mess and parked outside. He spotted Naomi emerging from the building almost immediately and his jaw dropped. She was also out of uniform and wearing a tight pair of jeans, high boots and a light green blouse with a matching silk scarf. But it was her hair that made him stare! A burnished red that was now flowing loose and falling round her shoulders. She laughed when she jumped in and saw his startled expression.

"What, never saw a redhead before Danny?" she teased.

"No, it's just that...... how on earth did you hide all that hair away last night when you were in uniform?"

"With difficulty, I can tell you. It's the bane of my life when I stand in front of some group of servicemen to discipline them with my red hair peeking out from under my hat!"

He shook his head.

"You could discipline me all you want and I would just enjoy looking at you. My God Naomi, you're just plain gorgeous! That husband of yours is some lucky guy."

She swung around in the seat.

"Speaking of Colin, what exactly did you say to the Colonel about me this morning?"

He glanced innocently across at her.

"Sorry, I don't know what you mean."

"Oh don't come on with that innocent face to me! You must have said something. He just up and volunteered that he was making some calls to have Colin and I relocated back home to the same posting. It could only have come from you. I have never even hinted that this is what I wanted. I know Colin would kill me if I did that, especially as he's in harms way right now and would want to stay with his team. Was it you Danny?"

He shifted in his seat, now embarrassed.

"Yeah, okay Naomi, I might have put a burr under his saddle about your situation. He asked me if he could do me any favors after sorting out the local problem in Aldershot. Sorry, I wasn't thinking of Colin's reaction if he got hauled out of an action spot ahead of time. I'd probably feel the same if I thought Fiona, my wife was pulling strings to get me a safe posting"

Her face softened into a smile.

"It's okay by me Danny, if it works. But at least I can swear, hand on heart, that I had nothing to do with it, if they do send him home. Wow, wouldn't that be something, especially if I ended up back there too."

She leaned across and gave him a long kiss.

When he came up for air, he sat back a bemused look on his face.

"What was that for? It's a good job I'm heading up to my wife in London! Another kiss like that and I'd be making other plans!"

She grinned impishly.

"Just practicing. You're in no danger Danny, I'm not trying to seduce you, though last night the thought was tempting. I was feeling kinda vulnerable until you set me straight on a few things. Like being in an action zone, where you have to focus on survival and not writing notes to your wife."

He grinned.

"Yeah, well, after that kiss, I'm wondering if being a marriage counselor was in my best interest."

They both burst out laughing and spent the next hour exchanging information about each other's situation.

They parted with a hug and Danny proceeded up to his home in London where he was greeted enthusiastically by his wife Fiona and daughter Allison. Wisely, he didn't mention the long kiss he had received in Aldershot.

He was back in Hereford three days later. He didn't get a medal for his Aldershot project but a commendation was attached to his record and his Commanding Officer was beaming when he received a crate of whiskey from a grateful U.S. military police Colonel. Of greater interest to Danny was a thank you card that he received some months later from Naomi to the effect that she and her husband were reunited back in California, where he was now involved in a training role with the Seals at Coronado.

The "Thank You" was underlined. He thought he knew why.

CHAPTER 6.

PRESENT TIME
LONDON, ENGLAND.

When Danny Quigley, now a civilian, wanted to be left alone in a bar, that's the way it was. On that particular evening, he didn't need any distractions. Still, there was something about her.

Even across the shifting movements of the crowded area, he was drawn by her quirky smile and the languid way she leaned back against the bar.

The fact that she hadn't taken her eyes off him since she'd breezed in earlier, piqued his curiosity.

Danny attracted women with his black Irish hair, tall muscular figure and the coiled sense of danger that he wore like a mantel around him.

He shook his head. The timing was all wrong.

He flicked a look at her again. God, she was the total package for sure!

From the tanned and toned body that must have been poured into the short black evening dress, to the slightly almond-shaped eyes that lazily surveyed the male occupants of the bar with some disdain. He loved the way her blonde hair was piled up on her head exposing a regal swan-like neck.

An idea started to germinate in his mind. She would be an excellent cover for his evening's work. Decision made, he stood up and strolled over to the bar. No pretence on her part. No turning away or breaking eye contact with him as he approached.

He positioned himself alongside her, plonked his glass down noisily, nodded to the barman and turned to her, a half smile on his face.

"Danny Quigley" he said.

She spun around slowly on the bar stool, facing him fully, her green eyes appraising him.

"Jacky" she responded, returning his smile which enveloped him totally. The noise in the bar faded away. From a distance he heard her voice add something and with a start, realized that she was not alone. A woman, a little older than Jacky, wearing clothes that were too tight for her as if in denial of her size.

"Danny, this is Rita. We work together."

He glanced sideways at her. His first thought was that she reminded him of a school-mistress he'd had at high school in Wales - tall and gangly with a face that just missed being attractive. She already appeared to disapprove of him. Her scowl and negative body language spoke volumes.

He struggled to recover his perspective and busied himself paying the barman.

"Nice to meet you Rita. Now can I get you both a drink? Perhaps you'd like to join me at my table."

Jacky shook her head.

"Drink-wise we're fine Danny, but sure, it would be nice to join you, right Rita?"

The other woman nodded grudgingly. Danny pushed away from the bar, and headed back across the room.

Despite the need to stay alert and focused on the evening's objective, he found himself drawn to Jacky. Her sensual walk to the table, only heightened his awareness and growing interest.

It didn't take long for her to be sitting beside him, chatting away like old friends. Her laughter tinkled, causing a small hush in the crowded bar, as if the patrons somehow found some satisfaction in the progress of their relationship.

She sat back and nodded her head disdainfully at the collage of characters draped across the full length of the bar.

"Danny you're probably just like all these other posturing, so called hard men, trying to impress the ladies."

He straightened.

"Hey Jacky, keep your voice down" he said touching her elbow. "This is one of the roughest pubs in London."

She made a face.

"Says you! I dropped in here to meet some of these tough characters you hear about. You know, the ex-forces, mercenaries, that sort. This lot couldn't even organize a good picnic, never mind fight a war!"

Her dismissive tone made him bridle.

"Hey hang on a minute. I've done my time in the Forces, so your evening isn't a complete waste. Anyway, you won't meet the really hard men you're talking about in this particular pub."

He scrutinized her closely.

"Why the interest anyway?"

She leaned forward.

"Oh, it's an article my editor asked me to do - you know, ex military types, what they get up to, body-guarding celebs, starting revolutions in Africa, training drug lords in South America, that sort of thing."

Danny decided to play hard to get.

"That sort of thing" he marveled, shaking his head, "and you think you can waltz into one of these meeting places, turn on that come-on smile, and they'll start gushing about which country they're going to liberate or which action they're planning next? Get real girl!"

Standing up and waving at them dismissively, he headed for the men's room.

Jacky's friend Rita thrust her head forward.

"I told you this was a crazy idea in the first place and he's just confirmed it. Let's get out of here."

Jacky shook her head.

"No, wait a minute Rita. Didn't he just say he had been in the Forces and he knows where these types hang out? He's our ticket in the door, and once I'm in - you know me."

Rita nodded gloomily.

"Unfortunately I do, but one of these days waving that fanny of yours around isn't going to save you're ass. Sooner or later you'll pick on the wrong guy and there may not be some nice bobby around the next corner to save you. I say lets go right now" she said, standing up and tugging at Jacky's arm.

Jacky shook her off.

"Look, the editor gave me this project and told me to get some real stuff, not what you can pull off the internet. If I blow this one, old tank-face from Birmingham will get that promotion that's coming up next month and my life won't be worth living if I have to work under her. No, I'm going to hang in here. Anyway you've got to admit, he's a hunk. See those shoulders?"

Rita pursed her lips

"There's something dangerous about the guy Jacky. I just can't put my finger on it. Notice the way he walked through that crowd of drunks like he was parting the Red Sea? Sure any idiot could see he was smitten with you, but what man isn't when you give him the treatment?"

Just then Danny returned.

"You girls still here? I thought you might have gone off the idea by now."

Jacky stood up facing him.

"Danny, I admit when we came in here I gave you the come-on from the bar. It was a mistake okay? Look, the truth is, I'm going to lose my job unless I get some insights into how these guys operate. What do you say we head off to this place where they hang out, and I promise I won't open my mouth or try to talk to anyone unless you give me the nod?"

She pirouetted in front of him.

"Anyway it won't do your reputation any harm with two good looking dollies on your arm. What do you say Danny?"

Danny wasn't sure about the inclusion of her friend Rita, but he liked the way she said his name...... almost like foreplay.

In any event, it suited his plan for the evening - kept the attention off him and on the two ladies in his company. He smiled and shrugged his shoulders like a good loser, holding out an inviting arm to each.

"Why not ladies? You talked me into it. Let's go."

Rita jumped back.

"You can leave me out of it. This is crazy. I've got a bad feeling about this Jacky. Hell, what do you know about Danny here anyway? He could be a bloody serial killer for all we know and you're just going to walk off into the night with him? Well I think you're bonkers, job or no job!"

She stormed out of the pub, knocking some glasses to the ground and causing a raucous cheer to go up from the bar.

Jacky looked across at him.

"Rita's my guardian angel you know. Never stops worrying about me. Are you one by the way?"

"One what? A guardian angel?" he asked.

"No silly, a serial killer!"

He grinned evilly.

"I've got my quota for this month so you're absolutely safe. At least until the full moon anyway."

Suddenly they were both startled by a man aggressively pushing in between them. Over six foot tall, with beefy weight-trained tattooed muscles straining at his sleeveless T-shirt and a sneer on his face, he swung his head towards Danny.

"You seem to be losing your women fast tonight mate. I see they're walking out on you. Maybe she'd like to see what a real man looks like."

Danny smiled disarmingly.

"Why don't you ask her MATE. She makes her own decisions" he replied evenly, nodding across at Jacky.

The man swiveled his head in her direction.

"How about it Miss? Want an evening with a real man?"

Jacky's face reflected puzzlement as she looked at the man and around the pub.

"Well sure, what woman wouldn't, but quite frankly I don't see anything in trousers in here that qualifies as a man."

She looked derisively back at him.

"You'd be right at the bottom of the pile, sunshine, as far as I'm concerned."

The pub was suddenly quiet as the man's face reddened. Some men at a nearby table started laughing. He turned aggressively to Danny, his fists already swinging.

Danny's right hand moved like a flash as he reached forward and pinched the side of the man's neck. His face paled, his eyes rolled upwards and he collapsed straight down to the floor. There was a collective gasp in the pub and three men started moving deliberately across from the bar towards Danny. Almost immediately the barman scuttled across and whispered something in the ear of the man in front. He stopped in his tracks, his eyes staring upwards at Danny as if seeing a ghost.

"Shit, you're Danny Quigley!" He said, his voice rising to a squeak.

Danny regarded him coolly.

"The very same." He stepped forward and reached out his hand. "Pleased to make your acquaintance."

The man shrank back and looked desperately around at his two companions.

"Let's get the fuck away from here lads."

He nodded at the man on the floor.

"Luke got what was coming to him. He was asking for trouble."

With that he grabbed his two companions and hustled them back across to the bar.

Jacky's jaw dropped.

"God, what was that all about? They looked like they were ready to tear your block off!"

He shrugged.

"Who knows? They suddenly lost interest in their friend lying there."

She looked down at the unconscious man.

"What on earth did you do to him?"

"Oh just some stuff I picked up along the way. Incidentally, I'm a financial planner. Useful technique when you run into too many objections."

She tilted her head back appraising him, as if seeing him for the first time.

"Financial planner my ass! I don't have to be a journalist to realize that you're pulling my leg. You better believe I'm going to come back to this later. Right now if you're still game, lets go to that other place you mentioned."

As if by some unspoken agreement, they both headed for the door.

Outside the pub Danny breathed in deeply of the fresh air mingled with the aroma of flowers from a nearby park. At least there was no longer any second-hand smoke in pubs, but nothing could eradicate the smell of booze, sweaty patrons and over-used toilets, in an eighteen hour a day pub.

He was pleasantly surprised by the natural way Jacky took his arm and leaned closer to him.

Easy Danny, he thought, easy. Remember your occasional girlfriend Siobhan back in Ireland.

More surprising was the scruffy man who accosted them out on the sidewalk.

"Get you a taxi Gov?" he asked eagerly.

Danny shook his head to clear it and commented to Jacky.

"God, this is the first time I've seen this service outside a scruffy pub! Must be the state of the economy…all those immigrants doing the jobs at a cheaper rate."

He nodded to the man.

"Sure why not. Worth a few quid not to have to hang around here."

He passed some notes across to the man who grinned, placed his fingers in his mouth, and whistled loudly.

A black taxi shot out of a side road, cut across directly and slewed to a stop in front of them. The scruffy man opened the door for them, at the same time asking Danny "Where to Gov?" as they both climbed in.

"Oh the Fox and Hounds in the East End" Danny replied.

The man shouted through to the driver who nodded and pulled away.

Danny was disappointed when Jacky broke contact and moved away from him in the seat.

"So, tell me about this place we're going to Danny" she asked.

He creased his brow wondering how, in a 20 minute cab ride, he could mark her cards - the meeting place where the hard men, as she called them, and their women, the tough slags, all hung out. How any of these women would gut her if they suspected that she was giving the eye to their man. Where the smarmy wannabes and the danger junkies liked to be seen in the company of men who had killed and could inflict extreme violence at will.

There was an accepted pecking order in the place. An unspoken thing that set the territorial limits on who you took into your confidence, or spoke to.

The action men, the Paras or ex SAS had an aura of violence about them. You could read it in their tight faces. The steely eyes that had witnessed unspeakable things and who still had nightmares about the faces of the people they had blown to bits. Few could keep a regular job for long as the boredom or the close contact with civvies forced them to

38

get lost in a fog of drink or drugs. Quite often the topic of conversation was who had 'topped' themselves since they'd last met up.

The clever ones started security firms in the U.K. and abroad, offering their services as bodyguards to politicians and celebrities, contract workers in Iraq or Afghanistan, and visiting princes on shopping sprees to Harrods.

All lived on their past glory days, the Falkland War, Northern Ireland, the first Gulf War, Bosnia, Kosovo and more recently discharges from Iraq and Afghanistan. They came to the Fox and Hounds for a few hours to pretend they could still cut it. A number of them still could, and they could barely hide their disdain for the phonies who bought them drinks and listened to their stories. Stories that got better with the telling to the hangers-on who listened raptly to their every word.

Danny liked to keep things simple.

"Just stay close to me and don't, whatever you do, get separated from me. Keep your head down and avoid eye contact. I don't want to have to fight my way out of here just because you gave the glad eye to some ex-squaddy who thinks you're after his body."

"Oh my God this sounds very primal" she exclaimed.

"You said it…primal! I couldn't have picked a better word myself, but then you are a hard-bitten journalist aren't you? Oh by the way, don't whatever you do, tell them that, and don't be seen taking notes."

He glanced at her.

"Are you sure you're ready for this Jacky?"

She straightened up.

"You'd better believe it. Ready and willing, so stop worrying about me. I've been handling come-ons since I was twelve years old."

He smiled wryly at her.

"I can't say I blame them, you're a hell of a lot of female."

He nudged her.

"Hey what's your last name, in case someone asks?"

She grinned.

"Not 'cos you want to know yourself eh? Okay, it's Spellman. I like the sound of yours by the way……. Danny Quigley……. Danny… hmm."

The cab sped on through the dark streets of London.

CHAPTER 7.

The man sitting in darkness in an upscale apartment, showed no surprise when the phone rang at two in the morning. In one swift movement he picked up the receiver.

"Blackstone" he answered.

"Morcambe here. We've been watching Quigley since we spotted him at Heathrow on your instructions yesterday. He's been cruising round the tougher pubs, not staying long before moving to the next one. Not drinking much in any of them. Hasn't talked to anyone apart from the last pub where he appeared to accost two women. One of the women left in a hurry and Quigley and the other woman just left in a cab. She's quite a looker."

"One of our cabs Morcambe?"

"Spot on, and they're being taped right now from my vehicle just behind them. The reason I called you is that they're going to the Fox and Hounds, so we're setting the team up there. The other thing is that the woman with Quigley is a journalist."

"That's okay, don't worry about it. I've got a handle on it. What about the other woman?"

"Followed her home.... lives in an apartment.... two names on the front door. The good looker probably lives there too. We ran their names through the system and they both work for the Daily Mail."

Blackstone breathed in evenly.

"Still no panic here. Now let me have her address and if Quigley leads you to the target, take them both out, the woman too. Quigley will have served his purpose. His part in this is still a mystery, but I don't really care if he's instrumental in wrapping it up. What I've learned about him since we talked yesterday is that he went into the parachute regiment some years back and seemed to vanish. Reappeared as a self employed Financial Services rep over a year ago, and around that time became a person of interest to the police in three thugs getting killed. A lot in the papers about him being ex-SAS and a trained killer. Probably true, so be careful when you tackle him. I dare say eighteen months on civvy street would take the edge off his combat skills. He was subsequently cleared of any involvement in those three deaths. By the way did you see who picked him up at Heathrow yesterday?"

"Someone, a chauffeur probably, met him at arrivals with a sign held up, then Quigley disappeared into a limo with tinted windows parked outside. We never saw who else was inside. He was dropped in central London so we had to use our assets to follow him. We don't know where the limo ended up."

"Damn! It would have been useful to know who's in contact with Quigley. We need to know if we have some new players in the game right now."

He paused for a moment.

"Okay, proceed as planned. No other civilian casualties where possible if our target turns up. Don't want the press to go wild on a slaughter of civilians."

Morcambe laughed harshly.

"I'm not sure that the demise of the occupants of the Fox and Hounds would cause much criticism. On the contrary the press would be handing out medals for getting rid of that bunch of rednecks."

"Morcambe, that course you did with your parent company in Buffalo hasn't done you much good. You know I hate those American sayings....... rednecks indeed!"

He hung up.

CHAPTER 8.

When Danny preceded Jacky through the door, a blast of noise met his ears. A small rock band was playing in the corner but was completely being ignored by the noisy occupants who turned to take in the newcomers.

Danny started to wave to a few familiar faces when a glass crashed to the floor and a small lithe whip-cord of a man pushed away from the bar and rushed at him, pushing him aggressively up against the wall.

Danny held his hands apart, stunned by the sudden attack.

"Hey Scotty, what the........." he started.

Shoving him again the man hissed

"Pretend we're having an argument Danny."

Still shaken by the sudden apparent attack by his former regiment friend, he tried a tentative shove back.

Scotty slammed him again and leaned close to his ear.

"They've killed a number of them" he whispered, "and I'm being hunted."

"Scotty.... killed who for God's sake? Is that the missing troop that MI5 asked me to... look what are you trying to tell me?" he asked fiercely, wondering if his old friend had gone completely off his rocker.

"The fucking troop from our last job in Iraq. They've all disappeared, and I know some of them are dead already for sure."

"Dead, but how Scotty? The 'Sass' don't kill that easy."

Just then Jacky interjected.

"Who's been killed Danny? What's going on?"

Scotty half turned.

"Just who the hell are you?" he growled.

42

At that precise moment the doors of the pub slammed open and two men in masks dived inside, MP5s turning in the direction of Danny and Scotty, as if by pre-arrangement.

Momentarily, Jacky stood in the line of fire and the first man hesitated.

Danny slung a chair in their direction and lunged at Jacky, bringing her to the ground. The chair caught the first man on the shoulder and a burst of shots slammed into the ceiling. Everyone in the bar was diving for cover. Scotty threw two chairs in quick succession at the second gunman and rapidly crouched down beside Danny.

"See me at the castle near my grandfather's in Wales" he shouted as a series of bullets started chewing up the wall behind them.

Leaping up, Scotty sprung off a table and disappeared headfirst through the glass window followed by another burst of automatic fire. The two gunmen dashed out of the pub. More firing was heard from outside, then there was silence.

Danny gingerly picked himself up off the floor, lifting Jacky to her feet as he did so.

"Stay here" he commanded as he dashed through the door.

Outside, he emerged cautiously but couldn't see anyone holding a weapon.

Tires screeched as a solid black Mercedes with tinted windows took off around the nearest corner. The gunmen, he surmised.

He looked desperately around for any sign of Scotty, and was grateful not to see his body lying in the street. Scotty had just used up one more of his nine lives he thought, but why? What was going on? If he didn't know any better, he had just witnessed an attempted killing of his good friend and possibly himself too.

A number of the missing SAS troop had been killed according to Scotty! That didn't make one iota of sense. Those guys had antennas that would stop even the most dedicated attempts to eliminate them. Hell, he had done numerous missions with them over the years prior to his discharge, and he knew that they were practically indestructible. He would back them against any elite force in the world including the U.S. Delta, Seals, and U.S. army green berets. Something was terribly wrong.

A dazed Jacky emerged from the pub, her outfit stained with spilled beer and dirt.

"God Danny, I can't believe what just happened! Bullets flying all around! We might have got killed in there. What was all that about?" she asked, her voice quivering.

He grabbed her arm and started running, pulling her along with him.

"Don't ask questions. We've got to get out of here right now!"

"But what about the police?" she demanded. "Surely we should wait…after all we were witnesses."

"Trust me Jacky. You don't want to be here when the cops arrive. We have to move our asses right now. Let's go!"

CHAPTER 9.

With the action imminent at the Fox & Hounds, Blackstone hadn't gone to bed. When the phone rang he snatched it up. He heard Morcambe's apologetic voice at the other end.

"It all went wrong sir. We had them both positioned just inside the door of the pub...... perfect place for a hit away from the crowded bar area. The woman got in the way and the lead team member hesitated."

"Hesitated? What the fuck for? She was a target too for God's sake."

"I really don't know sir. Perhaps he'd never killed a woman before. Anyway Quigley threw a chair and the target did the same and then dived straight through the window of the pub. When they got outside, he was disappearing down an alley. We gave chase but we lost him. Sorry sir!"

Blackstone cursed.

"Let me guess, there were none of the team positioned outside the pub just in case this sort of thing happened! I mean these are guys who jump out of planes into war zones on a regular basis! Surely you weren't expecting them to sit there quietly and be shot at?"

"Well if Quigley hadn't.........."

"Quigley, yeah, I distinctly remember warning you about him a short time ago. More importantly now that the target's escaped, did he speak to him? That's the last thing we need."

Morcambe hesitated on the other end.

"Ah... looking through the window it looked like they were having an argument about something. Scotty, as they call him, had him pinned up against the wall and was screaming in his face. It was only for a brief moment. They certainly weren't having a conversation."

"Probably some petty grievance from their regiment days. We should be grateful for small mercies I suppose. Now, we need to make a change of plan because the target is still at large and Quigley is the only lead we've got. Let him run, and the press lady too for the moment. When they've served their purpose we can get rid of them both."

Morcambe gasped at the other end.

"But I sent one of my men to wait for them at the journalist's place in case they managed to survive the pub attack, with instructions to finish them off! I was just trying to cover all the bases."

Blackstone slapped the table in annoyance.

"For Christ's sake Morcambe, am I working with a bunch of boy scouts or the tough ex-military types I was promised you'd be?"

"What do you want me to do sir?" he stuttered.

"Get round there and stop your team member from killing Quigley and the woman. Whatever you have to do Morcambe, do it. Now get to it and don't screw this one up or I might have to report back to Buffalo about how incompetent you've turned out to be.

Blackstone hung up.

CHAPTER 10.

Danny and Jacky ran two blocks to a busier road where he flagged down a taxi. On his instruction, she had given a destination to the driver, which was two blocks from the 4th floor apartment she shared with Rita. He knew the police would soon be talking to cab drivers who had picked up fares in the general vicinity of the shooting. It wouldn't take them long to get a description of both of them and possibly Danny's identity from the club patrons. He needed some time to figure out what was going on.

When he'd met with the Director General of MI5, Rebecca Fullerton-Smythe in the limo outside Heathrow the previous day, she had astounded him with the news.

A troop of eight SAS men had disappeared (technically half a troop) after being given two weeks R&R leave following a secret mission in Iraq. Their Commanding Officer, a Major Wainwright was doing a follow-up phone call to clarify some points regarding the mission and discovered that some of the men had effectively disappeared and he was trying to locate the rest of the troop. Even their families were unable to shed any light on the strange situation. In the past, the odd trooper had gone AWOL, mainly because of marital problems or stress, but this was beyond comprehension. The story was kept strictly out of the media. MI5, whose responsibilities covered counter subversion, espionage, and terrorism, was brought in by the Home Secretary to do an initial investigation before involving the police. One of the DG's first actions was to place a vaguely worded small add in all the newspapers.

"MISSING YOU IN HEREFORD"

Hereford was the home of the SAS 22nd Regiment at Credenhill. The advertisement contained a mobile phone number and text message details, but was unsigned.

Within two days a brief text message came through:

"ONLY WILLING TO MEET WITH QUIGLEY" S.

The DG had tried to contact Danny on his mobile phone but with no pick up and she had left messages on his voice mail. Aware that he had contacts in Ireland, she put out an alert at airports and ferry terminals and found he'd taken a flight to Dublin. Then Danny contacted her out of the blue, and they arranged to meet in London on Tuesday morning.

Sitting in the back of the speeding limo, with the Director General, he had shaken his head in frustration.

"Why the hell didn't you say something on my voice mail. I would have come straight back for God's sake. The S at the end of the message was probably Scotty. Is he one of the missing troopers?"

She nodded.

"Yes we've confirmed it with Hereford. We also believe it's Scotty because none of the other men have that initial with their names. This is now a national security issue Danny and I couldn't say much on a voice mail. You know better than most how insecure telephones are today. Anyway I didn't see any sense in spoiling your weekend. After you contacted me from Ireland, I still needed a couple of days to place another add in the papers. It said:

"QUIGLEY STANDING BY TUE"

We had another text message which simply said:

"HAVE Q DO A PUB CRAWL IN THE TOUGH PUBS ASAP" S.

That had been the extent of Quigley's briefing from MI5 apart from receiving direct 24/7 contact instructions, which included a package containing a set of new mobile phones. She did however give him one more piece of information. Her arrangement with Danny was under the MI5 radar and was a completely deniable operation. If he got into trouble she would have limited scope to extricate him.

Great, he thought, as she had dropped him in central London.

Danny raged inwardly. How could he have missed such a blatantly obvious trap? The bloody cab was a set-up! Just how long had they been watching him? He wondered if DG's small advertisement had raised a flag in some organization. Checking plane arrivals would be an easy step from there. They'd probably picked him up at Heathrow and had been following him ever since. He groaned. God, he had gotten soft since he'd become a civilian. He'd have to sluff that civvy skin off fast or he'd be dead meat!

Just then the cab stopped and he and Jacky got out.

He waited until it was out of sight, and holding her arm, started walking rapidly along the darkened street. In a few minutes they arrived at an apartment block where she fumbled with her keys and gave a muffled sob as she couldn't locate the lock.

"Here, let me." He took the keys and swiftly opened it.

She stepped inside and turned quickly to face him.

"Thanks Danny, I'm okay now. Thanks for getting me out of the line of fire back there. It's all catching up with me.... how close I came. I should have listened to Rita.... she had a bad feeling about this."

He stepped inside closing the door behind him.

She looked up at him.

"Look Danny, there's a time and place for........."

He put his finger to his lips.

"We'll check your place first before I go anywhere. No arguments. There's some heavy stuff going down here Jacky and I want to make sure you're not caught up in it, okay? Trust me, this is my game and the players just got nasty."

"But Rita is upstairs, she'll........." she started.

"I know she is. You may very well be right" he replied, steering her towards the elevators.

The lift seemed to take forever groaning upwards. Finally it stopped. Jacky turned right and moved along the hallway to the last apartment directly beside the emergency door. She reached up to open the door but he removed the keys from her hand, quickly opened the door himself and stepped inside.

49

The hallway in the apartment was in darkness. She went to go past him but he thrust his arm out and stopped her.

"Stay here" he whispered. "I'll check it out first."

She looked exasperated.

"Look, I do this every night" she said, her voice rising.

He pressed her arm again restraining her.

"Just sit tight for two minutes."

There was a steely tone to his voice and she stepped back slightly, a faint line of worry starting to crease her forehead.

"You don't think......"

Before she was finished he was swallowed up in the darkness as he crept down the hall. There were no lights in the lounge apart from a flickering glow from the TV set which was still on and hissing with a blank screen. As his eyes adjusted, he could make out the layout of the lounge and some doors leading off that were probably bedrooms and a bathroom.

Normally he would have waited there longer, listening, but he knew that Jacky was on a short fuse. He decided boldness was the best approach.

He moved to the first door and opened it cautiously. In the glow from the street lights and the lounge TV, he saw a bedroom with a fully made-up bed. Must be Jacky's he thought. Closing the door he went to the second room and opened it gently, expecting to see a sleeping form in the bed. Another fully made-up bed.

For the first time a sense of disquiet descended upon him. Where was Rita?

Danny backed out and headed over to the last room, which he assumed was the bathroom. He found her.... in the bath.

He flicked on the light and saw her still form staring up at the ceiling with a small hole dead center in her forehead.

Before he could make a further move he heard a gasp from behind him and Jacky's shocked face appeared, a keening sound starting to come from her throat.

"Oh my God, what's happened to her?" she gasped. "She's not dead. She can't be. I only left her a couple of hours ago."

He put his arm around her and eased her back into the lounge.

"Look, I don't know what this is all about........"

She threw it off and spun around to face him.

"You got her killed Danny!" she hissed. "She said there was something dangerous about you. She was right wasn't she? That shooting back in the pub…. that was all about you too wasn't it? That's what killed Rita - us getting involved with you Quigley."

Some faint noise out in the corridor resonated in the back of his mind and without replying he pulled the bathroom door shut behind him, cutting off the light.

He touched Jacky's arm and leaned close to her.

"Get down on the floor" he whispered.

Then he spun round and crept towards the hallway. As he reached it, a hand holding a gun with a bulbous barrel began to emerge from the shadows, followed by a head covered in a balaclava. Danny never hesitated. Whoever this was had probably killed Rita and was back to finish the job.

He grabbed the weapon arm with his left hand and kicked directly at the side of the person's knee, hearing it break. The assailant started collapsing onto the floor and as he did so Danny, still holding the gun arm dropped straight down onto his rib cage with his right knee.

The man screamed and Danny knew he'd broken some ribs.

He wrenched the weapon from the man's hand and jumped astride him trapping his arms.

"Put some lights on" he shouted hoarsely.

He was surprised and pleased that she reacted so quickly and the room was flooded with light.

He found himself kneeling on top of a long skinny man, who was writhing beneath him, his screams now a series of heavy gasps. Danny reached forward and ripped the balaclava off his head. It revealed a hatchet face and small set ferret-like eyes glaring at him. Danny knew he was face to face with a merciless killer.

The man struggled to sit up but couldn't with the pain and the weight on him. If what Scotty had intimated, that the troop had been killed, the man beneath him was probably involved in some way. There was no mercy in Danny's gaze as he leaned forward and whispered

"If you're trying to kill me, then you know who I am and what I can do to people. I haven't even started on you yet. Now I want information. Who do you work for and why are you trying to kill me and why kill that woman in the bath?"

Bloody spittle was on the man's lips as he tried to spit in Danny's face.

"Fuck you" he hissed. Then as an after thought, "what woman?" Danny grinned.

"I was hoping you'd say that. You see I'm thinking of my mates in the troop that you probably helped make disappear. They'd be disappointed if I didn't inflict some pain on you."

He grabbed a small doormat and crammed it across the man's face. Then he slammed the heavy barrel down on the injured knee. He felt the man arch beneath him and an anguished groan came from his throat. He pulled the mat back from his mouth.

"Okay, let's hear it. I want some answers and I've only just started on you" Danny grated.

"Danny don't" Jacky begged from the side.

The man's eyes flicked towards her as if seeing some hope.

"Can't talk…. dead if I do……" he gasped.

"You either talk or you'll wish you were dead."

Danny moved the weapon until the opening in the barrel was directly against the man's good knee.

"Ever seen someone after they were knee-capped? I did in Northern Ireland and it wasn't a pretty sight…. hobbling along, or in a wheel chair, with everyone pitying you… not able to work and existing on the dole. Your decision. Start talking. What's this about? Who's involved?"

The man's eyes were bulging out of his face.

"Don't shoot… please….. okay I'll talk."

"Go on." Danny pressed.

"The last mission…. buried out in the desert somewhere… bring us all down."

"Keep talking!" Danny shouted, pressing the gun harder against his knee.

The man lifted his head slightly, his lips opening and at that moment the side of his head disappeared and a spray of blood and bone drenched Danny. He threw himself backwards, expecting more bullets from what he assumed was a silencer.

Danny fired three shots from the captured weapon towards the doorway, hearing a cry as he did so. He heard the rapid pounding of feet in the corridor and sprinted outside, just in time to see the emergency door slamming shut. He dashed over and wrenched at the door but it was stuck fast, a piece of wood protruding from the bottom of it.

Someone had come well prepared.

At the same time he heard the sound of someone pounding down the stairs. While he was bending over he noticed drops of blood on the floor, which confirmed that he had wounded someone. Probably the person who had shot the man inside. He was tempted to continue the chase by taking the lift downstairs but he had a bigger mess to sort out inside the apartment.

Inside Jacky appeared surprisingly calm, sitting down and staring straight ahead. She was still in shock. Finally she looked up at him and whispered

"would you have done it?"

"Done what?" he replied as he rapidly went through the dead man's clothes, pocketing anything he found, including his wallet.

"Shot him in the knee?"

"At one time - oh yes. Yes indeed! It would have been a pleasure. Since I met a man called Clive Courtney over a year ago in Ireland, I've had to evaluate how I use violence. In terms of seeking retribution for my former mates in the service, you better believe it! We were more than family to each other and any survivor would do exactly as I would. It now looks like a bunch of them have been wiped out. I intend to find out why and who is involved and when I do" he pointed to the dead man, "this is nothing compared to what I plan to do."

"By the way" he continued, "how come none of your neighbors came out to see what was going on? This guy screamed to beat the band. I would have expected sirens by now."

"We're the end flat for starters and the people on the other side are away on holiday in Spain. Rita and I had agreed to water their flowers for them."

Danny pointed to the dead man.

"He probably killed Rita you know."

She thought about it for a long while.

"No police again?" she asked.

"Not just yet. We need to get some distance from this mess before we can do anything about it. Calling the cops would tie us up for days"

She shrugged helplessly.

"But won't the police start looking for Rita's flat mate.... me? How do I explain all this? I can't, 'cos I don't know myself" she exclaimed.

"They may think you were abducted by the killer. It will take them some time to sort this out. They'll tie you into the pub shooting sooner or later when they start comparing a picture of you and the stunningly good looking woman who was there. Right now we have to get out of London and start running. I need to reset my mindset because, Jacky my girl, right now we're at war!"

Her head came up, shock still registered on her face. Gradually a gleam came into her eyes "Danny can I ask you something? Do you think Rita would mind if I followed the story on this, or would it seem too callous?"

He looked at her in wonder.

"You little mercenary, you. Your friend is lying dead, there's another body lying here and all you can think of is the story? There's more to Jacky Spellman than I first figured. If I can keep you alive long enough, you might just be the edge I need to beat this thing. Let's go."

They sprinted out of the building.

CHAPTER 11.

Blackstone wasn't surprised when the phone rang a third time that night. He picked it up with a sense of anticipation.

"Yes" he said impatiently.

"Morcambe here. Bit of a screw up again I'm afraid. When I got to the flat our chap had obviously gone in to finish off Quigley and the girl but it must have gone wrong."

"Wrong? Dammit what are you trying to say man? Spit it out"

"When I looked around the door jamb Quigley had our team member on the ground interrogating him. It appeared that he was spilling his guts to Quigley so I had a clear shot at the other team member and shot him. Unfortunately Quigley blasted back at me with the weapon he'd taken from our chap and wounded me in the shoulder. I just managed to escape down the emergency stairs thanks to a wooden cleat I'd taken with me that I jammed the door with. Then I headed back to base where I am right now."

Blackstone groaned loudly.

"Screw up is right. So now we have a dead team member at that address. One that probably could be traced back to us, not to mention DNA evidence - blood from your wound. Make sure you don't go anywhere near a hospital. Get that illegal immigrant Indian doctor that we use occasionally to fix you up. Any sign of alarm at the building - lights going on and so forth?"

"I don't think so sir. We were both using silencers for a start and I didn't pick up any alarm on the police band. Other than that I didn't hang about, especially with Quigley now in possession of a weapon."

"Sounds like Quigley hasn't lost much after all since he hit civvy street - taking out one of your professionals like that. Okay I'll get a team over to sanitize the place. Quigley won't stick around, nor will the girl. I want you to go back, wait for the team and lead them in. The body is to disappear. Oh, and Morcambe?"

"Yes sir?"

"Have them check the bathroom as well. I believe they'll find the body of the other press lady.... collateral damage I'm afraid. She's part of the cleanup too, understood?"

"Yes sir.... understood.... my God the body count is mounting! But what about Quigley and the girl?"

"Obviously Quigley is fully alerted now and armed as well. I still have him under surveillance so we'll let the rabbit run and hope we're led to Scotty's burrow."

Morcambe's voice had a hint of admiration.

"You got a device on him sir? How'd you manage that?" he asked.

"You don't need to know. Trade secret my good fellow. Now I want you to organize a bigger team with the resources to move to any part of the U.K. at a moments notice. We can't kill Quigley yet. I need to know what if anything, his mate Scotty told him and just how much your dead colleague spilled to him before you finished him off. Good reactions there by the way Morcambe... killing him."

Blackstone hit the button on his phone and began dialing straight away.

CHAPTER 12.

Danny Quigley had only survived in a variety of dangerous situations over the years by being alert, aware and extremely careful. His training in the parachute regiment had taught him to look after himself in every imaginable situation that a soldier could find himself in. His eventual selection into the SAS had put the finishing touches to his skills. Only twenty out of every one hundred men trying out for selection into the SAS made it through.

The brutal testing regime in the Brecon Beacon mountains in Wales sent broken and injured men back to their units every week until the selection process came down to the final few survivors. Danny Quigley was one of them.

Then their SAS training began in earnest: weapons training using every advanced and unorthodox weapon on the face of the planet, advanced map reading and parachuting, (HALO) High Altitude, Low Opening and HAHO. High Altitude, High Opening (gliding into targets). The training was non-stop: coordinating close air support with NATO and U.K. Forces overseas, lasering targets for air and artillery strikes, the sophisticated use of explosive materials, how to eliminate an enemy by making it appear like an accident, advanced skiing and battle tactics in the Norwegian mountains, the use of small boats which they learned in Poole, Dorset with the Special Boat Service, the equivalent of the U.S. Seals, rappling down mountains and the sides of buildings and dismantling alarms and locks, learning to assault buildings in the Close Quarter Battle (CQB) house, or Killing House as it was called, and unarmed combat.

The SAS didn't fight for the sport of it. They fought to kill and disable and to do it silently with their hands, feet, elbows, head and any

weapon they came across. There were no fancy Bruce Lee high kicks or superfluous movements. The SAS unarmed combat trainers were very impressed with Danny. He had tremendous upper body strength and seemed to have some sort of built-in software that made him aware of an opponent's move, even before the man himself knew of it. His explosive speed and power made him deadly in combat. The use of weapons came naturally to him, especially the pistol and sniper rifle. At just under six feet he was tall for a trooper. On average, they tended to be small, lean, whip-cord types.

Danny's exceptional talents and his family's Irish background, had brought him to the attention of MI5, The Secret Intelligence Service, who had used him in a number of dangerous missions during his time in the regiment.

With MI5 he had picked up other skills like surveillance work, how to maintain contact with his controller while working, using vehicles to escape roadblocks and assassination attempts. He had also attended a U.S. marine sniping course in the States. In the SAS the training was never ending and Danny soaked it all up.

Under pressure from his then wife Fiona, he had taken release from the regiment, only to subsequently have her divorce him anyway.

While Danny had been busy during the past year building a financial planning business, he was still fanatical about keeping fit. He ran twice a week and had joined a martial arts club which taught a variety of styles that he felt would compliment his tough military methods. As a youth in Wales he had taken judo for four years. He believed that he was even more effective in martial arts now than he was when he was at the peak of his training in the regiment. However he knew too that being out of the daily mock-training situations of the regiment, his reactions had slowed down considerably.

They left the flat in Jacky's car and found a second rate hotel on the edge of town with a twin-bedded room which he paid for with cash. Jacky was now asleep. He knew he was caught up in something that could have deadly consequences for himself and anyone associated with him. He slipped out of the hotel, and using his pre-programmed mobile phone, called the Director General at her home.

She listened quietly, then told him to follow up with Scotty in Wales. Before hanging up she elicited the address of the flat where Jacky and Rita had lived and promised to sanitize the scene.

An hour after his conversation with the DG his mobile vibrated and he switched it on.

On the screen was a text message:

CALL ME. R.

He looked across at Jacky who was still asleep and slipped outside again.

It was picked it up on the first ring.

"Rebecca"

"Danny here…. ah Rebecca" he answered, still not entirely comfortable using her first name.

"We got problems Danny. When we got to the building it was already sanitized, completely cleaned up, including the two packages you mentioned. Nice cleaning job on the emergency door you mentioned too."

"Holy shi…. this is mind blowing!" he whispered into the phone.

"You said it Danny. You know what this means?" she asked.

He paused thinking.

"Well I'm not sure. I'd have to think it through."

"Understandable, but it means that we're up against a big organization that can provide this kind of service at a moments notice. These are heavy hitters and that means they have the resources to do what we can do and you know what those are."

His mind was reeling.

"Who could be this big?"

"Well, for starters our own people MI5, though that's unlikely seeing as how I am after all the Director General, MI6, the CIA, organized crime, some terrorist organization with a highly sophisticated computer hacker on their payroll, U.S. military intelligence or even Homeland Security - Israeli Mossad being another. The list is endless."

He was silent at the end of the phone.

"Are you still there Danny?" she asked quietly.

"Yes I am, but I'm wondering just how far I can run with this now, considering you can't provide me with any resources like weapons to fight back, or transport. I may need to travel, possibly out of the country and I can't do that as Danny Quigley because they obviously know my name."

"You're right, and while you're still under the MI5 radar right now I'll start working on some back-up. I still need you to hang in there. We're talking national security in a big way here, and right now you're my secret weapon in trying to break this wide open. Here's the thing. I'll have someone contact you in that village Scotty mentioned to you. The code word will be 'Rebecca' and don't worry about the security of this call as my line is scrambled. Okay?"

"Sure, fine. Now what about the lady from the press? Will she become a liability once it's known she's missing? Her face may be all over the papers."

The DG chuckled.

"Never knew you to refer to an attractive lady as a liability before Danny. Look, I'll contact the paper and have them sit on it for a few days. They're going to wonder what's going on with two of their people missing, but I can promise a scoop on any future story that emerges. This Jacky may indeed be useful, as you mentioned before. If we can't solve this shortly we may have to blow the head off it in the press. However a word of caution. My advice is to stay on focus and avoid any emotional attachment even though it's probably the farthest thing from your mind right now."

Danny grinned despite himself

"I hear you Rebecca and you're right, I do have a lot of other things on my mind, like staying alive, and thanks for the vote of confidence. I'll try not to let you down. Anything on that name I gave you from the dead man's wallet, Ian Jenkins?"

"Sorry Danny, not enough time. It is the middle of the night after all, and I obviously didn't want to use the metropolitan police resources. I'll get back to you when I have something."

They finished on that note and Danny made his way back to the hotel, letting himself in quietly.

Jacky was still asleep.

Danny liked a woman who woke up in a good mood. His former wife Fiona used to be very grumpy in the morning and needed time to come round. Jacky surprised him when she jumped out of bed, shouted a cheery 'good morning' and headed into the bathroom. He heard the shower running and fantasized about how she would look with the water cascading down her sleek body. Then he remembered the advice of Rebecca, quickly got up and put his outer clothes on.

He did some loosening up exercises as he waited for Jacky to emerge from the shower and his mind was also busy assessing their situation.

It wasn't good.

Some big organization was trying to kill him and Scotty and had almost succeeded the previous evening. Scotty was no doubt the primary target but anyone in contact with him apparently became a target too. Even poor Rita had ended up dead. They were quite prepared to eliminate their own people to prevent them from talking, and had done a professional job of cleaning up the flat after the event.

It all came down to Scotty and the missing troop. He had to meet up with him and get the full story. Something was driving this whole thing and there were obviously high stakes involved. He had to start putting the pieces together and that meant an immediate trip to Wales.

Just then Jacky came back into the room.

She had looked fantastic the night before and Danny thought she looked even better with her damp hair framing that finely boned face and those impish eyes, but they didn't stay impish for long when she saw the look on his face.

"How bad is it Danny?" she enquired tentatively.

He sat down in a chair and crossed his arms as he reflected on her question.

"Reality check? Well something bad has happened to a bunch of SAS troopers, just back from Iraq according to my friend Scotty, who you saw briefly in the Fox and Hounds. He maintains that they've been killed, and some group are trying to kill him too, and anyone apparently who comes in contact with him, even your friend Rita."

"But if you're right, why kill poor Rita? She never even met your friend Scotty."

He nodded.

"In retrospect I think the cab we took from the first pub was bugged and they picked up that yourself and Rita were with the press. They put two and two together and figured that I was about to introduce you to Scotty and blow the thing wide open. They must have followed Rita home and killed her, and were waiting to do the same to us. Nasty people Jacky."

He paused wondering if he should tell her the rest.

"There's more Jacky. Remember that phone call I made? Well, I had someone nip round to your flat to check it out and the bodies had been removed and things cleaned up. These are pretty methodical people we've come up against."

She gasped.

"Bodies gone! I can't believe I'm standing here in the light of day discussing the fact that Rita is dead and that there are people out there who are capable of such things and prepared to kill me too. It's just incredible!"

She plumped down on the bed, her face suddenly pale.

"This is getting real scary Danny. I don't like what I'm hearing. Where does it leave me right now?"

Danny sighed, and stood up, walking back and forth as he spoke.

"I don't know exactly Jacky, that's the truth. We could call a cab and have it bring you straight to work where you could just tell your story of what happened last night at the Fox and Hounds. Don't even mention going back to the flat. Think up some reason - you didn't want to wake Rita or whatever at that late hour, or that your new boy friend talked you into going to a hotel with him. Your boss would call in the police and they would have their own questions for you - why you left the scene of the shooting for example. Just claim you were frightened out of your wits and scarpered. You'd probably be perfectly safe then and you'd still have an exciting story to tell."

"And what's the downside Danny?" she asked.

"The downside? That they are set up to make sure you don't get to work this morning at the Daily Mail. Also you had a glimpse of the assassin's face, who they have since disposed of, so you could identify him which might lead back to them. Sorry to put it so bluntly."

"So they might just kill me anyway?" she whispered, her eyes moistening.

Danny sat beside her on the bed and put his arm around her.

"Hey, it's okay Jacky. I'm not going to let that happen. Is there somewhere you could hide out for a few days till we get a handle on all of this?"

She jumped to her feet.

"Absolutely not! I'm not letting go of the story now. This is big! Really big! It could make my career Danny. I'm going with you and don't try to stop me. If you do I'll blow this wide open believe me, and that includes the bodies at my flat. I want to see them pay for killing Rita too, she was a good friend" she muttered, her eyes misting. "What about the paper though when both of us are missing this morning? " she asked.

"Some people of influence that I know will call your boss and convince him to sit on it for a few days on the promise of any story that emerges. That story can of course, be on your byline Jacky."

"Okay, I can run with that. What's your next step Danny?"

"Get out of London without being picked up. I don't know if the people who are after us have access to all those bloody cameras set up around the city, so we have to be careful. My plan is to get a train to Luton where there's a trucking company I know that'll give us a ride to where I think Scotty may be hiding. I won't mention where that is for now. Once there, we can get a car and try to locate him. I'll pay the hotel to look after your car for a few days. They're used to tourists doing that. We travel from here by subway to catch the Luton train, but not walking together as they'll be looking for a couple. Okay?"

An hour later they were on the train. Three hours later they were thundering down the M4 motorway in a heavy truck, heading west towards Wales.

CHAPTER 13.

It was late afternoon when they were dropped in Chepstow just across the Welsh border. The driver waved to them as he took off.

They headed uptown to get some badly needed personal items. Danny was used to traveling light but Jacky was getting slightly desperate by then with only the contents of her purse for the unexpected trip. They agreed to split up and meet in a public parking lot just below the famous Chepstow Castle.

Danny gave her some money which she started to refuse until he reminded her that she couldn't use her credit card as it would be traceable. He purchased some toiletries, a change of clothes and underwear and stuffed them in a small backpack. He also stopped at a newsagents and bought the national papers, some chocolate bars and bottles of water. He knew what it could be like staking out a place and didn't know how long it would take to meet up with Scotty.

He quickly scanned the Daily Mail but didn't see any mention of Rita or Jacky. There was a short article on the attempted shooting at the Fox and Hounds and quotes from some of the hard cases who were there that night. The event would merely enhance the reputation of the bar and attract more thrill-seeking customers. No mention of his or Scotty's names, which was a relief.

Danny walked back to a used car lot that he'd spotted earlier and haggled over a beat-up Ford Granada that still had a good sound to the motor. He parted with 1,500.00 pounds cash and was still first back in the parking lot. He spent some minutes scanning the other papers, none of which referred to him by name, or mentioned the missing women. Soon Jacky appeared looking somewhat discomfited and out of breath. He found himself looking at her pronounced cleavage and jerked his head away.

She grinned and plopped a gym bag down on the ground.

"God, that's the fastest I've ever shopped in my life! Didn't even try anything on. I'll be glad to change out of this outfit. You may recall that I wore it last night to see me through London's seedy pubs."

She looked at the car.

"Traveling in style I see."

"Don't want to draw too much attention to ourselves.... anyway the motor's good. Did a basic mechanics course in the military. Quite often we have to patch up vehicles in the field as there aren't always garages around."

She looked impressed.

"Man of many skills I see. Tell me, why are we here in this place anyway?"

For the first time he told her about Scotty's message prior to his jumping out the window. Without comment she went to pass him back some change but he waved her off.

"No, hang onto that for the moment. You might need it. Some good news. No mention of your name or Rita's in the papers. Just an account of the shooting at the Fox and Hounds, and no mention of me either. That surprises me because my name was certainly known by a number of people there last night, but then they never were a bunch that believed in supporting the local police."

She creased her forehead.

"So what does that mean for us?" she asked.

"For starters, we don't have your picture splashed all over the front page which would make movement rather difficult. There's no manhunt out for me either, so I can still operate, however carefully, and try to start unraveling this. I mentioned being careful, and remember this is good news also for the people coming after us. They were watching the headlines this morning too, wondering if you'd faxed or emailed a story in to your paper. Make no mistake Jacky, whatever organization is involved here, they'll be turning every stone in their efforts to locate us, and Scotty too."

She was weighing it all up in her mind as they started walking back through the parking lot. At the entrance they passed a small beggar squatting on the sidewalk with an old blanket covering his head. As they approached the beggar held out his hand.

"Any chance of a few bob mate?" he pleaded.

Jacky had a look of distaste on her face but Danny took out a couple of pound coins and dropped them into his hand.

"Thanks Gov." the beggar muttered.

Jacky looked surprised.

"D'you always do that Danny? Where's that hard-nosed macho man gone to?"

He shrugged.

"There but for the grace of God.... bad luck can strike any of us."

She sniffed.

"Why doesn't he get a job like the rest of us. When I see beggars with their hand out I figure they're just trying to raise money for their next drink."

"You may be right most of the time but I find it helps not to judge. Who knows, he may not have eaten today at all."

She looked sideways at him as they crossed the road.

"The more I see of you Danny, the more of an enigma you become. The question is, which is the real Danny or have I even seen him yet?"

They went into the first café they spotted, as they were both starving at that stage. Once inside they sat as far back from the door as possible and, when the waitress came over, ordered one of the specials with some soft drinks. Then they both sat back, not speaking, appearing to relax for the first time since leaving the hotel that morning.

Jacky was the first to break the silence.

"Some of the research I did on taking on the assignment for the paper was checking into the security clearance you guys get prior to being accepted into the military. As you know it's quite extensive and I could appreciate how someone with an Irish background would have really been looked at very closely. Today it's probably an Islamic background that would come under the microscope."

He leaned back looking at her.

"So what's your point?"

"Just this. The research I did showed that they check back as far as the grandfather, just to see if there's anything that might represent a threat to the government. You know, criminal background, terrorism or what not. It means that these people, if they have resources like you're suggesting, would have run a trace back to Scotty's grandfather already, in their efforts to locate him, even before the debacle at the Fox and Hounds."

Danny's eyes gleamed with approval.

"Well spotted Jacky and you're absolutely right, apart from this case. You see Scotty's grandfather lived in Scotland up until he retired recently, then he moved to Wales, so his new location wouldn't be on file. As a matter of fact he hung onto the Scottish property. Myself and Scotty used to go there on our leave to fish and climb mountains. Of course everyone is traceable today in the post 9/11 era. Apart from social security, motor vehicle and voting records, you wouldn't believe the numerous methods available for locating people that exist today. Hopefully Scotty's grandfather has stayed outside the net, though we can't assume anything at this stage."

Just then their meals were presented by the smiling waitress and all conversation ceased as they attacked the generous portions.

It was dark when they emerged from the café. They crossed the road to the parking lot and noticed that the beggar was gone. Suddenly Danny tensed as two large men in police uniforms materialized in front of them.

"Mr. Quigley? We'd like to speak to you for a moment please. You too Miss Spellman."

Danny swore inwardly.

How on earth had they been traced so quickly? How had the police got involved? How did they even know their names? He decided to bluff it out. For all he knew they were the resource promised by Rebecca who knew of his plans to travel to Wales.

"What's this about officer? And how on earth do you know our identities? We only got into Chepstow a couple of hours ago."

By this time the men were alongside them and had gripped Danny and Jacky firmly by the arms.

Jacky jerked back.

"What's going on Danny?"

One of the men, wearing sergeant's stripes, who had first addressed them, spoke again.

"All in good time Miss. Just take it easy. We don't want any trouble. We'll be happy to answer all your questions down at the station. Now let's just move over to our vehicle there."

He nodded to a dark unmarked van parked about twenty feet away.

Bells started to go off in Danny's head. He stopped suddenly when the van was a few feet from them.

"Sergeant, this is a peculiar patrol vehicle if I may say so."

"Oh we use unmarked vans for catching poachers on the river Wye. We were on a stakeout when we were asked to pick you two up."

He started to move Danny forward again.

Danny swung his head round.

"Did they also give you English accents to go with the Welsh police uniforms?" he asked.

The two policemen looked across at each other. At that moment Danny glanced down and saw that their shoes were decidedly not police issue and he started moving.

He slipped the Sergeant's grip on his arm and levered it upwards in a wristlock, at the same time, using his other hand, he slammed the man's forehead explosively into the side of the van. As he did so he was aware that the other policeman had thrown Jacky aside and produced a large homemade cosh that he drew back to strike at Danny's head.

At that precise moment a shadow streaked around the side of the van, grabbed the cosh hand and then delivered an almighty head-butt to the policeman's face sending him moaning to the ground, blood spouting from his nose. A swift kick to the head silenced him.

Danny turned from delivering two savage chops to the back of the sergeant's neck and kidneys to see the beggar standing there grinning. He wasn't wearing the blanket on his head now.

It was Scotty.

Danny stared speechless.

"Scotty! Where the hell did you spring from, and dressed like that?"

"Good job I was. Figured you'd stop here and wanted to see if you were being followed. Nobody sees a tramp sitting in the street." he nodded towards Jacky, "especially your friend here. Wouldn't have had much lunch on what she threw me."

Jacky flushed.

"Sorry Scotty. Guess I have a lot to learn."

She looked accusingly at Danny.

"Did you know it was him?"

"Swear to God, I hadn't an inkling" he protested.

Scotty intervened.

"Let's get these two out of sight before someone comes along. I spotted them when they drove in here and it didn't take long for me to figure out that they were phony coppers, even talking about 'getting Quigley' as they walked past me. That's how invisible a beggar can be."

He strode to the back of the van and threw it open, then whistled.

"Holy shit, will you look at this!"

Danny moved around the van and craned his head. Jacky leaned over too and gaped at the sight. It was crammed with assault weapons and pistols of various kinds and makes, all hung and stacked neatly along the sides. There were also boxes of stun grenades, hand grenades, night vision glasses and boxes of ammunition. Scotty pointed to two slabs of C4 explosives, detonators and fuses while Danny spotted two sniper rifles anchored in wooden cases near the front. He scratched his head.

"Just what the hell have you stirred up here Scotty? There's enough stuff to outfit a small army."

Scotty nodded soberly.

"This is something isn't it? What organization could muster all this at a moments notice? And you know what?"

"What?" said Danny, still puzzled.

"We've lucked in with this lot. I figure these guys were the quarter-masters for the rest of the group whoever they are, providing weapons where needed in the U.K. They must have been pulled off their role to try to pick us up, dressed as cops."

Scotty stopped talking, grabbed some plastic cuffs from the back of the van and put them on the two phony policemen. He also tied their feet and gagged them with their own socks and they both heaved them into the van. He quickly searched them and relieved them of their wallets. There was nothing in the van except some ownership papers which he also stuffed in his pocket.

Danny went and brought the Ford Granada and they transferred a number of assault weapons over from the van, including both slabs of C4 and the night vision glasses. He also grabbed both sniper rifles and the appropriate ammunition. Then they slammed the door of the van shut.

Both Danny and Jacky got in the Ford while Scotty went and recovered an old brown Mazda he'd been driving. He led the way with Danny following in his car.

At the edge of town, Scotty pulled over as had been arranged. Danny got out of the car and took out one of the mobile phones the DG had given him. He called 999 and gave them a message about terrorists in a van parked in the castle parking lot. He gave the license number of the van but refused to give his name.

Before he jumped back in, Scotty had wandered over and stood at the open door. Danny punched his arm.

"That should keep them busy. Those two phony coppers will have a lot to answer for when the Welsh police descend on them."

Just then they heard a series of sirens go off in the center of town and they quickly gave each other a high five.

Before climbing into the car, Danny turned sideways towards Scotty and asked him a question that had been puzzling him since they had been accosted by the two phony police officers, who also knew both their names.

"How did they find us so fast Scotty? No one knew but myself and you know who in London."

Scotty pointed his thumb backwards at Jacky in the back seat.

"Ask her. I followed her uptown. She was using her mobile phone for about ten minutes."

Jacky gasped inside the car.

"Now wait a minute…." she started.

Danny went around to the other side, wrenched the door open and hauled her out.

"You were using a mobile phone? Just who the hell were you calling?" he demanded.

Her eyes flashed angrily at him.

"I don't like your insinuations Danny, nor do I appreciate your tone of voice for that matter."

He shook her.

"Who did you call Jacky?" he insisted.

"Not that it's any of your business. I still have a life you know. If you must know I called my mother. I was supposed to go up this weekend to visit, but that's obviously off now."

Danny spoke through gritted teeth.

"You impressed me with being a savvy young female reporter, yet it never occurred to you that mobile phones could be monitored, and you quite merrily spent ten minutes chatting. That's more than enough time for them to tie down our location, which they did, and you saw the results back there."

He reached in and snatched her handbag from the back seat.

"Dig out that phone right now" he instructed.

Looking somewhat defiant and contrite at the same time, she fumbled around in her handbag and reluctantly pulled out her mobile phone.

Danny snatched it from her and was about to drop it on the ground and smash it when a thought occurred to him.

"Where is your mother located?" he asked.

"Northampton" she whispered.

He then asked her for the number of the phone he now held. She readily gave it to him and he memorized it.

Danny pushed Jacky back into the car and moved away several paces.

Using his own phone, he hit the button for his direct number to the DG and brought her up to date on events since coming down the country. She was frantic for him to debrief Scotty but appreciated that the situation was very fluid right then. He explained what he wanted from her….. to trace the last call from Jacky's mobile phone, supposedly to her mother in Northampton.

She had some news for him too on the dead assassin, Ian Jenkins.

"Got out of the service five years ago - ex guards sergeant who went to work for one of those private American security firms in Iraq - company called Empire Security Services. Got dropped from the service by the way for shooting a bunch of Iraqi civilians without any apparent provocation. Reading between the lines I'd say he was a bit of a psycho."

Danny grunted as his mind spiraled around the new information. Suddenly he remembered the other thing he wanted her to do. He read off the two names of the phony coppers which he had taken from their wallets, and asked her to do a background check on them.

"You've been a busy man since we talked last night Danny and things may indeed be starting to break. I'll get onto the police down there and let them know we're interested in those two. I can get someone down to Chepstow tomorrow morning to do our own interrogation. Might give us more to go on. I'll send Sophia down independently as our go-between. She'll have some other material for you as well. She's my PA but I've been training her for the past 12 months with the idea of using her in the field. As I mentioned she'll use the name 'Rebecca' to establish her identity with you. Wait outside the police station for her. Use her as you see fit for the moment. I'll call you back when I have that intercept information, and by then you should have Scotty debriefed."

That's where they left it.

Danny stuck Jacky's phone in his pocket and got back in the car. He drove for several miles with her still smoldering in silence in the back.

He followed Scotty's directions before pulling into a poorly lit driveway beside a small bungalow which was situated back some distance from the road and directly overlooking the River Wye. Scotty explained that it belonged to the friend of a friend, as he didn't want to risk going to his grandfather's cottage. He parked the car and indicated that Jacky was to remain inside, then he walked 20 paces away.

It was time to debrief Scotty.

CHAPTER 14.

THE PREVIOUS MONTH.
HEREFORD, U.K.

Sergeant Scotty McGregor was lounging back on his bed after a hard night downtown with the lads the previous evening. They had just come back from a 3-day exercise in Germany where their role was harassing a NATO exercise group with nightly attacks. The knowledge that the SAS would be part of the opposing force had kept their enemy on edge and their nerves in tatters. Now back at headquarters in Hereford, with no imminent tasks on hand, the troop was letting its hair down.

Just then a head appeared round the door of his room - one of the male admin clerks from the CO's office.

"Sergeant McGregor, the CO wants to see you right away" he said, grinning at Scotty's disheveled appearance.

"Holy shit!" said Scotty, jumping out of bed. "What's it about anyway Benny?"

The man shrugged.

"Haven't a clue Sarge, but he wants to see you right away. Forget about the shower."

Scotty leapt into his uniform, which was still lying on the ground from the German exercise. He looked in the mirror and groaned. It looked like the cat had dragged him in. He quickly splashed some water on his face, ran a comb through his hair and hurriedly laced up his combat boots. Then he walked briskly through camp, thankfully feeling the life coming back into his limbs. At five feet seven inches there wasn't much to Scotty anyway, but what there was made him an awesome warrior in battle. Any group going out on a mission felt better with him along.

His thoughts flitted to his old mate Danny Quigley who had left the regiment over 18 months ago. Many a morning they had strode through camp together, their hearts pounding in anticipation of some impending action. While Scotty hadn't replaced Danny as a reliable partner in action, with anyone else in his unit, he had moved on purposefully in his career and had now been promoted to Sergeant. Quite often that meant that he led a troop on missions where no senior officer was designated.

When he got to the CO's office, Benny was already seated at the reception desk and nodded for him to go inside. Major Wainwright was of medium height but possessed of incredible upper body strength, and was a British weightlifting champion at the dead lift. Scotty had seen him lift the side of a jeep on his own, when it was stalled in a sand dune in Afghanistan. Despite the physical side he carried almost a professorial air about him. His eyes were alert and intelligent and he was fiercely loyal to the regiment and the men under him, to the extent that his career was probably blocked at his present rank for the duration. His men returned that loyalty and would virtually go to any lengths to avoid disappointing him.

Now he looked up at Scotty who had stepped through the doorway and stood at ease there. The regiment was not much for standing on rank as such, but respect for the Queen's commission was always present.

The CO chuckled as he looked up.

"Sergeant McGregor, you look terrible. I didn't think that NATO exercise would have such a detrimental effect on you lad!"

Scotty looked embarrassed.

"Sorry sir…. tied one on last night downtown. Wasn't expecting an early start today…. understood we had some time off to clean our gear up."

"That was the plan Scotty but I'm afraid that's all changed."

He reached for a sheet of paper.

"Here's a list of seven men. I want yourself and these troopers to be ready to fly out at noon today to a desert location. Prepare for, on the outside, to be away for approximately seven days. Standard weaponry for potential enemy contact, though it's not expected. However I do want you to get you're hands on an M60 and some belts of ammo and a couple of MK-19 Grenade Launchers just in case. Supplies and vehicles, which are Humvees, with fuel, will be standing by on landing. Full briefing in two hours for all nine of us. Oh yes, I'm coming along as senior officer. Someone, a civilian from London is coming down to brief us. This is highly confidential like most of our work, but even more so. That's all. Oh and Scotty, well done over in Germany."

Scotty resisted the temptation to ask further questions but was still reeling at the knowledge that the CO would be coming too. Normally if a commissioned officer were along on a vital mission, it would be someone of lower rank, not the commanding officer. He didn't have any more time to think about it. He had seven men to locate and get ready, including himself, within two hours. A troop consisted of sixteen men so he only had to locate approximately half that number. That wasn't impossible, but extremely tight considering they would have to get an issue of desert gear from the quartermaster, and be supplied with live ammunition and other weaponry including the M60. Some of the men might not even be in camp, and that presented other problems of having the military police locate them.

Like any SAS team they were chosen for their attitude, characteristics and complimentary practical skills. By coincidence, four of them had been in the regiment for over seven years, which included Scotty. The other four averaged about half that, though most had spent time in other branches of the service before selection to the SAS.

This four comprised of Terry Buckley from Bristol, whose favorite pastime was reading action novels; Taffy Jones from Swansea, a body builder; Grant Birchall, a brooding giant from Birmingham; Tony Archer from Yorkshire, and the team medic.

The more senior members were Scotty McGregor; the team sergeant, also deadly in using a knife and crossbow; Clyde Stoner, a brooding whip-cord of a man from Manchester, who was a natural with weapons and especially useful when they jammed; Nigel Hawthorn an ex-engineer officer who chose to try out for the SAS and passed selection. He was actually a 4th Dan in Judo and had helped out in unarmed combat training at the regiment - useful with vehicles too. Lastly, the Irishman from Belfast Jimmy Patton who was a creative expert in explosives and fearless in combat. Rumors abounded that he had gained those skills long before joining the parachute regiment and transferring into the SAS.

Fortunately Scotty managed to get all seven seated in the briefing room on time. They had seen and heard an unfamiliar helicopter land a half hour earlier and assumed that the civilian standing in front of them beside Major Wainwright had been the passenger.

The civilian was tall and well built, over six feet, somewhat overweight, which was well disguised by his Saville Row suit. He was in his early forties with receding black hair that he combed across to hide the fact. He was chunky and bad-tempered looking with an air of authority about him. Scotty suspected that he probably didn't like the apparent lack of discipline or respect shown by the scruffy group of NCOs sitting facing him in the room.

Scotty covered the grin on his face. He had seen it all before. Major Wainwright brought them to order.

"As you were previously informed, we have been notified of an impending trip abroad in support of Her Majesty's government policies, and you are the standby troop for carrying out this particular mission. A Mr. ...... ah Blackstone from London is your briefing official this morning."

He stepped aside.

"Mr. Blackstone...." he invited, his hands extended.

Blackstone stepped forward and surveyed the group with a confident smile.

"Right then. You're the selected troop for this task, and I must say you look impressive. Done an excellent job in Germany over the past few days I'm told. Now it may surprise you to hear me say that this task will probably be much more straight-forward than harassing NATO troops. That's our expectation anyway, but the importance and classification of the mission cannot be over emphasized. It goes beyond top secret which explains the total isolation of the troop from this moment and when you land in Kuwait. That's the plan.

You take off from Lyneham airbase in some hours time by special flight.... small civilian aircraft... a Lear jet.... no one else on board..... no mail for the troops or anything like that, which shows the importance of this particular mission. On arrival in Kuwait you will be met by a Colonel Minter from the U.S. Forces - a Marine Officer. He will brief you on your task from there and take care of your overnight stay. You will be housed and fed separately from other units there and Colonel Minter will fill you in on your destination and co-ordinates. He will also provide you with the transport, Humvees and supplies for your trip. Your objective is to collect a special cargo being delivered to Kuwait by aircraft and transport it to a U.S. unit which is approximately two and a half days away, inside the border in Iraq. You will encounter lots of coalition military traffic initially on the road out of Kuwait: supply trucks being run by civilians and of course military units, but this will reduce considerably once you cross into Iraq where your direction will swing west. You will have no contact with other units en route, nor on your overnight stops. Major Wainwright has been fully briefed on the need for this. You may run into military police check-points, but your orders will specify that they are to provide full cooperation to your mission. On arrival at your destination, you will hand the cargo over to the General in charge of the unit and return to Kuwait for extraction in the same plane you flew over in.

It's a simple straightforward task and one that's well within your capabilities considering the variety of tasks you have been asked to carry out in the past."

Here Blackstone paused and looked around.

"Now, any questions?"

Scotty stuck his hand up.

The civilian nodded to him.

"Yes?"

"What's the cargo.... ah Sir?" he asked.

Several of the troop nodded.

Blackstone cleared his throat.

"You don't need to know that Sergeant. It's not relevant."

Scotty's voice was firmer this time.

"With respect sir, I believe it is! How large is it? Where do we carry it, and how do we load it? Does it need any special treatment or handling? Is it sensitive equipment for example, like computer equipment which has to be protected from the sand, or does it need refrigeration? If it's such a simple job why not have the transport section bus it out there? Why do you need an SAS troop to carry out this job.... Sir?"

Suddenly the civilian's face flushed with anger and irritation.

"Now look here Sergeant, your job is to get that bloody cargo to its location, not ...."

Just then Major Wainwright stepped in and caught the civilian's arm, at the same time whispering in his ear. Blackstone looked quite prepared to continue to reprimand Scotty, but after a few moments he nodded, turned quickly and left by the side entrance without another word.

A few moments later they heard his chopper taking off.

Major Wainwright turned and smiled disarmingly at the group.

"Bloody civilians, even if they are ex-officers. They haven't a clue have they?"

He shook his head as if in frustration.

The group grinned, relaxing as he sat down in front of them.

"Okay listen up. Good question from Scotty. The cargo is a wooden crate about three feet tall and weighing about a hundredweight. No special treatment needed. We just manhandle it into the back of one of our four Humvees and leave it there. I don't know what it is, and quite frankly I don't want to know. However it's important enough that they want the SAS to deliver it to its destination, so whatever it is, they want the best of the best to guard it and that means the SAS. We take turns guarding it from the moment we take possession in Kuwait, and at night when we camp out in Iraq. Now the rest of the information we'll get in Kuwait, so just hold any further questions you have for the moment. I know it's the SAS way to dissect a mission down to it's finest detail and that's been our strength in the past, so we'll walk through all the stuff once we're fully briefed in Kuwait by Colonel Minter. Trust me on this guys. Now let's start moving. We have a plane to catch."

Scotty shrugged. They knew some more but he still didn't know why the CO of the regiment, a Major, was needed to ramrod the job. It sounded like a basic transport job.

Scotty had flown into Kuwait a number of times previously on various missions, however he wasn't prepared for the reception they received this time. Their plane, on landing, was directed off to a corner of the massive airfield. When they climbed down the ramp they found a U.S. military troop carrier backed up practically against it, and a Staff Sergeant directing them straight into the back. As soon as they were on board the tarpaulin was pulled down across the back of the truck which immediately moved off. The men sat in semidarkness on the slatted seats, some stretching after the long trip out from the U.K., others recovering from being awakened abruptly on landing.

When the truck came to a stop the tarpaulin was pulled back and they found themselves inside a large hangar, with vehicles and equipment parked around the side and doors leading off to various offices. The Staff Sergeant spoke briefly to Major Wainwright and the troop headed over to a door which led into a good-sized meeting room.

Inside, waiting for them, was a large bald flinty-eyed Colonel wearing marine patches who, they assumed, to be Colonel Minter. The Staff Sergeant slammed the door behind them and left.

The Colonel shook hands with Major Wainwright and they spoke together for some minutes while the troop dumped their bergens (packs) on the floor. Finally the two officers finished conversing. Major Wainwright sat down and the U.S. officer turned to the assembled soldiers.

"I'm Colonel Minter, U.S. Marine Corps. I understand you've had a general briefing back in the U.K. so it leaves me to fill in the rest. I may repeat some of the information you already know but that's probably not a bad thing. I would like to emphasize however the absolute top-secret nature of your mission, which explains the no contact with other personnel at this base or on the trip to your destination. For this reason you will be housed and fed here in the hangar tonight. We have limited but adequate accommodation for all of you. The good news is that we'll truck over food from the mess hall tonight, and from personal experience I know it's better than the stuff you Brits get in your mess."

There were some grins of acknowledgement at that. He went on. "However you're limited on the trip, as you would expect, to MRE's (meals ready eat) and no camp fires for that horrible brew you Brits call tea."

There were good-humored groans from the group.

"Now the cargo is being flown in tonight on a Lear jet. You are to meet it on the apron, load it onto one of those jeeps out there and bring it back here. It requires that one of you will guard the cargo 24/7 with two people traveling inside the jeep until you deliver it to your destination over the border in Iraq, and hand over to a specific team who will be waiting. Your CO has the names of the people there.

The nature of the cargo need not concern you. Your Commanding Officer here, Major Wainwright doesn't know either, and quite frankly doesn't want to know. Now I've worked with the 'Sass' before. I know how detail-orientated you lot are and that's good. The reason we asked for you is three-fold:

1. it's a valuable cargo and we want the best guarding it;
2. confidentiality is a by-word in your regiment and we know there'll be no loose talk about this mission either during or after it's completed.
3. the area where you are traveling to is still a fluid situation where control on the ground is concerned and sporadic small unit militia attacks are still happening, especially on the supply convoys. We don't expect it to happen to your group because you'll be much farther west, but we know from experience that you lads can handle yourselves if it does happen.

There are four Humvee jeeps for the nine of you and the cargo, so you can use one for your gear and split the others as you see fit, as long as there are two traveling with the cargo during the day. I'm supplying the Major and your Sergeant with the GPS coordinates of your destination, GPS equipment and suggested stopping off places for the two nights you're out there. The actual stops will of course be at Major Wainwright's discretion. You will be in constant communication with myself at base here, again using equipment we'll supply you with, and of course I want to be informed immediately if you run into any difficulty."

One of the men raised his hand.

Colonel Minter nodded to him.

"Yes?"

"Can we call in CAS (Close Air Support) or other coalition forces if we get hit by Al Qaeda or insurgents out there Sir?"

"Unfortunately no soldier, and for one good reason. The wider we spread this mission the more difficult it is to maintain secrecy. Can you imagine how many people would have to sign off on having air support just standing by on the possible chance that you lot might need bailing out? Absolutely not! And this is one of the reasons we wanted the SAS to head up this mission - your aggressive stance when you get hit in combat. The area is well known for the sand storms that spring up with little notice, so this makes air support difficult at the best of times. Any more questions?"

Scotty raised his hand.

The Colonel nodded to him.

"Sir I'm struggling to understand why you would even consider placing what is obviously a valuable cargo anywhere within harms way, when you could chopper it out in a few hours."

Major Wainwright must have felt that he should take the heat of Colonel Minter at this time and stood up, turning slightly to the U.S. officer.

"Ah Colonel Minter, this is the SAS way of going into a task. We like to look at every possible scenario and work out possible reactions to them. It's saved our bacon many times in the past."

Turning back to the troop.

"I've discussed this very point with our colleague from London and Colonel Minter by secure telephone. As regards using a chopper, there are an increasing number of these being shot down in Iraq so this was part of the reason for our selection. The frequent sand storms make it difficult for helicopters and they could suddenly end up flying blind and finding a solid landing pad can be almost impossible. If a chopper goes down the odds are that the personnel on board are killed as well, so the cargo would be vulnerable. All things considered, it was decided that a tough battle-ready SAS troop would be the best bet."

Colonel Minter jumped in again.

"Before someone asks the question, why haven't a Seal team or Delta force been given the job, after all it's an American operation? Quite simply there were none of their units available, what with our Forces pulling out from Iraq and with increasing demands from Afghanistan. If the truth's known, most of the Special Forces are at the point of exhaustion from too much frontline work. You lot coming back from the NATO exercise just slipped nicely into the window of time available."

He looked around as if expecting more questions but the troop stayed quiet.

Colonel Minter then proceeded back into the hangar with the unit and went over the equipment and vehicles. The Major and Scotty were briefed separately on the coordinates for their nightly stops and the eventual destination, the fuel required, and took possession of their GPS equipment. After an hour the Colonel departed while the troop sat around in a circle and continued to evaluate the various challenges facing them, including fighting formations and the use of weaponry if they were attacked.

The meeting carried on for another hour before the group broke up and went back to re-check their vehicles and equipment. Two of the troop were given a quick refresher on the radio equipment and call signs. Vehicles were assigned, equipment loaded up, and the group went off to sort out their accommodation for the night, which was in the same hangar.

The food truck appeared an hour later and they got stuck in as if it was their last meal. Shortly after Colonel Minter appeared again and spoke to Major Wainwright who beckoned to Scotty. All three jumped in the jeep with Colonel Minter driving. He carefully negotiated his way across the base until they ended up alongside a small civilian aircraft, which had presumably just landed. Standing at the bottom of the ramp waiting for them was a beefy American wearing denims and operating as loadmaster. He asked Colonel Minter and Major Wainwright for some identification and after scrutinizing these briefly led the three of them up into the aircraft.

The cargo looked exactly as Major Wainwright had described it - a wooden crate about three feet in height. Through the slats they could see sacking covering the contents. The loadmaster untied some stabilizers that had kept it anchored during the flight. They could still see the two pilots up front sorting out paper work as Scotty and Colonel Minter lifted the wooden crate between them and started towards the exit. It wasn't really a heavy load for two men, weighing as it did about one hundredweight, but the container made it somewhat awkward when they inched down the ramp.

Major Wainwright grimaced as he leaned towards them.

"I got this bloody stomach cramp lads. I need the toilet in the worst way. I'll see if the pilots will mind me using the one on board."

The two men hauling the load were fully concentrating on getting down the ramp and just grunted as the Major lurched off up the aisle of the plane.

Colonel Minter and Scotty completed the transfer of the crate into the back of the jeep and had just completed tying it down with some rope when Major Wainwright reappeared.

"That's better" he said wiping his forehead. "I think it was that bloody flight that did me… my guts have been churning ever since. Must be getting too old for all this shit!"

The Colonel and Scotty chuckled as all three climbed in and headed back to their hangar, where the crate was loaded into a Humvee. Then one of the troopers was assigned to start the guard duty on the cargo.

The real task began the following morning at sunrise.

They were on the road at dawn after a sizable breakfast had been brought over from the Mess. Once clear of the city they could see they weren't the only ones with the objective of getting to Iraq. Dozens of vehicles, mostly supply trucks driven by civilians, were heading like a giant snake towards the Iraqi border. On the other side of the road similar convoys, now empty, as well as military vehicles and equipment being evacuated from the de-escalating Iraqi mission, headed back into Kuwait. One of the troop had brought a small union jack triangular flag which he'd fastened to the jeep's aerial, which raised several cheers from U.S. combat troops returning from the front line.

The troop made several attempts to pass the slower moving convoys but this was making it difficult for the last jeep to keep up and creating some close calls. In the end the Major instructed them to stay in line until the convoys thinned out, which they did later in the morning. Helicopters shot overhead, heading for the border and they passed several military police huts whose main job was to keep the traffic moving.

After a long day they crossed over into Iraq, having gone through a brief check by military police and been waved on. They started heading in a westerly direction and noticed an immediate difference in the volume of traffic.

A few hours later they made their first camp for the night. The Major had decided to ignore the coordinates supplied by Colonel Minter and moved on a further five miles. The campsite he selected was set back among some old gnarled dead trees and what appeared to be a dried up water hole, about thirty feet deep.

The bottom of the well was cluttered with rocks, pieces of scrub and what looked like the bones of animals, possibly sheep or goats, that had fallen in at some time in the past.

The jeeps were set up in a defensive position and fields of fire allocated in the event of a night attack. The M60 was mounted and covered with a tarpaulin to keep any sand from getting into its parts. Major Wainwright instructed Scotty to have two of the troop fill half a dozen sandbags for defensive positions.

Scotty set the roster for the nights guard duty, with Major Wainwright, volunteering for the most difficult watch - 4 am to 6 am.

Scotty took the shift prior to that, and after a cold supper the troop bedded down. The night proceeded without event and Major Wainwright woke them up at the completion of his watch. Scotty was impressed that he had already dumped out the sandbags, which were stored away in one of the jeeps. The troop was dying to brew up and have something warm but no one complained, at least not too loudly. Finishing up their packet breakfast, and after tending to minimal washing, brushing of teeth and latrine duties, they started out again. The M60 was left mounted, but with a tarpaulin cover over it. The major instructed the unit to switch drivers in the cargo vehicle every four hours. An unusual order at best but being soldiers no one queried it.

They still continued to spot the occasional convoy, mostly military, who skirted them cautiously, until they recognized the U.S. markings on the vehicles and the British flag.

Some convoy leaders they encountered indicated that they wanted to stop, but Major Wainwright stood up in the jeep pointing urgently ahead, and they kept going. His only concern was that they might have been passing on intelligence of enemy activity ahead, but Colonel Minter had instructed him to avoid any contact whatsoever. None of the convoys appeared to take issue with this behavior.

The second night they set up next to an abandoned shepherd's hut and some rotting railings that might have held a herd of goats at one time. There was a man-made stone wall off to one side which made for an excellent defensive position in the event of an attack. The evening's routine was exactly the same - meals, guard duty, allocation of defensive positions and sleep.

SAS troops liked action, and all their training was geared to applying sudden deadly force, as a team. That was where their fierce concentrated firepower usually broke the spirit and will of any attackers. Right now it was looking as if it weren't going to be a trip they would be telling their grandchildren about. Some began to wonder again why a transport unit hadn't been selected for the task. It's the nature of soldiers to grumble and they did, but good naturedly and out of the earshot of their officer.

In the morning their spirits lifted, knowing they would reach their destination by late afternoon. The wind started picking up as the day progressed and sand whipped around them.

When they stopped briefly for lunch the Major gave them an unusual instruction

"We're on time to reach our destination late this afternoon as you know. Theoretically we're coming into a friendly U.S. military camp but I want you to stay alert and keep your weapons at the ready at all times. I'm not saying 'in their faces' as such, but what I don't want is you chilling out because you're inside their camp. Put the vehicles in a defensive formation and when I'm not in my vehicle don't make it too obvious that the M60 and the grenade launchers are primed and ready for action. I don't know what the overnight arrangements are for us but we may just hand over the cargo and head off to find our own camp site for the night."

Wainwright noticed the stunned looks and knew that he'd have a dozen questions flying back at him in a moment.

"No questions!" he barked jumping into his vehicle and heading off.

He left a bunch of confused troopers racing to catch up to him. They'd never had a briefing like that prior to action before.

CHAPTER 15.

The winds had got progressively stronger and the sandstorm that had been flicking at them, gradually ramped up over the course of the afternoon and slowed them down considerably. It was dark and late when they finally limped into camp and were stopped by perimeter scouts. They were amazed to find that these were heavily armed civilians, part of a private U.S. security company who normally protected contractors and visiting politicians in Baghdad. They couldn't see any U.S. servicemen around.

Their vehicles were directed to a spot between four trailers and some tents now flapping wildly in the wind. One of them reminded Scotty of the weapons trailers that Colin Powel had shown to the U.N., which underpinned his weapons of mass destruction presentation.

The Major alighted and was immediately accosted by a large crew-cut individual who caught his arm and pointed through the swirling sand to one of the trailers.

"Just two of you…. the General's waiting" he shouted.

Major Wainwright nodded to Scotty to accompany him, and the rest of the troop, without any prompting, swung the vehicles into a defensive formation.

They banged on the trailer door and without waiting pushed their way in where they found themselves facing three individuals. One was a squat, bald-headed man in fatigues, with one star displayed on his collar. He immediately stepped forward and stuck his hand out.

"General O'Donnell. You must be Major Wainwright. Pleased to finally make your acquaintance."

He then nodded to the two men with him.

"This is Tom Bradley and Ray Hardwick, executives with the Empire Security Services company out of Buffalo New York. You met some of their personnel outside."

Major Wainwright grinned.

"The Empire State. I get it."

Both men turned and nodded but didn't offer to shake hands.

One of the men, Bradley, was a tall gray-haired man with the studied look of the ex-military about him. He appeared to be measuring them and the way they had their weapons at the ready. His companion was a younger man with hard muscles protruding from a sleeveless jacket, a holstered 45 automatic on his belt, and wearing khaki cargo pants and an Australian bush hat. There was a half grin on his face as he looked at the two disheveled troopers standing there, however he said nothing.

Scotty didn't like the look of either of the civilians. There was something very watchful about them and the way they were appraising them.

The General turned back abruptly to the Major.

"Right, you've got the cargo and no problem on the trip I gather.... we've been kept informed by Colonel Minter back in Kuwait."

At that particular moment there was a stunning explosion close by and shrapnel sliced through the top of the trailer, catching the General across his back and sending him flying into a corner. The two civilians, the Major and Scotty all dived for the floor. Bradley stuck his head up a fraction.

"That was a RPG rocket.... can't mistake the sound.... sounds like an attack by some insurgents or Al Qaeda. Christ they weren't supposed to be anywhere near this location which is why we picked it."

Another rocket blasted nearby and a number of weapons joined in with the sound sweeping closer.

The General pushed himself up into a sitting position, the shoulders of his fatigues soaked with blood, and shouted across the trailer.

"Get out and bury that fucking bomb! If the bastards get a hold of that we're in deep shit."

He sagged back onto the floor.

The Major and Scotty, who were lying face to face, looked in stunned silence at each other before clambering to their feet. Right then Ray Hardwick, the man with the 45, leapt across the trailer and beckoned to them aggressively with the weapon.

"All right you two, you heard the man" he ordered.

The Major stared at him angrily.

"Get that fucking weapon out of my face or I'll be forced to take it off you and shove it right down your throat" his voice grated.

Hardwick looked stonily at him for a moment, then let his weapon hand fall to his side.

"Your turn will come Major, better believe it. Right now we better do as the General ordered…. hide that fucking cargo. Now let's move our asses."

The Major glanced momentarily at Scotty who just nodded and slapped the stock of the assault rifle he was holding reassuringly.

They went outside into virtual chaos. The wind was whipping tents and belongings right across the camp and sand blasted like a hailstorm. Bullets were scything from all directions and more explosions rocked the campsite. A number of terrorist vehicles had been hit thanks to the SAS M60 machine gun and the grenade launchers and were burning fiercely. The flames were casting ghostly shadows that were helping both the attackers and the besieged camp defenders.

Major Wainwright's troop, because of their initial defensive positions, were firing back strongly. The chatter of the M60 machine gun was steady and distinctive.

Hardwick ran alongside as the Major pointed to his Humvee jeep, the one with the M60, now engaging the insurgents. Once up to it he grabbed a shovel out of it and indicated to Scotty that he should get a second one from another vehicle. They both started digging directly behind the jeep with Hardwick crouched down on one knee as the battle seesawed around them. One of the troopers, Terry Buckley, was hit and was immediately pulled under one of the jeeps and treated by Trooper Archer the medic, before jumping back to his station.

Once the hole was down about four feet, Major Wainwright slapped Scotty on the shoulder and they both stood up and ran round the side of his Humvee, the one with the cargo in it. Scotty opened the side door and reached in for the crate.

Hardwick took the other door across from him.

There wasn't time to untie knots. Scotty hauled his commando knife out and slashed through the ropes that had held the cargo stable. With Hardwick pushing from the other side and the Major pulling, the crate slid across and was grabbed and lifted by himself and Scotty, who immediately shuffled with it around to the rear of the jeep.

The Major shouted up close in Scotty's ear.

"Get in the hole Scotty and grab this quick!"

In what seemed like seconds the crate was down in the hole and both Scotty and Hardwick started shoveling as if their lives depended on it. As the hole started to fill up the sounds of battle gradually began to fade. However the storm took on a fury of it's own, and apart from the flickering lights of the burning vehicles, vision was extremely limited and impossible for the troopers to see without some sort of protective goggles.

Once the hole was filled completely, Hardwick stepped over to the Major and shouted

"Let's roll the jeep over it for further security."

The three of them put the jeep into neutral and rolled it forward. Just then the second civilian Tom Bradley ran across and pulled Hardwick off to one side. After a couple of moments of conversation, Hardwick came back and shouted in Major Wainwright's ear.

"I'm to stay with the jeep overnight. It's our responsibility for the cargo now, so you're relieved. You and your men can cram into a couple of those trailers until the storm finishes. It'll take several hours to pass over."

Wainwright nodded and passed the information to the troop, who were starting to relax now that the attackers had fled off into the night. They would check in the morning for enemy casualties, as the troop believed they had killed a number of them.

Major Wainwright saw his men stretched out on the floors of two of the trailers and crammed in behind them. The storm continued to howl around the trailer as the hours passed. During the night some of the men stepped over him as they went out to relieve themselves, or the really dedicated smokers to have a puff.

It was a long night.

It was the silence that woke them. The wind had died down and the sound of the gritty sand striking the trailer had stopped.

Major Wainwright led the stiff, red-eyed group outside into the morning light. They hadn't seen the area in the daylight anyway but the storm had almost obliterated what must have been a well-established camp.

The smoldering hulk of two deuce-and-a-half vehicles lay at the top section of the encampment. Sand was piled up everywhere and the four U.S. Humvees that had been driven by the troop had sand sloping all the way up to the driver's doors. Some tents were still standing while strips of canvas and sleeping bags were strewn and wrapped around vehicles and trailers. The troopers carried out their wounded mate Trooper Buckley, brought him over and sat him in the Humvee with the M60 positioned in it. Major Wainwright stuck his head into the jeep as Trooper Archer did a quick check on Buckley's condition.

He seemed to be somewhat feverish, but alert and getting over the shock of the wound from the attack. Buckley struggled to his feet and immediately started to clear off the cover on the M60 and sweep the weapon clear of sand.

The medic gave the thumbs up to the Major who turned to see General O'Donnell, Bradley, and several of his security personnel, emerging from some of the other trailers.

The General strode over to Major Wainwright.

"Okay, where is it?" he asked abruptly, his eyes flicking around.

The Major shrugged.

"Hell we buried it right under my Humvee there, and Hardwick said he was now taking possession of it officially from us. Even said he was staying in the vehicle with it overnight."

He looked around in puzzlement.

"Just where the hell is he? The vehicle was empty when we crawled out here two minutes ago."

The General turned and shouted at some of the security detail.

"Check the toilet and those two tents and that other trailer. Shit, he knows not to leave this cargo alone. I specifically instructed him to sit right on it until we dug it up this morning."

The British troopers began sweeping the sand from their vehicles and started milling around as the civilian security personnel ran back across the camp checking tents, trailers and the toilet area, which was on the edge of camp with the canvas still miraculously strung up.

The men ran back to the General.

"No sign of him anywhere Sir. We checked the places he might be and there's nowhere else he could be. He's disappeared Sir, and there are no vehicles missing"

General O'Donnell cursed.

"I don't believe this! The guy had specific instructions to baby sit this fucking cargo until daylight."

He swung his head angrily towards the Major.

"Just where exactly did you bury it ?" he demanded.

"Right under my Humvee, Sir. We buried it and Hardwick told us to push the vehicle over on top of the site, as further protection. Then he climbed into the vehicle and basically told us that our mission was finished at that point. He was assuming responsibility for it. We weren't asked to provide additional security so we were just glad to get in out of the bloody storm, which is what we did" he finished.

The General stared at him silently. Finally he nodded to the security detail.

"Okay, push that Humvee forward, get some shovels from these Brits and dig that cargo up…. be careful with those shovels… easy does it."

The Humvee was shoved forward and two men started clearing the top sand off. They started digging and went down two feet……… then another two. Still nothing.

O'Donnell looked at the Major.

"Just how deep did you go for Christ's sake? I can't imagine you went very deep what with the attackers sweeping the camp and the sand storm."

Wainwright stepped forward and peered into the hole, his face puzzled.

"Hell I'm not sure we even went down this far. You're right, it was chaos out here and we didn't know if the attackers were going to be on us at any moment. It was panic stations. We just scooped out a hole and pitched the crate in. You know I'd swear there was only about a foot of sand on top of it when we finished. I don't understand this."

The General strode forward to the hole and looked down into it.

"Shit I don't believe this! You two, keep digging a few more feet."

He turned to the Major.

"Get your men digging too. Try a few feet towards the other end of the Humvee."

Major Wainwright nodded and two of the troopers ran, got more shovels and started digging. The first hole was now down several feet and the men stopped. Soon a second hole was uncovered with the same result.... nothing. General O'Donnell's face was no longer registering alarm but sheer disbelief.... even fear. All vestige of military discipline seemed to desert him. He jumped forward and grabbed the Major's arm, his eyes wild, his voice strident.

"Get your fucking men digging under those other vehicles Major, right now. You're just trying to fuck me up here! I'll have your ass for this..... your career! Do you hear?"

Major Wainwright calmly pried the General's hand off his arm and pushed him away.

"General I'd suggest you control yourself right now. We handed the cargo over to one of your security detail last night and he took charge of it. To suggest that we had something to do with its disappearance is ludicrous to say the least! We were all crammed in that dammed trailer for the whole night. The person who we handed it over to is missing. Okay, so there's no vehicles missing, but who's to say he wasn't picked up by someone during the night and just took off with the cargo? Even with the raiders perhaps. Hell of a coincidence, them hitting you right then."

The General's face paled.

"That's total bullshit Major. Hardwick was one of the primary movers on this whole mission. He's not going to sabotage it like this for Christ's sake!"

Major Wainwright sighed.

"Okay General, if that's what you want."

He turned to the troop.

"Okay lads, shove the jeeps forward and start digging in the sand where they were parked. Just down to about four feet."

The troop responded with alacrity, placing their weapons in the jeeps and slicing into the sand until three more holes were uncovered.... still nothing.

The General had been striding around impatiently, hovering over each hole. Now he pointed a few feet further along in front of where the jeeps had rested.

The troop looked up at their CO who shrugged and then nodded. The men started digging again but with less energy this time.

Same result.

At that moment Major Wainwright suddenly became aware that something had changed in the atmosphere around them. An artificial stillness had settled around the group which was broken only by the sound of safety catches being snicked off and rounds of ammunition being jacked into weapons. He swung around to see the General and Tom Bradley standing off to one side and several of his security detail with their weapons pointing directly at the troop. Most of the men were standing in 4 foot holes in the sand, with their rifles stuck uselessly in the back of their jeeps.

The Major stared at the General.

"Just what the hell is going on here O'Donnell? I'd advise you to think carefully about what you're doing and back off. I'm going to take my men out of this camp right now under my command, and you have no authority to stop us."

The General laughed.

"Oh but I do have the authority Major…. and it's right there in those weapons pointed at you. For your information I am a General, retired but still a General, and you have just fucked me up something wicked. For that I'll take pleasure in sticking you and your lads in those holes you just dug up. It wasn't intended that you leave here in any event, but I'm going to take more pleasure than I expected doing this because I have a feeling that somehow you sabotaged this whole deal on us, for whatever reason. You have no idea what you just screwed up Major and you never will."

The Major held both his hands up.

"Look Sir, we can discuss this….."

He was too late. The General nodded to the security detail who steadied their rifles, fingers tightening on triggers.

Wainwright knew that he and his troop were moments from death.

Just then there was sudden explosion of noise as the M60 opened up from twelve feet away, mowing down the line of the security detail, like corn before a harvester. The M60 kept stuttering away, and the bodies of the men on the ground twitched as the heavy bullets chewed into them.

The Major ran forward and jumped up on the Humvee to discover the wounded Trooper Buckley wrapped around the M60, his eyes closed but his finger still on the trigger. He reached forward, pried him off the weapon and laid him back gently on the seat.

Silence fell on the camp.

It was suddenly interrupted by the sound of a jeep starting up, over beyond one of the trailers. Scotty stuck his head into the Humvee.

"That so-called General and that civvy Bradley are doing a runner Major. They're heading out of camp."

Major Wainwright jumped out of the vehicle and grabbed Scotty's weapon, swinging towards the sound of the receding motor. It was still obscured by a trailer and only came into sight as it went up and over a sand dune.

He fired several shots at it, more in frustration than with the expectation of hitting anything. He handed the rifle back to Scotty. They both stood looking at the carnage around them.

"Major, just what the fuck have we got ourselves into?" Scotty asked haltingly.

"I don't know Scotty. I really don't. Right now check through the camp for any more of the U.S. team and then get through to Colonel Minter in Kuwait and fill him in as to what's happened. Ask him for instructions. This whole thing's beyond comprehension. I've no idea what's going on Scotty."

Scotty looked at him keenly.

"Sir, you must have had some inkling that things weren't kosher. Remember the instruction you gave to the troop about not assuming we're among friends. That's a first for us going into an allied camp" he said carefully.

The Major pursed his lips reflectively.

"Let's just say I was picking up some static about this mission and wasn't happy about some things. I can't say any more right now but we'll talk later. Get in contact with Colonel Minter straight away and come back to me."

Scotty dashed off and the Major turned to his men who were still standing around looking stunned at the chain of events. They had seen dead bodies before but not a bunch of allies who had just tried to kill them in cold blood.

He indicated for them to gather round and they crawled out of the holes they had been digging and stumbled over. He looked each of them in the eye for a moment, forcing himself to look in control of the situation and speaking calmly.

"I've been on several missions over the years and so have a number of you. What's just happened here is unprecedented under any set of circumstances. Quite frankly I don't understand it. An ally who, just like that, tries to eliminate the whole troop! It's beyond comprehension lads. We were carrying out a legitimate mission for our government in conjunction with the U.S. Military as we understood it. Now it looks like they intended to terminate the whole fucking squad right here in the desert, having delivered that bloody crate to them. They would have succeeded too if it wasn't for poor Buckley who, despite his wounds, was alert enough to man that M60. Just as well for us. Scotty is at this moment contacting Kuwait for instructions and in the meantime we have work to do."

He instructed them to lay out the dead civilians for burial and try to retrieve identity documents from each of them where possible. One of the troopers had a camera and was told to take pictures of the dead security personnel for the record, and GPS coordinates of the graves for possible future reburial. He was then told to take detailed pictures of the camp, including vehicles and the trailers, inside and out. He also had them collect up all the weapons from the camp and bury them in the sand.

Major Wainwright then went over to the trailer where he had first met the General, and spent time gathering all the paper work that was lying around. He only had time for a cursory look at some of the papers but nothing leapt out at him in terms of vital information on the mission. He went through the other trailers as well.

Just then Scotty stuck his head in the door of the last trailer.

" We haven't found any further members of the General's team in the camp. Can't raise Kuwait at all. No response whatsoever. Checked my call sign and frequency. Nothing but static coming back."

"This gets more curious by the moment Scotty. Just keep that news to yourself for the moment. We need to clean up this camp and head back. Go and check on the burials and scavenge any petrol you get hold of. We were supposed to get tanked up here, as you know. For the return journey, we can reduce down to three vehicles and I don't intend to take three days to get back to Kuwait. We have to sort this out a.s.a.p. before all hell breaks loose, so let's jump to it."

CHAPTER 16.

KUWAIT

They limped back into the American air base having made the trip back in 20 hours with minimum stops for rest and food. Even for the tough SAS troop who were used to deprivation on missions, it had been a hard and challenging trip. The injured trooper Buckley never complained on the journey and was grateful it had come to an end.

Once inside the base they drove around to the hangar where they had over-nighted prior to the journey into Iraq. Everyone climbed out and started dusting the sand off their uniforms.

The Major and Scotty walked swiftly over to the hangar doors where they had gained entry before. They were locked. They hammered on the doors but got no response. They looked at each other and of one accord went in two directions around the corner of the hangar, to check the other entrances. None of those doors were open either. They met back in front of the first door again.

"What's going on Sir?" Scotty queried.

The Major threw his hands up in frustration.

"Christ only knows Scotty! As you know we were supposed to debrief here before catching the same plane back to the U.K."

They both looked at each other as the same thought came to them. The Major gestured to the troop who were milling around uncertainly.

"Tell them to stay in their vehicles for the moment and then you come with me Scotty. We'll check out that bloody plane for starters."

In a moment they were carefully maneuvering their way across the base to the isolated area where their original flight from the U.K. had been diverted to. The apron was completely deserted. Not a plane in sight. They both sat in silence for a long moment. The Major peered uncertainly around at Scotty.

"This is getting scary Scotty. Just what have we got ourselves into? Who the hell are these people? he asked quietly.

Scotty sat there baffled, saying nothing.

Finally the Major stirred and turned the jeep around.

"I know one group of people who would have a record of when this plane took off - Air Traffic Control. Perhaps it's coming back in for us tomorrow or even later. We probably weren't expected back so soon from Iraq."

A British officer's uniform opens most doors even in a U.S. base. Shortly they were sitting across from Mr. Trevor Taylor, a civilian supervisor up in the Air Traffic control section. He was tall, middle aged and tanned, with a Texas accent and a tight angled face, which now looked quite anxious.

"As I understand it, you flew in last week on a civilian aircraft from the U.K. on a special mission and were expecting that same aircraft to be here waiting for you to take you back. Is that right Major?"

"That's correct Mr. Taylor. We were housed overnight in one of the hangars on the other side of the base and our liaison there was a U.S. Colonel Minter. We got our vehicles and supplies there and understood that on the conclusion of the mission we would be flying back on the same aircraft. Unfortunately there's no one at the hangar right now. We checked before coming round to see if our plane was here. It's nowhere to be found. We're back a couple of days early, but we understood that the aircraft would be staying here on the ground waiting for us. I'd like to know when it flew out, and also what the arrangements are for getting us out of here and if the plans have changed somehow."

Taylor looked sympathetically across at them.

"You boys look bushed for sure. I can see why you must be wondering what the hell's going on."

He pulled the computer around and hit some keys.

"Let's just look at when that aircraft flew in for starters and then we can see if we have a flight plan registered for the return trip. This is the

U.S. Air Force, but screw-ups do occur now and then, but when they do we don't advertise it. Just give me a moment here."

For the next ten minutes his hands flew across the keyboard and as they did so his face looked increasingly puzzled. His hands flew faster and his gaze flicked up more and more at them. Finally he stopped, pushed his chair back and hurried from the room.

He didn't return for a full hour. When he did his face was flushed and harried.

"Ah, sorry gentlemen…. ah Major…. strange goings on here. There's no record of a civilian flight into this airport on the day you mentioned, nor indeed a second plane from which you claim you collected some crate. I've checked with base personnel and they have no Colonel Minter in any hangar on the base."

Both Scotty and Major Wainwright jumped to their feet.

"Now look here" the Major snapped, "this is getting downright ridiculous, Taylor! I have a whole troop of men who flew in with me and were met and briefed by Colonel Minter. Just what the hell are you trying to pull here? That plane existed and Colonel Minter existed. Now come on, level with me. Just what the hell's going on here?"

Taylor's eyes refused to meet his and he retreated around behind his desk.

"I haven't a clue Major. It's a mystery to me. Sorry, no record of the events as you lay them out. Confusing I admit."

"Confusing! I should damn well say it is confusing! Right, if you want to play games Taylor, then I want an immediate interview with the Base Commander. Surely he knows what the hell is going on inside his own base. That's his job isn't it? Seems reasonable to me that he would know what planes would be taking off and landing on his turf."

Taylor coughed.

"That's going to be a problem. I tried to contact him. You see he's tied up on some exercise right now. However the good news is that his second-in-command has arranged another flight back to the U.K. for you and your group. It's…. ah…. actually sitting on that apron right now where you claim the other plane landed."

Scotty whistled. The Major shook his head in disbelief.

"You leave the room and a flight is arranged, just like that? I heard the U.S. Air Force is efficient, but this is crazy. I've hung around for days on bases like this trying to get out."

Wainwright scrutinized Taylor closer.

"They just want us out of here right? Washing their hands of us. They can't wait to get rid of us Taylor, is that it?"

Taylor's face was a picture of indecision. He stared at the Major his face ashen after the exchange. Finally he leaned close and whispered.

"Don't ask any more questions Major. Just get on the plane."

With that he turned and left the room.

Within twenty minutes they had collected the rest of the troop and driven around to where a U.S. Air Force plane was parked with engines running. They clambered out and abandoned their vehicles right there on the apron.

A civilian was waiting at the foot of the aircraft stairs. He wasn't happy when the troop started to board with all their weapons including the M60. The Major ignored him and they all climbed aboard carrying Trooper Buckley on a stretcher.

The plane took off immediately.

There was no attendant on the aircraft and they never spoke to the pilots on the trip. They discovered food and drink piled up in one corner of the plane, the flight obviously prepared in a hurry. The troop had never completed a mission in this manner before and it was a confused group that settled in uneasily for the long haul back to the U.K. Even the least experienced realized that the repercussions of the mission could be devastating for all of them.

CHAPTER 17.

WALES.

Danny wasn't aware that he been holding his breath during the last minute of the story. Now he let it out in a long relieved breath.

"My God Scotty.... I was worried there for a moment with your lads left standing on the tarmac. That's an incredible story! What happened when you got back to the regiment?"

Apparently the Major stormed off to see his commanding officer. He was gone three hours and when he came back he informed the troop to take two weeks off, but to stick around home soil to facilitate any inquiries that most certainly would be following. Each of them had to make a statement regarding the whole mission and these were handed over to Major Wainwright"

"Two weeks off. That's not hard to take! So what happened then?"

Three days later Scotty had received a call from the Major in the middle of the night. He was shouting down the phone. Words to the effect that some group was killing off the troop one by one, and that Scotty should go to ground and be on the alert for any attempt on his life.

The attackers were using the Major's name to get to the troopers and while he had no idea how many of the men had been killed, he wanted Scotty to attempt to contact the remnant of the group and meet up with him at his fishing boat in Polperro, on the south coast.

Danny's mind went back to the Fox and Hounds.

"So that's what you were trying to say when you slammed me up against the wall of the pub in London – that some of the troop were dead. What makes you think that?"

Scotty had received a call the same day that the Major had phoned, from someone who claimed to be representing the Major and asking him to meet with them urgently. He agreed to the meeting but didn't keep it. However he positioned himself early at the meeting place, a disused railway station outside Chippenham, at least an hour before the meeting.

Danny was all ears.

"So what did you see?"

Three vans had swept into the place at exactly the time arranged and a bunch of people spilled out carrying assault rifles. They looked like professionals by the way they carried themselves and held their weapons. The group blocked both roads out of the old station and posted people front and back. Scotty had set up a hide that they would have had to walk on to see him. Otherwise he felt that he wouldn't have had a chance to survive the meeting, especially if he'd gone unarmed.

"Did you see any faces? Recognize anyone?" Danny asked.

"Afraid not. It was dusk anyway, so all I could see was a bunch of pro's with weapons. Everybody knew what to do and where to go.... smooth as silk."

"So what happened?"

"Nothing. They left after fifteen minutes. I waited another hour before slipping away. All I can say is that if any of the lads got caught in that type of situation without a weapon, they'd be dead meat. Sorry to have to say it, but that's it." Scotty said despondently.

Danny jerked his hand up.

"Wait a minute Scotty. You got a warning in time from Major Wainwright. Is there any chance some of the others might have too - not fallen for the fake message and realized something was up. Went to ground like you did?"

"Who knows at this stage. The Major was frantic when he called me, so some of them must have been lifted by then."

He shook his head gloomily.

"It all goes back to that fucking debacle of a mission to Iraq. It's like the hounds of hell have been let loose."

Danny stood there for a long time, his mind struggling to take in the incredible story he had just heard. He started as his cell phone vibrated. It was the DG.

Danny motioned to Scotty.

"Go keep an eye on Jacky" he suggested.

Scotty turned and went over to the car where Jacky was waiting.

He gave an abbreviated version of Scotty's story to the DG. Despite this, it still took a good twenty minutes with questions being fired at him as he recounted the start and finish to the mission. He could tell from the stunned silence at the other end that she was struggling to understand the enormity of the events surrounding the Kuwaiti mission. She showed great interest in the description of the civilian who had come down and briefed them in Hereford. Finally she was completely silent at the other end. Danny waited too.

"Still there Rebecca?" he finally interjected.

A long sigh at the other end.

"Yes, unfortunately Danny. This started with an SAS team going missing and I got you in to try to locate them and somehow unravel the situation. Now it's exploding out in all directions. Sounds like members of that troop are being hunted and eliminated as we speak. Surely whoever is doing this will have to stop once it becomes common knowledge. Once the cat's out of the bag in other words. For example, I now realize I'll have to brief the police on the present situation as MI5 have no police powers in the U.K."

"I think you're missing one important point here" Danny countered.

"Oh, what's that?"

"Anything you know Rebecca, or I know, or the police shortly know, is strictly hearsay and wouldn't count as real evidence. These people are trying to eliminate all the first hand witnesses who went on that mission to Iraq. If they can do that, they can just cover their tracks and deny everything."

"You may be right Danny but that sounds too simplistic to me. There's a bloody bomb involved here somewhere which has disappeared in Iraq. There's U.S. military involvement and a U.S. civilian security firm as well, not to mention the civilian who came down to Hereford and instigated the SAS mission. I don't know how this could happen without full government backing. It couldn't get initiated out of our office, without Home Office approval and my authorization, and we don't operate outside the U.K."

"What about MI6? This was outside the U.K. so wouldn't they be the drivers on anything like that?"

"Well yes of course. MI6, which is the equivalent of the CIA in the U.S., operate outside with the foreign secretary's approval. I now have to approach MI6 on this. They don't always share their operational secrets with us, by the way."

Danny sounded frustrated.

"For crying out loud, there's U.K. nationals being murdered right now on U.K. soil! This goes beyond bloody turf wars between yourself and MI6."

"Well to prove murder Danny, we have to produce some bodies and so far we haven't got any and that includes your friend Jacky's roommate. She might not be your friend much longer when I tell you of the call to her mother that she mentioned. Her mother died four years ago, so I'd suggest you have a little talk with her as soon as we hang up."

Danny groaned.

"Oh shit! She must have been sicked onto me at that pub the other night. What I don't understand is why they go and kill her room mate."

"Ever think you're talking to two different groups here Danny? It might explain a few things. Oh by the way, those two phony coppers in Chepstow also belong to that U.S. civilian security firm and recruit mostly ex-military. They have a U.K. recruiting arm in Britain set up in Southampton. We're trying to chase down the U.K. directors of the company as we speak."

"Hmm…. you've given me lots to think about Rebecca. Now here's the question. Has my brief changed or do you want me to continue to try to locate the remnants of the troop where possible?"

"This is only the tip of the iceberg on this mission Danny. It's only started to unravel at all since you came on board, so keep your investigation going and for Gods sake keep Scotty safe. He's the only living witness we've got so far. I'm sending Sophia down on the early train to Chepstow to liaise with the MI5 interrogation team at the police station and then report back to me. She'll also have two Canadian passports in case you have to make any trips out of the country. This has got international implications written all over it. Your passport has a new name for you because it looks like they know about Danny Quigley."

"Two passports Rebecca. Who is the second one for?" Danny asked.

"Sophia of course. She's a cute little blonde but tough as nails. You'll like her. I need someone in close liaison with you from now on and it creates less scrutiny when a man and woman are traveling together - as man and wife."

"Man and wife!" Danny exploded. " For Christ's sake Ma'am….. it's…."

Danny was left standing there shouting into a dead phone.

In disgust he flung the mobile phone on the ground and crunched it under his foot. Fortunately the DG had given him several more to use.

His head came up sharply. Time to interrogate Jacky.

Danny strode rapidly back to the car, opened the trunk and extracted some items from inside. Then he threw open the rear door, reached in, slapped a handcuff on Jacky's nearest wrist and hauled her out of the car.

She screamed loudly, trying to push back at him with her free arm which he promptly grabbed and snapped the other cuff onto before unceremoniously dragging her towards the house.

Scotty leapt out of the car.

"Danny, what the hells going on?" he demanded.

Danny pointed to the house.

"Inside Scotty. I have some questions to ask this little bitch and she'd better have the answers."

Jacky was stumbling along trying to keep up with his rapid pace.

"Danny please tell me what's going on?" she pleaded. "What d'you mean about questions you want to ask me? What are these cuffs for? You didn't have to do that. I'd have come inside if you'd asked me to, for crying out loud."

Scotty dashed ahead of him, extracted a key from under a plant pot and opened the door in time for Danny to storm through. Scotty flicked some lights on and proceeded to pull thick curtains across the windows. Danny slammed Jacky into one of the kitchen chairs.

Scotty came back over and whispered to him

"Hey what's going on here? I thought she was on our side."

"I thought so too" he said grimly, before turning to the woman.

"Okay Jacky, tell me once again about your phone call to Northampton."

She tried to stand up but he pushed her back down as she shouted at him.

"I don't have to tell you anything, you thug! Let me go right now or I'm going to get the police onto you. You have no authority to handcuff me and hold me prisoner against my will.... hell that's ten years inside at least. I should know, I've covered enough trials at the Old Bailey."

Danny laughed cynically.

"Reality check Jacky. My former mates and Scotty's troop are being hunted and killed as we speak. Now if you're involved in any way in this, I can tell you, you won't have the opportunity to speak to any police. Scotty and I'll be judge and jury and you won't be leaving this room.... at least not alive. Now tell me about your telephone call."

She paled suddenly, looking over at Scotty desperately.

"Scotty please. I thought we were becoming friends out there in the car chatting. This is crazy. Tell him he can't get away with it - holding me here against my will!"

"I'd advise you to level with Danny, Miss. He's right, if you have anything to do with my mates disappearing into thin air..... being murdered.... you won't get much sympathy from me. On the contrary...."

A long moment of silence fell on the room.

"Tell me about that phone call" Danny insisted.

Her head came up.

"I told you I called my mother."

"Your mother died four years ago Jacky. Pull the other one."

Jacky's face crumpled in shock.

Scotty came forward and leaned towards her.

"Look Jacky, you're in over your head on this. Danny's not saying you're responsible for our mates getting murdered, but you're obviously playing a part in this whole thing. You're reporting to someone who's more than likely involved, and that means you're equally guilty in the eyes of the law. You could very well be the one doing ten years unless you level with us right now and start giving us some answers."

She started sobbing then, which went on for a full five minutes.

Scotty got the key from Danny and unlocked the cuffs from her wrists while Danny went and got her a glass of water from the tap.

After some more sniffles she started to talk.

CHAPTER 18.

LONDON.

Rebecca Fullerton-Smythe was only the third female Director General of MI5. Stella Rimington, who had been the first woman DG to be confirmed in 1992, broke the pattern of male heads of the organization, and she was the first head to be publicly disclosed.

Rebecca was an attractive, tall and extremely fit lady in her early forties, but who could have passed for ten years younger. Her dark hair framed a pair of startling green eyes which had a tendency to turn a paler shade when she was angry. As Director General she had a lot to live up to, not the least of which was the attitude of security organizations such MI6 and the various police forces in the U.K. who still relied on the 'old boy' network. They frowned on women holding the top spots and were reluctant to view them as equals at the table. The various police shows on TV led one to believe that women were becoming a driving force in crime detection and acceptance by their male colleagues. The reality was that these were the exception rather than the rule and any woman who did make it to the top ranks had got there through exceptional talent and determination.

This epitomized Rebecca Fullerton-Smythe who had fought her way up through the various levels of the Metropolitan Police to eventually claim the top spot. Her law degree from Cambridge had helped considerably. However her detractors, and there were many, had complained that it had been equal opportunity pressures for women's advancement that had been her shortcut up through the ranks. In fact it was probably her keen intelligence and finite grasp of organizing people and resources that had made her stand out from her predecessors and the deciding factor in her being suggested for the top MI5 spot when it became vacant. The support of the Home Secretary, who had to work closely with MI5 on a regular basis, helped too. Rebecca had never looked back and the organization was now more appropriately positioned for the new equation facing security organizations world wide, terrorism and its particular application to the U.K. - home grown terrorism.

Rebecca and Danny had been thrown together a year previously when one of her senior MI5 operatives had set in motion a plan to assassinate Gerry Adams and destroy the fragile peace process. At that time she had developed a healthy respect for Danny's combat skills. Her ability too with a weapon had, at that time, saved Danny's life and won his respect and friendship.

Right now she was gathering her thoughts for the person she was going to meet inside a small intimate restaurant down near the American Embassy:

Charles Percival Saunders known as Percy, her opposite number in MI6 and rumored to be heading for a knighthood. Saunders was a tall fifty five year old greyhound of a man with a strong aquiline jaw, a keen intellect and over 25 years as a career intelligence officer in the military. He had finished up as a Lieutenant Colonel and was reputed to have close ties with a former CIA Tel Aviv station head Brett Zeitner, now posted back to Langley. Rebecca's problem was how much to tell him at this stage so as to continue to have some control of the situation. If she revealed the full scope of the operation beyond the U.K. and into Kuwait and Iraq, Saunders could claim that it was an external problem outside the U.K. and hence fell under MI6 responsibility. However she still had a troop of SAS gone missing and possibly murdered inside the U.K. which could have a bearing on national security and which did fall under the MI5 brief. They met on a regular basis and occasionally liaised on security for foreign diplomats visiting London for various reasons. She felt that she should have earned his grudging respect for her work on a variety of projects that required their mutual cooperation. Rebecca had the distinct feeling though, that he still regarded her as being on probation and was just waiting for her to mess up.

Today he had beaten her to it, and she smiled when she saw that he had picked the exact table she herself had chosen on two previous occasions when meeting other security personnel. It was positioned right at the back of the room, and as far away as possible from other diners.

He stood up when she approached and shook her hand firmly, his alert eyes examining her closely.

"Nice to see you Rebecca. You're looking great as usual. If I didn't know better I'd say you were thriving on all this stress."

She smiled at the compliment, sitting down in the chair he pulled out for her.

"What stress Percy? Is there something I've been missing?" she said feigning puzzlement.

He leaned back.

"I'd say you were winding me up Rebecca. I have heard through the grapevine though, that your organizational skills are starting to pay dividends."

She made a face.

"Well, it's nice to know I'm finally starting to earn some brownies. I thought I'd have to turn water into wine before the establishment took notice."

He chuckled good-humoredly.

"Touche. I must admit you could have counted myself among the unbelievers when you landed the top spot, but I have to say Rebecca, you've won me over and a lot of other hard-nosed people as well."

She was startled but pleased at the tone of the conversation. They chatted for some moments as they ordered drinks and meals. When she had a glass of white wine in her hand she leaned back and thought about how to introduce the subject. Did he already have some knowledge of what was happening? Nothing would surprise her knowing the MI6 tentacles that stretched across various Government Agencies and Police Forces. Saunders had twenty five years of building up contacts and was known to play his cards close to his chest. She decided to launch straight into the subject, knowing that he wasn't one to beat around the bush.

"Percy, I have a brief from the Home Secretary to locate nine SAS people who've just returned from some mission overseas and have virtually dropped off the edge of the planet."

Saunders placed his glass on the table and leaned forward.

"Dropped off? In what way? Deserted? AWOL? Kidnapped? What exactly do you mean?"

"They've just disappeared Percy. All of them including their Commanding Officer a Major Wainwright who went with them on the mission. They're not AWOL because they all received two week passes, and desertion is not plausible as they're all career soldiers."

Rebecca could see that he was genuinely surprised, shocked even.

"Christ Rebecca, I can see the Home Secretary getting his knickers in a twist over this. If terrorists got a hold of SAS uniforms they could get aboard North Sea oil platforms, or even penetrate Heathrow and other airports under the pretence of an exercise. Hell, this is mind-boggling! Why weren't we briefed sooner?"

Rebecca suddenly realized that he was putting a completely different complexity on the disappearance of the troop, probably because he wasn't aware of the full implications of the SAS mission.

Saunders cocked his head looking thoughtful.

"Wainwright…. I actually met him a few years back…. good solid chap. Was a Captain then but had a great grasp of detail as I recall. I had no doubt he was heading for the top, but he would probably have had to switch out of 'Sass' to make it. Strange they sent a Major to head up the mission. Quite often it's one of those hard-nosed Sergeants or even a Captain. How did the mission come about anyway?"

"You weren't briefed by the way, because we were trying to get a grip on the implications of what happened. Was it a straight missing persons matter which should involve the police or were there national security implications? Contacting MI6 at that initial stage wouldn't have made any sense. As I understand it, Major Wainwright summoned an eight-man troop together, well technically half a troop, and a civilian came down from London and briefed them on their mission. Wainwright, after coming back from the mission, apparently had some misgivings about it and went to see his Commanding Officer. At that time they realized there was some confusion as to how the mission had got it's operational approval in the first place. Major Wainwright stated that he'd assumed the chap who had briefed them was either from MI5 or MI6 and had already received the blessing of the Government."

"MI6!" Saunders looked shocked. "Hell this is the first I've heard of it. I'm assuming from your tone that your group knew nothing about it either."

"Absolutely. The first I knew was when the Hereford Commanding Officer made a direct contact to the Home Office looking for answers on Major Wainwright's return from Kuwait. They, in turn got us involved, and then the men from the troop started disappearing."

Just then their meals arrived and while Saunders was obviously bursting with further questions they settled in to eat, though all enjoyment of the food had suddenly evaporated for the MI6 head at that stage.

Rebecca was cursing herself for mentioning Kuwait and knew that Saunders' incisive mentality would bring him back to it eventually. She was already scrambling in her own mind as to how she could curtail it to the U.K. end of the mission.

They both ate hurriedly, silently. The silences echoed with unspoken questions and Rebecca wondered if she could still achieve her own outcome of the meeting. Finally having finished and waved away the desert menu, they each settled for a coffee.

Saunders looked at her with pursed lips, his gray eyes now flinty.

"I play poker Rebecca. Did you know that? Is that in your little briefing file on Charles Percival Saunders?"

She was in the process of sipping her coffee and nearly spilled it.

"I didn't know, Percy, as a matter of fact, but why are you telling me this? Much as I enjoy hearing about your pastimes, I would have thought we had more urgent matters to discuss right now."

His lips curled slightly in an appreciation of her attempt at humor.

"Not just a pastime Rebecca. Twenty five years of interrogating suspects and gathering information. As a poker player I have a distinct advantage, I can tell when people aren't speaking the truth or at least fudging it. Right now I don't believe you're giving me the full story here. Could we start again at the beginning and let me have the name and a description of this civilian who briefed that missing troop in Hereford?"

Rebecca's expression didn't betray the emotions she was going through at that time. She admired the steel-trap mind of Saunders and was smarting from the rebuke. She played poker herself and actually thought she was pretty good at it. Obviously not!

She nodded, partly to herself and partly to Saunders who took it as acknowledgment of the point he'd just scored.

"Okay Percy. It probably comes with the territory, keeping our cards close to our chests as one might say. Now as to the individual and a description.... his name was Blackstone. As I recall it the guy was fortyish, somewhat blocky and starting to put on a bit of weight but well concealed by a saville row suit. Probably ex military from his deportment and authoritative manner. Apparently looked somewhat pissed off, but that could be from having to mix with some scruffy squaddies who show little respect for ex-commissioned officers. Hair starting to recede, but some vanity demonstrated in the way he combed it across."

She stopped, her mind searching for more details but at the same time she noticed an imperceptible widening of Saunders' eyes. Gotcha, she thought. You're not as good at poker playing as you thought! Out loud she asked

"Does that description ring a bell with you?"

He shook his head, eyes becoming hooded as he glanced at his watch.

"No can't say it does Rebecca. Could probably fit any one of a hundred ex guard officers I've come across in my career. Now I've just noticed that my next meeting is imminent. Shows you how time passes when you're enjoying the company. I'll see what my sources can throw up on this whole thing and get back to you."

Rising from the chair, he glanced at the bill and threw a wad of money onto the table.

"Keep in touch" he called to her as he marched smartly out of the restaurant.

She quickly reached into her handbag, extracted her cell phone and hit a pre-programmed number.

"Yes Ma'am?" the expectant voice at the other end.

"He's just leaving. Alert the others and don't lose him.... and I want pictures " she instructed.

She switched off and sat back in her chair thinking 'Percy, whatever are you up to? You certainly recognized the person I described. Now where on earth are you dashing off to? There were a dozen other questions you should have asked me…. hmm.'

She ordered another coffee, relaxing for the first time since the meeting started.

CHAPTER 19.

Jacky's story didn't add to the information that Danny had hoped for but it clarified some areas. She was a regular journalist with the Daily Mail and was seated at her desk when she heard the news that a Miss Paula Bloomingale could very well land the promotion coming up for a senior reporter. Paula was a newly arrived member of staff who had come down to London after working on a Birmingham paper for two years. Jacky had been slogging away at the Daily Mail for six years and felt she had earned the kudos to expect that reward. Rumor had it that Paula and her married boss David Prescott were seeing each other outside of office hours, and that her promotion was earned on her back rather than out in the cut and thrust of everyday reporting. Whatever about that, Jacky just couldn't stand her broad whining Birmingham accent, and if Paula got the career advancement she would be Jacky's boss and she couldn't bear the thought of that. What she needed was a scoop, with national or even international implications, to put her right back on the front page and in the face of her boss David Prescott.

Unfortunately on that particular Tuesday morning, there were no scoops around and no apparent possibility of one. Until she got the phone call from someone who claimed he had a massive potential story and wanted to meet with her to discuss it. Normally female reporters, like estate agents, had learned to take certain precautions when meeting strangers. Jacky asked her friend and fellow reporter Rita to go with her, hoping that would not put off the man she was going to see. The meeting place he had suggested was a small café in Soho and he said that he would recognize her from the picture in her regular byline.

They were about five minutes late but when they walked inside. A man waved to them from the back of the café which was practically empty at that time of the morning. When they sat down he didn't introduce himself straight away but instead waved the waiter over and ordered some coffees. The man didn't seem in a very good mood and was obviously not pleased at Rita being there.

After a few moments he settled down and introduced himself as Ronnie Blackstone. He was a burly, bluff, middle-aged man with receding hair and the air of someone who was used to people doing what he told them to do.

He produced an identification card and muttered that he was with the Government and quickly put the ID away before she could properly scrutinize it. He claimed that they needed her assistance on a matter of national security. Something that would wipe everything else off the front pages of the papers and she could have the inside track on the story. Initially he couldn't provide her with all the details, but these would unfold as she got involved in the situation.

Rita being a more in-your-face reporter, asked him directly whether he was MI5 or MI6. He just smiled and pointed out that if he was, he couldn't or wouldn't admit to it. Her task, she was told, was to convince her boss to let her write a story on the ex-paramilitaries and some of the legends associated with them. Having done so she would be picked up that evening in a cab and taken to a pub as yet un-named, where those types hung out. Someone would meet her outside the pub and escort her inside where they would point out a man called Danny Quigley. He was an ex SAS trooper with whom she must then get acquainted. The contact was the key to the evolving story and she must stick to him like glue. Her assignment was to report on his activities and whereabouts using a pre-programmed mobile phone he was giving her. Jacky would then be positioned right inside the mega story when it burst and Blackstone would supply all the additional details to make her disclosures credible when she wrote it up.

Jacky asked how they knew that this Quigley person would be there that evening. He didn't respond.

Rita enquired about the possible scope of the story or the timing of it. Was it a political bombshell, a politician caught in bed with some boy, a massive financial swindle, or something else entirely? Blackstone didn't supply any further information, merely adding that the story would unfold as they followed his instructions, and as Jacky badly needed a spectacular story that would give her a head start in the promotional stakes, she didn't push it.

Blackstone suggested that Rita go with her on the evening's adventure. They agreed and he passed her the mobile phone with his number programmed into it, adding that they would have some regular meetings to update her on the developing story. That's how she ended up in the same bar as Danny and giving him the glad eye. Hearing that she might be killed trying to get to work, she had chosen to run with Danny. The potential story still loomed large in her assessment of her reactions as well, she admitted. Despite her growing doubts, she had rung the pre-programmed number on the cell phone that Blackstone had given her and reported to him their location in Chepstow. She got the impression that he already knew where they were.

That was pretty much her story.

Jacky sat on the chair looking both guilty and downright miserable. Danny and Scotty looked at each other in silence for a moment. Finally Danny stirred.

"Stand up Jacky and take your clothes off," he instructed.

She shrank back in the chair.

"Oh God no! You're not going to...." she started.

He held his hands up placatingly.

"Hey, it's okay, you're not going to be assaulted or anything. However if Blackstone already knew where we were, he's obviously planted a bug on you. I don't know how or where, but we need to know fast as we may already be in danger at this location. With today's technology, as you well know, they can trace you through your mobile phone. Oh and by the way, I now think that Rita was murdered by this man Blackstone because she could identify him, and you would have been next."

She stared at him trying to analyze the information coming at her.

Scotty had gone into one of the side rooms and come out with a blanket, which he held up for her.

"Come on Jacky, start firing those clothes across and let Danny have your handbag and phone," Scotty told her.

Without any further grumbling she proceeded to pass her items of clothing under the blanket. Danny started with the handbag, dumping everything onto the floor. He groaned at the plethora of items spilling out: pens, eyebrow pencils, lipstick, breath freshener, comb and hairbrush, Tampax, even three condoms, which made him smile. A set of car keys attached to a plastic security fob, a bottle of tablets and a small container of pancake makeup. There was other stuff too but Danny was searching for items that could have a monitoring device installed and with the miniaturization available today, any of the things he'd dumped out of the purse could have been utilized.

In the meantime Jacky had all but finished with undressing. Her voice came around the blanket.

"Not my underwear too surely?" she asked plaintively.

"Just your bra Jacky, because of the attachments" Scotty replied starting to look embarrassed at this stage.

"Thank God for small mercies" she exclaimed as her bra came flying over the top hitting Scotty on the head.

He handed her the blanket, which she promptly wrapped around herself and sat down watching them at work.

Danny who was on the floor, scooped up all the items from her handbag and placed them in an empty fruit bowl off the table, then walked over to her. She clutched the blanket tighter around her at his approach. He knelt down so that his eyes were level with hers.

"Now Jacky, is there anything in this bowl of stuff that you don't recognize?" he asked.

She looked carefully at the items and shook her head.

"No, those are things I definitely put in my handbag myself."

"Okay, good. Now I've been thinking, there's three possibilities where they could have planted a monitoring device on you. Blackstone could have slipped something into your pocket or handbag or indeed the cab driver, who brought you into the Fox and Hounds. That would be a foreign object in your handbag, which we've now eliminated. It could of course be another lipstick, which you might not notice unless you decide to freshen up your make-up. The mobile phone as I mentioned, is an obvious one and we'll look at that in a moment… perhaps too obvious in case we checked it. Putting a bug inside it would probably be overkill anyway as they can use it to plot your position as it is. Thirdly, they might have got into your flat even before they broached you about the story and planted something in your apparel."

Despite her predicament Jacky found herself interested.

"How would they know what I might wear that evening? That would be pretty hard to predict, wouldn't it?" she asked, now intrigued.

Danny considered for a moment.

"Well, an evening handbag would be an obvious choice, but it depends just how many evening outfits you have with matching handbags. A man wouldn't be too good at trying to figure that out, but shoes are quite another thing. How many pairs of shoes have you sitting in your wardrobe that you might wear for an evening out?" he asked.

"I'm not big on shoes really. Rita is...." she averted her face, "was. I've probably four pairs of shoes that I might wear out" she nodded at her apparel on the floor, "including that pair, I just took off."

Scotty leapt up from the floor and disappeared over to a small cupboard with various tools hung on nails on the wall. He grabbed a hammer and swiftly knocked the heels off both shoes. A small metal item, about an inch in diameter, tinkled out on to the floor. All three stared at it, fascinated.

Danny stood up and smashed his heel down on the object, flattening it. A look of relief swept across Jacky's face.

"So it wasn't just down to me. I feel such a fool being taken in like that. If it wasn't for my stupid ambitions Rita would still be alive. It all seems so pathetic now."

Danny's face softened as he saw how stricken with guilt she actually was. He touched her shoulder briefly.

"Okay, we still need to work fast here. Check the lipstick in the bowl please and make sure it's yours. Scotty check the rest of her clothes and let her have them back. Somehow I don't think they spent time sewing imitation buttons onto her clothes when they visited her flat. They would have wanted to get in and out fast, but a good shoe man could have done the job quick. Jacky, you probably have a few more shoes with bugs in them back in your flat."

Jacky confirmed that the lipstick was hers and retreated into the corner to put her clothes on again.

Danny wrote down the only number that was programmed into her mobile phone, which had been her contact number to Blackstone. He hoped that with her help they could lure him into a trap at a later date. He then smashed the phone under his heel before he and Scotty had a brief strategy meeting.

Scotty slipped out and did a quick reconnoiter of the area around the building. While he was outside Jacky came back over combing her hair. She looked up at Danny, a shadow of uncertainty on her face.

"What happens to me now Danny? I was obviously mislead right at the beginning of this whole thing. Through my own blind ambition, I'll admit, but I'd never have anything to do with murdering people or breaking the law. I'm really sorry and if there was any way I could make it up I would. You scared me when you mentioned me doing time in jail. You weren't serious were you?"

Her eyes were tearful as she finished and Danny gave her a brief hug.

"No, not really Jacky, though this is a serious business you've got yourself mixed up in and people are going to go to jail.... if they're lucky. As for you, I'd like to take you with us for two reasons. First, Blackstone will most certainly kill you at the first opportunity and he has men either in the area or closing in on this location. Second if you're willing, we might be able to use you and the number on the cell phone Blackstone gave you to get our hands on him and find out what part he's played in this whole thing. I have to say though that it could be dangerous if you do agree to come along with us."

A gleam came into her eyes.

"You mean I could still get this story then? I now know there's a mega story here somewhere. I'd like to be there when it finally unravels.... for Rita too" she added.

Just then Scotty slipped back in the door.

"All clear outside. Nothing up or down the road. They must be low in resources now that we put those two phony cops away. They could have more people on the way though."

Danny nodded thoughtfully.

"They may have bracketed this location roughly before we smashed that bug, so we need to spend the night somewhere else. I have to meet someone in Chepstow in the morning."

Scotty clapped him on the shoulder.

"I happen to have another cousin back in the hills who would be glad to put us up."

Danny grinned.

"I thought I'd met all you're cousins by now."

Turning to Jacky.

"Don't ever fall out with this guy. He's related to half the population in Wales. Speaking of which Scotty, you were going to phone your grandfather up the road. Is he okay?"

"Yeah I did, he's fine. We have a code arranged in case he's got unwanted visitors. As it is, he's got the three German shepherds out and I wouldn't want to be in anyone's shoes if they try to get to him."

They left in a hurry.

CHAPTER 20.

Rather than waiting outside the police station, Danny met the early train from London and tried to guess which young woman was Sophia, the liaison from Rebecca. He was still inwardly seething at the DG who, as he saw it, was burdening him with an extra passenger to carry on the operation. The original plan was that he would accost her after she visited the two MI5 agents at the police station. However he wanted to pre-empt this arrangement and make contact early. He finally settled on a trim, youthful looking blonde, who was walking purposefully along the train platform pulling a small airline bag behind her. He had to admit that the DG was correct, she was cute with a terrific figure. She appeared to be exuding energy as her eyes swept left and right. Her eyes caught his as he leaned against the door-jamb, leading into a waiting room and her step faltered. Then she strolled over and stopped in front of him.

"Danny Quigley isn't it?" she enquired looking up at him. "I thought we were supposed to meet in a more cloak and dagger fashion at the police station - you know, I give you the code word and so on."

He was momentarily startled.

"How the hell did you recognize me?" he asked, somehow miffed that she had sprung it on him rather than the other way round.

She grinned, pleased at his discomfiture and he noticed that when she smiled her whole face lit up and her hazel eyes literally danced with good humor. He felt some of his reservations evaporate. She bit her lower lip as if debating how to answer him. Then as if coming to some conclusion she shrugged.

"Twelve months ago when you were involved in the situation with Colonel Crawford and Gerry Adams, we pulled your record from the

E.J. RUSS MCDEVITT

regiment and it had your picture on it. I nearly didn't pick you out as you've changed a lot since that photo was taken. Your hair is longer for starters, but the DG warned me to keep my eyes open and stay alert. Oh I did take the MI5 course on surveillance and counter surveillance, so I'm applying those skills too."

She mentally berated herself for trying to impress him but he smiled graciously, taking her bag. They made small talk as they strolled down the platform and into the parking lot where the old Ford Granada he'd bought was waiting. They both climbed in and stowed her bag on the back seat.

He took advantage of the short drive to the police station to update Sophia on the situation and Jacky's confession.

When he'd finished she asked him

"Do you trust her now? I mean enough to take her with you? She could be still leading the opposition right to those troopers you know."

He looked unconvinced.

"Yeah, I kinda do at this stage. If you'd seen her state after we interrogated her, you would too. Well it wasn't much of an interrogation really, but she was pretty shook up. It was her obsession for a story that got her into trouble in the first place, but we might still be able to use her as a trump card to draw out this so-called Blackstone. We'll take her along, but it doesn't mean that we won't keep a close eye on her, and you could certainly help where that's concerned Sophia."

"Hmm…. I'm still somewhat dubious about that but you know what you're doing so I'm happy to go along."

She canted her oval face sideways.

"That's the first time you used my name Danny" she said softly. "It sounded kinda nice."

He straightened suddenly, slightly embarrassed at her tone.

"Let's get you down to the police station and see if your colleagues have made any progress. The more information we have at this stage the better."

He didn't park directly in front of the station as he was still carrying the material they had taken from the bogus cops, but instead stopped a hundred yards down the road in a small parking lot. She gave him a smile and jumped out. He watched her all the way back up the street in the rear view mirror. My God! he thought. She was definitely attractive.

The way she walked and the outfit she wore didn't leave anything to the imagination! He saw several other male heads turning. Not someone he'd have selected for undercover work. She wouldn't exactly blend into a crowd, as a good surveillance operator should.

It couldn't have been more than ten minutes later that he saw her running, or rather stumbling back down the street, towards the car. He jumped out in alarm, not knowing if someone was chasing her. Apart from some people who stopped and looked curiously after her, she didn't appear in any apparent danger. She jumped into the car and Danny did also. She looked sideways at him and her face crumpled.

"Let's get out of here Danny for God's sake!" she gasped.

He started up and carefully edged out onto the street, turning right towards Scotty's location and picking up speed. He glanced at her several times as he did so.

Finally she whispered.

"You can pull over now Danny, please."

He eased over to the side of the road and stopped, switching off the motor.

"Shit, shit, shit!" she exploded. "All that bloody training I've had and I thought I was real cool. I could cut it out there with the best of them. I could even show them! The sight of two bodies and I fell apart."

He looked sideways at her startled.

"What bodies?" he asked.

"Those two phony cops were found shot dead in their cells early this morning for Christ's sake!"

He shook his head as if in denial.

"But how? I thought two of your people were coming down to question them."

"That's the problem Danny two people turned up at 5am this morning claiming to be from MI5 and carrying the proper paper work. The two bogus policemen were brought to an interview room and the MI5 people asked to be left alone with them. A while later the desk sergeant was checking back and found both prisoners shot in the head and the MI5 team gone. They'd apparently slipped out a fire door."

"Let me guess. They were not from MI5 at all."

"Exactly! When I went in, the legitimate MI5 team had just arrived and there was total pandemonium I can tell you. The police inspector had called the DG in London to try to unsnarl it and I was allowed in to view the bodies. That's when I nearly threw up and fell apart. I quickly excused myself and dashed out. I bet they're all laughing at me back there" she lamented.

He shook his head soberly, his mind racing as he tried to take it all in. Finally he stirred and, reaching across, he took her hand in his.

"Hey, let me tell you this Sophia, and you can take it to the bank. I bet there isn't a cop in there, and that includes your two colleagues from MI5, who haven't heaved their guts up when they encountered their first body. You can include me and a number of my tough mates from the regiment in that as well. I'm afraid it's just par for the course in this business and I guarantee you get over it fast. I hate to say that one gets hardened to it but it's a fact and a necessary shell you have to build around yourself to help you recover your focus."

She peered up at him.

"Is that really true Danny? That one actually gets used to it? All that blood and gore. God it was horrible!"

"Death is horrible anyway Sophia however it happens, but when violence is involved, it can be messy. You just learn to disconnect mentally so you can carry on, but it does catch up with you later when you get home, and then you can have a strong reaction. I know cops who turn to drink and drugs and even those people who do postmortems, I'm told, pay a price too. So let me say this, your reaction is quite normal and nothing to be ashamed of."

She squeezed his hand.

"Thanks Danny."

He started the car again.

"Let's go connect with Scotty and fill him in on the new events. Keep a sharp eye out as there's obviously some phony MI5 agents floating around the area. You'll need to contact the DG shortly to see if she has any further instructions on the situation. Things are moving fast and we need to be planning our next move."

CHAPTER 21.

Rebecca had just hung up the phone after talking to Sophia in the Chepstow area. She was shocked at the turn of events at the police station which had resulted in an early morning telephone call to her home from the agents she had dispatched to question the two bogus policemen. At the moment there was a full-scale investigation being carried out at the station and the MI5 involvement was still being regarded with some suspicion.

There was a growing feeling that if MI5 had underscored the importance of the two phony policemen, a ring of steel would have been thrown around the police station.

Instead two 'agents' had waltzed in, murdered two prisoners and got safely away. Rebecca herself admitted that they had been lax in briefing the local police and she still had the problem of how the killers had obtained false MI5 identity papers, which the desk sergeant claimed were bona fide. But then he would wouldn't he?

She also found the expose of Jacky interesting, especially the description of the so-called man Blackstone who had recruited her, which also fitted the name and description of the individual who briefed the troop at Hereford. It fitted the picture she now held in her hand of a man coming out of the American Embassy, with Percy Saunders. Percy had been followed by her team to the Embassy and had gone inside. He emerged a half hour later with another man who very closely fitted the description of Blackstone. Right now she had people in the MI5 building trying to match the picture with a name, but unfortunately the team watching Percy Saunders had lost him when he left the American Embassy with the other man. They had got into a black cab, and when the driver turned the car it was swallowed up in a whole fleet of other black cabs.

Rebecca's mind raced ahead. American Embassy…. CIA London station…. civilian aircraft involved with the Hereford troop's mission…. the CIA's reputation for crossing various borders with impunity, with captured terrorists on board.

She slapped the photograph down on the desk. Just what the hell was going on here? she wondered. Where did she start to unravel the various strands that were popping up? She had already arranged a dispatch rider to take the picture to the police station in Chepstow for Scotty and Jacky who had seen Blackstone face to face, to examine it.

Well there was one other obvious place to start: Percy Saunders, who had dashed out after their lunch and made a beeline for the American Embassy and probably the CIA. He obviously knew a hell of a lot more than he had divulged to her yesterday when they met. Well he would have to now that she had him dead to rights.

She grabbed her phone and dialed Percy's direct number at MI6. After four rings it was picked up at the other end and a woman's voice answered.

"Hello, who is that please?"

"Rebecca Fullerton-Smythe at MI5. I'm looking for Percy" she answered.

There was a pause at the other end. The voice now had an urgency to it.

"Oh Ma'am, I was just about to call you. This is Tracy Barton, PA for Mr. Saunders. Mr. Saunders didn't come home last night and his wife called missing persons. Normally the police sit on these for 48 hours as you know, but in view of his position it's set off alarm bells."

"Not come home? Good God what can have happened to him? Why we met yesterday and…."

"I know Ma'am. That's why I was going to call you. You see you're the last person he saw yesterday. He never kept any of his appointments after that. I'm sure the police will be in touch with you but Mrs. Saunders, his wife, is in such a state I thought I'd call you and see if he told you where he was going after he met with you. You see he was supposed to come straight back here. I know because I manage his diary."

Rebecca's head swam.

Percy gone missing…. not seen since their meeting yesterday….

Instinctively she felt that she shouldn't at this time divulge her knowledge of his trip to the American Embassy.

"Tracy, I'm still shocked at what you just told me…. Percy missing and the police involved, so it could be serious. As regards your question, Percy left the restaurant where we ate yesterday, in a hurry because he apparently had an imminent meeting. He didn't say where he was going I'm afraid. I assumed it was back to his office. Is that where his next meeting was scheduled for?" she asked.

"Well yes it was, but I'm surprised that he left in a hurry because it was not until two thirty. He should have had lots of time for the meal. Can you recall what time he left you Ma'am?"

Rebecca cast her mind back.

"Well let's see. Our meeting was at 1pm and he was already there. Our meal came quite quickly. Then we had a brief chat and he left, probably about one forty five. He had loads of time to get there for two thirty. I got the impression he was running late Tracy."

"On the contrary, he could have got back here within ten minutes so he would have been in plenty of time. I can only assume that he went somewhere else. I can't imagine where as I handle all his incoming calls and there was nothing out of the ordinary about them that morning. We checked his emails too but there's nothing there unless he wiped it out, but that's unusual for Mr. Saunders. He always keeps me in the loop."

They talked for a few minutes longer and Rebecca got the name of the police officer who was in charge of trying to locate Percy. Apparently it had been kicked up to Scotland Yard from missing persons due to the status of the person involved.

Rebecca for the first time started feeling little gremlins of concern creeping into her gut. She was in a massively protected building with all sorts of personal and operational security at her disposal. Yet she still felt secure enough to go out for lunch or private meetings in London, without an entourage of security along and she understood that Percy Saunders operated along the same lines. Rebecca's face had not been in the papers and her identity not disclosed, but if MI5 received information that indicated a potential threat, then a whole wall of protection would spring into place.

June, her secretary, stuck her head around the door.

"Ma'am there's a gentleman in reception, claims to be the head of the CIA London station, a Mr. Basil Sinclair, who asked for an urgent meeting with you. I had them check his ID thoroughly and they checked back with the agency in the Embassy. He's kosher. Shall I bring him up?"

She hadn't heard his name before. Normal courtesy would dictate that she knew the various intelligence people at the various Embassies though some, like the Israelis, Americans, the Russians and others, still liked to play things close to their chest. Her interest now piqued, she told June to fetch the CIA man up.

A few moments later the door opened and a man appeared in the doorway. She felt her head spinning. It was the man in the picture! The one she assumed was the elusive Blackstone who now turned out to be Basil Sinclair, CIA station head, London.

CHAPTER 22.

Sophia went back into town by herself in Scotty's brown Mazda car and collected the photograph taken outside the American Embassy and sent by the DG to the police station. She had difficulty getting away from the investigation. The MI5 involvement was creating strong criticism for its sloppy procedures.

Danny was getting worried by the time she rolled up to the supermarket parking lot on the edge of town where himself, Scotty and Jacky were waiting in a second vehicle. On joining them inside she opened the envelope with the picture and passed it to them in the back seat. Scotty's reaction was immediate.

"That's the bastard all right. Him and his bloody officer airs. He's got a lot to answer for - he's set this up."

He looked at Sophia.

"Do we know who he is yet?"

"Unfortunately no. The DG just got the picture back from the lab and is running it through the ID systems. They'll know soon."

Jacky cut in.

"That's the same man who approached me as well. I'm getting confused listening to what's being said. Is he really from the Government as he hinted?"

Danny took the picture back and examined it closely.

"We don't know yet as Sophia just mentioned" Danny said tersely, "but when we do, and if he has any involvement with the lads disappearing, then you're looking at a dead man. Whether he's with the Government or not I promise you it's only a matter of time."

Jacky shuddered at the steely tone in his voice and Sophia glanced across at him as if trying to measure his anger. Scotty just nodded in agreement, his mouth closed in a tight grim line. There was silence in the car.

Finally Danny stirred.

"Okay, we can't just sit here. The plan now, which Scotty and I discussed, is to head south down into Cornwall for a meeting with someone who can throw some further light on this. I'm not mentioning names and places just yet. However we need to start taking the battle to the enemy, or with their resources they'll pick us off one by one. We know that the American security firm have a recruiting unit in Southampton. We know from the description of the people who tried to get Scotty, that they have heavy weapons and they know what they're doing. It's quite a long trip but we'll be stopping on the way. Don't use any credit cards when we do and no phone calls, except Sophia will call the DG for an update. We'll take both cars just to have some options in case the opposition spots one of them. That reminds me Scotty, we need to check these two vehicles again, just in case they've managed to plant something. For instance the Mazda that Sophia drove has been parked in town while she went to the police station. Someone could have got to it."

"I can help sweep one of them Danny" Sophia offered.

Danny had forgotten that she had had MI5 training so he left her and Scotty to get on with it as he and Jacky got out and stretched. He could see she was feeling a little left out.

"Hey Jacky, how are you at driving on motorways?" he asked.

She perked up.

"Pretty good actually. My boyfriend and I went up to Scotland last year and I drove most of the way there and back. He hates driving and I enjoy it. I'd love to help Danny. Thanks for asking."

He thought about asking about the boyfriend to see if the relationship was still current but decided to avoid the topic.

"Well you just got the job of being my driver. Don't think me rude if I drift off to sleep. It's an old regiment habit. Sleep and eat when you can. Scotty, though, wouldn't be happy unless he was in control behind the wheel."

She looked pleased for a moment but suddenly her face got serious again.

"Do you really think I can help somehow? I mean, play a part in finding that chap in the picture? Scotty's confirmed that he's the one who was at Hereford and now I've told you that he set me up too. Is there anything more I can actually do?"

Danny nodded.

"It's possible we can trap this chap with a phone call from you. If you happen to be speaking with this Blackstone, you could say that I got suspicious when those two phony cops turned up in Chepstow. Then tell him that I destroyed your phone, but that you managed to jot down his number. If he questions you about whether you've changed your shoes tell him you did, as they weren't suitable any longer. He may wonder why your bug stopped working. In any event the cops will want to talk to you about him because he more than likely killed Rita and he'd kill you too if he got the opportunity, so you're better sticking with us for the moment" he explained.

"And until I get my story" she retorted with a cheeky grin.

He shook his head in wonder.

"You bloody reporters!"

Just then Scotty gave him the thumbs up about the vehicles and Danny explained the arrangements as they traveled south, and how the two cars were to keep in touch. Sophia had brought down a package of fresh mobile phones and they quickly programmed in the numbers for both cars.

Sophia looked disappointed that she wouldn't be traveling with Danny but waved to him as they all jumped into their cars and headed for the M5 motorway south. They had a good five hours drive ahead of them.

CHAPTER 23.

When the DG looked into Basil Sinclair's cold eyes, the man she now knew to be also using the name Blackstone, she had no doubt that she was looking at a killer. He seemed larger and more formidable than the U.S. Embassy picture had portrayed. His hand, when he shook hers was cold, and she shuddered slightly. He peered closely at her as if sensing her disquiet.

She went through the preliminaries of introducing herself and asking him to sit down as if someone else was speaking through her lips and looking at him through the wrong end of a telescope. She settled back in her chair, glad of the support and the fact that her large desk was between them. She now looked cautiously across at him.

"I understand you're the CIA Station Head at the Embassy Mr. Sinclair. Sorry about the security downstairs, checking your identity and so on."

"No need to apologize Ma'am. At the Embassy you'd never get inside to see me in under a couple of hours. The security there is totally ludicrous, but that's the world we live in now. Thanks for agreeing to see me at such short notice."

She coughed.

"I'm at a disadvantage here as I haven't been made aware of your posting to the Embassy. The last information I have is that Don Bradshaw was station head. It's normal practice to update MI5 and MI6 on any new appointment."

There was a slight reprimand in her voice. He grimaced as if in regret. The regret didn't quite reach his eyes.

"I was only appointed in the last three months and Don Bradshaw is already back in Langley. I meant to get around to it, but getting a grip on the local situation has been taking all my time. Sorry about that."

She held his gaze for a moment feeling control flowing back into her limbs.

"So…. here we are. I'm surprised to hear the English voice. So the CIA finally appointed an Englishman to the London station. What's your background then Mr. Sinclair?" she enquired, leaning forward.

"Well actually I was with MI6 prior to this appointment. My last station was Tel Aviv. I had various contacts with the agency over there and must have made a good impression on someone, hence the appointment. I understand 9/11 created an awakening in the agency for the need for local on the ground intelligence instead of relying on the more sophisticated satellite stuff they were using. The potential threat of the U.K. home grown terrorists is of great interest to the Americans. Hence my appointment."

Despite her tight control her face registered surprise. Now she knew why Percy reacted to her description of the man Blackstone who had briefed the SAS team at Hereford. He knew exactly who she was talking about. The knowledge was probably the primary cause of his disappearance too…. and probably his death. She was certain that she was now sitting across from the very man responsible. Another bell went off in her head: an ex MI6 agent would probably know the process for authorizing an SAS operation and might still have the contacts inside to carry it off.

Her eyes flitted across to the closed doorway that separated her from her PA's office. Suddenly she wished Danny Quigley was in the room with her.

Sinclair peered closely at her.

"You all right Ma'am? You went a bit pale then."

She cursed inwardly not having wanted to alert the man as to her suspicions. She sat up straighter.

"Oh yes, fine Mr. Sinclair. Now may I enquire as to why you came here this morning? An urgent meeting I understand from the front desk. Unusual approach. A phone call could have made sure I was actually in the building and available to see you at short notice."

"Point taken Ma'am and I'll bear it in mind for the future. However it's come to my attention that you're investigating the disappearance of some SAS personnel. Is that true?"

"Well I'd be very interested in where you gained this information for starters. However I can't comment on what I may or may not be working on right now Mr. Sinclair. MI5, as you know, covers the internal security of the State, and we would rarely involve MI6 or your own organization the CIA, who both work internationally. Of course we might have cross-over responsibility where a suspected home grown terrorist makes plans to leave the country for Pakistan or Afghanistan, or indeed the U.S. On that basis we would have to involve other agencies such as MI6 or yourselves where we needed additional resources outside the U.K., or Scotland Yard if it needed to be kicked through to Interpol."

Sinclair shifted his heavy bulk impatiently.

"Yes, yes, I know all that Ma'am. However we have our resources on the ground here as well and we may very well be able to help each other out."

Rebecca allowed her face to look puzzled.

"Help me in what way? I don't quite follow where you're coming from."

"Well perhaps an exchange of information, and we can then start using our considerable local contacts to help you."

She realized then that he was just there to pump her for information. That was reassuring because it meant that he had lost the trail of Danny, Jacky and the remaining troopers. She wondered if he was aware that she was the last person to see Percy alive, apart from himself. She continued to allow her face to look perplexed.

"I'm sorry, but you've lost me completely Mr. Sinclair. You mention a hypothetical situation of some military personnel disappearing which I can't comment on and you're offering to help us. With what in mind? Where do the interests of the U.S. Government come into this? Please enlighten me."

His face got fractionally redder. He obviously had no use for women, Rebecca thought, and certainly didn't like being lectured to. Well tough!

"Look Ma'am" he started. "It's the old story, wheels within wheels. Trust me, there is a possible connection, which I'm not at liberty to disclose just yet. It would help us if you do locate these missing people, to allow us some access at that time. That's all I can say at this point."

Sure, so you can kill them, she thought.

There was silence in the room for a moment.

Rebecca decided to change the topic of conversation to see his reaction.

"Did you know that Percy Saunders has disappeared?" she enquired studying him closely.

His head shot up.

"Ah…. no, I didn't. When did you hear that Ma'am?"

"Just before you got here actually. He went missing yesterday after lunch according to his PA. You knew him?"

"Well yes I did of course with my MI6 background. This is terrible news!"

"Yes it is, isn't it? Did you see each other often?" she asked.

He shook his head.

"Rarely since I took up my new post. I'm sure the relationship would have developed as I got a grip on running the station. Saw him briefly when I came back from Tel Aviv to move across to the Embassy, but that was it" he answered.

Got you, she thought.

She also realized that Percy had not disclosed that it was she who had provided him with the information that made him dash out of the restaurant. Sinclair had not disclosed his source of information of the missing troopers either, she noticed. How long would it take him to find out that Percy Saunders' luncheon appointment had been with her and that she must be holding out on him?

There was an awkward silence again and his eyes closed into narrowed slits as he regarded her speculatively. It was obvious to both of them that the visit was over and that there was no meeting of the minds. Neither offered to shake hands when he got up and left a moment later.

She shivered involuntarily. She knew a killer had just visited her office.

CHAPTER 24.

M5 SOUTH

They had been traveling south for approximately three hours and getting ready for a break, when Danny's mobile phone rang. He had been sitting back with his eyes closed as Jacky made excellent time on the motorway. He sat up abruptly and switched on the phone. He knew it could only be the DG.

"Hello."

"DG here Danny.... some news.... astonishing really."

He sat up straighter as she filled him in on the recent visit of the CIA London Station Head Basil Sinclair, now known to be the man Blackstone who briefed the troops and recruited Jacky. When she had finished he whistled in amazement.

"This whole thing is going completely off the rails Rebecca.... CIA involvement! I can see where you tie it in with civilian aircraft and the whole smell of the operation. Sinclair has the know-how to set it up at this end with his work at MI6, but what's it all about? Where does it link together, and why kill off the troop? Why not just complete the mission and no one would be the wiser? The SAS never talk out of school. I'm more confused than ever."

"Yes, me too Danny, but the players are beginning to emerge and that's a start."

"Pretty big player, the U.S. Government. So where do you go from here - straight to Langley? With the MI6 head also missing, you could go direct with your information, couldn't you?"

"Perhaps I could but I intend to gather more information first. With that in mind I've just put a 24/7 surveillance team on our friend Sinclair."

"They'll need to be good Rebecca. He'll catch on pretty quick if someone's following him. Probably sweeps his car and house clean every day and has his contacts everywhere if you try to access his phone records or start going deeper into his background. Why not have Scotland Yard pick him up? After all he's the last person to have seen Saunders alive and we have an ID on him as briefing the team at Hereford."

She sighed audibly.

"Can you imagine the flack if I'm instrumental in pulling in the head CIA honcho without some sort of tangible proof of a plot to subvert justice here in the U.K.? I need more proof Danny. The surveillance may throw up something, and we have a team of thirty people with a fleet of cars on it right now. I've had to cancel some very important stake-outs to do this, so I can't sustain it for long."

Danny grunted.

"What if the bastard goes after you Rebecca? He didn't show much respect for Percy Saunders. He'll soon know that you were the last person to see him and that you were holding out on him. Do you want me up there to watch your back?"

She was silent for a moment.

"I'd like that, but remember you're operating under the radar right now Danny. Don't worry I can surround myself with a protective team just by a phone call. What you're doing right now is vital. That means trying to locate the rest of those missing troopers and Major Wainwright. I suspect that only he can shed light on this whole debacle. Oh by the way, those two who were murdered in their cell in Chepstow were also working for that security firm in Southampton. That's a police case now so they'll be calling on them in due course. I'll let you know what they find out, if anything. Stay in touch."

She finished the call on that note and he was thoughtful as he crunched the phone under his boot and threw it out the window onto the meridian.

Jacky glanced at him, her journalistic nose practically quivering.

"What was that all about?" she enquired.

Danny realized that trying to curtail the information at this stage was all but impossible as she had heard his side of the telephone conversation. In his opinion, she had been unwittingly drawn into the situation and was now solidly in their camp. She still had to sit on any potential story until they had unraveled the whole background, which was taking on more sensational details by the moment.

As they were coming up to Exeter and were probably all in need of a break, he called Scotty on the cell and agreed to pull off at the next exit.

He glanced over at Jacky.

"I'll save it until we get off the motorway and find somewhere for some grub. I know Scotty travels on his stomach anyway and I'm not too far behind him on that."

Soon they spotted an exit sign and Jacky eased off the motorway, slowing the car down. She stretched her back and grimaced.

"I used to be able to drive forever but now I'm aching after just a few hours. It could be this damn seat! It's not the most comfortable car I've driven in" she exclaimed.

Danny chuckled.

"I know what you mean. Scotty would be disgusted at how soft I've become since I got out of the regiment. I used to eat up this stuff too. Could drive for ages and still leap out of the vehicle and kick ass without having slept for 48 hours."

Her eyes flicked sideways as she drove off at the exit.

"Getting soft? You could have fooled me Danny! Back there in London, the way you took out that guy with the gun, that was the work of a pro. From my perspective you've lost nothing and you probably saved my life. I owe you one."

They cruised along in silence looking for a café or restaurant, aware that Scotty was close behind them.

"Over there" Danny pointed, as a family style restaurant loomed up ahead with a large parking lot now half full. In a few minutes they were parked and all four were standing outside the vehicles, stretching. Danny watched the traffic for a moment to see if anyone was showing an interest in them.

Scotty sidled up to him.

"I was watching when we pulled off at that exit. No one was following us. I think we're in the clear so far Danny."

"Hope you're right. With the technology they've got today we wouldn't know anyway, but I think the cars are clean so that's something. Okay let's get inside. I have some more interesting information I just got from the DG."

The next several minutes were taken up with washroom breaks and ordering meals. They had taken a corner table well away from the door and windows and now they sat back as Danny updated them on the latest developments. Their jaws literally dropped when he told them of the disappearance of the MI6 Director and the involvement of the CIA.

Scotty was the first to react.

"Let me get this. We were actually briefed in Hereford by the London station head of the CIA? The U.S. Government initiating a U.K. military mission without their knowledge or consent? This is the stuff of a paper back novel that you'd dismiss as being total bullshit!"

He looked around, suddenly uneasy.

"You know with the stuff they got, they could have a plane overhead right now and be listening in to us. We need to re-evaluate what we're planning to do Danny. They've got both the intelligence capacity and the military whack to stop us dead once they locate us."

Danny nodded soberly.

"Yeah, I don't want to come up against one of their Delta or Seal teams. I've worked with them before and they're fearsome warriors, make no mistake about it. However it would create an international incident if they ran an operation here in the U.K. This rogue CIA unit are probably using the British recruits in that security firm as muscle at the moment. Most of them are probably ex military and not to be underestimated. We still have a big edge though with the caliber of our lads, if they are still alive and well, and with Wainwright, south of here."

Sophia looked troubled as she listened to the to and fro of the conversation.

"I don't like the turn of events. It sounds like the DG could be in some danger back there from this CIA agent. If he can lift the director of MI6 off the street to keep a cap on this, she could be next on his list once he finds out that she was Percy's last contact. I'm beginning to think that perhaps I should be with her right now watching her back. I know she has security details she can summon at will, but I know her routines, having worked as her PA, and can go most places with her, being a woman."

Just then the platters of food were brought up to their table and they fell silent as they all got stuck in. Jacky made a face at Sophia, nodding at the two men who were virtually attacking the food. Scotty spotted her looking at them in amusement.

"Old regiment habit. Eat and sleep when you can. Hard one to let go of. Look at Danny, he's a bloody civvy now - you only need to look at his hair - but he still eats like a trooper."

When they were finished and at the coffee stage Danny nodded to Sophia and she followed him outside. He turned to her.

"Look, I've been thinking about your concerns regarding the DG back in London. You've got a point there. Why not contact her and suggest that you come back in. We could stay the night in Exeter and get you on the first train out of here in the morning. What d'you think Sophia?"

"As much as I'd like to stay in the field with you, I'd feel better if she had someone with her who knows her habits and movements."

He nodded.

"Here's a thought too: suggest that she send that picture of Sinclair and Percy Saunders taken by the surveillance team, to the metropolitan police. She could do that anonymously or have Jacky's paper publish it on the front page. Put some pressure on the bastard and take it off us."

"A-ha…. I like it Danny. Let me give it a shot."

She moved away a few feet and started using her mobile phone.

He stretched again as he listened to the murmur of her voice. Ever on the alert his eyes roved around the parking lot looking for signs of interest in them. He heard her discontinue the call and moved closer to her.

"That was quick. What did she say Sophia?"

"She's open to me coming back in and staying close to her. She intends to move into a safe house tomorrow evening, located in South London somewhere so I can be part of the protection team. She'll still go into work at Thames House though."

"Good move but don't let her relax Sophia, just because she's in a safe house. The CIA have tentacles everywhere and may already know where the MI5 safe houses are. Wouldn't take too much groundwork to achieve that and Sinclair's old MI6 job might have provided those details anyway. Now what about my idea of the running the picture?"

"In principle she liked the idea of putting pressure on Sinclair but he would immediately know that he was being watched and so her surveillance would be impossible, or he'd just avoid any move that might compromise him. With the surveillance team in place he might lead them to the location where Percy Saunders is being held."

"Yeah, if the poor bugger is still in the land of the living" Danny muttered. "These people aren't taking any prisoners."

They were silent for a few moments, each with their own thoughts.

Finally Danny stirred.

"Hey, I'm going to miss you Sophia, even though I just met you this morning. You are one impressive young lady and I'd be happy to have you on the team at any time."

Her eyes misted over and impulsively she hugged him.

"Thanks Danny I appreciate that, especially after this morning's debacle at the police station. Yes, who knows, we might just work together again. That passport the DG gave me showing me as your wife in case we had to travel together - I guess it's now redundant. Hmm.... that might have been interesting!"

He laughed, holding her at arms length and looking intently into her eyes.

"You know something Sophia. It might at that" he said softly.

Just then Scotty and Jacky came out and they filled them in on the proposed change of plan.

Twenty minutes later they were booked into a Travelodge, which Danny paid for with cash. He had separated the DG from a large portion of cash for taking on the mission prior to realizing that his old SAS regiment was involved. Ten minutes later they were in their separate rooms preparing to settle in for the night.

He had stripped down to his shorts and was almost asleep when he heard a slight tapping on the door and was immediately wide awake. He crept silently out from under the covers, grasping the Glock that he had placed under the pillow, and moved over to the door. He listened for a moment.

The tapping came again. He cautiously opened it a crack, standing off to one side and peered around the door jamb. Sophia was standing there dressed in a short nightie. He opened the door wider and she stepped through, closing it behind her.

"I kept thinking about that passport Danny. Being your wife I mean, and being cheated of a honeymoon" she whispered.

She never got a chance to say another word. Danny's lips settled gently yet urgently over hers.

CHAPTER 25.

Jack McAllister who had been placed in charge of the surveillance operation by the DG felt shock run down his spine. He had followed Basil Sinclair to Heathrow airport and watched him flash his card at the traffic policeman outside arrivals as he left his car there. Jack had done the same himself a number of times and the security people always cooperated. Then he had followed Sinclair at a safe distance to international arrivals and watched as the man pushed into the group of people waiting. Passengers were streaming off various flights, being greeted by friends and business acquaintances and then being swept on through.

After 20 minutes he saw Sinclair wave and move forward to greet one of the arrivals. It was then that Jack felt the shock.

The person coming off the flight was a blocky male, mid thirties with a large square head and eyes darting around as if measuring everyone near him. He had ink-black long hair that fell down over the collar of his coat. A big man, he appeared to walk very lightly on his feet and casually pulled a suitcase behind him.

Jack immediately moved back behind a pillar and took out his mobile phone, then hit a pre-programmed number. A voice answered immediately.

"Yes Jack?" It was his 2nd in command Greg Watson.

"Greg, pull the surveillance cars immediately but just keep the one watching at the Embassy. Tell them to move well back though."

"Okay Jack, consider it done. Want to say why at this stage?"

"No but meet me back at the DG's office. I'll try to get an immediate meeting. This will blow her mind!"

Jack didn't even take another look around the pillar at the target. He turned, exited the terminal swiftly and waved to a car parked further back down the line. As it came level he jumped in and turned to the driver, an older man, with steel gray hair and a tough lived-in face.

"I've pulled the surveillance cars. Greg's dispersing them right now."

The driver glanced sideways at him.

"That's a sudden decision Jack. Does that mean I'll get a night home for a change?"

"Look we'll brief the team later Tommy but for now take it as given that you can have the night off. In fact, why not slope off after you drop me at Thames House. If the DG complains I'll tell her that you guys have been flat out for the past two weeks even before this Embassy job."

"Thanks Guv.... we can sure use the break, and let me know when you can what's going on."

"I'll have Greg give you a shout as soon as we decide where we're going with this, Tommy."

Not much was said for the following forty minutes as the driver battled the thick traffic congestion back into central London.

When he got out at Thames House, the MI5 building, Jack hurried through security and took the elevator up to the DG's floor. As he came into the reception area, the secretary nodded to him.

"She's waiting for you Sir.... oh, and Greg's there already."

He nodded, thanking her, then opening the door, stepped into the DG's office. Rebecca stood up as he came in.

"What on earth is this flap all about Jack? A simple surveillance operation and you've pulled off the whole crew without as much as by your leave."

Jack could see that she was more curious than annoyed.

Greg, his 2nd in command was obviously more frustrated than curious as he'd had to cancel some other surveillance work and pull people in who were off duty. Jack didn't keep them waiting.

"The CIA man Sinclair met someone at Heathrow that I recognized immediately.... Reuben Wyborski. Does that name mean anything to either of you?"

Both Greg and the DG looked blankly at each other and back at Jack.

"Can't say it does" she answered.

Greg shrugged his shoulders.

"Me neither Jack."

Jack's face was animated.

"He's Mossad for crying out loud! When I was on that security course run by the Israelis two years ago, the same chap gave a session on surveillance. It wasn't said openly but we all knew he was Mossad. Probably a Katsa as they call them, a case officer to us, who recruits and runs agents in different countries."

"But why the panic Jack?" the DG asked. "Surely it would be interesting to see where they were going after Sinclair picked him up."

Jack shook his head.

"Ma'am we're good at what we do and some of the team are positively shit-hot, but the Mossad gets three years initial training on surveillance tactics and this chap would have sniffed us out in five minutes flat. No question about it. That's all we needed to blow this operation Ma'am."

The DG looked impressed.

"Well, you're our resident expert on Israeli security Jack, and if you say so then I'm in total agreement with your swift reaction. You still have a watch on the Embassy so it might still result in some useful information. What I'm trying to figure out is why someone from the Israelis, and at his apparent level, is in London and at this particular time? Is it a coincidence or is there an Israeli connection to this whole thing. What on earth could that be?"

"Perhaps not Israeli but Mossad Ma'am. They get up to all sorts of schemes and they're a law unto themselves. The Prime Minister of Israel and military intelligence quite often haven't a clue what they are up to. Whatever Wyborski is involved in might be a completely black operation. Hell they're not even mentioned in the normal defense budgets and they have all sorts of irons in the fire for raising extra cash anyway."

"Such as what?" she asked

"Well they quite often train both sides in a conflict and then sell them the equipment and arms to kill each other. Rumor has it that they've trained some Asian Government army units and their opposing rebel forces on the same base at the same time in Israel, and had a hell of a job keeping them apart."

The DG nodded.

"Well we do know that the Israelis look after number one regardless of the consequences and that is their country's security. Perhaps if we had a holocaust in our history we might be somewhat paranoid as well. Is there any chance Jack that this Wyborski is over here to hunt down the missing troopers and eliminate them?"

Jack shook his head.

"No, a Katsa like him might come in and suss out the situation and if it merited a killing they would send in what they call a Kidon unit, an assassination squad to carry it out."

"But don't they have lots of resources here already? I mean they have a pretty large Embassy here."

"Well of course they would have their standard spooks at the Embassy but they wouldn't get involved in assassinations. Their role would be gathering intelligence information on potential threats to their country."

"Threats… such as what?" Greg intervened.

Jack leaned forward gesturing with his hands.

"Think of all the Muslims now living here and the thousands who go back home every year. They're not all going to military training camps I'll grant you, but still a rich source of information. They would keep an eye on those radical mosques here in the U.K. that preach hatred of Israel and monitor the people frequenting them. They also have thousands of young Jewish people here in the U.K., mostly students who they call Sayanim. A number of them maintain Israeli safe houses and get paid for it. There are also established business people who help them. These people are just part of the great Jewish Diaspora who can be counted on to help out with money or contacts as required. For example, hotels, car hire firms who could help them without any paper work involved. There's also another category - legitimate businesses specially set up by the Mossad, which allow their agents to travel openly to countries that would not normally welcome them. It's formidable, believe me!"

The DG strolled across to the window overlooking the Thames. She was quiet for a few moments, then turned to him again.

"A lot of the background Jack is fairly common knowledge among the security forces of most countries including MI5 here. I must say I'm an admirer of Mossad and the freedom they have to solve problems under the radar, as it were. However if they're planning an operation in the U.K., that certainly falls under our watch. I wonder if this Wyborski came in under his own name today?" she asked.

"My research has shown ma'am that case officers like him come in legitimately using their own name, to the major base countries like the U.K., France etc. They wouldn't risk being caught with false documentation. In other countries, where they're not among friendlies, they would have no problem in setting up a separate identity and the Mossad are the best in the business when it comes to false documentation. If they do bring in a Kidon unit to assassinate someone, they'll be traveling under false papers for sure, but we're speculating now over something we haven't a clue about."

Greg spoke up.

"Jack has done a special study on the Mossad, ma'am and I respect his take on this. Now, following Sinclair the CIA chap was a good idea. It might provide us with the information we need to lift him, even if he is CIA and has diplomatic immunity. We already know he set up a false mission for the Hereford lads and may have made the MI6 chap disappear, probably permanently. Could we not resume surveillance when this Mossad person isn't with him? For example stay at a distance in the interim, but close up when the Israeli goes to his hotel."

The DG looked at Jack.

"Sounds like a wise plan. What do you think?"

He pursed his lips thoughtfully.

"Greg's got a point. I'm still leary of getting anywhere close to this Mossad character. On balance I'd say the possible gains probably exceed the risks involved. I'd like myself and Greg to handle this one ourselves. Oh, I told Tommy to go home and have a night off. The whole team is weary as hell right now."

"That's fine Jack. However you'd better let Greg organize that, as I have another job for you. You know the two who were murdered in their cells in Chepstow? Well I dropped the information to their Chief Superintendent down there of the connection with the security firm in Southampton. They would have picked up on it sooner or later. Now here's the thing. I've talked him into letting you, Jack, go along with his team tomorrow to interview their head man down there in Southampton. You won't be there as MI5 but as a DC from the Chepstow police. It would be useful if you got a chance to look over the place without us showing our hand. I have to tell you that the local police in Chepstow are not happy bunnies right now with the way we handled this whole thing. They maintain that those two would have been under special watch if we'd indicated our strong interest in them right from the start, so you have some fence mending to do Jack."

He shook his head ruefully.

"They have a point Ma'am. They must suspect that we probably left the two men trussed up like turkeys in that van with the stack of weapons. They know we haven't any powers of arrest in the U.K. so they figure we did a runner. But yeah, we could have handled it better."

He looked keenly at the DG.

"I'm assuming you did have something to do with this whole thing Ma'am?"

She avoided his eyes.

"Don't ask Jack and I'll tell you no lies. Suffice it to say that I have some other irons in the fire right now. Let's just leave it at that okay?"

They talked for a further ten minutes organizing travel plans and communication for Jack and the ongoing surveillance of the CIA agent.

CHAPTER 26.

Back on the M5 again heading south, Jacky and Scotty were in one car following Danny. They had left Sophia at the station after a quick breakfast while awaiting the arrival of the train. Jacky was driving as Scotty, for once willing to surrender the wheel, sat back relaxing with his eyes closed. She glanced sideways at him.

"They looked pretty close this morning" she commented.

He opened one eye.

"Who?"

"Danny and Sophia of course. Did you see how she clung to him when he hugged her goodbye" she said with some irritation in her voice.

He shrugged, a faint smile tugging his lips.

"Danny's just like that you know, demonstrative. Anyway he helped her yesterday when she nearly freaked out seeing those bodies."

"Yeah sure, helped himself you mean. He looked pretty beat this morning I thought."

" I'm not sure what you mean Jacky. He looked pretty normal to me and I've been his mate for years. At least until he got out and became a bloody civvy!"

"That shook you didn't it?" she asked. "Him getting out of the regiment."

He was silent for a moment. Finally he sighed.

"Yeah you could say that. Danny was the guy always guarding my back and I his. We could almost read each other's mind at times. It was difficult going into action with someone else. I mean the regiment guys are all first class and we're like the bloody musketeers, all for one and one for all. You know all that crap, but Danny was something else.

What really pissed me off was that his wife forced him to get out of the service and then started divorce proceedings after four months. He was struggling like mad to get going in civvy street. Danny's a warrior and should have stayed on in the regiment."

"He's making a go of it though in financial services, isn't he?"

Scotty nodded in disgust.

"Yeah sure, but at what cost? The man's the best killing machine the regiment's ever recruited. Hell they even use one of his operations in Afghanistan as a case study for new SAS recruits. I heard recently that some Special Forces in other countries have got hold of the details as well and incorporate them in their survival training."

Intrigued now, her journalistic nose quivering, she tapped his knee.

"Hey, this is interesting Scotty! Come on, give with the details. Were you there at the time as well?"

"Yeah sure, but this is official secrets stuff and I've signed the form so you didn't get it from me.... promise?"

She nodded vigorously.

"Oh absolutely! This is a bloody boring road at the best of times so it'll make the time go faster. Let's have it. I'm all ears Scotty."

CHAPTER 27.

LONDON

"How the hell has it come to this?" Reuben Wyborski demanded. "You were supposed to clean this situation up and cap it, and now you've got three of your people dead and one wounded."

Basil Sinclair, even though he was sitting in his impressive office at the Embassy was looking decidedly unhappy.

"Well in a way it's not my fault. Those troopers were not supposed to come back out of the desert and somehow they did. They managed to get out of Kuwait before we were informed about it and ended up back here on their home turf. Then I'm tasked with locating and eliminating them - a team of SAS troopers, and all I have to work with are some security people, admittedly ex-military, but still not top drawer by any means!"

The Mossad man paced the room, obviously not pacified by the CIA man's excuses.

"You had to kill three of your own men for God's sake! You can't blame that on the SAS!"

"Well the two in Wales went and got themselves captured" Sinclair protested, "with a van load of weaponry that we'd organized for locating the rest of the troopers. We had to terminate them or they would have led the police back to us. The same applied to the chap who was caught at the flat here in London. It was sheer bad luck really."

Wyborski stared unblinkingly at him.

"Bad luck you say? I'd say incompetence. You make your own luck in this type of work Sinclair. You realize of course that those three dead men will sooner or later lead back to the security firm down in Southampton? Have you warned them to expect a police visit, possibly with a search warrant?"

"Well, I've got my ear to the ground and my contacts haven't heard that the police are making that connection, at least not at present. I was in the process of beefing up our search teams to go after the remnants of those troopers."

Wyborski sighed, wearily rubbing his forehead.

"Rome burnt while Nero fiddled! Look Sinclair, your ass is on the line here and that high profile future you got planned with the company. Start using your head for a change. Get onto the American security company at the Southampton office at once and have them clean out their recruiting files. Move any of the team who are there out to the warehouse at the compound and lay on some interviews over the next few days to make it look like a normal recruiting center, which it started out as anyway. Got that?"

Sinclair nodded and reached for the phone.

Wyborski went over and poured himself a cup of black coffee as he started running his mind over the deteriorating situation developing in the U.K. He was only half aware of Sinclair's voice in the background as he spoke to someone called Morcambe. Suddenly his head jolted up as he caught the tail end of Sinclair's phone call. He turned to him as he put the phone down.

"What name did I hear you mention just now?" he asked urgently.

Sinclair looked nonplussed.

"Oh, Morcambe you mean. He's my chap...."

Wyborski slapped his hand down on the desk.

"No, no you idiot! Something about losing contact with this person... Danny...."

"Oh Danny Quigley. We were following him, hoping he'd lead us to the troopers."

The Mossad man looked agitated.

"It can't be the same person! It's too much of a coincidence."

He leaned forward and grasped the CIA by his arm.

"Quick tell me all you know about this man and how he's involved in all of this" he demanded hoarsely.

Sinclair quickly went over the series of events that led them to be aware of Quigley flying into Heathrow and the surveillance they had arranged. He'd set up a press lady to get close to him and how they nearly took out Scotty McGregor in the Fox and Hounds. He reiterated the details at the flat where Morcambe had been forced to kill one of the team who was being held down by Quigley. He recounted how, on becoming aware of the name 'Quigley' being involved, he had researched the name. That had led him to some newspapers, a year old. In it was a story that Quigley had demolished three thugs in an underground parking lot and was subsequently blamed for their sudden demise. Eventually he was cleared and went back to his civilian job as a financial planner.

"He's the same person for Gods sake! Quigley, Danny Quigley" Wyborski whispered.

Sinclair's face suddenly looked concerned.

"What about him? Hell we nearly took him out in that pub."

"What about him? Apart from you deliberately involving the press in this, the most stupid thing of all is not knowing who you're dealing with…. Quigley! Just last week I was a visiting lecturer at our Special Forces school in Israel and sat in on the previous lecture, which was survival training. You know who the topic of conversation was about? Danny Quigley, and what he did in Afghanistan. My friend, you nearly walked into a meat-grinder!"

CHAPTER 28.

POLPERRO, CORNWALL, UK.

Jacky took her eyes off the road momentarily and swiveled her head around towards Scotty.

"Why did you stop the story? What happened to Danny in Afghanistan?" she asked impatiently.

He pointed ahead.

"Danny's pulled into that big parking lot at the top end of town. I remember he said it was a one-way, incredibly narrow street like those Spanish villages have, and that we'd walk down."

"Okay but you're going to have to tell me the rest of the story soon. It's mind-blowing."

Scotty grinned and shrugged. He wasn't above teasing her.

"Hell, you can see he survived it Jacky, he's right there in front of you. You've probably heard enough by now. It's a pretty mundane story anyway."

"Now look Scotty, I'm not going to be left hanging in the air. I want to know...."

She paused suddenly, catching his grin.

"You bastard Scotty, you're winding me up. All right I can wait, but the first chance we get I want the rest of this. Can't you see what a story it would make?"

He raised his hand.

"Hey, remember the official secrets act I've signed. I don't want my ass caught in a wringer over this Jacky" he cautioned.

"Have no fear Scotty. Remember we journalists always protect our sources" she added flippantly.

They pulled in alongside Danny's car and he was already standing outside talking on his mobile phone. He closed it with a snap as they got out and strolled around to Scotty's side where Jacky was unwinding herself wearily from behind the wheel.

Danny caught Scotty by the shoulder and turned him aside.

"I used the contact number you gave me for the Major and I'm meeting him down in the village on my own. He's instructed me to wait inside a specific restaurant and he's going to check for surveillance before he approaches. He's suggested that we book into that B&B a 100 yards from here for tonight. He'll meet you later Scotty."

If Scotty seemed disappointed that he wouldn't be seeing the Major right away, he didn't show it.

"Fine Danny but as you can well imagine, I'm anxious to know as soon as possible what happened to the rest of the troop."

"Okay, I understand Scotty. I know they're your mates too and you were like family. I'll get right back to you. Oh, he suggested that you try for a front room and start watching for anyone suspicious following me when I leave there. There's lots of tourists around but a surveillance team should stand out."

Danny caught Jacky's eye and thought she looked at him rather strangely.

"You okay Jacky? Boring old drive wasn't it?" he queried.

"Oh yes, it was Danny" she stammered.

His gaze swept back to Scotty accusingly.

"You haven't been telling her about me have you?" he demanded.

Scotty spread his arms wide.

"What's to tell? Hell, you're not even one of us any more. You deserted us for civvy street remember? You even look like one of them with that bloody long hair."

Danny looked from one to the other skeptically. Then he brought Jacky up to date on the immediate plan. They walked the short distance down to the B&B and booked in. Danny and Scotty managed to get a room with twin beds and Jacky got a tiny room with it's own washroom, up in the attic. They would move their small belongings in later.

Danny took off down the narrow street, trying to act like a normal tourist, at the same time watching for anyone following him. He found the restaurant and ordered a pot of tea with two cups, sitting off to one side but close to a window that allowed him to watch passers by. He finally spotted Wainwright outside, as he casually bent down to tie his shoe lace before standing up and coming in. It only took him a moment to spot Danny and he walked over to the table.

Danny had meant for appearances sake, to be very casual, but seeing the drawn, haunted face of the Major, a man he had worked with on many occasions, he stood up and hugged him. Not a word was spoken.

Wainwright sat down and poured himself a cup of tea. Finally he looked across at Danny.

"Have I ever got a story to tell you, and I hope to God when you've heard it that you can help us because we're as good as dead if you can't.

"By the way Danny, stop calling me Major for Gods sake. You're a flipping civvy now and I'm Bob, okay?"

Danny smiled.

"I seem to recall we weren't too good at recognizing rank back then anyway.... Bob."

Wainwright laughed.

"You can say that again! Now just to clear the decks, who are you representing here? I'd like to know who I'm dealing with."

Danny had been thinking about that and realized he could no longer honor his agreement with the DG to stay under the radar. She had told him that he was engaged on the basis of a deniable operation, if he got into trouble. However he now had to level with Wainwright and bring him up to speed on events.

"I'm working under the radar with MI5. They were brought in when the troop disappeared and they ran an oblique ad in the papers aimed at contacting them. Scotty replied to it. However he only agreed to meet with them if I acted as go-between, so that's how I first got involved."

Wainwright leaned back in the chair, relief showing on his features.

"Thank God we're getting some help" he whispered. "We couldn't hide out down here much longer with that crew looking for us. Now tell me the rest of the events since you got involved."

Danny spent several minutes going over the situation since he'd been brought in. Wainwright listened without comment or interruption. A dawning realization was flooding his face by the time Danny was finished.

"So the chap who briefed us, Blackstone, is actually called Sinclair and works for the CIA? Can you believe it?" Wainwright said wonderingly. "Some bloody nerve!"

Danny waved to the waitress and pointed to the teapot, then turned back to him.

"How about you take it from there Bob. Scotty's told me the story of going to Kuwait and the trip into Iraq. He felt that you knew more than you were letting on to the troop at the time."

Wainwright nodded, marshalling his thoughts. Then he started to tell Danny about the strangest trip he'd ever undertaken for the SAS.

Danny quickly interrupted him.

"One quick question first Bob. The troop?"

Wainwright lowered his head, shaking it.

"They got two of them Danny. They've disappeared completely. I can only assume they're dead. Why would they keep them alive? The rest of the lads are on that fishing boat, down in the harbor there. The one I used to do my fishing in, remember?"

Danny nodded glumly.

"Only too well Bob. Only too well. Okay, now give me the whole story."

Bob started talking with a brooding intensity like a man reliving a bad dream.

"I felt something was wrong with the mission from the word go. Oh nothing I could put my finger on at the start. I got the usual notification that came from my Commander that a mission being initiated by the Government was imminent, MI6 to be exact, and I was to expect a call from a Mr. Blackstone. As you heard from Scotty, this Blackstone turned up, briefed the troop and myself and left. It was from then on that I started to feel uneasy about it. I've done lots of these ops with MI6 and MI5 and there tends to be a pattern to them. You know lots of contact back and forth, telephone, emails, sometimes even further visits or briefings from other people in the Government with input for the mission. With MI6, who operate outside the U.K., we might have people come down and tell us about the culture or politics in a country - how to liaise with other services who might have to get us out in a hurry; off-shore pick-up by submarine for example, should things go wrong as they sometimes do; contacts in foreign countries such as other intelligence agencies or friendly embassies. None of that happened. I did call a contact number that Blackstone had left me but was always fobbed off by some chap who said that he wasn't available. Now of course I discover from you that he was actually CIA all the time!"

"Do you remember the name of the chap you spoke to?" Danny asked.

Wainwright snorted in derision.

"A damn lot of good that would do at this stage. Probably wasn't his real name anyway. As I recall it was Brownlea or Browning, something like that, oh and the extension number was 206."

Danny made a note of it on a sheet of paper in front of him. He looked up.

"Okay carry on. Sorry for the interruption."

"Well anyway we get to Kuwait and I try to pump Colonel Minter of the U.S. Marine Corps for more information beyond the briefing he gave the troop. He just stonewalled me. It would have been normal practice to have invited me round to the mess for a drink, but we were all kept isolated in that hanger overnight. Not allowed contact with anyone. At the plane, when we were taking the crate off, I faked a sick stomach and went back in to use their toilet with the intention of chatting with the two pilots. I heard an exchange between them. One of them was just saying, 'did you see the reading on that fucking crate. It was hot. Off the bloody wall. Hell I want to have kids one of these days. I'm glad it's out of the goddamn plane'!"

Danny leaned forward.

"Shit, this is starting to get hairy Bob!"

"You better believe it! I eased into the cockpit making a face as if I wasn't feeling too well, introduced myself casually and asked if I could use their toilet. They looked a bit surprised at first but waved me to the nearest washroom. I congratulated them on the delivery and just as casually did a Columbo on them as I turned away - "oh where did you fly out of today?" I asked. The younger of the two said Tel Aviv and as he did so the older man shot him a warning look and that was the end of the conversation.

We left the following morning for Iraq."

Danny stopped him there.

"So you knew you had something hot with you?" he prompted.

"Damn right and it was nuclear! Flown out of Israel on a civilian plane. Who flies civilian planes and ignores borders since 9/11?"

"CIA" Danny muttered. "We're starting to see the dots being joined up here. Did we tell you that your Blackstone, who is really Sinclair, was station head in Tel Aviv up until recently?"

Wainwright was shaking his head.

"How could the Israelis release a nuclear bomb to a slip-shod outfit like that? Shit, they nearly lost it to a raiding party in the desert."

Danny eyed him levelly.

"Where did it come from in Israel I wonder? Any ideas?"

"Well we've known since 1960 from that American U2 flight that they have a nuclear plant at the Dimona research center in the Negev, about 40 miles northeast of Beersheba. We also know that there's a much smaller reactor, a nuclear research facility in Nahal Sorek, inside an air force base just south of Tel Aviv. I suspect they may have acquired the weapon there and flown it out directly to Kuwait. I'm just guessing really but it would be a logical choice and the simplest."

Danny nodded.

"So you knew or suspected that it was nuclear? That's why you disposed of it isn't it? How did you manage that?" he asked.

Wainwright chuckled.

"Privilege of rank my boy. It's handy when you can give orders and set the stage. Oh, I got the drivers to switch every few hours to reduce the effects of radiation. I'm hoping there is no future health problems for the lads as a result. The first night we stopped at an old well and I had the men fill six bags of sand for protective purposes. I'd ignored Colonel Minter's suggested stopping place by the way and chose one further along the route. Your mate Scotty looked at me funnily when I gave that order regarding the six sand bags. The place was well protected as it was. Then I impressed them all to hell as a leader when I took the worst shift of the night for watch duty. Prior to dawn when the men were in their heaviest sleep I simply took the crate apart and lowered the item that was in there down that dried well."

Danny stared at him impressed.

"Hell that thing was heavy! It took two of you to get it off the plane."

He laughed.

"You're forgetting, I'm a dead lift weightlifting champion Danny. It was easy. The bomb, and we may as well call it that, was shaped very much like a beer barrel. I had no real problem shifting it around and lowering it on a rope down that damn well. Guess what I did then?"

Danny raised his arms in the air.

"I've no idea, but you have the floor. I'm all ears."

"I dumped the six sacks of sand down on top of the bomb, covering it completely. Then I filled the crate with boulders and tapped it back together again. My only concern was that I might wake some curious trooper who discovered me hammering nails into the crate, but you know troopers."

"Yeah, sleep when you can, that's the rule. Then what. You had a real problem when you got to the camp?" Danny responded.

It was Wainwright's turn to hold up his arms.

"Let's stop right there Danny. I do have a real problem and right now, before we go any further, I want to pass part of this burden over to you."

"Well, I guess that's why I'm here in the first place. In an un-official capacity admittedly, but with an ear to the throne as it were. Go ahead."

Wainwright bent down and undid his shoe, then, reaching into it, drew out a small piece of paper which he passed over to Danny.

"Do you still have that photographic memory Danny or has civvy-street erased that?"

He looked down at the paper.

"What exactly is this Bob? Why is it so important that you hide it in your shoe?"

Wainwright looked around carefully then leaned forward and whispered

"It's the GPS coordinates of that fucking bomb! Up to now I was the only one who knew where it was. I was so conscious that if anything happened to me it would just lie there until some people stumbled across it. Who knows just how stable the thing is anyway."

Danny breathed out slowly.

"So this is what it's all about? This is what's behind the killings. As far as the people who set this up are concerned, the whole thing's gone off the rails. Now it's cover their tracks time and there's a massive fall out if it does come out Bob."

"You're not kidding! We have the U.K. involved, the U.S. Government, the Israelis. I can tell you this, anyone of those governments would put a lid on it any way they could, and I include our own in this too. For starters the U.S. President and the Israeli President would have to resign, even if they claimed it's a black operation. I know that the U.S. President has to sign off on any covert operation, and it has to have Senate oversight as well, so there'd be no hiding place."

Danny pushed the paper back across the table.

"Okay, I've memorized the coordinates. What do you want me to do with them?"

"For the moment hang onto them. I'm just relieved to have given them to someone else at this stage. Use your own judgment as to who to pass them onto. Now as to the rest of the story…."

"Well Scotty told me the next part of it - the firefight at the camp. I want to know how you made the empty crate disappear, and one of their men to boot."

Wainwright struggled as if reluctant to go further. Finally he sighed.

"Okay, it was obvious that we weren't supposed to come out of that camp alive. It was written all over them especially that bastard Hardwick. He could hardly wait to waste us. Well it was like a picture of hell in that camp. The attackers eventually withdrew leaving behind a bunch of burning vehicles. The wind was screaming and the sandstorm was blasting against the torn tents and trailers. The troop and I were all sprawled across the floor inside the trailer trying to get some sleep. I made a point of staying right at the door. During the night some of the troop went out, possibly for a smoke, and stepped over me both going out and coming back in. I waited until the small hours when they'd settled down and then slipped out. I walked over to the jeep which was parked directly over the crate. Hardwick had insisted on staying in the vehicle to guard the cargo. It was still blowing sand but not as bad as before. I came up behind his door, opened it swiftly, pulled him out by the hair and cut his throat in the sand. I didn't want the seat in the jeep to show evidence of him being killed."

Hardened as he was, Danny still looked startled. He was about to say something but Wainwright stopped him.

"Let me finish, please. I then hauled the dead man across to the back of a large sand dune and covered him with sand. It was already drifting across him as I left so I figured he'd never be discovered. Then I went back, shoved the jeep forward and dug up that crate. I'm strong Danny, but at times like that it's surprising where that extra strength comes from. I dragged the crate even further beyond where I'd hidden Hardwick, kicked all the wooden slats off it and tossed them around. The rocks I left there. They would be covered minutes later and wouldn't mean anything to anybody, separated as they were from the crate. I went back, filled in the hole where the crate had been buried and pushed the jeep back over it. By then I was completely exhausted and believe it or not, I went back to the trailer and slept for about two hours. The sleep of the dead. The rest you know. General O'Donnell and the security guy Tom Bradley went berserk when they discovered that the bomb had disappeared."

Silence fell between them for a good five minutes.

Danny finally looked across at him. There was admiration in his gaze.

"Bob what you did was amazing. Absolutely amazing, and in a way you did it all on your own. Oh you had a troop there to call on, but you didn't, and more importantly you got them all out of there and home."

Danny was shocked to see tears starting to rim Wainwright's eyes.

"I got them home all right Danny but they've killed two of them since we got back, and it's all my fault. I should have twigged that this was a black operation from the word go. Here's a question for you Danny. Why not use that press lady you have with you and just run the story? Blow the whole thing wide open?"

"Good question, Bob and believe me I've asked myself the same thing. The problem is that the bad guys would all go to ground - disappear into the woodwork. We'd never find the bastards and the governments would just stonewall and deny everything. No, I want to find these people and exact the maximum price for taking our guys out, and that's the next stage. We now have to start taking the initiative and fighting back."

Wainwright nodded his head fervently.

"I agree with you Danny but unless you brought a magic wand with you my friend, it won't take them long to catch up with us, sitting down here."

He reached into his pocket and extracted a crumpled envelope.

"Oh this came in for you at the regiment when I got back from Kuwait. I guess someone had an old address of yours. I was going to pass it on to Scotty in the hope that he had some contact number for you."

Danny took the envelope and shoved it in his back pocket, his mind already on something else. Suddenly he became aware that he had missed a question from Wainwright. He looked up.

"Sorry Bob what was that?"

"Looks like shortly I'll have another Danny Quigley story to add to the saga, as if it wasn't mind-blowing enough as it was: the military decoration presented to you at 10 Downing Street in a private ceremony for your mission in Afghanistan; an equally private presentation at the American Embassy by the Vice President of the United States for their highest decoration; the Afghan President had you specially flown over to receive their highest decoration, and now this…. God!"

Danny looked embarrassed for a moment, then turned and waved to the restaurant proprietor, who came over to them.

"Yes Sirs?"

"Can you get us another cup of tea and some of those scones please?"

The man nodded and hurried back to the bar.

Both men sat looking at each other in silence. Finally Wainwright sat forward.

"You're really intend to follow through with this Danny? You might be better leaving it to the authorities at this stage. They have the resources and the police powers, and as you say, you're under the radar with MI5. It could be your undoing. From our experience we know that nothing is as it seems in these operations. You can plan and rehearse all you want, but on the day anything and everything can go wrong"

"Yeah I have to go through with it Bob. Even if the police could prove that this outfit killed our troopers and some of their own people, they would end up getting their wrists slapped and probably do time. That's not good enough. I would never forgive myself if I didn't have a go at the people who killed our regiment mates. Oh by the way, there's a story I need to tell you when we get through this, about an experience I had over in Ireland last year. It kinda changed me and the way I look at my life, in particular the way I have used violence in the past. It's been quite a journey and I'm still working it through in my mind."

"Jesus Danny! You tell me now, in the middle of this extremely dangerous situation! I was hoping, and so were the lads that we had the old Danny Quigley behind us. Can you still handle all this? If you can't we're lost before we even start!"

He reached across and grabbed Danny's arm. Danny stared directly into his eyes.

"In some sort of strange way Bob, I'm even more effective than when I was in the troop. No ra ra ra like before when we were going into action, but a detached clinical approach, almost like I was given a gift. If you believe in good and evil, then I'm using it on occasion to defeat evil. Sounds like a load of crap out of a comic book I know, but there it is."

Wainwright threw his hands in the air.

"Danny, we always said civvies were a weird lot and you just proved it in spades. If you don't mind I won't tell the lads about this conversation. We might just lose some of our volunteers. Now here's the tea and scones, but you've got my interest piqued so you can just go ahead and tell me about what happened to you in Ireland."

Danny's brow furrowed as he struggled with the challenge of his experience there the previous year. How could he succinctly put into a few words his most life-changing event to date?

"Okay Bob, just an overview. I owe you that at least. A year ago I got into some bad trouble. You may have read about it in the papers if you were in the U.K. at that time."

Wainwright shook his head.

"We were out in Iraq around then. Some of the squaddies make a point of reading the papers but we were out in the field for three months and cut off from the usual stuff from the U.K., you know, mail, papers and so on."

Danny raised his hand.

"Right, it doesn't matter. I'll fill you in. I was accused of killing three thugs in London and the cops were going to arrest me so I left the country for Ireland, a place called Sligo to be exact. I met a strange individual there, a chap called Clive Courtney known as C.C., a Brit who worked in the U.K. and was supporting a women's rescue organization in Ireland. He started helping me too, and in the process told me that he discerned a spirit of violence in me."

Wainwright chuckled.

"Sure, years in the 'Sass' will do that! Come on, did he have a crystal ball or something?"

"Let me finish Bob, then you can slag me if you want. I pointed out the very thing you just did, my military career and all the people I'd killed, but he said that the spirit of violence came from somewhere in my upbringing. The 'Sass' was just the vehicle I'd chosen to express that violence. He did some work with me and I discovered that it was the experience of having my mother beaten and abused by my stepfather that had created the core of anger in me. He helped me get over it and release all that anger. It was an amazing healing experience Bob. I just felt freed up and somehow cleansed. Sounds corny I know."

Wainwright whistled and peered closely at him.

"If it was anyone else telling me this Danny I might take them seriously, but you're the deadliest fighting machine on two feet that I've ever seen in action! Look at Afghanistan for God's sake. Does this mean you can't take offensive action any longer? If so we might as well forget avenging the lads up in Southampton."

Danny reached across and patted his arm reassuringly.

"I struggled with it as well Bob but was thrown back into action again almost immediately which was probably a good thing. I was surprised to discover that I was even more effective than I had been in the troop. It didn't mean I liked violence, but when placed in the position of taking proactive action, I was focused and highly efficient."

Wainwright sat back looking at him reflectively.

"Sounds too much like Superman or Batman for me Danny, but if it works for you so be it. Personally, if you were backing me up in the field I'd worry that you might hesitate at the wrong moment with all this stuff going through your mind. Give me the old Danny Quigley any time. The lads would feel the same so for fuck's sake don't breathe a word about your so called conversion to them! Anyway, where is this guy Courtney now?"

"Sadly, he's deceased as far as we know. When I last saw him he had only 3 months to live, terminal cancer, and that was over twelve months ago."

Danny said nothing for a moment, then continued.

"You know Bob, since that experience in Ireland I'm at peace with myself for the first time in my life. I was all screwed up before I joined the Forces, and the 'Sass' was an outlet for my rage. Now I see the tension reflected in your face and body language as well. I'm curious why you didn't move out of the regiment as most officers do after a few years."

Wainwright shook his head and looked away momentarily.

"Look, the regiment was my family and you bloody troopers were practically my kids for God's sake! There's lots of people who hate the 22nd SAS Regiment and would cut the legs from under it given the chance. I was always up there fighting for more funding, training and high priority operational roles. There was never an opportunity to bail out and pursue my career in another regiment. I probably left it too late."

Wainwright tried to laugh but only half succeeded. Danny could see his haunted eyes behind the mask and recognized it. He used to see that same look all the time when he saw his own face in the mirror. Wainwright reached forward and slapped him on the shoulder.

"You take the biscuit Danny, you really do. I wish I'd recorded our conversation back there because tomorrow I'll be wondering if I had a bad dream! Now lets get out of here before I change my mind about this operation!"

Danny restrained him.

"Hang on here a minute Bob while I go outside and brief someone. Have another pot of tea. I expect I'll be at least 20 minutes."

Danny retreated to an outside extension in the garden of the restaurant and called the DG.

"Call me" was his cryptic message.

In a moment his phone buzzed. Rebecca's voice was as clear as if she was standing next to him.

"Yes Danny."

Danny summarized the details of his debriefing with Wainwright. He was impressed with the DG's presence of mind who, despite several gasps during the story, remained silent until he had finished. Even then she remained silent for a whole minute before....

"Danny this is absolutely mind-blowing! It's the stuff fiction novels are made of. You laugh at the author's imagination and reassure yourself that, hell this couldn't happen, but it's happening right here and now! My head is absolutely reeling as it is."

Danny cut in.

"Wainwright's right on the edge Rebecca. He's been carrying this on his own for so long and he blames himself for the death of his men. My suggestion would be to leave him out of any proposed action we take for now. He can work in a supportive role of course."

"What exactly do you mean by action Danny? This means an immediate visit to the Home Secretary who will most certainly bring in the Foreign Secretary. It's out of your hands now. You've done your job and earned your fee and you're going to have to back off. It's a police operation now Danny."

"Wait a minute Rebecca. You know darned well that as soon as you raise the alarm the people involved will scatter and there'll be no justice for the lads who've been murdered. What I'm asking for is 48 hours to settle some scores, and then you can let the police loose. How about it?"

She was quiet for a moment.

"What did you have in mind Danny?" she asked cautiously.

"I want to take out the security people who work up in Southampton" he replied. "That's where the killers came from. They may not specifically be working out of the main office, but are certain to have a place where they train and keep a stock of weapons - a warehouse, or a deserted building for example. I need to locate that center first and then move on it."

"Well you should know that the police visited their main recruiting office yesterday and one of my people was with the team. You're right, it's just a normal front office building, recruiting security people with military experience. The police had a search warrant which they exercised and took away a number of files. Jack McAllister's our chap and his feeling is that the visit was expected and they were prepared for it. Hell they were even interviewing potential recruits during the police visit. The files of those people who were responsible for the killings were probably sanitized."

He grunted.

"Okay, not the most encouraging of news, but here's the thing Rebecca. How about you get someone to dig into any purchases of properties in the Southampton area, made by the company during, say the last two years? Could you do that for us please?"

Danny kept his fingers crossed waiting for her answer.

"Danny I want to tell you why I'm going to say yes. McAllister's been trying to keep Sinclair and this chap he claims is Mossad under surveillance. It's a tough one because the Israeli apparently invented the practice of following people. However Jack figured that they probably sweep the car clean in the mornings, so he managed to attach a monitoring device to their car when they were having lunch in a restaurant off the M40 heading out of London. He hoped to recover it from the vehicle before it ended up back in the underground parking lot in the U.S. Embassy. You could say that Jack likes living on the edge. Anyway they followed the car to High Wycombe and do you know where it ended up?"

"Haven't a clue but I'm sure this is going somewhere" he answered impatiently.

"It is Danny. It certainly is. The car ended up at a crematorium on the outskirts of the city and both men went in and were there for over an hour."

He felt a cold shiver run up his spine. The missing troopers had probably ended up there. They were probably already reduced to ashes. He felt the anger build up in him.

"You're obviously thinking the same thoughts I am right now. Does this mean we get our 48 hours?"

"We can't sit on this information Danny because the DNA evidence of those troopers would probably disappear if it hasn't already. We're getting search warrants and organizing a police unit to secure the building and establishing who the owners are. We have pictures of Sinclair and his Israeli friend visiting there so if we get the DNA evidence that we suspect is still there, we can move on them. The Israeli may very well have diplomatic immunity, we just don't know yet, but we could wrap up the CIA man Sinclair. After all he's a British citizen and we're looking at a murder charge here. Okay, you have your 48 hours Danny but I want to be kept informed. Is that understood?"

"Yes Ma'am" he answered formally. "By the way, could you make sure they don't get a phone call out when you descend on the crematorium people.... no phone calls to solicitors?"

The DG sighed.

"Did I ever tell you that you'd be a very good dictator, denying people their rights under the law? But I suppose we can pull the national security card in this instance. The police won't be too happy though."

"Thanks Rebecca. And by the way, Wainwright recalled that he tried to contact Blackstone at MI6 to clarify some points and kept getting someone called Brownlea or Browning on an extension 206. Could you run that lead down?"

"Wait a minute Danny. The name rings a bell. We get circulated when a flag goes up on anyone in security. Hang on a second there, I'm just trying to locate an informational email that came in a couple of days ago."

There was silence at the other end.

Danny moved the mobile phone to the other ear, feeling a headache coming on. Mobile phones simply didn't seem to agree with his head. He didn't accept the so-called findings that claimed they caused no mental damage.

Rebecca's voice came back on the line.

"Here it is. A body was fished out of the Thames and identified as a Phil Browning. Subsequently we were informed that he was a low echelon employee at MI6. It's routine to inform all intelligence agencies but quite frankly we had no reason to take any notice of it."

"Well there was no reason to obviously, prior to Wainwright's information. So they're cleaning house right across the board. You need to watch yourself too Rebecca. By now Sinclair knows you had lunch with Charles 'Percy' Saunders. He's a slippery customer by all accounts as we're seeing."

She snorted.

"If Sinclair shows his face within twenty feet of me I'll blast it clean off his head. Remember how I used that shotgun last year Danny?"

He grinned despite himself. He also felt a grain of sympathy for anyone who was unfortunate enough to come into her sights as a potential enemy.

They chatted further as they agreed on future communication and tactics, then Danny want back inside to rejoin Wainwright.

They were now going on the offensive.

CHAPTER 29.

HIGH WYCOMBE, U.K.

Sinclair was speeding back down the M40 humming to himself as Reuben Wyborski sat thoughtfully beside him. After a while he stirred.

"You know of course where Quigley and the remnants of that troop are going to turn up Sinclair, don't you?"

The car swerved as his head flicked around to the Israeli.

"Just how the hell can you predict that? I've got watchers trolling hotels and guest houses looking for a small number of male guests. I have the government listening post at Cheltenham as a favor to the CIA, monitoring telephone calls on landlines and mobile phones. I have contacts in police forces on the watch for an influx of military-type personnel turning up in their area. How can you waltz in here and tell us how to do our business?"

Wyborski smiled.

"Elementary my dear Watson, to coin a phrase. You lost a man in that press lady's flat, shot by Morcambe I understand. His ID was probably checked by Quigley at the time. That's what I would have done, and passed on to whoever he's working for. That will lead back to Southampton. The other two that you eliminated in the police cell will be traced back to the same source.... Southampton. Quigley is trying to find you just as much as you want to find him and I'll bet you a pound to a penny that's where he'll turn up."

The car swerved again as Sinclair fumbled for his phone.

"Shit I better get onto them and warn them then."

The Mossad man reached out and stayed his hand.

"Better still Sinclair, just take the next right turn for the M4 and head straight down there. I'd like to meet this Danny Quigley. Does the myth measure up to the man I wonder? Might be interesting to find out."

The other man thought about it.

"Reuben, you have the reputation yourself for being one tough son of a bitch from what I've heard. Okay, I know you're not one of those assassins from the institute, what do you call them, Kidons, but your reputation goes before you. D'you think you could handle Quigley if it came right down to it?"

Wyborski tapped his fingers together.

"As you say Sinclair, my reputation. Wouldn't do any harm at all if I took down Quigley who's already looked up to in my own country among Special Forces as some sort of icon. No, no harm at all. There's your turn off by the way."

Danny's phone rang a half hour later. It was the DG.

"Danny I don't think I need to run down those properties in Southampton. Jack just contacted me and it looks like our friend Sinclair and the gentleman from the Mossad are heading in that direction. They'll probably lead right to the location you were trying to find."

"Sounds good. Tell me, has he got the bug still in place on their car?" he asked.

"Affirmative Danny. Good hunting."

She hung up.

CHAPTER 30

POLPERRO, CORNWALL, UK.

They were all assembled on Wainwright's boat which he had taken a mile out of the harbor and anchored. Danny discovered that the two troopers who were presumed murdered were Taffy Jones the bodybuilder, and Terry Buckley from Bristol who loved action novels. That left Major Wainwright, Sergeant Scotty McGregor, Troopers Grant Birchall the giant from Birmingham, Clyde Stoner a weapons expert originally from London, Nigel Hawthorn the ex engineer officer with skills in vehicle maintenance and a 4th Dan in judo, and Jimmy Patton from Belfast, a demolition expert. They also had Tony Archer, the medic.

Despite some reservations they had allowed Jacky to come on board as well, recognizing that they might need some sympathetic press behind them by the time they had finished with the mission. As it was, she agreed that she would not go to press until the text of the article was approved by Major Wainwright.

Wainwright opened the meeting after large amounts of tea and coffee had been brought in and people grabbed the nearest place to sit or perch. In his brief opening remarks they had a minutes silence for the two murdered troopers, then he turned it over to Danny.

Danny looked around the room, catching each man's eyes before starting. He cleared his throat.

"Bob is as angry as all of you about this and he wants to avenge the two troopers who were killed. However he recognizes that, as a serving officer in the British military, he's not going to head up vigilante action here in the U.K., even if it is to settle the score. He is, however, quite happy for me to take on this lead role, and on that basis wants to volunteer the use of his boat for the operation which he will captain. He's especially not going to order you, his troop, into getting involved. It's up to each of you to make your own decision. There are obviously grave risks involved here, not the least of which could be your future career in the military, or possible criminal charges. On that basis, who wants in? Remember this is pay back time. Some of you know me and some of you may have heard stories about me, and you may have gathered that I don't muck about."

Every hand in the room shot up as of one accord.

Danny looked around, his face lean and hard, but proud of the group's reaction.

"That's it then. We're all in on the operation. Bob and I have discussed an action plan to start taking the battle back to the enemy. The enemy we face is not the standard one that we're used to engaging with on the battlefield. These are men wearing suits and ties, hiding behind security clearances, and able to muster a vast array of resources in intelligence, technology and trained personnel. They're a formidable force to be reckoned with and not to be taken lightly. I've just discovered that they have an interest in a crematorium in High Wycombe and we believe that is where they probably disposed of Taffy Jones and Terry Buckley."

There was a murmur of anger among the men and some of them sat up straighter.

Danny continued.

"Yeah I know, that's how Major Wainwright and myself felt when we heard the news. Now things are moving as we speak. MI5 and the police will be moving on the crematorium site and doing their stuff, taking people into custody and gathering DNA evidence. The evidence we have so far is that the London station head of the CIA appears to be up to his neck in this whole thing in the person of Basil Sinclair, better known to you all here as the man Blackstone, who briefed you at Hereford for the mission."

There were whistles of amazement and several hands shot up. Wainwright cut in.

"Look, leave Danny to finish the briefing first and then you can ask your questions, okay?

It took a few minutes for the men to settle down again. Jacky was busy scribbling notes while Danny waited for silence.

"Another unusual development is that a top ranking case officer from the Israeli Mossad has flown into London and visited Sinclair. Both of these men went to High Wycombe together. The interesting thing is that we have a bug on their car and the latest news is that they appear to be heading down towards Southampton. We hope they'll lead us to their operational base down there, not just their public recruiting center, and when they do we intend to make our move. If we're lucky we'll discover all the rats in their hole together and you know how we deal with rats don't you?"

Clyde Stoner sliced his finger across his throat.

"Yeah you exterminate them" he muttered.

Danny nodded.

"Now the people we're up against have already killed three of their own to stop them talking and a low level contact at MI6, so they're a pretty ruthless bunch. They also lifted the head of MI6 and we fear he probably ended up in that crematorium. The names all lead back to a recruiting center in Southampton for ex servicemen to work as security personnel overseas: Iraq, Afghanistan and numerous other trouble spots. It's a satellite office for Empire Security Services in Buffalo New York State. Scotty was nearly scooped up by them. Tell us your impression of those people Scotty."

Scotty scratched his head.

"Hmm….. focused, professional, appeared to work well together, heavy assault weapons and they held them as if they knew how to use them. Used standard blocking methods to contain the area. Essentially any one of us wouldn't have had a chance to escape even if we were armed. My advice is, don't underestimate them."

Danny's voice was grim.

"We don't intend to. Now Bob and I have already worked out a rough plan of action to be refined once we get more information on the destination of that car that's being followed right now. Essentially we split into two teams for the moment. Scotty takes team number one and the weapons from our vehicle across by boat to Southampton. Once there, he will liaise with my team, which will be going up by road using both cars. We can't risk being stopped on the road by police and having weapons with us. I have some work for Scotty when he gets there and will brief him separately. We haven't much time as I've been given just 48 hours to wrap this up or the authorities will move in and those rats will have scattered."

Nigel Hawthorn the ex engineering officer raised his hand.

Danny nodded.

"Yes Nigel."

"You say you've been given 48 hours. By whom? Are we in some way official on this Danny?"

"It's unofficially official Nigel. That's all I can say. However we're all sticking our necks out here, have no doubt about it! You know the penalty for carrying guns in the U.K."

"So finish the job and don't get caught. That's what you're saying?" Jimmy Patton prompted.

Danny looked across at him and nodded, saying nothing.

Within ten minutes the boat was heading back into port and Danny was closeted with Stoner the weapons expert and Patton the explosives chap as they picked his brains on the weapons they had confiscated from the two phony policemen in Wales. Then he spent the remaining time with Scotty.

The worm had turned.

CHAPTER 31.

Jack McAllister the MI5 operative followed the vehicle driven by Sinclair across the M4 still heading south. The monitoring device made it simple and avoided any chance of discovery. The car ahead picked up the M3 motorway and the speed increased. Jack closed the space until he was about half a mile back. An hour and a half later he noticed that the vehicle ahead had stopped. He slowed down as he spotted an upcoming exit for the city of Winchester which the target vehicle had probably taken, and swung off, keeping a close eye on the monitor to make sure he didn't get too close. Once off the ramp he pulled over to the side. There was no movement in the vehicle ahead so he returned to the road and drove at the normal speed a car would progress, and in a few moments flashed past a restaurant where he spotted the target vehicle. There appeared to be no passengers in it and no one standing around the entrance.

A quarter mile down the road he spotted a fast food restaurant and dashed inside, placing an order at the counter. After using the washroom. Jack grabbed his food and some napkins and dashed outside again, breathing a sigh of relief when he saw that the target vehicle was still stationary. He made a quick call to the Director General informing her as to his location. He had one question for her:

"Ma'am, when these people get to their destination, what do you want me to do?"

"Continue to keep the place under observation, because this is probably the site we're looking for. However if they move at all, follow them" she instructed.

"Who's we Ma'am?"

"OK, I want you to liaise with a Danny Quigley when he gets to Southampton in a few hours. I'll contact you then. In terms of saying any more at this time Jack, you're better off not knowing."

There was silence on the line as Jack thought this through. Eventually he sighed.

"My next question was going to be, who is Danny Quigley, but I gather I don't ask that?"

"You always were quick off the mark Jack. In this case spot on. You'll be meeting him shortly in any event. If you decide to help him any further I don't want to know about it, understood?"

"Yes Ma'am, I certainly do! I'm beginning to look forward to meeting this Danny Quigley."

The call ended on that note.

She sat silently for a moment after hanging up, realizing that she was putting her whole career on the line with the 48 hours she was giving to Danny. Time to help him close off some bolt-holes and exact a penalty for the murdered troopers and the lower echelon MI6 employee. Knowing him as she did, she had no doubt that the penalty he would exact would be pretty extreme. She flipped the intercom. Her PA's voice came across.

"Yes Ma'am?"

"Have Sophia bring the car round the front. I want to speak to security at reception on the way out."

"Very good Ma'am."

Her vehicle was parked in the underground car park beneath the building. Sophia had been working as her close protection officer since she'd come back from Exeter. She had been warned to expect some reaction from Sinclair once he realized that she had met Sir Percy prior to his visit to him at the Embassy. Sophia had taken over the job of driving for her boss and accompanying her to lunch and various meetings.

In a short while the DG was striding into reception where an alert security supervisor Jock Andrews stood up to greet her. At that precise moment the whole reception area shook as a powerful explosion rocked the building. A building that was virtually bomb proof and could sustain rocket attacks if necessary. The security man stared at her, his face shocked.

"That's come from the underground car park Ma'am" he shouted.

Her hand flew to her mouth.

"Oh God, Sophia!" she gasped, as she dashed over to the elevator. The security man went to go with her but she stopped him.

"No stay here and raise the alarm. It could be a diversion to hit us up here. Get more security down and call for the police, an ambulance and the bomb squad."

Ashen faced, Jock dashed back towards his desk.

The DG jumped into the elevator and pressed the button for the below level garage, thankful that it was still working. Once the doors opened to the garage she stepped out into a scene of utter carnage. The place was filled with smoke and a number of cars were already burning, some fiercely from punctured petrol tanks. One exploded twenty yards from her sending shards of metal flying around the garage, narrowly missing her. She spotted two male figures lying motionless on the cement floor. It was then that she noticed her vehicle. It was consumed in flames. She grabbed a fire extinguisher from the wall beside the elevator and ran over in the direction of the car, feeling the blast of fierce heat. A cry rose in her throat when she saw the figure in the car. Sophia. She tried again to get nearer and use the extinguisher but the heat beat her back. She knew no one could have survived and fell to her knees sobbing. Suddenly she was aware of arms picking her up and hustling her back to the elevator. It was the security man accompanied by other shocked staff members.

"Come on Ma'am, we need to get out of here. This whole garage could go up. The fire department will be here any moment and we've already started evacuating the building."

Her mind reeling, she allowed herself to be helped back into the elevator.

How could anyone penetrate the secure underground MI5 parking lot? she wondered.

Going up in the elevator she looked across at Jock Andrews.

"Jock were you on the front desk when that CIA chap Sinclair came in to see me two days ago?"

"I was Ma'am."

"Did he park underground at that time?" she pressed.

"Not initially. He sent his driver around to park there but the attendant stopped him and called through to us at security. It wasn't until you OK'd the meeting and we verified his identity that we allowed the driver to go inside. Why, is anything wrong here Ma'am?"

He darted an anxious glance across at her.

"Nooo….. not as far as I know Jock. Just crossing all the T's right now. We'll come back to this when we make our enquiry. I'm sure security wasn't responsible for this lapse."

She sagged back on the side of the elevator as a fit of coughing racked her body. The smoke inhalation was catching up on her. She had no doubt that the bomb was meant for herself, and poor Sophia had paid the price. The fact that Sinclair and his driver had been allowed into the secure underground garage could have given them the opportunity to place a delayed explosive device on her vehicle, which they must have activated today. Obviously they knew which one she drove.

Sinclair's motive for the visit was not to gather information from her but to eliminate her. As an added precaution, she believed he had waited until he was out of the London area in High Wycombe to provide an alibi for himself in case he needed it. More than ever she was glad she had given Danny time to create closure on the whole situation. She hoped his plan would pull in the bombers and exact the ultimate vengeance on them. If not, she vowed that she would personally find out who was responsible and do the job herself. To hell with her career she thought as her mind tried to grasp the enormity of the atrocity and her personal loss.

CHAPTER 32.

Wainwright was already ploughing along the coast with Scotty and half the troop. That left Danny and Jacky in one car and the remnants of his team in the second vehicle, which had left ahead of them for Southampton.

He was happy to let her drive and he kept an eye on the route for her, using a map he'd got earlier. They drove along in a comfortable silence and he was glad of that as his mind was spiraling around the various threads of the operation.

After a while she patted his arm with her left hand.

"Scotty told me the story about Afghanistan, Danny, while we were driving down the M5. He finished it back in the Bed and Breakfast. That was an incredible experience! Was it true about the number of Taliban and Al Qaeda you were instrumental in wiping out? I found that mind blowing!"

He wondered how to reply to her question. The contrast between being dropped in a hostile environment where people would kill you, and driving along in the quiet English countryside was difficult to explain.

He rubbed his face and sighed audibly.

"I appreciate that you're a journalist and used to debriefing people about accidents, tragedies and so forth. Notwithstanding that, it's difficult to fully explain to someone who hasn't been in action, the process you go through mentally and emotionally to ensure your survival. You might have come from a friendly game of darts in a pub or taking your dog for a walk, then suddenly you're on a plane heading for enemy territory where people are planning to kill you any which way they can. You're carrying all sorts of gear to kill them too. It's a shock to the system. That IED may already be planted and waiting for you. You either switch on your defense apparatus fast or you're dead. I've always had the ability to do that, and when I hit the ground in Afghanistan I was ready and willing to do what I had to in order to stay alive. Yes, I killed a lot of people over there Jacky. I don't take any satisfaction in it and actually don't like getting medals for it. And yes, I still have nightmares about it. In the process of the operation though I came to believe in the mission and what we were trying to accomplish there. I didn't start off believing that, but soldiers do what they're told to do and that's it. One of these days when hopefully, Afghanistan has a better future, I may take some satisfaction in accepting that I played a part in it. That's all I'd really like to say. End of story Jacky and no offence."

"None taken Danny and thanks for the explanation. Now what about that girl Scotty mentioned? Whatever happened to her?"

He shrugged.

"Never heard anything from her again. It's that kind of place over there. I often wonder if she achieved her dream of helping her people as a medic or a doctor."

Jacky wasn't ready to give up just yet.

"Did you fall for her then? I heard she was pretty."

He shook his head.

"God you people never give up! Always the bloody story! The answer is I don't know. I was so insulated by the mental armor I put on that I really switched everything else off - emotions, feelings and so on. I was operating on automatic pilot and the human side was buried deep."

She shuddered.

"I'd never really thought about that aspect before, but I guess we produce people like you, pre-programmed if you like, to go and do stuff that we can't or won't do."

"Killers you mean" he said cynically.

"Sorry, I didn't mean it to come out like that Danny. One of the questions I was going to ask those hard men in the Fox and Hounds that night when I first met you was just how difficult was it to adjust back to civilian life afterwards?"

He grinned.

"To stop killing people you mean?"

She slapped his arm.

"I didn't mean that at all you moron! Come on give me a break."

He thought about it.

"Yeah, there are adjustments to make. For some like the SAS and parachute regiments, particularly those who have seen considerable action, quite a lot! Some don't make it. There's a lot of suicides Jacky. Just look at the lads from the Falklands war. We miss the action, the adrenalin high as it were. We haven't seen the legacy from Iraq and Afghanistan as yet, but it's coming I'm afraid. As for myself I tried to switch my energies over, peculiarly enough to financial services, and so far I'm managing to make the adjustment. Now can we leave it at that?"

Jacky got the message and started concentrating on her driving again.

Hours later she looked across at him as they came into a small town called Bridport.

"I need a break Danny. I'm about all in right now. How about we pull in for a coffee and a sandwich?"

He stirred himself, realizing how selfish he had been in not switching drivers.

"God, sorry Jacky, I wasn't thinking straight. You were expecting to have a good nights sleep back there at that B&B we had to cancel, and here we are driving through the night instead. Sure, pull into the first place you see and I'll take over after. How's that?"

"Sounds good to me Danny."

She smiled inside liking the way he was showing his concern for her welfare.

Shortly after they parked beside a small café attached to a petrol station and dragged themselves from the vehicle. Danny patted her on the shoulder.

"Hey, well done. You did some good driving back there. You sure know how to handle a vehicle."

She stretched, nodding her appreciation at his comment.

"As a reporter we're on the road a lot at all hours following different stories all over the country so this isn't exactly new to me. Speaking of reporting, I haven't been doing much recently as you may have noticed, but I have an idea that I've been mulling about and would like to run it past you inside."

"Yeah why don't we do that, but let's get some coffee inside us first."

With that they headed inside and Jacky's appearance drew a few admiring glances even at that late hour. Danny headed for a small table in one corner and from habit sat facing the door. A tired waitress appeared and they ordered a BLT each and a large coffee. Jacky disappeared into the washroom and emerged shortly after looking more refreshed and alert. Danny then made his way to the men's washroom and had just emerged as the two cups of coffee were plonked down on the table. Jacky reached gratefully for hers.

"God am I ready for this!"

She took a large swallow as he put two spoons of sugar in his and added some milk. He yawned as he stirred his cup.

"You and me both Jacky. By the way you look great for someone who's been slogging their way around from Cornwall to Dorset. Last time I came down here was when I was doing some training with the Special Boat Service at Hamworthy barracks in Poole. Nice country, but driving at night on these roads! So many of those bastards coming towards you don't even dim their bloody lights. Now what's this idea you're talking about?"

She took a long swallow and put her cup down.

"Okay here's the thing. You very kindly brought me along because of the possible danger to myself. This guy Blackstone or whatever his name is, was eliminating witnesses, my roommate Rita for example and the chap in our flat, not forgetting those two phony policemen in Chepstow. Now this event, from my observation, is heading for its conclusion. With the police involved at the crematorium in High Wycombe, the media will be on to it like sharks. I've been involved in this since the start, and if I'm not careful I won't even get an article into my paper before it breaks. I can't be in danger any longer surrounded by a bunch of SAS characters, so here's the thing. How about I contact my paper, explain why I've been missing - staying alive to be precise, and arrange for an article to be ready when you give me the go ahead?"

Just then the waitress came back over with their BLT's so they both fell silent as they virtually attacked their sandwiches. He paused between bites and grinned at her.

"You eat like an SAS trooper, did you know that Jacky?"

"I'll take that as a compliment Danny. Now how about my idea of the story?"

"Certainly it has some merit. Timing is critical on it's release though. We have an agenda here as you well know. If the bastards we're after get a clue that the finger is pointing in their direction the rats will desert the ship and scatter. You agreed that you'd clear any articles with Wainwright first, so that still goes. However he might buy a teaser article about the missing SAS troop back from Kuwait, how the police are investigating it, and that you have an inside source, and revelations will follow hard and fast under your byline. You could hint at rumors of dead SAS troopers and a crematorium in High Wycombe being investigated. How does that sound?"

Her face lit up.

"Wow! Terrific Danny, but will Wainwright buy it?"

"I don't see why not. After all we can't hold you prisoner. I know you want to work along with us until this plays out because there's a lot more of this story that hasn't even happened yet. As a reporter you'll want to hang in to the bitter end. We won't be talking to anyone else in the media so you'll have the whole scoop."

Danny's cell phone rang and he snapped it open. It was Rebecca.

He could barely take in her first few words. He stood up suddenly, his chair crashing to the floor. Everyone in the restaurant looked across at him and silence fell on the room. Danny's face had gone white.

Jacky reached up to his arm.

"Danny what is it?"

He shook her off, turning sideways away from her and speaking urgently into the phone. After a few minutes his glazed eyes passed over her face, not even seeing her. He snapped the phone shut and without a word strode across the restaurant floor and out the door. Jacky hurriedly passed some money to the waitress, waved off the change and dashed out after Danny. She found him standing by the car cursing.

"What is it Danny? What's happened?" she pleaded.

"Shit, shit, shit" he muttered. "Sophia's been killed! Blown up in an underground parking lot at MI5. She was collecting the car for the Director General. The bomb was meant for her. Oh for Christ sake, not Sophia!"

She stepped backed shocked. They had said goodbye to Sophia only two days ago. It seemed unreal now to think of her as dead.

"Have they learned any more about how it happened? Who's involved in it? Have the police any clues at this stage Danny?"

He nodded his head grimly.

"Rebecca has a good idea that it was that CIA bastard Sinclair who was using the alias of Blackstone. He visited her a few days ago and managed to get into the underground parking garage in their building. She figures they must have known her car and planted a device, activated to go off when Sinclair was out of the city. They had to evacuate the whole bloody MI5 building."

"But can they prove anything Danny? Can they pin something on this bastard finally?"

He took a few deep breaths and his form went still, his face taut with a cold stirring anger.

"It doesn't matter about proof any more. This guy won't end up in any court. He's already dead meat walking around."

Jacky felt cold shivers running up and down her spine. She was glad she wasn't in Sinclair's shoes right then.

When Danny strode into McDonalds in the center of Eastleigh early that morning, a tall man dressed in casual sports clothes waved to him. He had a sharp intelligent face and his dark hair was starting to show some steel gray. He looked fit and lean and his brown tan made Danny think that he was a golfer or a keen gardener.

The DG's description was pretty spot on. She had contacted him earlier and told him of the meeting she had arranged with Jack McAllister who had been following Sinclair and the Mossad agent down from High Wycombe.

Jacky had followed him in and was now lined up at the counter ordering him a breakfast bun and a large coffee. On his suggestion, she intended to eat alone until the two men had discussed certain issues.

Danny smiled and stuck out his hand.

"Danny Quigley. I guess you're Jack?"

Jack smiled easily his shrewd eyes taking in his form and stance.

"She said you were a civvy now but you still walk like one of those troopers we read about."

"Oh how's that?" Danny enquired.

"Like a coiled spring ready to commit bloody mayhem!"

Danny's face clouded.

"When I catch up with that bastard who murdered Sophia, that's exactly what I intend to dispense. You can bet your life on it."

"I'd kinda like to be there when that happens Danny. Sophia was a lovely person and a good friend."

Just then Jacky popped his breakfast and coffee on the table and without a word steered her way through some tables and sat down near the wall.

Jack's eyes flicked over to her.

"The DG filled me in on her. Sure you're doing the right thing there Danny, planning mayhem and carrying the press along with you? I would have thought you'd be avoiding them like the plague."

Danny shrugged.

"You could be right Jack. I might just regret it but I might also need some friendly press coverage when this is over. The story's going to break anyway once the High Wycombe connection becomes public knowledge. We'll see. Anyway fill me in on what you know of the target vehicle you've been following."

Jack nodded.

"Okay, here's the scoop. They ended up close to here."

He pulled out a local map and pointed to an area.

"It's a large warehouse and it's in the flight path of the airport, which might suit their purposes if they have some training with firearms. Now the road they're on is a dead end so I wasn't able to follow them in all the way in my vehicle."

Danny leaned forward about to interrupt him. Jack stopped him with a gesture.

"I said I couldn't follow him in my vehicle. I did however hide the car and slipped up through the surrounding woods. It was still dark so it was easy enough to do so without being spotted. I had a pair of night glasses so I had a good visual of the site. The only place back there was a large building set back on a big chunk of land. It has what looks like a new high chain link security fence with a fiber-optic stress-sensor line enmeshed throughout. The bottom of the fence looks like it's buried in cement, which prevents any digging under it. The gate into the ground is constructed of solid steel, as is the actual door to the building."

"Any sign of cameras or dogs?" Danny enquired.

"No dogs, not while I was there. I would imagine they have cameras installed going from the caliber of the fence and the doors. There could be a pressure-sensor system under the topsoil as well to detect intruders above a certain pre-set weight. So, some pretty heavy-duty deterrents in place Danny."

"Any other entrances that you could spot? What about on top of the building? Any obvious vents or openings?"

"Sorry I couldn't risk getting any closer. For all I know they had sensors outside the fence so I stayed well back. Oh yes, I did see one window vent on top of the building on my side. There may be others as well farther back or on the opposite side which I couldn't see."

"No, that's good Jack. Now what about electricity and telephone lines?"

"There was a generator going around the back somewhere, so they get their power from that obviously. I saw no lines going in, nor telephone lines for that matter. Mind you they could have had them installed underground or just rely on mobile phones."

Danny nodded grimly.

"Hmm, we can't cut their power nor have we the time to investigate if they have land lines installed so we can't cut their communication either."

McAllister looked questioningly at him.

"So what's the plan Danny?"

Danny looked levelly at him.

"I don't have one at present Jack. Even if I did, are you sure you want to know?"

Jack nodded vigorously.

"If this was yesterday I'd already be out that door and on my way back to London, but Sophia was blown up today Danny. Whatever you plan to do, I want in. .....Clear?"

"Fair enough, you're in as of now. You can help me with a couple of areas. How well do you know the layout around here Jack?"

It turned out that McAllister had a weekend cottage on the Isle of Wight off the shores of Southampton, which he visited regularly, taking his car across on the ferry. He advised Danny to have Wainwright bring his boat into the harbor at Woolston, which he pointed out on the map. Wainwright would be berthed as close as possible to where the opposition had their enclosure, a fifteen-minute drive away. Danny could then liaise with his team on the boat and hammer out an action plan.

Danny immediately contacted Wainwright on his mobile phone as he sailed past Cowes on the Isle of Wight. He briefed him on the suggested berthing location. The Major was familiar with the Woolston area and had a contact who berthed there and would allow him to tie up alongside. Then Danny settled back to gain as much information as possible on the target site.

"Now Jack, some more questions. Will the police hear us if we start some action there tonight? What about their response times if they do? How much time would we have? Could we block them coming in somehow and still have a way out for the team?"

Jack made a face.

"It's a built up area around the airport and people would certainly call into the police station in Eastleigh. Of course if there's a plane taking off it could disguise the sound of automatic weapons or cause some confusion. This is old hat to you 'Sass' chaps Danny. Remember we MI5 people have no police powers in the U.K. so this scenario is not included in our training. Our role is normally gathering information and we have to call in the police to apprehend suspects. I gather you don't intend to apprehend anyone?"

"You can take that as gospel Jack" he replied grimly.

"Okay, here's the thing. The nearest police as I mentioned are here in Eastleigh, so they would probably respond and investigate the sound of automatic weapons or explosives. If you intend to blow your way in, that would set the alarm bells ringing for sure and they'd most certainly call in support from Southampton as well. Oh, and there is a police training college in the immediate area, so they could swamp the area with trainee cops if need be."

"Okay, I hear you Jack. This is going to be a tough nut to crack for sure. Any ideas on getting out once we hit them?"

Jack grimaced.

"Depends how much noise you create going in there and how long you take to close down their operation."

He pointed to the map.

"There's a secondary road that goes straight down from the airport to Woolston where Wainwright would be berthed. If you wrapped the operation up swiftly your lads could slip down that route in fifteen minutes depending on traffic, and be out to sea before a major alert is established. Now there are three other exit routes out of the area. One is west on the M27 for a short distance and then cut off on the A36 to Salisbury. Another is east on the M27 heading in the Portsmouth direction. I'm not sure that route is a good choice as you are heading further south and may get caught in a police lockdown with very few side roads to escape on. The last possible route is north onto the M3 heading straight for London or getting off it shortly onto the A34 heading in the direction of Newbury and the M4 Motorway."

Danny was following the different routes on the map as Jack traced them.

"Hmm…. some of the lads would be heading back to Hereford so the northern route to the M4 would suit. I reckon Scotty would go for that in his car, which he wouldn't want leaving in the area as it could be traced back to him. The rest of the team could head straight down to Woolston and the boat. We'd have to do a trial run to familiarize ourselves with the roads."

Jack tapped the map again.

"It's a busy road during the day so the timings will be off."

Danny nodded.

"Understood. However the exit strategy is key. One wrong turn and we could be compromised big time."

Jack chuckled dryly.

"Especially if you're carrying a bunch of dead security people. I assume you won't want to leave any evidence behind."

Danny looked at him thoughtfully.

"This is starting to look a bit hairy Jack. I need to talk to Wainwright again to clarify a few points. Go and grab some more coffees while I go outside and call him."

When Jack returned a few minutes later balancing two cups of coffee, Danny was coming back in, his face clouded.

"Not good?" Jack enquired.

"Afraid not. Wainwright says the berth is one of those floating ones out from the quay and he has to get a tender to bring his men ashore, so we can't evacuate our terminated friends that way. It would take too long and they would be very exposed. That leaves only one way out. We'll have to borrow a van, fill it with those dead security people and one of Scotty's mates can drive it north to the M4 and then west. I'm told there's lots of old mine shafts in Wales where sheep fall in and are never seen again. Ideal for disposing of bodies."

"When you say borrow, you mean steal don't you Danny?"

"Whatever. Now one more thing. Using your MI5 card could you manage to get me a swing past the target site today sometime? If it's possible could we use a genuine mail van and get me a uniform as a passenger, possibly someone they were training in. A plumber's van would be too obvious and your Mossad friend, if he's still there, would twig it right away. Here's the thing, he could stop at the entrance to the site and ring the bell if there is one, and say that he's checking on how many people got their last directory. Complaints were coming in of people who didn't get theirs. How would that go down?"

Jack pursed his lips skeptically.

"Too many holes in that one Danny. As we discussed, they may not even have a landline so calling on them enquiring about a telephone directory delivery would be a dead give away. I can understand you needing to get a visual on the target building before working out a plan to hit it, but we need to do it some other way. Oh, and a word to the wise. Don't kill the Mossad agent if you can help it."

"Why not?" Danny demanded. "He's probably up to his ears in this whole thing."

Jack nodded.

"Probably is involved in the overall plan, but he wasn't in the U.K. when your lads got topped. Now I can tell you that if you kill a Mossad agent they won't rest until they've terminated anyone involved in it. That means they could go after you or anyone in your team or their families, no matter how long it takes them…. even years!"

"Okay, thanks for the advice Jack" Danny said evenly.

"There's one other thing. I told the DG that I met Wyborski the Mossad chap a few years ago when I was attending a security training course in Israel. I understand he's supposed to be pretty deadly at unarmed combat, so watch yourself Danny."

"Fine, that could be useful information. I just hope he stays out of my way. Now how do we handle getting a visual on the compound? I've found that planning is everything in this kind of operation and I don't want to lead the team into a location we know nothing about."

Right then Danny's solution walked up to him in the form of Jacky. His jaw dropped. He reached up and pulled her into the seat beside him.

"Jacky, just how easy would it be for you to arrange an over-flight with your paper, of a compound we intend to hit tonight?"

CHAPTER 33.

Apart from Scotty and Nigel Hawthorn, they were all on the boat at Woolston. Scotty was on surveillance duty at the recruiting center in Southampton and Nigel Hawthorn was out working with McAllister. Jacky had contacted her paper and, to their delight and amazement, they had arranged for a Southampton firm to place a helicopter at their disposal. They had already completed a photo run over the target building.

Jacky was in Southampton at the local office of her paper. She was emailing her first report, which was going to hit the front page the following morning. Danny had acquired a bunch of walkie-talkies for the group and Scotty was already in possession of one and had been briefed on frequencies.

Now they were huddled around a bunch of digital photographs of the building in the opposition compound, which the chopper had flown over earlier. It reminded Danny of the old days in the troop when they started to plan an operation. Nothing had been sacred and rank didn't come into it at all. Ideas and approaches were discussed and challenged. Nothing was red-lighted and everything was considered.

The building they were looking at was about 50 yards in length and 30 yards in width. The roof was covered in green tiles and had two window vents embedded in it. It was completely surrounded by a 12-foot fence topped with razor wire. Outside the fence there was a section of trees, which extended back about 100 yards with a clearing between the fence and the trees of approximately ten feet. Danny pointed to it.

"McAllister checked locally and the section of trees belonged to someone else, not the security firm. So the odds were that there were no security devices planted within the tree areas. McAllister got up close the first night he followed them in there but didn't spot any dogs."

There was a murmur of relief around the table as Danny continued.

"We estimate they may have up to ten people in there with an arsenal of weapons and from what we hear they know how to use them."

He stopped and pulled out a slip of paper.

"Their offices were raided a few days ago and the police scooped out their recruiting files which they suspected had been sanitized. However they must have been in a hurry because I just heard prior to the meeting that two ex SAS peoples names were discovered in the files."

The giant Grant Birchall looked up.

"Hey man we don't like having to fight our own here. They'll have a good idea of how we'll hit them, that is if they suspect we're on to them. Do we know their names?"

Danny checked the piece of paper again.

"Yeah, Bull Bignell and Nick Nicholson" he replied.

Tony Archer the medic nearly choked.

"Bignell is one right bastard. Hell I've patched up a dozen troopers he's put a beating on. He got kicked out some time ago. I haven't heard of Nicholson though. Has anyone else?" he asked looking around.

Jimmy Patton, the explosives expert nodded.

"He was in a different troop but I understood he was a good head, competent and focused. To be honest, I'm surprised he ended up with this lot."

Someone else cut in.

"That's civvy street for you lads. You get out 'cos the wife's nagging at you and the first time you go to the job center with your curriculum vitae, and you tell them that you're a sniper, guess what?"

Danny snorted.

"Yeah I've been there and it's pretty demeaning after you've put your ass on the line for your country and some snotty nosed little kid is deciding your future for you at the job center."

Clyde Stoner stood up.

"Hey look guys this isn't solving the problem of getting inside that fucking building. That fence looks pretty formidable. We could get our asses shot off if we get stuck at that gate. I've checked the weapons on the way up in the boat and we have some nice stuff there. No heavy weapons though like for example an M60 and they may very well have some set up. Jimmy Patton had a look at the C4 explosives you grabbed back in Wales. Right Jimmy?"

Patton the Irishman leaned forward as Stoner sat back down.

"Yeah. I'm getting an idea for the main door of the building which looks like reinforced steel."

He looked around the group.

"Does anyone remember that failed IRA attack in Northern Ireland some years back? What was the village called? Loughall or something like that. It was a pretty gutsy raid actually. They put gas and explosives on the front of a JCB and drove it at the police station entrance. Unfortunately for them we got a tip-off and were lying in wait. The poor bastards didn't have a chance. Not with 'Sass' teams waiting for them. Anyway I'm thinking I could do the same approach to the door with the limited amount of C4 we have and some gas canisters."

Wainwright cut in.

"But why not the front gate? Why not blow that first? What's the good of planning to blow the front door of the building, if we get stuck at the front gate?"

Danny grabbed one of the photographs and held it up.

"I can see where Jimmy's coming from. We can penetrate the gate some other way because it's not as solid. However it'll take the C4 to demolish that building entrance."

Nigel Hawthorn stuck his hand up like he was in grade school.

Danny nodded to him.

"Go ahead Nigel".

"Jimmy was talking about memories a moment ago. Well who remembers the movie The Untouchables?"

Several of the men nodded.

"Yeah, Elliot Ness. He'd have made a good trooper. What of it Nigel?" asked Wainwright.

"Remember how he used what looked like reinforced garbage trucks to smash through steel doors before the bad guys had a chance to hide anything? Why can't we do the same on the front gate?" he said, excitement in his eyes.

There was silence in the room as his excitement started to catch on.

Danny grabbed his phone and keyed in some numbers. No one said a thing as Danny fired his words out rapidly.

"Jack, we need three more things, a JCB, a big solid garbage truck and a work shop to make some adjustments to the truck. Oh and some gas canisters. Can you do that?"

Danny grinned as a stream of invective came back down the line. He held the phone out so the group could hear. Finally he cut in.

"Hey look we're right in the middle of a briefing for the operation. I'll get back to you, but Jack, we need those vehicles and that workshop, oh and don't forget the van for the trip to Wales."

He hung up and looked around the room.

"Looks likes the plan is coming together."

Patton caught his eye.

"I've been thinking about the possible police involvement. What we need is some more time to pull this off.... a little distraction for the cops while the lads are off doing their stuff. Let me give you some examples."

Just then the walkie-talkie rang in Danny's rucksack. It could only be from Scotty but he'd been told not to call except in an emergency. Tentatively he picked it up and switched it on. The voice at the other end was one he'd never heard before.

"Danny Quigley I presume. Foolish of your friend Scotty to leave his walkie-talkie set on his contact frequency, and him a trained trooper at that. Let me introduce myself. Blackstone is my name. I'm sure you've heard of me by now and I hope to meet with you shortly. Oh yes, we found the bug this morning so we know that you're aware of our other property. Very clever of you. We intend to have a chat with your friend Scotty in a little while. After we have supper. He won't be joining us unfortunately. We want to introduce a little water boarding to him. You know the Americans use it now of course."

"You bastard Blackstone!" Danny hissed. "I've already got your death notice written out for what you've done to those two troopers. Now if you torture Scotty it's going to take longer for you to die."

"Tch, tch, such threats Danny. You're not in a position to make any right now. However we will give you a chance to help Scotty avoid our little chat with him after supper. Up to you of course."

"What exactly have you got in mind Blackstone?" he asked, his voice savage.

"Simple really. Should have thought of it before but it didn't twig until he dropped into our lap so to speak. Dressed as a beggar up the road from our recruiting office! Come on Danny, such trade craft! Beggars haven't ever been seen on that street before. However we lucked in didn't we? Now what do I want? Well for you to come to the compound alone and unarmed later this evening and discuss a little trading with us. Scotty's life depends on it."

"What do you want to discuss Blackstone?" Danny asked.

"I'll expect you this evening…. and Danny, I wouldn't leave it too late. We may have started our little chat with Scotty and he won't like it. See you then."

The line went dead. The room was completely silent as all eyes were on Danny. They had already gathered that something was wrong. He looked around at them one at a time.

"They've got Scotty. I've been invited to the compound this evening or they start water boarding him. I'm going of course, but we now need to re-examine the plan we were working on, and Patton, I want to hear your ideas on distracting the police."

CHAPTER 34.

The perspiration was soaking Bull Bignell's T-shirt when he stepped back from working on Scotty who was now slumped forward in his chair. The restraints held him securely and stopped him from falling. Scotty lifted his head with great effort and glared at him.

"Shit, my old man hit me harder than that Bignell! No wonder they canned you from the regiment."

Bignell roared in anger. He reached forward and grabbed him by the hair, his right fist coming back for another murderous blow. His mate Nick Nicholson stepped forward and caught his arm.

"Come on Bull, he's only wanking your chain. He's not going to tell you anything at this stage. Hell you've been pounding on him for the past hour."

Bignell shook his hand off.

"I'll teach the bastard…." he started.

Another voice cut in from behind them. It was Blackstone who had just come into the room with Wyborski.

"Your friend's right Bignell. He won't talk, however we don't need him to talk now. I've arranged for his friend Danny Quigley to visit us here this evening alone for a little negotiation, so we don't want our prisoner to be too roughed up do we?"

Bignell and Nicholson both froze. It was Nicholson who spoke first, his voice almost a whisper.

"Danny Quigley's involved in this? Jesus no one told me that! Hell we don't like coming up against our own Blackstone."

Wyborski cast him an amused glance.

"So you've heard of him then?" he pressed, moving closer.

Nicholson nodded.

"Who hasn't? They use his Afghanistan operation in training at the regiment now for escape and evasion exercises. He's a one-man killing machine. I wouldn't want coming up against him."

The Israeli's eyes gleamed.

"Yes, they started using it recently in Israel too with Special Forces training. As a matter of fact I sat in on one of their sessions. From experience I've found that those so-called heroes fall short of their reputation when you start to sift them through. When he gets here I intend to do just that. We'll see just how hard a man he is."

Bull Bignell snorted.

"I agree. I was never impressed with the shit they put about on Quigley. I'd like to have a go at the bastard myself when he gets here."

Scotty lifted his head again.

"You wouldn't even provide a warm-up for him Bignell. If he comes here," he slowly swung his head around taking in the group and other members of the team who had gathered around "most of you will be dead by midnight, or wish you were."

Bignell moved forward again to strike him but Wyborski gently caught his arm.

"Let's go into the next room Bignell and you can fill me in on the SAS methodology of unarmed combat. That could be useful to me."

He led the man off through the door followed by Blackstone. The other men in the team scattered to various tasks around the building.

Scotty held Nicholson's eyes.

"When Quigley gets here Nick, find a way to cut me loose and get me a weapon too."

"Why should I do that Scotty? I have my reasons for being here and I don't intend to blow it."

Scotty stared at him, watching to make sure no one else was coming too close.

"Why exactly are you here Nick? I would have picked you for an operation at the drop of a hat. You were an up-front guy in the regiment. What the hell has happened to you for Christ sake?"

Nicholson's eyes flickered back to meet his.

"What's happened? Cancer's happened.... to my twelve-year-old daughter, Yvonne. The National Health Service has done all it can. Our only chance is a clinic in Switzerland that has a record of curing people who have been given up on, but it costs money."

"How much money Nick?" Scotty asked.

"A hundred thousand pounds sterling" he replied.

"And Blackstone's promised you that amount Nick?"

"Yeah, that's right Scotty. Cash on the barrel when this op is put to bed and it sounds like we're nearly there."

Scotty laughed bleakly.

"Two things Nick. One, Blackstone has been mopping up witnesses as he's been going along on this - a female reporter in London and one of his own people, two of your team he had killed in the jail in Chepstow, and a lower echelon MI6 employee in London. Plus he's trying to wipe out the troop that are live witnesses to a botched operation they tried to pull off in Iraq. You and your mates are not going to come out of this alive. Blackstone will clean house first. He's got too much to lose mate."

"And your second point Scotty?" Nicholson asked, listening intently.

"Quigley will give you the money for your operation Nick, even though you and I know that a lot of those so called cures are just catering to the desperate and don't work out. But if you want to pursue it, Danny will come up with the money for it."

Nicholson's face looked skeptical.

"Quigley has that kind of money? Come on pull the other one Scotty!"

Scotty nodded.

"Why do you think he's even involved in this right now Nick? He's a civvy for Gods sake! He's involved because a special government department has pulled him in to sort it out and are paying a massive fee to do so - five hundred thousand pounds."

Nicholson's breath was inhaled sharply.

"Five hundred thousand, and Government backing? Why isn't this place surrounded by heavily armed teams right now then?"

Scotty winked.

"Because the Government screwed up and want the entire thing done under the radar. No big police operation when the objective here is to bury the whole episode and everyone involved in it. Get it? That's why Danny Quigley's involved. When he walks into the building this evening you're either on our side or you're dead. There's a death sentence on every man in here. That's the truth. And your little Yvonne will be dead with you. Now start thinking with your head mate before it's too late."

"How do I know he won't kill me anyway Scotty?"

Scotty looked bleakly at him.

"Tell me one thing Nick. Were you involved in the killing of our two lads? 'Cos if you were, I can't help you. You're history."

"Hell no, as God is my witness! I was here at home base when they got hit. Bignell was there though and most of the team."

Scotty studied him for a long moment and finally nodded.

"Okay here's the deal. When Danny gets here, wait until no one is near me, cut me loose, hand me your weapon, then hit the dirt and stay there. I'll make sure no one takes you out Nick. If Danny's walking calmly in here, believe me he has a plan and he won't be taking any prisoners."

CHAPTER 35.

As night was falling, Danny walked slowly up to the gate. The bright arc lights gradually exposed him as he approached. His mind was completely relaxed while his whole body felt taut as if it was sheathed in invisible armor. He had mentally prepared for this moment and was alert and poised for action.

Two men in camouflage uniforms and holding assault rifles were waiting inside the gate, which was still locked. They peered nervously through the wire at him.

"Danny Quigley?" one of them asked harshly.

Danny chuckled good-humouredly.

"The very same. Now lads, how about you relax a bit and open up this gate. I have no intention of killing you, at least not yet."

One of the men shouted at him.

"They said you wouldn't be armed. Now do an about turn and let's take a look at you."

Danny slowly turned around holding his arms slightly up in the air.

The chains on the gate rattled and one of the men pushed it open. The other one leapt through and went behind Danny, holding his weapon against his back. He then pushed him through the gate while other man locked it behind him. The same man then searched him roughly and stepped back.

"He's clean Tommy" he said.

Tommy produced a set of plastic cuffs and threw them to his colleague.

"Put these on the bastard" he instructed.

Danny moved slightly sideways and laughed.

"Sorry, that wasn't the deal lads. No cuffs."

Both men lifted their assault rifles and prodded his chest and back.

"Put these fucking cuffs on or we'll blow you all over this yard" Tommy shouted harshly.

Danny yawned.

"No I don't think so. Your boss wants a little chat with me. You see I have something he wants. He wouldn't like me delivered full of holes. I'd suggest you call him on that."

Danny nodded to the mike attached to his collar. Both men glared and looked like they were going to use their rifle butts on him. Finally Tommy walked back a few paces, turned round and spoke into his radio. He listened for a moment, then turned back.

"Okay no cuffs. Let's get the bastard up there."

He leered at Danny.

"We'll get our chance later mate."

Danny smiled. "I can't wait…. mate!"

Tommy and his colleague escorted him to a door in the back of the building which was opened quickly, then he was hustled down a long corridor with rooms running off left and right. He couldn't see what the rooms contained as the doors were closed, but he was impressed with the solidity and interior structure of the building.

They pushed through into a large area which looked like a food hall at one end, with tables and chairs set up in a corner. At the other end several SUVs and vans were parked while the sides of the hall contained racks of weapons of varying sizes and descriptions.

Danny could also see that the building contained a second level. This had what looked like offices and overlooking decks on which stood a number of armed men looking down on them. He counted at least ten, and right away he knew that they'd underestimated the number of combatants they might be up against. Another four, including the two gate escorts stood around downstairs, and an additional three people who were not armed.

Tommy slammed him in the small of the back making him stumble forward. Ignoring the pain he recovered his balance and strolled towards the two men. He recognized the Israeli from Jack's description.

Danny stuck his hand out.

"Wyborski, I imagine. Heard a lot about you" he said casually.

The Israeli looked startled but returned his handshake cautiously while maintaining a defensive stance.

"Danny Quigley of course. You do indeed fit your description…. but heard of me? Pray tell how?"

"We picked you up at Heathrow. After all as a Mossad Katsa, you came in on your own name as usual. You don't usually play games on friendly turf isn't that right? Oh we know you're the resident specialist on surveillance back there in King Saul Boulevard in Tel Aviv, so we gave you a long leash when following you."

If Wyborski were shocked, he covered it well. He canted his head sideways regarding Danny with an amused smile.

"If you're so smart, why are you standing here as my prisoner with us holding all the cards?"

Danny looked at him gravely.

"Look, you wanted me here for some negotiation. Now here's my deal Wyborski. If you've had nothing to do with the murder of my colleagues, you can still walk out that door and be on a plane out of the U.K., no questions asked. I can guarantee it. If you have been involved, then the deals off. Blackstone here is a different story, or should I say Sinclair our friendly local CIA agent."

There was a gasp from Blackstone/Sinclair who jumped forward mouthing obscenities as he swung a fist at Danny.

"You fucking bastard. You screwed everything up. How do they know about me?"

Danny casually blocked the punch and pushed Sinclair, sending him stumbling back.

"They had you dead to rights from day one Sinclair. Pictures of you with Sir Percy who disappeared and probably ended up in that crematorium in High Wycombe."

Danny made a quick guess.

"Oh yes, Scotland Yard have pulled in the directors of that site and they're spilling their guts. You won't be getting on any plane shortly Sinclair unless your CIA buddies can arrange another special flight out for you."

The third man stepped forward producing a pistol from the small of his back and raised it to Danny's head.

"One thing you forget Quigley. Right now you don't hold any cards. All it takes is one squeeze of this trigger and you're history. I owe you one anyway for winging me back in London."

Danny screwed his eyes sideways.

"Ah, the killer of a helpless woman. I'm supposed to be impressed?" he retorted with disgust in his voice.

Sinclair stepped between them.

"Hold it there Morcambe! Remember we need certain information before we do anything permanent to Quigley here. Now fall back and put that gun away."

Morcambe glowered and stepped back, reluctantly shoving his weapon into it's holster.

Wyborski raised his hands.

"Look this is getting us nowhere."

He nodded to Morcambe.

"Bring Scotty into the room and keep him over there against the side of the wall. I'm going to offer an interesting challenge to Quigley here. Let's see if he's a gambling man shall we?"

In a few minutes Morcambe and two other men dragged the chair with Scotty tied to it, into the room.

It was Danny's turn to gasp, which he quickly smothered when he saw the bloody state of him, sagging forward against the restraining ropes.

His cold eyes turned to the Israeli.

"Who did this to him?" he demanded.

"I believe your old SAS trooper Bignell had some contribution there. So much for this regiment loyalty we hear about."

Danny filed it away.

"Okay what's your proposition Wyborski?"

"Ah yes…. the proposition. Well there's some speculation as to just how tough you are Quigley. The stories abound, but stories tend to get exaggerated out of all proportion with the passage of time, as I believe has happened in your case. You're not even a serving SAS member but a financial planner as I understand it."

He laughed disdainfully, looking round at the other two men before continuing.

"Here's the deal, Quigley. I have a certain reputation myself in unarmed combat. Let's just say I believe I'm much better than you in that particular area, and I want a chance to prove it. I'm willing to fight you for Scotty's life. If you beat me, you both go free provided you give me the location of a certain device in Iraq, which I believe you know."

"And if you beat me?" Danny enquired.

Wyborski laughed.

"Let's just say I want to provide you with sufficient motivation to put up a good show Quigley. If I beat you I'll make sure not to kill you in the fight. However we will then proceed to work on your friend Scotty until you give us the information, and I promise you, you will. Now what do you say?"

Sinclair jumped forward.

"Look this is fucking ridiculous! Let's just start on Scotty right away and get the hell out of here. It sounds to me like the cops are not too far behind Quigley. Get your fucking ego out of the way Wyborski and let's get down to serious business!"

Wyborski ignored the outburst, keeping his eyes on Danny who nodded.

"You got yourself a fight. Let's do it. First let me have a quick look at Scotty. I'd appreciate it."

Sinclair started to protest but was quickly silenced by the Israeli. Danny was then escorted at gunpoint over to the side of the hall where Scotty still sagged against the restraints in the chair.

Danny leaned forward and whispered.

"You okay mate?"

Without opening his eyes Scotty whispered back.

"Kick his ass Danny!"

Danny looked over at Wyborski.

"For fuck sake he's out cold! At least cut these damn restraints off him and let him lie on the floor. Keep an assault rifle at his head if you want to but he's past hurting anyone right now."

Blackstone nodded to Nicholson resignedly.

"For God's sake let's get going with this! Nicholson cut those ropes off him and put him on the floor. If he moves even an inch don't kill him but shoot his knee off."

Danny watched as Scotty was cut loose and slid forward onto the floor. He was conscious of Nicholson's eyes watching him closely. Finally he sighed and turned back into the room.

"Okay Wyborski, let's fight" he said through gritted teeth.

Danny had had to forge his stepfather's signature in order to take up judo at his school in Wales when he was thirteen years of age. His stepfather thought he was taking soccer, but for the following five years Danny worked on his judo skills and was given an old uniform by his trainer who liked his aptitude and attitude. A friend took the uniform home regularly and had it washed for him. Unfortunately for Danny he wasn't able to take off on the grading weekends with the rest of the class until his brutal stepfather was out of his life. Then he quickly proceeded on a fast track grading and ended up a 4th Dan black belt. He particularly liked foot sweeps and hip throws. The principle of a leg sweep is to get your opponent as his weight is coming down onto his front foot just an eighth of an inch from the floor, sending him crashing down heavily.

When Danny joined the SAS he was taught a completely different style of fighting. Apart from the close-quarter battle (CQB) house, or killing house, which set the SAS apart in any assault operation, he was taught how to kill or disable the enemy swiftly, silently, effectively, using his hands and a variety of weapons. Danny's instructors were amazed at his speed, mental agility and natural ability at unarmed combat. His inner computer appeared to sense an opponent's next move even before he attacked. However he never underestimated the ability of anyone he was up against, and right now as he took his jacket off he knew that he had a difficult battle in front of him. Fighters have a way of judging others by the way they stand, walk, and carry themselves. All the signals he was getting from the Mossad agent were that he was up against a highly dangerous and worthy opponent. He noted the square Polish head, set on a short chunky neck and tapering shoulders, and the solid stance on two well-balanced legs. The eyes that had been amused before were now regarding him with the ferocity of a Doberman Pincer. Danny could tell that the man kept himself in tip-top condition.

They were standing six feet apart. A silence fell on the room as all eyes were on the two fighters. The stakes were high for both of them.

Danny launched himself straight at the Israeli, striking hard towards his throat and finding it instantly blocked by a rock-like elbow and a return strike which he also blocked and stepped back. The Israeli circled around him smiling. A smile that didn't quite reach his eyes.

"Nice try Danny, however your friend Bignell already briefed me on the SAS attack principles so you'll have to do better than that."

Then the Israeli moved straight in and fired several short savage punches at Danny's ribs and stomach, followed by an incredibly fast kick to his shin-bone. Danny blocked all the blows automatically, keeping his focus on the eyes of the Israeli. He almost got caught with the kick as it came at him so fast but he turned his leg sideways just in time. The boot skidded off his calf muscle with such impact that he came to an awful realization: the Israeli was using steel-tipped boots! A direct kick from one of them would disable him immediately.

When he was in the parachute regiment prior to qualifying for the SAS, some of the soldiers did extra off-duty work as bouncers at nightclubs in the city. Many a time Danny had watched them prepare prior to their evenings work. He had noticed that they quite often wore solid boots, sometimes steel-tipped, and jock straps with protective cups. He now had to make an assumption that the Israeli had prepared similarly for the fight. He also had to reassess his strategy. If he launched a kick at the Israeli's crotch and it bounced off, he would immediately be vulnerable to a damaging return kick.

Danny bore back into his opponent, throwing several fast punches and chops and finding himself being blocked, slipped sideways throwing a back knuckle strike, catching the Israeli on the nose which immediately started streaming blood. The man roared with rage and jumped at Danny with several short savage kicks which he blocked with the side of his boots and moved slightly to one side making the Israeli miss, sometimes only by inches. Danny knew that just one of those kicks would finish him.

The men strung around the hall were now shouting and encouraging the Israeli to finish him off. Dodging the last kick, Danny's guard was open for a moment and he felt a solid blow on the side of his forehead. His head was ringing as he stumbled back, and the Israeli sensing his advantage leapt at him, throwing a flurry of punches.

Danny recovered his focus, blocked and returned blow for blow, causing the Israeli to miss on his last one overbalancing slightly and falling against him. He immediately spun into a high Judo throw, causing the Israeli to crash to the floor. As he landed Danny leapt at him with the idea of finishing him off, but his opponent sprang back onto his feet, backing off and falling back into a fighting stance.

"Nice try Danny" he panted. "You won't get away with that one again."

"Oh, didn't Bignell tell you about that technique? I have a few more he doesn't know about either that I'd like to show you. Sounding a little out of shape aren't we? What's the matter man, been out of the field too long have we?"

The Mossad man threw himself at Danny again, his steel-tipped boots lashing at Danny's lower extremities. The man's speed was incredible and it was all Danny could do to evade the assault, as he felt a solid kick skidding off his thigh. He managed to poke the damaged nose again with a short snappy straight knuckle strike and had the satisfaction of hearing the man gasp and roar with pain.

Danny glanced quickly down at his watch. Nearly time.

He decided to try a different tack, backing off gradually as the Israeli came towards him throwing combinations of kicks and punches. While still watching the man's eyes he was on hyper alert as to how the Israeli was planting his feet as he came forward. He was waiting for the right moment.

As the Israeli stepped forward onto his right foot, having just drawn back his left following an abortive kick, Danny knew this was the one. Everything felt right.

Danny's legs swept explosively across the other man's lower leg at precisely the right moment and, as the Israeli went crashing to the floor he followed him down, his knee crunching into the man's rib cage. His keening scream filled the room.

It was obvious to everyone that the Israeli was seriously injured and totally defeated.

CHAPTER 36.

As Danny climbed to his feet some of the men started lifting their assault weapons and at that moment the sound of a low flying plane penetrated the building. The roar increased until the whole building shook. Morcambe shouted to Sinclair.

"What the fuck's going on? They've never been this low before!"

Sinclair's gaze was torn between the hurt Mossad agent and looking up at the ceiling where the noise became so loud some of the men dropped their weapons and covered their ears. Just as the noise of the plane started waning Danny looked down at the Israeli and found himself staring into the barrel of a Glock pistol, held steadily by the man.

"You may have beat me Quigley but the last laugh is on you" he hissed.

"What about the device mate? Forgotten about that? I'm the only one who knows where it is" Danny said levelly, trying to stall for time.

"Fuck the device! Let others worry about that. All I want right now is to see you dead you bastard."

His finger tightened on the trigger. Then everything started to happen at once. A shot rang out and a hole appeared in the Israeli's head. Danny looked sideways and saw Scotty standing over against the wall with an assault rifle held against his shoulder.

Danny heard himself say "oh shit" thinking of the consequences of killing the Mossad agent. Two explosions rang out up on the ceiling and both window vents came crashing down into the room. At the same time there was a massive explosion and the front door of the building flew half way up the room. From the open holes in the ceiling, where the window vents had been, two figures in black with face-masks came rappling down, firing automatic weapons.

Figures started falling on the top deck of the building and others began firing back. Through the dissipating smoke from the blown door, more black clad figures came racing in, accompanied by an increasing volume of fire from several weapons.

Danny had leapt into action just as soon as Scotty killed the Mossad agent. He grabbed the Glock pistol and whirled towards Sinclair and Morcambe. Both men were still shocked by the suddenness of the assault but Sinclair recovered first and was already running for one of the doors leading into another room. Morcambe was on one knee, his face snarling as he spotted Danny coming towards him. He started tugging at his pistol from his belt holster.

It snagged.

Danny didn't believe in hesitating in the middle of a battle. He'd seen good men die doing that. He shot him twice in the chest, both bullets not even an inch apart. He turned and kept running towards the door Sinclair had gone through.

Scotty ignored Nicholson lying on the floor, who had earlier thrown his assault rifle across to him. Now he turned towards Bignell.

Like a lot of bullies, Bignell had never expected the situation to reverse so suddenly. He was still half in shock when Scotty jumped forward, dropped the rifle and grabbing his shoulders, delivered a massive head butt, smashing the man's face into a bloodied pulp. Still moving, he spun the man around into a strangle hold and dropped straight down, hearing his neck snap. He then jumped to his feet picking up the assault rifle as he did so.

Nicholson's head came up and Scotty screamed at him "Stay down or you're a dead man. Don't move an inch," before racing off to a fire-fight that had started up further back in the building.

Danny opened the door only to be greeted with a stream of bullets from a second door across the room. He ducked back, then pointing the weapon in that direction, let off three quick shots. He dived into the room doing a forward roll and coming up to the ready position. No shots came back so he raced over to the door and kicked it open, keeping well to one side as he did so. It led outside into the back compound of the site. In the half light ahead he spotted a running figure and started after him. Thirty yards farther on he nearly ran smack into the back fence of the compound and stopped, looking about frantically. Where the hell had Sinclair disappeared to?"

Suddenly his feet clanged against something and he knelt down to discover a metal plate about a yard square. Pushing it aside he saw a hole disappearing into the ground.

A tunnel!

So Sinclair had arranged a bolt-hole for himself. It was probably a short tunnel under the fence. If Sinclair was that cautious he probably had it booby-trapped and with a vehicle on the other side. If Danny had had some hand grenades he would have lobbed a couple down on the off chance of collapsing the tunnel in on Sinclair. He debated grabbing a vehicle and making his way out the front gate and up along the fence in an endeavor to locate the other end of the tunnel. However time was of the essence now with the police probably on the way, with possible other resources such as choppers. Frustrated, he turned and dashed back towards the building where the firing was tapering off. At that precise moment the door he had come out of previously, crashed open and two men sprang through carrying assault weapons, swinging in his direction. Instantly he recognized that they were not from the SAS team and dropped to one knee, the Glock held steady in both hands. Time froze as if life were giving him a still picture of the moment. He normally liked to hit an enemy twice to make sure, but he only had time for one shot each. He felt the kick of the Glock and one of the men was slammed backwards. The other fighter pulled the trigger and Danny saw a trail of bullets chewing up the ground and coming towards him. He snapped off a quick shot. The man dropped as if pole-axed.

He checked and confirmed that both were dead.

The firing inside the building had now completely stopped. Danny discovered that all the opposition excluding Nick Nicholson had been killed. No mercy had been shown. No prisoners taken. These men had been responsible for the death of two regiment mates. It was now time to mop up and evacuate the compound, leaving as little evidence as possible. Fortunately they had planned this down to the smallest detail.

The plan to have a plane fly low over the building to cover the sound of a helicopter, with two troopers dangling from ropes and landing them on the roof had worked perfectly. It had also covered the noise of the front gate being rammed and the front-end loader with explosives approaching the building's front door.

The troopers had done the rest.

Now they had to get back to that boat and clear of the area. Patton had created a diversion in Eastleigh by suddenly appearing at a petrol station wearing a mask and carrying an AK 47. He chased the staff and a few motorists away screaming 'Allah Akabar!' and 'Jihad' while firing into the air. Then he proceeded to set the pumps on fire by clamping the nozzles open and throwing a phosphorus grenade into the wash of fuel, before jumping onto a motor bike that he had liberated, and tearing back to the compound in time for the cleanup.

The result was that the SAS team were in and out of the compound without encountering any police presence. The petrol station attack had drawn the police like a magnet.

First the SAS team had to sanitize the compound, taking all the evidence with them. Danny ran his mind over the available vehicles again. Scotty planned to take his back to Hereford because the ownership could be traced back to him.

Danny and Jacky had arrived in the car he'd bought in Chepstow. He was going to abandon it in Woolston as he had bought it for cash using a false name. He would then depart with Wainwright in the boat.

Trooper Nigel Hawthorn, who had been helping Jack in collecting all the resources needed to attack the compound, had hot-wired a large van. It was to carry the dead personnel northwest into Wales for disposal, driven by one of the SAS unit, with Scotty leading ahead in his own vehicle. Jack was to shuttle the remainder of the team who couldn't fit in Danny's car, down to the boat and then head back up to London with Jacky and Nick Nicholson. With his MI5 card he wasn't concerned about police roadblocks.

They had a lot to do in a short time.

CHAPTER 37.

It seemed an eternity, but it was actually only twenty minutes before they were back at the boat in Woolston. Wainwright calmly shuttled the team members who were coming with him, onto a small craft out to his boat. Four of the SAS team had sustained injuries in the action, none of them serious. On reflection, after a hurried conversation with McAllister, he'd left the body of the Mossad agent at the compound and the dead Morcambe holding the rifle that had fired the fatal shot. This contrived scenario though, wouldn't fool a forensic team for very long. McAllister had told him that the Israelis had a thing about the repatriation of the remains of their soldiers and agents, and they wouldn't accept the total disappearance of Wyborski. Jack was extremely anxious for Scotty's longevity if the Israelis ever discovered that he'd fired the fatal shot. If they did, they would dispatch a Kidon or assassin to take him down. As it was they would not accept the death without a full investigation being carried out.

By now the troopers were on board the fishing boat and Wainwright was waiting to ferry Danny across.

Once they cleared the harbor he planned to head straight out to sea rather than through the Solent which was closer to shore, to avoid any possibility of being spotted as they made their escape. Then he would head for Poole in Dorset, the home of their sister unit, the Special Boat Service. He had arranged for a chopper ride for the rest of the squad back to Hereford while he returned his boat to its normal berthing place at Polperro.

McAllister was getting ready to take off back to London with Nick Nicholson and Jacky. Her paper had agreed to fund the medical costs for Nicholson's child in Switzerland, saving Danny one hundred thousand pounds, which Scotty had previously committed him to. Jacky had had a quick one-to-one with Wainwright regarding just how much she could write about in her revelations without divulging the SAS unit's involvement, or indeed her own. The whole U.K. situation was now blown wide open leaving her free to do a fuller overview of the strange case of the SAS unit coming back from Kuwait and being stalked by an unknown killer team who had now flown the U.K. She wasn't to disclose that they had disappeared permanently!

The doors on McAllister's car slammed shut and Danny was about to cast off the small boat and jump aboard when Wainwright shouted across to him.

"Danny did you ever read that letter that came to the regiment for you?"

Danny stopped and struck his forehead.

"God I completely forgot Bob," reaching into his back pocket. "Give me a second in the light here."

He ripped the envelope open and unfolded the one page letter inside. His eyes flicked to the bottom and froze! It was from Jamila!

His mind flew back to the time he was inadvertently left behind during a combined SAS/Delta team operation in Afghanistan, some years previously. At that time, he had been helped by a young mountain village girl, Jamila, who was instrumental in his escape from the Taliban.

Now, after all this time, a message from her. He held it up closer and started to read.

'Dear Danny, sorry I didn't keep in touch as my aunt took me from Kandahar right away. She said it was better as I was from a Taliban family and the Government would find out and question me or worse. I'm in London, working on a doctor's qualification. I didn't try to contact you as I know you're married and I didn't want to complicate things for you. Now I'm forced to get in touch as I'm getting phone calls at night asking for the sapphires back and I'm being followed. I don't know who else to turn to. The authorities here would probably send me back if they discovered my background. Can you please help me?

Yours, Jamila.'

Danny's mind swirled as he tried to assimilate what he'd just read.

Jamila in the U.K. and being followed! Demands for those sapphires after all this time! His eyes darted to the top of the page. It had an address and was dated two weeks prior. He was probably too late if she really was being stalked!

In his peripheral vision he spotted Jack's car starting to pull away and dashed over in front of it waving frantically. The car stopped. Jack wound the window down and stuck his head out.

"What's up Danny?"

"I need a ride back to London Jack. I just learned about a situation there, and I need to get back pronto. Can you fit me in?"

"Absolutely old chap. Jump in the back with Jacky."

Danny dashed over to Wainwright who was obviously confused by Danny's movements. He threw the boat lines across to him.

"Got to get back to London a.s.a.p. Bob…. problems…... be in touch."

He waved to Wainwright who didn't waste another moment, and as Danny jumped into the car the small craft was already pulling quietly away.

Jacky grinned cheekily.

"I knew you couldn't stay away for long Danny" she teased.

He sat there dumbly as the car edged away from the river and headed straight for the A3 and the M3 north to London.

Jamila in London!

CHAPTER 38.

On the way up the M3 Jack pulled into a service station at Nick Nicholson's request to use the washroom. He'd started shaking in the front seat and Danny figured it was a reaction to the violent action he'd seen back at the compound. Jacky also took advantage to dash inside and Danny leaned forward in the back seat.

"Jack, if it turned out there were some Taliban operating in London on some sort of operation, that would fall under the MI5 area of responsibility, wouldn't it? You know, national security?" he asked.

Jack swung round and looked back at him in astonishment.

"Good God Danny! We've just wiped out a whole assassination team and I'm looking forward to a well-deserved break, and you spring this on me! Where the hell did this pop up from?"

"A letter I just opened. Wainwright gave it to me a few days ago and I forgot all about it until he reminded me back there. Can't say too much right now as I don't know much more until I meet with someone in London, but my initial understanding of the situation is that some Taliban are following a woman I first met in Afghanistan"

Jack's face looked puzzled.

"The Taliban in London, and following this woman? What on earth for?" he demanded.

Danny avoided his gaze.

"I can't say much more right now Jack."

"Can't or won't Danny? Come on, this is national security information and the DG will want to get right on it. You need to tell us everything you've got so we can move on it."

"Yeah I hear you Jack but I need this evening first to suss it out some more. Tell you what. Raise the flag with the DG and arrange for me to meet with her tomorrow morning. I promise to give you the whole deal then, when I know it. How's that? Oh by the way, the Thames Building, is it still in use after the bomb?" he asked.

"The underground garage is totally demolished and the first floor badly damaged. The second floor was caught too but mainly smoke damage. The third and fourth floor were OK' d by the fire department for use and the lift is thankfully still working, so the DG can meet you there. We've been authorized to park on the street for the moment with a special temporary badge, and we've hired security to patrol the parked cars. The rest of the staff from the fire damaged floors have been given a week off while we try to arrange for temporary accommodation. We're talking probably six months of construction, so it's a real mess Danny. Now about this Taliban thing.........."

Jack was about to have another go at him when Jacky and Nick returned and jumped in the car. Jack turned back and switched the motor on.

The traffic into London wasn't too bad at that time of the evening, so they made excellent time. Jack dropped both Jacky and Nicholson at the Daily Mail office where she, no doubt, would have a massive welcome, having earlier notified them of her imminent arrival.

Danny had Jack drop him in North London, near Duckett Road, but not so close that the MI5 man, still curious from their earlier exchange, would have an inkling as to his destination. Standing beside the car he leaned inside the drivers window.

"Jack, would you have some official identification I could use for this call just in case I need it? I could return it to you at Thames House in the morning."

Jack snorted, looking at him.

"You've got a fucking nerve Quigley. After......"

Danny cut him off.

"After what you were involved in earlier this evening? And you worry about lending me your ID? Come on Jack!"

McAllister said nothing more. He thrust a leather wallet into Danny's hand, slammed the car into gear and took off, forcing him to jump back out of the way. He watched Jack drive away and then started walking.

Before he turned into Duckett Road, he checked again that Jack hadn't tried to follow him. He was now very glad of the MI5 course he'd taken over a year ago when he'd been introduced to the skills of surveillance and other tactics.

Once he reached the address, a small three-storey apartment building, he walked cautiously up the front steps to the doorway. Cars were parked on both sides of the road so it was impossible to determine if any watchers were present.

There were six names posted up on the doorjamb. Hers jumped out at him.... J. Mehsud. He took a deep breath and pressed the doorbell.

There was no response.

He tried again. Still no response.

He tried a few more times with the same result and deliberated what he should do. Jamila could very well be out somewhere and might not be back for some time. Equally, if she knows she is being followed she may not want to answer the door. As he thought about it he noticed a smartly dressed young woman striding up the street in his direction. He was well aware how luck could sometimes fall into one's lap and hoped that the young lady was coming to this building. She turned and walked up the steps towards him, taking a key out of her purse. He gave her a big Danny Quigley smile that had melted the hearts of more than a few women in the past.

"Hi, was supposed to meet Jamila" he said to her." She must be in the shower, not answering her doorbell. Can you let me in please?"

She looked at him warily.

"Come on, get real, this is London. As a woman, I wouldn't want anyone letting a stranger inside the building looking for me. I'd suggest you come back later."

Danny smiled again.

"I appreciate you being so security conscious Miss, especially as I'm with MI5. Jack McAllister is my name."

He briefly flashed the security card, his thumb half covering the picture, but the Government heading was unmistakable.

"I'm really concerned about Jamila's safety" he added. "As you noticed I do know her first name which is not on the door bell there."

She struggled for a moment digesting the new information.

Again he gave her a large reassuring smile.

She smiled in return.

"Oh why not? Especially if you're with a Government Security Service."

She opened the door, preceded him inside and pointed to the lift.

"Jamila's on the third floor. Give her my regards. I'm Juliette. I'm on the ground floor."

In a moment he was in the elevator and heading upwards. It stopped with a sudden lurch and he stepped out. There were two separate flats on that level and he spotted the one with Jamila's name on it. He noticed that there was a spy hole in the door and knew that it would help him get inside if she was in.

He knocked, standing in front of the spy hole. No response. He knocked again, louder. A muffled voice came through the door.

"Who is it?" a woman's voice demanded.

"Danny Quigley, Jamila. I just got your letter."

There was a muffled gasp from inside and a scraping sound against the door. He assumed she was looking through the spy hole and stood still. There was a small cry from inside and in a split second he could hear the locks being slid back and the door opened.

It was Danny's turn to gasp.

Standing in the doorway was a modern sophisticated woman, taller than he'd expected, with beautiful dark hair flowing down her back. Her dark exotic eyes were staring at him in shock and amazement, her lips slightly parted. She wore a wine-colored pant suit with a scarf loosely arranged around her neck and no make up. She didn't need any. She was a stunning beauty without it. He hadn't appreciated before that she had perfectly proportioned features and bone structure. She now carried herself with an easy confidence.

Without a moment's hesitation she threw herself into his arms sending him rocking back slightly on his heels. He returned the hug, feeling her body molded to his all the way down, and smelled the perfume from her newly washed hair.

"Da-ne, Da-ne, Da-ne, she gasped on his shoulder as she clutched him tighter. Danny felt his eyes moisten. He patted her back.

"Hey, it's okay Jamila, it's okay. I'm here. We'll take care of any problem that's come up. Trust me."

She stepped back still holding his arms.

"Let me look at you after all this time. Yes, you've got older and your hair is longer, but it looks good on you, like a rugged Hollywood western star. My Da-ne" she breathed wonderingly.

He deliberately ran his eyes up and down her figure appreciatively.

"And so have you Jamila! What a beauty you've become. A long way from the young girl in the cave with the wounded shoulder. You'll have to tell me all that's happened to you to end up in London at a medical training college. Oh, and by the way, I've been living here in London as well. I've been out of the military for nearly two years."

"Here in London at the same time as me? My goodness, if I'd only known. I assumed you were still a soldier. You were so good at it Da-ne."

He grimaced. "Well my wife persuaded me get out of the service. She didn't leave me much option. She was fed up with me being away all the time. Fat lot of good it did me though. She divorced me shortly afterwards."

"Oh I'm so sorry to hear." Sympathy flooded her face.

Danny could see that she genuinely meant it. She canted her head sideways.

"And your daughter, do you see her often?" she asked.

He nodded.

"Yeah, I see her every second weekend and occasionally on special days like her birthday and at Christmas. I hope to drop in on her tomorrow because I missed my last weekend as I was out of London."

He nodded to her smart evening clothes.

"Were you going out this evening Jamila?"

"No one says my name like you Da-ne. It brings me back to that time together in the mountains. How it changed my life! Many times when I wanted to give up I remembered how encouraging you were back then. Oh yes, I was going out tonight to a small going-away party for one of our teachers who is emigrating to Canada, but I certainly won't go now, and they won't think anything of it if I don't turn up. Let's sit over here and talk. I'm sure the letter intrigued you and worried you at the same time, so let me bring you up to date on what's happened to me since your Major took me to my aunt's place when we landed in Kandahar."

Jamila told the story of how her aunt spirited her out of Kandahar the following day to Kabul, where she immediately changed her name and started her working in the medical clinic there. She hadn't wanted the Afghan government to hear about her as her family were well known

Taliban supporters and she would have been held for interrogation. The new Afghan army still used torture methods of getting information from prisoners. Shortly afterwards, a Dr. Hawthorn, who took an interest in her, managed to get Jamila over to the U.K. and into medical training college under a special fast track program sponsored by the U.K. Government for the re-construction of Afghanistan. She still had another two years to go to graduate.

"How did you pay for the school fees?" he asked wondering if the sack of sapphires had been of some use and if she'd managed to get them exchanged.

She smiled.

"Da-ne, you were so good giving me all those sapphires for myself and my dream. My aunt in Kabul regularly met with all the different western charities and truck drivers coming in with material for the clinics. She made many friends, some quite close. In fact one became the fiancé of my sister who is a year younger than me, and they now live in the Netherlands. This man smuggled the sapphires out, sold them and had them split into three accounts in the Cayman Islands."

"The Cayman Islands? My God that's sophisticated for an aunt in Kabul. Why three accounts Jamila?"

She smiled and, getting up, walked over to a small desk opened a drawer and took out some paper work. She handed it to Danny.

"Have a look at that Da-ne." she urged.

It was a passbook with his name on it. There was an amount entered inside - one point three million euros! He stared at the figure. Then he looked up at her.

"Jamila, I don't understand! This is a pass issued by a bank in the Cayman Islands, for one point three million euros made out to me! What does it mean?"

She smiled again, almost triumphantly.

"I mentioned three accounts. You see I offered the whole thing to my aunt in Kabul when I saw the abject poverty of the people there and especially the women. It was heart breaking, but my aunt said that I would do more good becoming a doctor and coming back to minister to them, rather than just handing money away. She accepted one third to open and support six more clinics. She insisted that it was only fair that the remainder be split equally between you and myself, because you deserved it and my education would be more than covered by one third, so that's how we set it up. I knew your name of course and all you have to do is turn up in the Grand Cayman with your passport and you can do with this money whatever you want."

Danny looked dazedly at the passbook.

"My God that's over two million U.S. dollars" he exclaimed. "But why euros?" he asked.

She tossed her head.

"Oh my Aunt is into these things. She said the dollar is sinking too low" she replied nonchalantly.

He shook his head.

"I gotta meet this aunt of yours! But seriously, I don't need two million dollars. Why don't you keep it for the full cost of your education or even transfer it back into your aunt's account for your country?"

She came and sat beside him.

"Oh Da-ne, Da-ne, still the same generous person, always thinking of others. No, this is for you and that's the end of it. Now can I ask you a question that I've wondered about since I became westernized?"

He shrugged, wondering where this was leading.

"Of course" he answered.

She looked directly into his eyes.

"When we were in Afghanistan together, I felt very strongly that you liked me. Do you still like me, now that you've met me again, Da-ne as a modern woman?" she asked.

He nodded.

"More than I can tell you Jamila."

He put his arms around her and she leaned into him. They sat there for a long time, just holding each other, almost as if their beings needed to absorb the lost time and get re-acquainted. Finally she stirred.

"Thanks Da-ne" she said quietly. "Now my other problem."

He straightened up.

"Taliban here in London following you? Demanding the sapphires back? How can this be? How are they contacting you?" he asked.

She sighed.

"Yes indeed. I wondered how myself. I get these phone calls at night demanding the gems back, from a man with an Afghan accent speaking broken English and threatening me. I'm sure I'm being followed on foot on certain days and routes too. My car outside has been trashed, tires slashed, windscreen and rear lights smashed in."

"How do you know it was them who trashed your car?"

"Because I got a call the following night and he asked if I'd got the message they'd sent. There was no misunderstanding. It was they who did it."

"Any violence to you personally?" Danny asked. "Outside the apartment? In the subway? At work, in the parking lot ....?"

"No nothing. Nothing like that."

He stood up rubbing his hands together.

"Okay, I'm seeing MI5 tomorrow about this. If there's Taliban operating in London, it's right up their alley. We'll get surveillance set up on the flat and on yourself and we'll flush them out, so don't worry."

He touched her reassuringly. Her face paled.

"But we can't Da-ne. I don't want that!" she protested.

He blinked, looking puzzled.

"But you said..........."

She turned away wringing her hands.

"I know, I know, but you still can't. You see, since I sent you the letter, I've recognized the voice on the phone. He got angry one night and let off a stream in the Afghan language."

Danny reached over and turned her around facing him.

"And?" he insisted.

"It's my brother from home. The one who was fighting for the Taliban. He would know of the sapphires and they must have questioned my aunt, and when I say questioned I don't mean polite conversation. I tried to contact her at her normal number in Kabul when this started but it's cut off. If she talked, and it looks like she did, it was under torture. Don't you see, I can't turn in my own brother to spend the rest of his life in a U.K. prison. It would kill him! Oh Da-ne, what can we do?"

CHAPTER 39.

Danny spent the night on a pullout sofa bed in the lounge of Jamila's flat and had his best night's sleep in a long while. They had spent the previous evening catching up on events in both their lives. He couldn't believe what a sweet and gentle-natured person she had developed into in the time since they had briefly said goodbye in Kandahar. They both realized the special relationship that had existed between them had somehow survived, and he wanted to avoid doing or saying anything to upset it.

In the morning they decided to go out for a snack, just to spend some normal time together and Danny wanted to use the occasion to see if she would be followed. He made a quick call to his ex-wife to tell her that he couldn't pick up his ten year old daughter Allison for his weekend with her until the afternoon.

After a few hundred yards he decided they weren't being followed, unless it was a highly sophisticated operation involving lots of resources which he doubted the Taliban could mount in London. Jamila wore her bourka as they strolled three streets over to an early morning Polish restaurant. With the diversity of London, no one looked a second time at her head- gear, apart from a few males who stole quick glances at her slim lithe figure.

Inside they both ordered coffee and some scones, freshly baked out of the oven, with extra butter. After demolishing two of the scones quickly, Danny sat back and looked around the restaurant. It was Saturday morning and a number of hung-over men and women were lounging around drinking large mugs of coffee. Other couples were avoiding each other's eyes as they came to terms with the previous evenings 'catch', which was probably calling their judgment into question, in the harsh morning glare.

Jamila glanced around too and looked back at him smiling. He could tell she had come to the same conclusions and he was glad that he had decided to take the softly softly approach of getting to know her all over again.

"So, a young Muslim girl coming to London all by herself. Was it difficult to adjust from the mountains of Afghanistan and Pakistan to the freedom of the U.K. and it's capital city?" he enquired, lifting his cup and taking a large swallow.

She bit her lip lightly as she raised her eyes to the ceiling reflecting on his question.

"Yes and no Da-ne. Fortunately I had some basic English as you know. I practiced this at my aunt's clinic in Kabul, speaking with her visitors, the charity workers and teachers and sometimes coalition soldiers. Really anyone who would talk to me. I knew I needed to master English to fulfill my dream. My aunt encouraged me to discuss the various countries that these visitors came from and find out what life was like there."

"Wow!" he interjected. "You really worked at it Jamila. Your English is just amazing! I mean I picked up back in Afghanistan that you were determined to achieve your goal of becoming a qualified doctor and helping your people, and I'm really impressed how you went about it. How did you get to England?"

"An English doctor, Elisa Hawthorn, who worked at Cambridge University as a lecturer in their medical program, helped me. She used to come out and work in the clinic during her summer holidays and must have seen something in me. Dr. Hawthorn started the whole train of events that got me to the U.K. as a legal immigrant and into medical school. She also arranged for this apartment for me for the duration. I understood that she had some useful high up contacts in Government, who were involved at that time in the long-term reconstruction and establishment of democracy in Afghanistan. My basic education was lacking, however I got in on this special program where they fast tracked me through. Their priority was getting local Afghan people educated to the level where they could start taking responsibility and help the country become stabilized and self sufficient. So there it is. Very hard work but I'm on track and I must confess I love England

and the personal freedom it gives me as a woman. I still practice as a Muslim, but I don't pray five times a day as one is expected to. I just try to be a good person."

"Well, that's quite a mouthful Jamila! I can certainly testify that you are a good person. After all you saved my life back in those mountains, and yes, your story does give me an idea of how events have played out in your life. Now tell me, a beautiful desirable young woman like you, are there many suitors chasing after you?"

She blushed, putting her cup down.

"I can't believe what you're asking! If I didn't know you better I'd say you were a bit jealous" she exclaimed.

He grinned sheepishly.

"Well maybe a trifle" he admitted. "Anyway you are a free woman to see anyone you want to. I just wondered if there's anyone special in your life right now" he added.

Her eyes softened.

"Not in the way you mean Da-ne. Oh I have various friends in college but mostly women. We really have very little time for socializing with the amount of study involved, and if we go out it's usually as a group. As a Muslim anyway, I wouldn't feel comfortable in a lot of the places that young people go to on a night out. Does that answer your question?"

Without waiting for an answer she reached forward and covered his hand with hers.

"Now what about the same question to you Da-ne? Fair's fair!"

He wondered how to answer that without getting himself into hot water. He didn't want to lose her just after finding her again, yet he didn't want to mislead her either. He decided to bite the bullet.

"Well" he started cautiously, "divorced some time ago but too busy trying to start my business to take advantage of my newly single status. I wasn't deliberately practicing celibacy for any religious or other reasons. I enjoy a woman as much as anyone I guess. It was just a time where I couldn't afford any distractions, and financially I couldn't afford it either. I did find a woman in Ireland called Siobhan who I got close to and recently went back over after a year's absence. There was something there. Still is probably, if I'm honest, but I'm not sure about the future of it. She's committed to her work as a nurse and I'm pretty tied down to getting my business up to the next level. It could be another year before I see her again, if then. I still have a small business involvement over there. I did meet a journalist recently that I like and that could develop, given time. I don't know if that answers you're question Jamila, but I'm trying to be completely straight with you."

She looked seriously at him.

"You didn't have to go into such detail at all Da-ne. I have no right, nor do I wish to question you on your past relationships or indeed present involvements. That's your business. Enough to know that we are here together and as to the future… Inshallah…. who knows? Living in my village, men would go out to fight and not come back. There was always wailing in some house, but the women were strong and accepted the situation and just got on with their lives as best they could. It usually meant being looked after by some member of the family, a brother, uncle or cousin. I know enough to enjoy the present moment and not take on unnecessary burdens about a future that might never come."

Not much was said after that as they both sat, her hand still laid on his, lost in their own thoughts, but an unmistakable bond slowly growing between them.

He excused himself for a moment as he ducked over to a nearby table where a man had just put down a Daily Mail newspaper and started eating. Danny tapped him on the shoulder.

"Excuse me mate. Could I have a quick scan of the front page please?" he asked smiling.

The man glanced up.

"Sure go ahead. That's quite a story there."

Danny quickly ran his eye over the various articles. Jacky had done an impressive layout, starting with a troop of SAS back from a secret mission to Kuwait and being stalked by a team of mercenaries who had now fled the country. They had killed two of the troopers including the head of MI6, and cremated them in High Wycombe. There was a brief mention of her flat mate being killed, the attempt on her life as well, and the murder of two of the mercenaries in the jail in Chepstow. The directors of the crematorium were in custody and the local head of the CIA London station was being sought internationally. There was no mention, as had been agreed, about the violent action in Southampton the previous evening though the police there, Danny realized, must already be investigating the abandoned compound and the body of the Israeli. The article left many questions unanswered and the media would be having a feeding frenzy, trying to catch up on the Daily Mail article, which had the byline of Jacky Spellman.

He thanked the man and laid the paper back on the table.

When he sat down again, Jamila raised her eyebrows in an unspoken question, but he just mentioned spotting something about the SAS, his old unit.

When they got back to her front door he carefully checked to see if there was any surveillance. While it was difficult to assess all the parked cars and their possible occupants, he still felt that she was not being watched at that particular time. Unfortunately he had to head back into the city for his meeting at Thames House.

He kissed her for the first time and felt her respond. He felt a silly grin on his face as he turned away and headed downtown. God, it's good to be alive he thought as he felt his spirits lift after the grim events of the past week.

CHAPTER 40.

The smoke-blackened face of Thames House stopped him short on the sidewalk. He could still smell burning rubber and petrol fumes in the air and shook his head thinking of Sophia being caught below in the conflagration. The was a barrage of construction activity around the building which he weaved his way through to the temporary security passageway set up for visitors.

Upstairs he was greeted by the Director General, a pale and shocked Rebecca Fullerton-Smythe who gave him a hug and poured him a large coffee. Jack was already there, sitting across the room. Danny went over and shook his hand, at the same time handing his MI5 pass over to him in the palm of his hand.

The DG sat across the desk and managed a weak smile.

"Well, when you take on something Danny you really finish the job don't you?"

Danny raised his hands and looked innocently across at Jack.

"Hey, what does she mean here Jack? Is there something I missed?"

Jack looked thoughtfully at him.

"Well it could be that she gave you a task, under the radar as it were, to locate a missing troop of SAS who were being picked off one by one. Right now those lads are on a chopper being flown from Poole to Hereford where they'll have some pretty tight security put in place. We suspect this may no longer be necessary as the bastards who killed two of the SAS troopers and Percy Saunders are now lying at the bottom of some mine shaft in Wales, so game over Danny."

Rebecca seemed to perk up.

"Absolutely first class job Danny. Well done! Jack hasn't had so much fun in a long time, isn't that right Jack?"

Jack nodded.

"Well losing Sophia wasn't fun, but I'll tell you something Ma'am. I can see why you hired this guy! I wouldn't want him chasing me, that's for sure!"

Danny feeling restless, stood up and walked over to the window looking down on the construction workers below. Finally he turned.

"The bastard who caused all that damage below, Sinclair, and murdered Sophia, is still on the loose so it's not game over just yet. I'm going after him Rebecca" he added grimly.

She got up and moved across to the window beside him.

"Now look Danny, you've done a brilliant job finding the troop, getting them out of danger and eliminating that ex-military scum. It's probable that one of them planted the bomb that killed Sophia so we've settled the score on that. Now the task of locating Sinclair goes international and is pretty much out of our hands…. MI6, Interpol, obviously Langley, who have the embarrassment of a rogue agent on the loose. You've earned your fee so I'm a happy bunny on that score right now."

"Well I'm not and whether you authorize it or not I'm making a trip over to the head office of that security company in Buffalo to see if he's holed up there. I'd like to use the passport you sent down with Sophia as my name might ring some bells wherever I fly in."

Rebecca looked at the stubborn set to his features and glanced over at Jack.

"What do you do with someone like that Jack? Do I kick his ass out of here?"

He grinned, standing and yawning.

"I wouldn't recommend trying to kick his ass at all Ma'am. Anyway there's the other bombshell he dropped last night coming up from Southampton."

"Oh, I was going to ask you to do the kicking" she said, grinning wickedly.

"Figured as much" he muttered gloomily.

She turned back to Danny.

"We'll talk later about any trip to Buffalo. Right now give me an update on your news that there are some Taliban in London. That's a first for MI5 I can tell you. We're watching hundreds of people who might, just might, have contacts with various terrorist groups worldwide. We have people planted in the radical mosques here in the U.K. and we routinely check on the four thousand or more young Muslim men who go back to Pakistan or Afghanistan to get re-acquainted with their culture. Most are legitimate visitors abroad but some get poisoned by radical Iman's or Al Qaeda sympathizers. These are the ones we keep a close eye on. Home grown terrorists Danny, carrying British passports, and they are our worst nightmare. The Americans are now actively profiling British Muslims entering the U.S. The Taliban would love to strike a blow at the heart of England for our military efforts in Iraq and Afghanistan. Quite frankly they haven't the resources or the sophistication to organize something like that, so update me on your information. Jack said you would get a fuller picture last night when you met this person back here in London. Is that right?"

Danny had been dreading this conversation since finding out that Jamila's brother was one of the people involved. Lives could be at stake however, if he concealed information from MI5, as well as sabotaging the trusted relationship he'd built up with them.

He re-filled his coffee cup and stirred in some milk and sugar as he marshaled his thoughts. Finally he turned and faced them.

"I need to tell you a story first to lead into this. I was in Afghanistan working with a Delta team approximately two years ago and got cut off when the choppers left without me. I tried to walk out and ran into some Taliban. I killed two of them but my weapon misfired on the third one and a young girl of seventeen saved my bacon by shooting him. He was her cousin."

"Jesus why did she do that Danny?" asked Jack.

"Her name was Jamila and her uncle and cousin were coming on to her on the trip. I just happened along at the appropriate moment. She must have figured her chances were better with me. Said something about praying for some help and there I was. Anyway she agreed to help me get through the mountains back to Kandahar where she hoped to join her aunt. She dressed me up in some gear from the dead Taliban, dyed my skin with mud and worked out how to get past any curious people we met along the way. Before we hit the road I checked out their packs, and apart from a load of IED's I found a small sack of sapphires, apparently from the mountain area of Pakistan across on the Indian side. Apparently they produce the best sapphires in the world. I figured they must be worth a few million dollars at least."

Rebecca reached across and touched his arm, interrupting his flow.

"What on earth was a small mangy bunch of Taliban doing with a sack of sapphires worth millions Danny? That's what I can't understand."

"Yeah, I wondered that too" he said "so I asked her. She said it was to pay for weapons, ammo and explosives for the Taliban when they got to Kabul. Apparently that's how they paid for them."

She shook her head wonderingly.

"My God, military intelligence would have been interested in that information!"

She thought for a moment.

"I've seen your military file on the Afghanistan operation. Quite extraordinary. However I don't recall reading about sapphires Danny. Correct me if I'm wrong here."

He nodded absently, his mind back in those hostile mountains four years ago.

"You're right Rebecca. I told her to keep them and use them to get educated and become a medical doctor, which she is doing here in London. She still has some years training ahead of her. Her aunt, a very capable woman from what I heard last night, sold the sapphires for her."

"That wasn't a good move Danny. It would have been useful intelligence for the coalition forces to figure out that loop. Could have saved some lives, who knows" she chided.

Danny made a face.

"Sitting here right now safely in London, I couldn't agree more. But then my focus was on getting out of those mountains and avoiding being killed. The U.S. intelligence people who met me really pissed me off anyway with their attitude. To be honest I wasn't thinking beyond the moment right then Rebecca, and that kid was so determined to rise above her upbringing in a backward mountain village and help her people. I really admired her determination to make something of herself."

A slight smile touched the DG's lips as she glanced across at Jack.

"Danny always did have a soft spot for the ladies, but a sack of sapphires? She must have been something! Her education level can't have been very high coming out a village. How did she get accepted into medical school over here. I hear it's not even easy for English kids to get in. The competition is tough. "

Danny shrugged. "I don't know the full facts there Rebecca. Apparently the U.K. Government have a special fast track program to get young Afghans qualified in various disciplines and back over there re-building the country."

Jack coughed.

"Why do I feel we're coming to the whole point of this story Danny?"

Danny nodded. "Well spotted Jack. You're not a spook for nothing. The bottom line is that I got a note from Jamila, sent to Hereford. She must have figured that I was still in the 'Sass'. She's now living in London and has started getting demands quite recently for the return of the sapphires. Last night I discovered that she believed she was being followed. Her car was trashed one night and she got a call the following night, basically telling her that they were responsible. She hasn't been approached or harmed physically but she's obviously terrified."

"I don't get it Danny. Two years pass and nothing. Now suddenly out of the blue she gets demands for the sapphires back! How do you explain that?" Jack asked impatiently.

The DG nodded.

"Yeah, I don't get it either."

"As I understand it, someone eventually made the connection. The aunt had disappeared in Kabul and if the Taliban interrogated her she would have spilled everything. It probably took time to run Jamila to earth here in London."

She looked warily at him then.

"There's more isn't there Danny? Tell us the rest" she asked quietly.

He looked up miserably.

"Yeah she finally recognized the voice one night of the person phoning her when he lapsed into his local dialect from Pakistan. It was her brother who has been fighting with the Taliban since he was fifteen. I told Jamila I would somehow try to look out for him. She said a U.K. jail would kill him."

Jack and the DG exchanged glances. The DG reached across and held his arm.

"You poor sod Danny. Of course you knew your chances of that were pretty slim once we got involved. You like her don't you?" she asked gently.

He nodded, looking away.

Nothing was said in the room for the next few moments. Finally the DG stirred.

"Okay, we have work to do. Jack lets discuss with Danny how we plan to carry out this operation. We need to synchronize your team with his meetings with this… ah…. Jamila. First we get all the information we can about her, address, place of work etc. Have a listening device installed in the telephone in her flat and a bug in her car. I assume she'll cooperate with this. I'll start debriefing Danny on what we need and you start getting a team to launch a 24/7 watch on our target. Okay, hop to it."

Jack disappeared out of the room.

The DG glanced at him, as she lifted a writing pad and pen from a drawer in her desk.

"There's more about the sapphires you haven't told me isn't there Danny? I promise you I'll get back to it later. Now let's start getting this down."

CHAPTER 41.

After he left Thames House, Danny made a quick trip home by subway to his flat in Croydon where he showered and changed. He had practically lived in the same clothes for the past week and was glad to get into something fresh. He flipped through his mail, and seeing nothing of interest switched on his answer phone and checked his messages.

A couple of business calls from his secretary in the office and a brief thank you phone call from Siobhan in Ireland. He had used the large fee he'd received from Rebecca to bail out her hostel for women which was on the verge of closing down. He felt a twinge of guilt on hearing her voice but quickly dismissed it.

Then he drove round to his ex wife Yvonne's house, which had been given to her as part of the divorce agreement. It had nearly been burned down just after he took his discharge from the regiment, by a gang who had been pressuring him to assassinate a leading politician. The door was opened by his 10 year old daughter, Allison, who threw herself into his arms and squealed in delight.

"Oh Daddy Daddy, you finally got here. I couldn't wait. I was just about to call you but Mum told me not to be silly, that you were probably on your way. Where are we going?" she asked, her voice rising. He put her down patting her red hair and noticing that her freckles were more pronounced than ever, but he knew it was more than his life was worth to mention them to her.

"Tell you later Sweetheart. Let me have a brief chat with your mother and then we can go, okay?"

She nodded and dragged him inside as Yvonne came through from the kitchen, smiling.

"She's been on tenterhooks all morning waiting for you Danny" she said, giving him a brief hug and pointing to the chair.

"Coffee?" she asked.

Allison dashed off to collect some things for her day out with him, while he sat down and started stirring in some cream and sugar.

Yvonne was a looker! Tall with red hair and wickedly green eyes, she carried herself like a model and was a rising star in a successful interior design company. After the initial shock of the divorce Danny had worked at building a new relationship with her, knowing the pain it could cause Allison otherwise. She teased Danny continually about potential girl friends and didn't appear to have a jealous bone in her body. Danny protested that he didn't have time for new liaisons but she only half believed him. They had both moved on and were reasonably comfortable, even relieved with the new relationship.

She now appraised him.

"We missed you last weekend Danny. Were you busy or out of town?" she probed.

"I was actually over in Sligo in Ireland for the weekend. Came back Tuesday, then got caught up in some stuff. Got back into London late last night" he answered.

"Ah yes, the old connection in Ireland from a year ago. Do you still try to help that woman's hostel out? What about the nurse who worked there, what was her name?"

"Siobhan. Yeah, I still help out when I can, but there's not much I can do, what with trying to build my financial planning business. They still look after over a hundred women who now have their babies instead of going for abortions, and they also now have a detox unit for the ones on drugs. It's a 24/7 responsibility for Siobhan" he answered.

She cocked her head, a mannerism of hers that used to make Danny's heart race.

"You were keen on her back then weren't you Danny? Still something there between you?"

"Well yeah, you could say so, but meeting once a year, you know how it is. Now there was someone else that I did want to tell you about, especially as I'd like Allison to meet her this afternoon."

Yvonne's eyes brightened with interest.

"Do tell Danny. You mean to say that you've finally got someone who you want Allison to meet? Wow! I've got to meet her too!"

He held up his hands defensively.

"Hey, wait a minute! I don't want you to read too much into this. Now here's the thing Yvonne, I briefly mentioned her in passing when I came back from that operation in Afghanistan, where I was left behind in the mountains, just before you made me get out of the regiment."

Her face cleared. "Of course….."

"You always complained back then that I never told you anything about where I was or what I was doing and I quite simply told you that I couldn't. Official secrets act and all that. However in this instance I did mention a girl who saved my life in Afghanistan who was so determined to get out of her village and get some sort of medical qualification so as to help her people. She wanted to become a doctor actually. Remember that?"

She leaned forward, refilling his cup as she did so.

"Now that you mention it, I do. Didn't she disappear after you got back to Kandahar?"

"Yeah, her aunt spirited her away to Kabul to make sure she wasn't questioned by the government police as she had a family connection to the Taliban. Anyway, what I'm leading up to is that she has re-surfaced here in London. Major Wainwright forwarded me a letter she sent to the regiment addressed to me. She must have figured I was still a soldier."

Yvonne looked stunned.

"My God Danny, that's some story! And she's now here in London after all that time? Have you met her yet?" she asked, her face bright with excitement.

"Last night for the first time. She's in medical school right now, and doing quite well. So she is well on her way."

Yvonne leaned forward.

"And tell me did bells go off when you met her? How old is she now?"

Danny started getting slightly embarrassed at that stage.

"Nineteen or twenty I guess. Well you know, there was nothing between us when we met in Afghanistan. I was too busy staying alive right then, and married to you as well which was important to me. She was only seventeen or so then, just a girl really, but now amazingly, she's a grown woman. Quite beautiful as it happens, and yes, in some sort of a way, there was a bond there when we met last night. I really like her and I think she likes me, but it's early days and she plans to go back to Afghanistan to help her people, when she graduates. So no big plans, no promises or expectations from either side, just an enjoyment of the moment so to speak."

Yvonne came and threw an arm round his shoulders.

"You deserve some happiness Danny, that's for sure" she whispered. "After all you've been through and done for your country. I'm sorry it didn't work out for us but you know I wish you well. You're right, enjoy the moment and who knows, life sometimes finds a way."

He squeezed her hand just as Allison came breezing back into the kitchen. She stopped, startled at seeing them, a grin coming onto her face

"You should see you too, like a couple of love birds. Does this mean…..?"

Yvonne straightened up.

"No it doesn't. Your dad was just telling me about an interesting lady he's met and he wants to introduce you to her when you go out."

Two emotions flickered across her face, disappointment at having to share him with someone else, and fascinated at the thought of meeting a female friend of her Dad's. That had never happened before. Her face brightened as she raced for the front door.

"Let's go Dad" she sang.

Yvonne patted his arm.

"You go and enjoy your daughter Danny."

CHAPTER 42.

Before heading off in his car to pick up Jamila, Danny made a quick phone call to Jack, apprising him of his plans. In their discussions, they had thought it unlikely that the Taliban would make any move while Jamila was in his company. It was more likely that they would way-lay her outside her flat or near her work place, possibly when she went for her car to return home. For that reason Jack had only organized a small team of two cars for the weekend, to be beefed up when she was on her own traveling to and from work. They also intended to have an MI5 officer on site overnight in the building where she lived, and another at the college on a daily basis, during the hours she attended there.

As the role of MI5 was one of gathering intelligence and did not have powers of arrest in the U.K., Rebecca was liaising with Scotland Yard in having a police presence in one of their surveillance vehicles. Danny felt that was an unwieldy arrangement and as he intended to be involved, found it frustrating that he could not carry a weapon. The laws in the U.K. regarding firearms could mean getting up to seven years in jail if caught carrying one. They had no option down at Southampton but the London police were continually on the alert after previous terrorist strikes there. Cameras everywhere also meant that during any one day a Londoner could be appearing on at least 300 cameras across the city.

On arrival at her address Danny jumped out and called Jamila on his cell phone. In five minutes, she was opening the front door and walking smilingly across to them. Allison jumped out and ran to meet her.

"I'm Allison, his daughter. He hasn't told me a thing about you so I want to hear everything!" she exclaimed.

Jamila gave her a hug and smiled with pleasure.

"Well I'm Jamila for starters. At least he's probably told you that much. He's told me a lot about you though."

"Oh, what did he say Jamila? Lots of good things I hope."

"Of course, how could he say otherwise? As far as he's concerned, you're perfect Allison" she teased as she got into the front passenger seat, turning to keep eye contact with her. Allison jumped into the back grinning, glad she had offered the front seat to Jamila.

"Well you're the first girl friend he's ever introduced me to Jamila, so that's progress" Allison volunteered as she fastened her seat belt and sat back.

Jamila swiveled her head back towards Danny, now starting the car up.

"Oh, he said I was his girl friend did he Allison? It's the first I've heard of it."

Danny sighed.

"Little girls tend to exaggerate Jamila, don't you remember when you were young?"

He caught Allison's eyes in the rear view mirror.

"I said she was a friend as I recall."

"You did so Daddy! Anyway I'm not a little girl for Pete's sake" she muttered disgustedly.

Jamila reached back and took Allison's hand in hers.

"You certainly aren't a little girl Allison. Anyone can see that. Just ignore him. You know all fathers think their daughter is a little girl forever. That's why they look so shocked on their wedding day when they have to give her away to her future husband."

Allison looked mollified, having a grown woman other than her mother on her side. She settled back and started enjoying the ride through the streets of London.

That was the start of one of the best days Danny had in a long time.

Usually his day out with Allison was a fun time, but with Jamila present, it took on an even greater significance. It was as if he had a complete family again and the togetherness appeared almost seamless. If anything took away from the afternoon it was his constant need for alertness in the people and their surroundings. He tried to spot

Jack's team but failed. That was good because if she had followers, they wouldn't spot them either.

They first visited the London Eye, a great spinning wheel high in the sky which one could ride up on and view the whole of the city and which Jamila had never been on. Then they took a short Thames cruise followed by a snack. On Allison's urging they ended up in Hyde Park where they strolled around for about an hour. He had managed to park in an underground car park close by. Danny and Jamila walked arm in arm with Allison running ahead, entranced by the ducks and swans on the water. Eventually they reluctantly headed back to collect the car and head home. The plan was for Jamila to cook something at her flat and then Danny would drop Allison back at her mum's house.

As they strolled down the incline into the underground garage Danny nodded at Allison who was still rushing ahead.

"God bless her energy. She wears me out over a weekend I can tell you. I don't tell her but I'm glad of a break when it's over. I sometimes wonder how Yvonne managed to bring her up practically all on her own, and keep a job going as well."

Jamila laughed.

"Modern women are marvelous at what they can do Danny. In my village we always had a big extended family to share the upbringing of the children. Mind you there's no way I'd choose that way of life at this stage. I've got too spoiled."

Danny was thinking of this remark as he hit the unlock button on the keys and opened the back door for Allison.

What happened after that was a blur.

He heard a voice shouting in a foreign language and Jamila cried out. Danny lifted his gaze and saw a man three cars down, pointing a handgun at them. Swinging his head he spotted two more men also standing three cars behind, both with automatics fully extended. Jamila had seen the two men behind them as well and gasped.

"It's Ahmed! My brother. Oh God!"

Without thinking Danny grabbed Allison and pushed her onto the floor beside the back seat.

"Keep down!" he shouted urgently.

Jamila was still standing there as if frozen in place. Danny grabbed her with one hand and literally threw her onto the back seat, her face only inches from Allison's.

"Keep your head down Jamila" he shouted.

"Danny don't...." She started to sit up.

He pushed her head back down again.

"Keep down, they've got weapons" he shouted frantically slamming the door and hitting the lock button on his key ring as he did so.

He inched his head up over the roof of the car and a burst of fire greeted him from both directions, whanging off their car and the ones in front and behind them.

He heard a cry of pain from the direction of the two gunmen and surmised that the three men hadn't positioned themselves very well, as they'd placed themselves in their own cross fire. Fighting in the Afghan hills may not have been a good training ground for setting up ambushes in underground parking lots. Or else they had thought that snatching Jamila would have been a simple operation. He noted that they hadn't fired when Jamila was exposed and assumed they wanted her alive.

He was a different story.

They had chosen an excellent place to spring an ambush and he berated himself for dropping his guard after the relaxing day. There might not be any more days like it.

He dropped to the ground and peered under the car. Two cars beyond his own he could see the feet of the first man standing in the middle of the vehicle. He crawled around the rear of his car without attracting any further fire. There were only two cars between himself and the nearest assailant now. He lay flat and peered under the vehicle. The man's feet were still visible in the same position. He couldn't risk being spotted coming around the rear end of it so he crawled underneath, inching along slowly in the confined space. He would be a sitting duck if his assailant dashed around to check on him. Fortunately he managed to squeeze through and kept his eyes glued on his attacker's feet which hadn't moved. He climbed cautiously to his knees trying to assess his next move. He was unarmed and up against three armed terrorists.

The firing had stopped but the men were shouting to each other.

Next moment Danny heard the sound of running feet and the noise of weapons being smashed against the windows of the car where Jamila and Allison were lying. Both women started screaming, fear and desperation in their voices. The men pounding in the car windows started shouting at the two people inside.

Where the hell are you Jack? he thought desperately.

His dilemma was solved for him.

Allison screamed again at the top of her voice.

Assuming the gunman would be distracted by the sound, Danny ran around the back of the car and launched himself at him. The man turned at the last minute, his weapon swinging towards him, a shocked look on his face.

As Danny's weight and momentum hit the terrorist he grabbed for the man's gun hand and caught it as they went rolling out onto the cement driveway. They both hit hard and immediately Danny was aware of the cord–like figure fighting back under him with a desperate ferocity. The gun in his hand, an Austrian Glock, went off twice, sending shots into the ceiling. The gunman clawed for his eyes with his other hand and Danny ducked his head away, slamming an elbow into his face and rolling backwards pulling the terrorist with him. As he came down on the cement he saw an opening and was able to slide the gun arm into an arm lock and snap it at the elbow. The man screamed in agony and Danny was aware that one of the other gunmen had run out onto the cement, his weapon focused on the two fighting. Danny separated the Glock from the injured terrorist's hand and kept rolling. At the same time the standing terrorist started firing at him. Danny could literally feel the bullets pass within inches of his face as he swiveled onto his knees trying to get the Glock into the palm of his hand. The gunman steadied himself and took careful aim. Danny knew he was going to be hit. Suddenly the horn blew loudly and the man's hand jumped as he fired. The bullet slammed into his colleague on the floor and his body arched with the impact. That gave Danny all the time he needed. He fired twice, aiming for the largest part of the individual in front of him.

The terrorist crashed backwards onto the cement.

Danny knew he had fired a fatal shot, but he also knew that earlier two terrorists had been firing at him. So he jumped up. At that moment there was a clatter of feet and Jack came running up the garage with two other people, one carrying a weapon. The man, on seeing Danny, screamed at him.

"Put the gun down on the floor now……"

Danny pointed towards the car where the two terrorists had been standing.

"There's another one over…..!" he started to shout.

The man with the gun dropped into a firing stance.

"On the floor now I said, or I fire!" he bellowed.

Just then there was a muffled shot from the side of the vehicle where the two terrorists had been. At the same time Jack jumped over to his colleague and pressed his weapon down to the floor.

"That's Quigley for Christ sake! He's with us!"

A look of confusion streaked across the man's face as he looked from Danny to the location of the shot. For safety's sake Danny carefully placed the Glock on the ground and stood up.

Jack ran over to the back of the car where the shot had come from. He emerged pale-faced a moment later, shaking his head.

"The guy totaled himself. Put the gun in his mouth. It's a mess."

Jack's colleague, the one with the gun, was now shaking uncontrollably and could barely holster his weapon. His first time in action Danny thought. He knew what it was like. He'd been there.

A piercing scream came from Danny's car and Jamila leapt from it racing backwards to where she'd previously seen her brother. Jack tried to stop her but she brushed past him and hurled herself down on the ground beside the terrorist who had just taken his own life. Then she started screaming again. A keening, tearing scream that rebounded from the damp walls of the underground garage.

Danny remembered her statement about the sound of keening women in the village when their men were killed. She had just discovered her dead brother.

He raced to his car.

Allison was still lying on the floor by the back seat, sobbing uncontrollably. He gently helped her up, and put both arms around her. After awhile her sobs slowed down and her tear-streaked face looked up at him.

"I thought you were dead Daddy. I heard the shots. Those men were trying to kill you weren't they?" she choked out, trying to get her breath.

"I think they were after Jamila" he answered. I just got in the way I'm afraid. Who blew the horn by the way?"

She sniffed again.

"It must have been Jamila. I was still stuck between the seats. I couldn't see anything. Are the men dead Daddy?" she whispered, trying to look round his form.

He nodded.

"Unfortunately yes. One was shot accidentally when Jamila distracted his colleague who was trying to shoot me. She saved my life by blowing the car horn. The other one killed himself. Probably didn't want to be captured and end up in prison. I'm afraid he was Jamila's brother who she hadn't seen since she left her home in Afghanistan."

Allison looked even more shocked.

"Oh God poor Jamila! Can I go to her Daddy? Maybe I can just hold her hand."

"In a moment perhaps Allison."

He was touched by her reaction and impressed at how fast she was recovering. They sat there for a moment saying nothing. Finally Danny sighed.

"You'll have to find out sooner or later Allison. I had to kill one of them. He was about to kill me. I'm sorry I had to do it but I had no choice sweetheart."

She nodded vehemently.

"I'm glad it was him and not you Daddy. I'd have killed him myself if I'd had a chance to save you."

"Thanks, but hopefully you'll never have to kill anyone, and whatever you do don't tell your mother what you just told me! She'll say I'm a bad influence on you. Speaking of your mother, I better call her right away. Is she ever going to be pissed."

She laughed then.

"Daddy, you just said a bad word" she accused, but her eyes were gleaming.

He grunted knowing she wouldn't let him forget it but at the same time he marveled at how fast she was coming round from the experience.

Gently helping her out of the car they walked over to Jack who was standing off to one side.

"Hey Jack, I've got to go outside and call her mum and get Allison some fresh air. She'll probably head right round here. Keep an eye on Jamila there for a moment will you and tell her I'll be right back?"

As he turned away to head for the entrance, his arm was grabbed violently from the side causing Allison to stumble. It was Jack's colleague who had the gun out earlier.

"Just where the heck do you think you're going mate?" he shouted. "You're not just walking away from the scene like that. I saw you standing there with a weapon in your hand. That's seven years inside at Her Majesty's convenience."

Danny looked down at the man's hand.

"Would you take your hand off my shoulder please…. like right now?" he snapped. "My daughter has just had a terrible shock and I'm taking her outside for some fresh air and to call her mother."

He turned as if to walk away but the man's grip tightened and he started reaching round for his weapon.

Jack tried to intervene.

"Look Jeff, he's one of us for crying out loud. What's the matter with you."

Jeff flicked a glance at him.

"Stay out of this Jack. This is police work and need I remind you that MI5 has no brief in this area. I'm hanging on to this one till my superior gets here."

His weapon was half out of his holster at that stage.

Danny was standing with his ten-year-old daughter and an idiot policeman, who had probably never fired a weapon in anger, was drawing his gun.

He reached up casually and grasping the back of the man's hand in a wrist lock, spun sideways, sending him straight down onto to his knees with a cry of pain. At the same time he just as casually removed the gun from his other hand and handed it to Jack. Still holding the man down with the pressure of just one hand Danny started to speak quietly to him.

"Now you listen to me my friend. You've obviously never used that weapon in your life, as evidenced by you shaking in your boots a few minutes ago. I, on the other hand have, innumerable times, and I don't appreciate some idiot even if he is a policeman from shaking a weapon in my face, especially when my young daughter is standing right beside me. Now, I'm going outside as mentioned and I'll be happy to talk to your superior when he gets here. If you get in my way between now and then I promise you a long absence from the Force on medical leave."

He increased the leverage on the wrist. "Is that clear mate?"

He leaned forward and stared intensely into the policeman's shocked eyes. The man looked desperately at Jack as if looking for a way out, but seeing none he nodded several times.

"Yes, yes.... very clear.... only trying to do my job" he stuttered, his face creased in pain.

Danny studied him for a moment and releasing his wrist turned and spoke to Jack.

"Don't let him have that weapon back until his boss gets here. If I have to take it off him again I won't be as gentle next time."

Danny took Allison's hand and strolled off towards the entrance. Jack looked fiercely at the policeman.

"Do you know who the fuck you just came up against you moron? He's won so many decorations for his work in Afghanistan from the U.K. and the Americans, there isn't any room on his uniform to display them. He killed a hundred and sixty Taliban and Al Qaeda over there on one mission, while serving in the SAS, and you try to put the hold on him when it's blatantly obvious that he's just saved the lives of these two women and himself from terrorists. If you hadn't been so bullheaded we might have got a prisoner here as well that we could have questioned as to how they got into the country and who their contacts are here in the U.K. As it is, it gave the bastard enough time to top himself. If I was you I'd keep this little incident to yourself when your boss gets here, otherwise your career at Scotland Yard might be very short term. I should tell you that Quigley is a close friend of the Director of MI5 and the American Ambassador here in London, so cool it Jeff or I'll slap you down myself."

With that he turned away in disgust.

CHAPTER 43.

Danny was right. Yvonne was pissed when he called her. She was even more pissed when she got there forty minutes later and heard the full details of the incident. Her eyes blazing she tore into him.

"You take her out for the afternoon knowing that people were after Jamila and even had a police team following her around! Just how dumb can you get Danny? You obviously didn't think for one moment that Allison might be caught in the middle. She could have been killed for God's sake!" she shouted.

He threw up his hands helplessly knowing in hindsight that she was right. Earlier MI5 had discounted the threat of anything happening when other people were with Jamila, but they had been proved wrong. For the terrorists it must have been an ideal opportunity to strike in an isolated location and with few witnesses. The MI5 team and Danny just hadn't considered the possibility of an early attack.

"Look, we didn't think.... " he started to explain.

"That's right Danny. You didn't think, and I thought you were finished with all that violence stuff when you got out! Well have I got news for you? I'm going back to my lawyer and this time I'm going for full custody. I'm not putting my daughter in danger any more in your company. If you see her again it'll be under my direct supervision, and that I promise, won't be very often" she raged.

Then she was gone dragging Allison with her, casting him a helpless look.

He was hit again two hours later.

All the statements had been taken by Jeff's superior, a Chief Superintendent, and the forensic and investigative team had taken over. However Danny thought that Jack had said something to the

Chief Superintendent as he hustled Jeff out to a police cruiser and unceremoniously stuck him into the back seat. Nothing more was said to Danny about the incident involving him earlier.

Towards the end Jack came over to him.

"We're driving Jamila home and a female officer will stay with her. We don't know if there are more terrorists around so we'll be protecting her for a while. I'm not making any more assumptions about those people."

Danny cut in.

"Look, I'd like to go along with her and……"

Jack shook his head.

"Sorry Danny. She doesn't want you anywhere near her again. She blames you for the death of her brother. Says you promised to keep him out of it and now he's lying dead over there."

He squeezed his shoulder sympathetically.

"Give her some time" he added, "who knows, she might come round."

Danny turned away, saying nothing. He knew she wouldn't. In the Pashtun tribal villages of Pakistan they taught you how to do one thing well - to hate.

A few minutes later he stood by, watching as Jamila was helped into a police van. She avoided his eyes completely. He turned and walked away towards the main road, not waiting for the lift that Jack had promised him. It was a Saturday he'd always remember. Apart from the dead terrorists, he'd just lost the two most important people in his life.

CHAPTER 44.

The next two hours were a blur. Danny took a cab into Soho and wandered around for some time without really seeing anything. The smell of food drew him into an Italian restaurant where he ate something without any real appreciation of what he was tasting. After leaving he wandered into a small old world pub and drank two pints of German beer, slowly nursing them as he started to realize that they wouldn't erase the pain. Some woman tried to draw him into conversation, but as he ignored her she went back to her table miffed. A man sitting nearby came over and gave out to him. Danny turned and looked at him saying nothing. Something in his eyes must have worried the man, for he scurried back to his table.

Outside the pub he was lucky to catch a cruising black taxi and had the driver drop him off in Croydon at his flat. He tensed, coming up to the entrance to his building, when a car door opened and someone got out. It was Jacky.

"Oh Danny, I just heard what happened. Jack contacted me. I'm so sorry. Just thought I'd pop down and see how you were."

He gave her a long hug, overcome by the day and her concern for him.

They went inside together and Jacky got busy brewing up a cup of tea which she knew he liked from their recent travels together. They caught a late news bulletin that mentioned the death of three terrorists near Hyde Park. She pointed to the screen as the bulletin ended.

"Jack gave me the heads up on the story so I'm not here to pump you. He said to tell you that your name won't be in the police press statement tomorrow. They'll limit it strictly to police involvement. When the enquiry comes up you'll have to appear, but MI5 will ask for a closed hearing on the grounds of national security so you'll still be okay."

He was finally starting to come round and respond.

"Strange really. In the Service I killed a number of people face to face. No problem to me. That's what the job was about at times. Even the episode in Southampton didn't get under my skin. They deserved killing as far as I was concerned, but somehow today was different. I didn't know any of those people. I was suddenly confronted with them and I was protecting my daughter, Jamila, and of course myself. Now all three terrorists are dead, in a way thanks to me and my reactions. My ex wife swears she's going to prevent me from seeing Allison again and Jamila blames me for her brother's death. Shit, what a day Jacky!"

She sat closer to him, turning off the TV.

"Danny, I think blaming yourself is a bit daft really. Those three terrorists made a decision to come here and were after Jamila. They would have caught up with her sooner or later. She's lucky you were there today or it would have had a different ending. You only fired in self-defense and killed one of them, and it wasn't even your own weapon! As far as the other two were concerned, one was accidentally shot by his Taliban colleague and the other chose to take his own life. He probably chose that over going to prison here in the U.K. If he's been fighting with the Taliban since he was fifteen, as Jack said he was, then he's lucky he lasted so long."

He sighed, sitting up straighter, and threw his arm around her.

"You're not a journalist for nothing Jacky. You have a way with words girl. The first time I saw you in the Fox and Hounds I thought to myself, there's something about her, and you know what? I was dead right."

She laughed.

"Funny, but I said the same thing about you."

She leaned further into him.

"Would you like me to stay the night Danny?" she whispered.

He grinned.

"I thought you'd never ask," he teased

With that he took her hand and lead her off in the direction of his bedroom.

Some days are not all bad.

CHAPTER 45.

Two days later he was flying into Pearson Airport in Toronto, Canada. He had talked the DG into allowing him to use the Canadian passport that Sophia had brought down to him in Chepstow. She had also given him an added package of credit cards, Canadian drivers license and an Ontario health card, all in the name of Brad Kincaid, a resident of Kingston, Ontario. She had emphasized that in no way could it be construed that he had the backing of MI5, as the organization had no responsibility outside the U.K. It was MI6 who carried the can for any international operations. It was not even an 'under the radar' operation and in no way could she intervene if he ran into difficulty with the authorities. In other words he was totally on his own.

She did, however, make a call to a contact at the CIA in Langley to try to discover the whereabouts of one of their agents, a Dianna Rayburn, who had completed the marine snipers course with him some five years previously. Her contact came back later in the day to inform her that Dianna Rayburn was no longer with the agency and lived on a small hobby farm in the southern part of New York State, near Erie in Pennsylvania.

The address and phone number were also supplied.

Before leaving the U.K. Danny contacted Major Wainwright at Hereford and asked him to play mum, or claim a loss of memory on the GPS position of the nuclear weapon that he'd hidden in the dry well in Iraq. He explained why and the Major went along with it.

He complimented Danny on the precision of the Southampton job and that there appeared to be no fallout from the action.

Danny was mentally bracing himself for the next stage of the operation - to bring to justice the remaining members of General

O'Donnell's crew, the Empire Security personnel from Buffalo, New York State. They were the people who had been waiting in the Iraqi desert to take possession of the nuclear weapon. It was obvious they had planned to eliminate the SAS team on delivery and probably issued a contract on them when the trip was aborted. He had gone over the descriptions of those men again with Major Wainwright and stored the information away in his head.

Now it was payback time.

Landing in Canada with a Canadian passport posed no problems, however the massive number of new arrivals going through emigration slowed him down considerably. It was two hours before he was out on the highway in a rental car, heading for the U.S. border. Due to the lateness of the hour he decided to get off the QEW highway at Niagara Falls and book into a hotel for the night. He had never visited the Falls before and spent an hour viewing the incredible mass of water cascading down. Even at that late hour the place was still full of tourists, mainly Japanese with their cameras buzzing, and everyone appeared to be having an enjoyable time. Twice he was asked to take the picture of couples with the Falls as a background, and had smilingly obliged.

After a while he spotted a KEG steakhouse and had what he considered to be one of the best steaks of his life, chased down with a pint of Canadian beer. Feeling much more relaxed he returned to the hotel and, even though it was late, he decided to try and connect Dianna Rayburn, south of the border.

The phone was picked up almost immediately.

"Hello".

"Is that Dianna?" he asked.

"Yes it is. Who's this? Her voice sounded cautious.

"Danny Quigley. I don't know if you remember, we met up on the marine sniper's course about five years ago."

There was a moment's hesitation, then

"Yes of course, the Brit from the SAS. We had a few good chats together. I remember you were supportive of having a woman on the course. That was more than I could say for some of the other macho types who thought a woman had no place being there. Where are you calling from Danny?"

"I'm in Niagara Falls right now on the Canadian side, heading over the border in the morning, and was hoping to drop in on you if possible."

Again the hesitation.

"Danny, is this a business call or just pleasure? If it's business, you should know that I've left the agency some time ago."

"Yes, I know that Dianna. We did contact Langley and were informed that you'd left. In fact they provided me with your contact details. It is business however. I just wanted you to mark my cards in a couple of areas."

"Well, how about that! They rarely give out information about ex agents. You must have some real heavyweight friends Danny. I picked it up when you said 'we did contact Langley'."

Danny mentally cursed the slip, especially having been warned about dropping MI5 into any of his enquiries. He laughed out loud.

"Still as sharp as a tack Dianna. You haven't lost a thing. Can I take it that you'll allow me to drop in on you? I can fill you in later. I trust your husband won't mind."

She laughed, and Danny picked up a slightly cynical tone in her voice.

"You don't have to worry about that Danny! We divorced some three years ago. My son Kieran who is sixteen, is man of the house now, and he certainly won't object. He'd love to meet someone like you, especially right now. Sure, feel free to drop in, and while you have the address I'd better give you some specific directions or you'll never find us. It's a small farm out in the boondocks."

The call finished a moment later. He wondered what Dianna had meant when she referred to her son Kieran, saying that he wouldn't object, especially right now.

CHAPTER 46.

Kieran knew he was in trouble again when he exited the school gate wheeling his bicycle. Billy Joe McGlebe and four of his cronies were waiting for him or anyone else who wandered out after the mothers had departed with their kids in their vehicles. Billy was a meaty seventeen year old who had been kept back a class and didn't like being in the same room as Kieran, who made him feel inadequate. Kieran had been roughed up before and pushed around but nothing that resulted in more than a few bruises and torn exercise books. His mother had noticed the bruises and eventually dug out from him that he was being bullied at the high school. She had visited the school the next day and gave out to the principal who insisted that they didn't really have a bullying problem.

Word got around that Kieran had complained and the taunting got even worse. There was something different though about the group waiting for him today. There was a silence that he found disquieting, and Billy Joe's eyes were gleaming as if in anticipation. They crowded around him and Billy Joe grabbed the bike, throwing it to the ground, driving his boot through the spokes and buckling the wheel. He looked up at Kieran.

"Snitching to the principal were we? I'll teach you to try to get me in trouble."

With that he punched Kieran in the face who staggered backwards, but was held by the other cronies. The boy tore himself out of their grasp and launched himself at Billy Joe catching him on the lip with a blow that made him cry out in pain. The bully rubbed his mouth, and when he saw blood on his hand his face flushed with rage and launched himself at Kieran who was again being held firmly. Billy Joe started flailing at him with both fists until he slipped to the ground, partly unconscious. At that point they all started kicking him.

Fortunately one of the female teachers was coming through the gate and on seeing what was happening, started shouting at the group. Billy Joe and his cronies looked up startled at the interruption and quickly dispersed in all directions.

The teacher knelt down and helped Kieran sit up. There was blood streaming from a cut lip and he was dazed and disorientated from the assault. The teacher took some tissues out of her handbag and started dabbing his face. She was shaking her head.

"Are you fit to stand up Kieran? I told the principal to get rid of Billy Joe before someone got hurt. All the teachers were told yesterday morning to keep a sharp look-out for bullying and his name was mentioned, but this is not just bullying, this is a pure assault on you. If I hadn't come out then, who knows how badly injured you could have been."

She helped him to his feet, glancing at his smashed bicycle.

"God, this is serious stuff Kieran. I'm going to call the police right now and have those bullies picked up."

He suddenly seemed to recover, his face showing fear.

"Please no! Don't call the police. They can't do anything to Billy Joe because of his age. They'll just slap his wrist and he'll be back at school tomorrow and my life will be hell Miss Jones. I'll be okay, really I will" he insisted, clutching her arm.

The teacher stared at him undecided, then sighed.

"Okay Kieran, but I'm driving you home and your mother can take it from there. We can get your bike in my pick-up and take that back too. I'm certainly going to make a report to the principal in the morning, whatever happens. The next boy they attack might not have a teacher interrupt them and who knows where that could end up. Come on lets get you home."

CHAPTER 47.

In the morning, Danny decided to take advantage of being in Niagara by taking the incredible Maid of the Mist trip up under the Falls itself. Then he bought a ticket for The Journey Behind the Falls. Afterwards he came out and crossed the road to a restaurant where he had parked his rental car. After lunch he started heading down the QEW towards Fort Erie just before the U.S. border. It looked directly across a short section of the Niagara River, at downtown Buffalo in America.

On reaching Fort Erie, still in Canada, he drove down to the Niagara Boulevard, parked alongside the river, in one of the many small viewing areas and started making enquiries about hiring a boat. The man he spoke to referred him to someone who rented out boats at a small marina a few hundred yards away for fishing trips. He had to produce his Brad Kincaid identity and leave a hefty deposit, but managed to arrange for a craft to be waiting upon receipt of a phone call from him. Satisfied, he headed back onto the clearly marked bridge to the U.S.A.

He was stuck in a stream of traffic going over the bridge, as the cars slowly inched up to the border patrol huts. Eventually he had just one car in front of him and watched as the female border patrol agent reached across and took the driver's documents and a brief conversation with him. Then she came out and went around to the open trunk of the car. She poked around inside opening some bags before slamming it shut, returning the keys to the driver and waving him away.

The green light showed so Danny eased forward until he was opposite the hut and handed across his new Canadian passport. The woman was youthful, alert, and looked trim in her uniform. She ran the edge of his passport through a machine in front of her and stared at the screen for a moment. He tensed slightly, noticing the short pistol in her holster.

He smiled at her, appreciation for her figure showing in his gaze. She didn't return the smile.

"Where are you going, sir?" she asked briskly.

"I'm visiting a friend in the southwestern part of New York State. It's close to Erie, Pennsylvania I understand" he answered.

"When are you coming back?"

"Probably in four or five days."

"Are you taking anything into the country that you need to declare?"

"No, nothing officer."

Her eyes roved over the car before coming back to him. She returned his passport.

"Enjoy your trip sir."

There was a hint of a smile in her eyes as she said it.

"Thank you officer." He felt a sense of relief as he put the car into gear and drove into the United States.

He got straight onto 90 West, collected a toll ticket after a few miles and drove for over an hour before exiting at Fredonia for a break and something to eat. He wandered around his first American Wal-Mart store, amazed at the variety of items they stocked, before going up the street to a Tim Horton's coffee shop where he ordered a BLT sandwich. He had encountered the chain in Canada and had been enormously impressed with their friendliness and efficiency. He was told that they were a Canadian franchise, starting to make headway in the U.S.

Sitting there he was amazed at how many of the occupants were seniors who were enjoying the laughter and repartee between the various small groups. Was there a new sense of spirit now that George W. Bush was gone? His British accent always raised a friendly smile. After all the Brits had backed their war in Iraq and Afghanistan, and shed blood with them on the battlefield. He finished his sandwich and coffee and got back onto 90 West, collecting another toll ticket. It was now late afternoon.

He was amazed how quickly he passed through the State and exited prior to hitting the Pennsylvania border. Despite the directions he still got lost and had to stop and ask the way a number of times.

Eventually he found the farm and walked straight into a family crisis. Kieran had just been brought home by the teacher. A police patrol car was standing outside. His timing could not have been worse.

When he knocked on the front screen door it was eventually opened by a smiling, dark haired young woman whose features vaguely reminded him of Dianna. She had long silky hair and gazed at him with interest.

"I'm…. ah" he thought quickly. "I'm a friend of Dianna…. is she here?" he asked, reaching out and shaking her hand.

The woman held onto it and pointed to her throat with the other. A small sound came from her as she attempted to say something. At that moment the door was opened wider and Dianna pushed her way through.

"Ah Danny, you came at a bad time. Kieran's been beaten up at school. The principal decided to call in the police. You met my younger sister I see. She looks happy to see you but unfortunately she can't speak."

Danny reached forward and gave her a hug, and as he did so he whispered.

"I'm Brad Kincaid if the cops ask, Brad Kincaid" he repeated before stepping back.

She looked startled for a moment and stared at him closely. Then she nodded.

"Brad Kincaid………"

Turning to her sister.

"Meet Jennifer, Jennifer meet, ah… Brad Kincaid. Now let's go inside."

They went straight into a large lounge with a kitchen at the other end. Two policemen were standing over a young man who he assumed was her son Kieran, but they appeared to be arguing with him.

Danny overheard the end of a sentence spoken by one of the policemen.

"…….. and we can put a stop to him."

Kieran, whose face showed bruising and who had some streaks of dried blood on his T-shirt, spoke fiercely back to the policeman.

"Parents have complained before. You people have been involved before, but he just ends up back in school. He boasts that the courts can't touch him 'cos he's under age. If I give you a statement now I just get a worse beating next time. Forget the statement. I'm not giving one."

The policeman, a lean leathery individual over six foot tall turned to Dianna.

"Can't you do something Dianna? Kieran's right in one way, juvenile court holds no fear for these young thugs." He pointed to Kieran, "but this is different. I mean this is a serious assault and we aren't going to let it lie. We'll charge him ourselves if we have to but Kieran's statement would make a big difference. We already have one from that teacher Miss Jones. We're going straight round to that young thug's father Puck McGlebe when we leave here."

Dianna laughed sarcastically.

"A lot of good that'll do Tim. Billy Joe's dad is a bigger thug than he is! Guess who taught the little punk?"

The policeman scratched his chin.

"They're a bad lot for sure, and it's got worse since McGlebe's wife ran off two years ago with that preacher. Billy Joe probably never had a chance and I hate to say it, but his future already looks like he's going to spend a lot of time in one prison or another."

Dianna pushed past him and sat down beside Kieran, putting her arm around him. She looked up at the policeman.

"Don't expect me to feel sorry for Billy Joe. As far as I'm concerned the sooner he ends up in jail the better."

She pointed to Danny.

"Oh this is…. ah…. Brad Kincaid, an old friend who just dropped by."

Tim looked at him keenly. From the possessive look he'd given Dianna before, Danny wondered if they had something going between them.

"Are you with the company too Mr. Kincaid?" the policeman asked.

"The company?" Danny queried, looking puzzled.

"The CIA, where Dianna used to work. We all know of her background. She does some police profiling for a number of the law enforcement agencies around here and as far over as Detroit. You look too fit to be sitting behind a desk."

"I'm afraid not officer. I just run my own financial planning business up in Canada" he smiled wryly. "I wish my life was a bit more exciting at times."

"What's with the British accent? I thought Canadians talked very much like us Americans?"

Danny smiled easily.

"Well, when I became a Canadian citizen there were twenty five different nationalities in the room. It's a real melting pot up there just like the U.S. was at one time. They still swear allegiance to the Queen, so lots of Brits emigrate over there."

Tim exchanged a glance with his colleague, a short blocky man with the look of an ex-soldier about him. Then he gestured to Dianna.

"At least get Kieran examined by a doctor and get some photos of those injuries in case it does end up in court. Useful if you decide to charge Puck McGlebe himself for damages. Might just stop him if he gets hit in his pocket book."

Danny frowned.

"Why do they call him Puck?" he asked.

"He used to be an ice hockey star before he got banned for breaking someone's teeth with a hockey stick. Played up in Canada quite a bit" Tim answered.

Not a lot more was said and they left shortly afterwards. They both cast a lingering glance at Danny as they went out the door.

Danny cursed his timing. Also most Canadians, even new citizens, would have made the connection between a puck and ice hockey. The last thing he wanted was coming to the attention of the police right then.

In the police car, Tim glanced at his colleague.

"Financial planner my ass! Did you see how he moved?"

"Yeah, military or ex-military for sure. I should know. I spent ten years wearing the uniform. I'll tell you something else Tim, he's no ordinary soldier either."

"Hmm…. this gets interesting for sure. For a Canadian he didn't pick up on the hockey puck connection either. They're passionate up there about the sport. Even as a new citizen you'd expect him to know that. Wouldn't do any harm to keep an eye on this Brad Kincaid. We have an excuse now to drop in again with young Kieran's assault. Let's go see this bastard McGlebe. I'd love an excuse to thump him."

CHAPTER 48.

Things fell back into some sort of routine after the police left. Dianna took Kieran down to a nearby health clinic for examination and Danny accompanied Jennifer as she went out to the barn to bring in a small herd of twenty-five sheep and goats waiting at the gates in two nearby pastures. He could see that the stalls were already spread with fresh straw and the water buckets topped up. Before the animals were allowed in, a small portion of grain had to be scooped out of two different sacks and deposited in their individual bowls in the stalls. He watched her quietly and efficiently measuring out the grain and quickly fell into the routine with her. She smiled with pleasure at his efforts and seemed to enjoy his involvement.

Jennifer took him by the arm and pulled him off to one side, indicating that he should stand there. Then she went outside and opened the first gate as the sheep came dashing in, heading for their stalls. There were four separate stalls and the sheep appeared to know which one was theirs as they rushed in and buried their heads in the bowls of grain. Jennifer followed, shutting the stall doors behind them, and stood watching as they fed.

Walking across to the other side, she opened the doors into a set of empty stalls, which Danny then assumed were for the goats.

Without being prompted, he moved out of the way for what he assumed was their entry. They bleated impatiently as she hurried out to the second gate and stood aside to avoid being knocked over as the goats, led by a solid horned ram, stormed through and started feeding on the grain. She dashed after them, going into the stall with the ram and pulling the door shut behind her. She caught the big animal, pulling it away from a smaller ram's feeding bowl. Danny could see that Jennifer was struggling and quickly opening the stall gate, hopped inside, grabbed the ram by the horns and helped her move it steadily across to it's own bowl where it started eating. Jennifer smiled across at him in acknowledgment. A couple of times the big ram attempted to go back to the younger one's bowl but Jennifer just nudged it back with her knees and some hard shoves. At one point she pushed too hard, started losing her balance and Danny grabbed her just in time. For a moment he felt an incredibly muscled body pressed against his, before helping her back on her feet to resume her watchful stance.

She stood there until the smaller ram had licked it's bowl clean and was starting to munch some hay from a wire mesh contraption attached to the wall, then indicated to Danny to vacate the stall. Once outside she secured the gate, then turned to Danny with a huge grin on her face and gave him a hug. He returned it automatically and wished he could have spoken to her about the animal routine he'd just witnessed. As most people would do, he found himself making faces at her and giving her a high five when the stalls were all secured. Then the barn was secured for the night and the lights turned off. They finished up feeding the cats in another section of the building.

Danny yawned and stretched enjoying the fresh country air and the complete change of routine. They headed back to the main house just as Dianna arrived in the driveway with Kieran. Danny opened the door for her.

"What's the verdict on Kieran?" he asked, as they started walking inside. Jennifer had gone to the other side of the car and was reaching to help Kieran out. He shrugged her hand off and headed into the house on his own.

As the two women scurried around preparing supper, Danny who was never great with teenagers, made an effort to converse with Kieran. What he did find difficult was trying to hold a conversation with him when he insisted on watching some soap on the television. Despite this Danny got the impression that he was a highly intelligent and sensitive young man and hoped to eventually become a vet.

When the soap finished, he turned off the TV and Danny queried him about the details of the assault. Kieran was reluctant at first but gradually opened up and seemed relieved to go over the beating he'd taken at school.

Danny was impressed that he'd struck back at the bully despite being restrained by his cronies, and told him so. Kieran relaxed after that and looked across at Danny.

"On the run back from the clinic, Mum said you used to be a soldier Brad. Did you ever kill anyone?" he asked, sitting forward.

Danny groaned inwardly. His efforts to take on a new identity were leaking badly. Already the local police were showing an interest in him and now his background as a soldier was coming out. Kieran would probably be boasting about it to his school buddies before the week was out. He actually was a financial planner now but that wouldn't help him if the authorities hauled him in and fingerprinted him. He had no doubt that the Americans had possession of the fingerprints of all the British Forces by that time. Tony Blair had given away everything but the Royal Family before he left office.

He was saved having to answer Kieran when Dianna stuck her head in the lounge and called them to supper. Despite Jennifer's inability to talk, and Kieran's recent ordeal, the meal proceeded smoothly and Danny felt accepted by the family.

Kieran and Jennifer took their desserts and dashed back into the lounge to watch American Idol, leaving Dianna and Danny alone. She took out a cigarette and nodding to him, headed for the back door, where she sat on the steps and lit up. Dianna was probably nudging forty but looked ten years younger. Her fine sculpted face was alert and watchful as she scrutinized him while she took a long pull on her cigarette.

"Okay Danny what gives, and I don't want any bullshit. I'm not in the company any more so I won't be talking to anyone in Langley."

He recognized that he would have to completely bring her into the picture. If Dianna discovered at a later date that he had misinformed her about some of the issues, he knew she would make a bad enemy, so he told her the whole story. It took the best part of an hour and she asked a number of questions. Finally he fell silent.

She lit up another cigarette. Blowing some smoke at him she grunted

"You just made me break my rule. I'd cut down to one a day, but what a day! Kieran gets beaten up and you turn up here with a story out of Robert Ludlum, and you know what? I believe all of it. Shit! What's this government coming to?"

She looked warily at him.

"Why are you over here now Danny?"

"I'm going to hit the Empire Security people in Buffalo, which co-incidentally is just a couple of hours up the road. In particular I'm interested in some of their people who were waiting in Iraq to take possession of the nuke - a General O'Donnell and a Tom Bradley."

"What do you intend to do with them?"

She squinted at him over a halo of smoke as she asked.

"They're involved in the deaths of two troopers in the U.K. I suspect they sanctioned the hits and would have wiped out the whole troop if I hadn't got involved. They're history Dianna, when I catch up with them."

She looked at him thoughtfully.

"Two things Danny. Leave it to the authorities to sort out. The justice system here in the U.S. will absolutely marmalise you if they discover that you were involved, even in a small way, in anything like this. The powers that the police and intelligence people now have since 9/11 are just plain scary. You could literally disappear off the street and no one would ever know what happened to you. They can do anything they want to you once they've incarcerated you. You've read about the water boarding, now banned by Obama of course, but that's just a symptom of a whole change in culture among police and the intelligence services. I hate to say it, but we're now worse than the bad guys I used to chase at one time with such fervor."

"And the second thing Dianna?" he asked.

"What do you want from me Danny?" She waved around her. "You can see my situation here. I have a sixteen year old in school. I'm supporting my younger sister. I run a small hobby farm, which doesn't bring in any income and I've built up some contacts as a profiler with some regional police forces. Why should I put all that at risk? Plus the cops are already sniffing around you."

He looked away, regretting the impulse to involve her.

"I wanted to get information on the London CIA chap Sinclair who just escaped us in Southampton. Is he back here now? What backing does he have? Is he just a rogue agent who got involved with the Israelis? What's his connection to General O'Donnell and the people at Empire Security?"

She blew out her breath noisily.

"Oh man, you're out of your depth Danny! Have you any idea of the flags that would go up at Langley on a number of fronts if I tried to gather information like that? I really don't know if I even have any contacts there any more after five years. They keep an eye on retired agents to make sure they're not getting back in the game, especially with some new player. Hell, with one phone call they could screw up my work as a profiler in the area. All they have to do is play the national security card and I'm persona non grata."

She reached forward and shook him by the shoulder.

"Am I getting through to you Danny?"

He nodded, but realizing that she could no longer see him in the gathering dusk, he replied reluctantly.

"I hear you Dianna and I apologize for my naivety in coming here in the first place. It was stupid of me to try to involve you in this. You certainly do have a huge amount at stake here, what with Kieran, your work connections and Jennifer too. What's wrong with her by the way? She's a delightful person. I really enjoyed working with her and the animals this evening."

"There's absolutely nothing wrong with her apart from the fact that she doesn't speak any more. I said doesn't rather than can't, because she did talk at one time."

"When did she stop speaking? What happened?" he queried.

She stood up, stretching as she answered.

"Our parents had a farm and when Jennifer was six, she witnessed her father accidentally back the tractor over her mother."

"Oh my God, what an experience!" he said shaking his head.

"That wasn't all" she added. "Her father went straight across to the barn and hung himself. She followed after him and saw it all. She hasn't spoken since that day. Oh she did go to college and graduated with some help from special needs, even had a boy friend once. She writes notes to people to communicate with them."

He stood there completely wordless, his mind trying to grapple with the shocking revelation he'd just heard about the sweet girl he'd helped as she did her chores.

Finally he whispered.

"That poor kid, and her only six years old! I just can't imagine it."

She caught his arm.

"Yeah, that's Jennifer's story and unfortunately she probably won't have a normal life as such, a career and so on, and will be dependant on me-unless some sort of miracle happens, but she seems to have taken to you."

She stepped back and cast a keen glance at him.

"Now, I've been thinking. There is one way I can help you but it involves a quid pro quo from you Danny. Let me show you what I'm talking about. Come on, follow me"

She turned and headed off in the direction of the barn. Inside she went over to a large section of hay bales and started climbing up a ladder propped against them. He followed her.

"Hey, you know what," he shouted up at her disappearing back" I fantasized many a time since we met on that snipers course, that I could get you in a hay barn like this all by yourself."

She laughed throatily, not entirely displeased.

"You should be so lucky Danny. But to tell the truth, I thought about you the odd time too, especially since I got divorced."

"Did I pick up that the cop Tim had something going with you?" he asked, still climbing.

"He'd certainly like to think so. He's asked me out a number of times but you know, getting involved would just complicate things right now. I don't have the time, or to be honest, the inclination to invite some male into my life. Oh at times like today with Kieran's situation, it would be nice to have a man around. But I haven't any plans to make changes at present, whatever Tim might like."

On reaching the top Dianna proceeded in a straight line to a wooden wall at the far end where she heaved some bales away revealing a door with a large padlock on it. Reaching up to a large beam she extracted a key from over the top and unlocked the door.

It revealed a small room, stacked wall to wall with weapons of all descriptions - C4 explosives and timers, hand grenades and an M 60 machine gun. He even spotted some air-to-air shoulder-fired missiles and stacks of ammunition. Danny gasped and stepped back, staring at her in amazement.

"You talk to me about keeping my nose clean around here, while you have enough weapons hidden away to start a revolution! What on earth for Dianna?"

She shrugged.

"We're not far off a real crisis here in the U.S. I believe a civil war is coming Danny, even with Obama in power, or perhaps because he's in power" she said fiercely. "Rebellion is very close to the surface in the American psyche and our democratic system is just not working anymore. CNN says it's broken, and they're probably not far wrong. Look at the hatred and bitterness around the country. This country will explode soon. The have-nots will just take whatever they want from those who have. The men with the guns will emerge and there's lots of those around. It'll be survival of the fittest Danny and no quarter given. The government will be unable to restore order. Look at Katrina still wallowing in water after all this time."

Danny was startled. There was nothing spoken for some time. Then he sighed and looked back in the armory.

"You can't live on weapons Dianna. What about food and water and all the other things you're going to need if the balloon goes up?"

"I've thought about those too Danny. Even you are not going to be told the location of our food supply. The animals of course, are the first line of defense food-wise but they would disappear overnight without the weapons to protect them. Now do you want to know the quid pro quo for the use of this cache of firearms?"

"I can't imagine what it is you want but I'm dying to hear."

She took a deep breath.

"Kieran has a sick note for the next three days. I want you to put your mission on hold and teach him how to defend himself. That's all. Can you do that Danny?"

His jaw dropped.

"In three days! My God girl, you're not asking for much are you?"

She pointed inside the room.

"Your decision Danny. Now let's head back in or the others will be wondering if you really did have your way with me up in the hay loft. Kieran's no slouch in those matters and I keep forgetting to call you Brad."

CHAPTER 49.

Dianna headed off early for a trip to Rochester in New York State and planned to return later in the day.

Danny had a new task - to help Kieran learn how to defend himself, and he had to do it in three days! Danny recalled the weeks and months of training he'd had himself, first in the parachute regiment and after an incredibly tough selection process, in the SAS.

His passion for martial arts started when he was thirteen with his introduction to judo. Some young men had a passion for football or golf but he'd lived and breathed martial arts. His training in the SAS had moved him to a much higher level, but despite that he'd continued to study various other forms of combat when the opportunity presented itself. He had outgrown the local clubs in Hereford, the home base of the 22 SAS Regiment, and traveled on weekends around the U.K. and Europe to further his knowledge, when he was not on standby for a Government Sabre team.

He was part of an SAS team that had trained Special Forces in two South American countries, the Netherlands and the Ukraine in unarmed combat.

The problem with Kieran was that he was a sixteen-year-old youth, whereas Danny's previous training projects had been with tough, highly-trained police and military personnel.

Still he needed access to that cache of weapons.

After breakfast, Danny washed up the dishes then explained to Kieran that he wanted to take him out to a particular type of sports store in the city of Erie to purchase some special equipment. Kieran looked excited at the prospect. Jennifer had been listening and dashed over to the table, scribbled a quick note and handed it to him.

'Can I come with you?' she'd written.

"What about the animals?" he asked.

Kieran answered for her.

"They're outside already. She just has to top up the water buckets after lunch."

Danny smiled at her.

"Sure, let's go then."

They all went outside, piled into the Nissan rental car and headed off for the city.

It wasn't as easy as he'd first thought. There were lots of sports shops that sold runners and equipment for all sorts of activities. He did make a purchase of some soccer boots at one of them for Kieran. However they had to make six stops before they found what Danny was really looking for - fighting gear for martial arts. He was just going to purchase protection gear for himself and Kieran but was surprised at how interested and involved Jennifer became as they browsed through the store. On impulse he bought a kit for her as well, taking the time to make sure the various pieces of gear fit her. Her face light up and her eyes danced as she looked at both of them as if reassuring herself. Kieran patted her shoulder.

"Hey, the man said he's getting you the gear Aunt Jennifer. Take it before he changes his mind."

He was scooping up his own as he spoke, heading for the cashier. A delighted Jennifer followed him. Danny paid in cash and carried everything out to the car. Rather than heading back Danny looked around the small strip mall.

"Kieran, anywhere around here we can have a coffee and a snack?" he asked.

The young boy knew just the place. His idea of a snack was a burger piled high with everything possible. Jennifer and Danny settled for a Danish and a coffee each. Kieran was two bites into his burger when Danny settled back, coffee in hand and looked across at them.

"Kieran, your training starts here. I only have three days to get you to a point where you can handle yourself in situations where you need to react fast and defend yourself. Three days is a very short time to attempt this, so I have to select those moves and defense tactics that you can take on board and use smoothly and automatically. Make sense?"

"Absolutely." Kieran answered, his burger forgotten for a moment.

"Are you going to teach me to kill people?" he asked eagerly.

"Afraid not Kieran. This is not a situation where you have to kill people. They lock you up for that and anyway, you should always only use as much force as is deemed necessary in any threatening situation. Never pick a fight. Never show off what you're going to learn over the next few days. Difficult for a young fellow brought up on Superman and Spiderman, I know. Keep the knowledge to yourself and use it only to look out for yourself, your friends and especially your family. When you decide to use it, do so explosively. Don't talk about it, just do it, understood?"

He nodded, his eyes wide as he picked up the serious tone in Danny's voice. Jennifer tapped his arm and indicated that she wanted to write something. She dashed over to the counter, grabbed a pen, came back and wrote. She pushed it across to him.

'Can I do it too please?' she'd written.

Danny blinked uncertainly.

He'd bought her some kit thinking that perhaps she could wear the protective gear to help Kieran throw some punches when he had to step to one side and direct him. He hadn't actually considered training her as well. There was also the time factor. He had to get Kieran up to speed in a hurry. Time spent correcting Jennifer would slow the process down.

Kieran nodded across at him.

"Okay by me Brad. She's fit, man! Should see her out on a bike on the roughest trails."

He looked across at her face rapt with anticipation. Shit, he thought, what the hell am I doing here? I'm supposed to be bringing down some bad guys and I've got myself involved in teaching a sixteen year old how to fight and now his aunt wants to join in too. God! He threw his hands up helplessly.

"What the hell! In for a penny, in for a pound" he answered finally.

"What does that mean Brad?" Kieran asked.

"It means yes, you dummy."

He suddenly realized what he had just said and reached contritely across and caught Jennifer's hand.

"Gosh Jennifer I'm sorry. I didn't even think" he said making a face.

She scribbled another note and pushed it across.

'I forgive you. I got it all the time in college. No one meant any harm.'

Danny expelled a breath, glad to be off the hook and finally leaned forward and placed his empty cup down.

"Okay, you're both in but don't tell Dianna. She'll kill me for sure. Now here's some good news and some bad news. The human body has a huge amount of vulnerable points where people can be hurt or disabled. That's the bad news. The good news is that it's pretty easy to learn how to protect those points, once you learn the correct stance and blocks. I can teach you how to strike an opponent's vulnerable areas and cause enough sharp pain to stop them in their tracks. Most fights are finished in under twenty seconds. Someone gets hit on the bridge of the nose and it starts streaming blood - end of fight. You deliver a sharp kick to the shin bone which inflicts terrible pain - end of fight. You poke someone in the stomach with your knuckle and they double over in agony - end of fight. From experience I've found that bullies quit fast when they feel pain, and especially when their victim starts fighting back."

Kieran jumped in.

"Yeah, I caught Billy Joe on the nose and I reckon I could have had a chance with him if the others hadn't grabbed me. How can I handle that Brad when his buddies all crowd round and pin me?"

Danny patted his arm and noticed that the burger had disappeared. Throwing some money on the table he stood up.

"All in good time Kieran. Now you two, let's get back and start training."

He started with blocks. Both were kitted out and they had cleared a large section of the lounge. He focused on the fundamentals at first, using the correct balanced stance and holding the elbows and hands up to protect the upper body and face. He kept moving around Kieran throwing mock but easy blows at him until he started looking comfortable with it. He had to stop him at one point.

"Kieran, the one thing you always do is to watch your opponent's eyes. Always maintain eye contact. I notice you tend to drop your eyes when I go to strike you, or try to look at where my hands are. A lot of people do that but it's the eyes that tell you when your enemy is going to go for you. Okay?"

Kieran nodded, standing there breathless and glad of the break.

"Yeah, got it. This is great Brad! I'm already beginning to see how I can stop someone from landing me one."

"Good man Kieran. Now let's get Jennifer out here."

She was a surprise for him. He wasn't expecting her to have such a quick grasp of what he'd been demonstrating to Kieran but the solid use of her hands and elbows showed that she had a natural talent. He upped the ante with her and pushed her harder, but she responded and fought back. He stepped back for a break. Kieran shouted excitedly from the side.

"Isn't Aunt Jennifer something else Brad?"

"You better believe it Kieran! Hey, she's a natural for sure."

She could see that he meant it and grinned happily. He then had them work with each other and stepped in occasionally to demonstrate a move. After a while he showed them how to use their feet and legs to block kicks and how effective the edge of the shoe was on the attacker's shin bone.

It was lunch-time by then and they stopped.

Jennifer raced outside to take care of the animals and Kieran prepared a sandwich and on Danny's request, a pot of tea. A while later Jennifer came back and they all sat down for lunch. The tea was terrible but Danny didn't say anything. He was busy answering questions from Kieran who was anxious to get going again. Even Jennifer scribbled a number of queries she had about self-defense. Most of those he knew would be covered over the next couple of days, but he was delighted with their interest and responded with equal enthusiasm.

He started the afternoon demonstrating how to punch with the fist while still protecting their vulnerable areas. He had them move back and forth together as they worked through the exercises. Then he donned some protective gear himself and faced off with both of them in turn.

It was block, block and strike. Block, block and strike. Then block, block, block and strike. Round and round until they were doing it automatically. He pushed them harder, tapping them in the face and stomach lightly when they dropped their guard. Finally he stopped as they were both breathless and obviously wilting.

He sent Kieran to bring a flip chart and stand that Dianna sometimes used in presentations for her work. Jennifer went to the fridge for a jug of juice and three glasses. Danny had a quick drink before positioning the chart directly in front of them, and picked up a flip chart pen. Quickly he drew a picture of the human form and turned to them.

"Everyone okay? Ready to go on? Any questions so far?" he enquired.

He was pleased that neither had any and proceeded.

"Okay, excellent! You're both doing fantastic and we're making great progress. Much better than I anticipated. Having Jennifer involved is actually moving things along even faster than I imagined, so well done."

He turned to the flip chart.

"I mentioned earlier that the human body has a lot of vulnerable areas. We're going to look at some of them, and it's not possible to attack all these points with the fist alone. It's too broad an instrument to do any harm, so we have to learn to use other strike points so as to disable an attacker. There are points on the body where you can literally kill someone with a blow or a strike, but for this exercise we're only interested in inflicting a limited amount of pain, to halt their attack and withdraw."

Kieran raised his hand. Danny nodded to him.

"Yes, Kieran?"

"What if they don't withdraw? What do you do then?" he asked, his face anxious.

"Good question. You raise the ante and increase the pain."

He looked closely at him.

"Believe me, when someone is on the receiving end of some of the blows I'm going to teach you, you won't find them coming back for more. Remember, it's all about sudden explosive action delivered with power and speed. Forget what you saw in the movies where the good guy stands there and lets someone hit him first. If you think you're just about to cop it in the face, strike first and strike hard."

"But won't you get blamed for starting it then?" Kieran queried.

"Fair comment Kieran. I'd recommend that you risk being the guy standing and getting blamed rather than the one in the right but lying on the ground with a broken jaw. Would you buy that?"

They both nodded.

Danny turned and started marking large X's on different parts of the body, then went over the different ways to strike an opponent: delivering a short snappy punch from the shoulder; how to chop with the side of the hand, using stiff fingers and knuckles to strike vulnerable areas; the devastating effect of an elbow strike to the side of the head; the use of knees and feet to weaken and shock an opponent.

After demonstrating each move he had them practice the strikes and blows themselves, continually stepping in to correct posture and delivery. They found it difficult to attack and still remember to protect themselves at the same time. They were now into using fists, elbows, knees, or the side of the hand, and using the ridged knuckles like a spear on the nose and into the soft stomach areas. He was really pushing them hard.

They had a short break, then went back on the floor.

There was an increased fervor about them now they had other tools to work with. He had to stop them a number of times when they caught a sensitive area or bumped heads as they fought in the small room. Finally he pulled Jennifer out and went against Kieran himself, pushing him hard and stopping him a number of times to correct a stance or an improperly delivered blow.

Then he sat Kieran down and stepped out to work with Jennifer for fifteen minutes. She had obviously benefited from watching them as she came at him with fire in her eyes, throwing punches with all her might. Kieran egged her on from his chair and Danny grinned in appreciation, feeling the sweat break out on his forehead. Finally they stopped and she fell into his arms laughing. Kieran jumped out of his chair and came forward, thumping her on the back.

"Aunt Jennifer, you were like a tiger going after him! I've never seen you like that before. Wow!"

Looking at Danny, "She really pushed you didn't she?"

He nodded in agreement, grinning as Jennifer turned and gave Kieran a high five.

"I wish I'd had an aunt like her back in Wales" he remarked, grabbing a paper kitchen towel and wiping his face. "She sure made me work. I haven't sweated like this since I was in the gym two weeks ago."

They had another short break before he pulled them back again.

"Now it's unlikely Kieran that this situation might happen to you in a school-yard scrap, however I need to warn you, some people use their head with devastating effect. They use it just like they head a soccer ball. They tend to signal what they're going to do by standing in close to you and perhaps even grabbing your jacket by the lapels or collar before slamming their head into you. It's always finished everyone that I've seen being on the receiving end of it. You're finished –a bloody mess, probably with all you're teeth smashed in as well. I have a mate, a buddy that is, in the U.K. who is absolutely deadly at it. He actually hits twice, straight down into the face and then a strike upwards. Game over I can tell you!"

The awe was in his voice as he said this. Kieran raised his hand and Danny nodded to him.

"Yes Kieran?"

"That sounds fierce! What can you do to stop them hitting you?" Kieran asked.

"What can you do? As mentioned they try to set you up for a hit by coming in close, so keep your distance. The other thing is to have your left elbow up as if you were scratching your nose but ready to throw across in front of you as they strike, like this."

He showed them a useful way to have their right arm held across their stomach with the left elbow cupped by the right palm, the fingers of the left hand touching their chin as if in a thoughtful pose. It was actually an incredibly effective way to deflect a sudden punch to the stomach or a deadly head butt. They tried the defensive move where they stood and started getting the hang of it. He halted them for a moment and asked a question.

"Kieran was concerned about the head butt, and I've given you a defense. Now bearing in mind what I've said earlier, what else could you do?" he asked, looking from one to the other.

Kieran stood there, puzzled. Jennifer dashed across to the counter and scribbled something down on a sheet of paper as fast as she could and hurried back to Danny with it. He looked at it and chuckled.

Kieran looked at him.

"What?" he asked irritated.

Danny handed him the piece of paper. Kieran flushed and looked up.

"Of course. Hit them first!" He looked at her. "Aunt Jennifer, you don't miss a trick. It's so obvious. If they're trying to set you up, just go for them first. Okay, got it" he exclaimed, his good humor returning.

With that she looked at the clock and indicated that she had to go out. Danny took advantage of the moment to tell Kieran how to protect himself from a kick in the groin, which would equally disable him. As additional insurance he'd bought Kieran a protective cup worn by athletes, which he suggested he wear when he went back into school, as a precaution. He'd also bought Kieran a pair of soccer boots with hard tough leather toes, so as to deliver a painful kick to the shin bone of any attacker should the need arise. He hadn't gone for metal tipped boots as they could easily do real damage and the weight of them could slow Kieran down. He talked to him about his mental attitude in approaching a fight, being confident, expecting to win, and being absolutely ruthless once it started. Bearing in mind that these were only high school kids, it was still worth remembering that any dangerous or unpredictable assailant you let up off the ground, could pull a knife and finish you off.

With that they ended for the day

An hour later Danny got a phone call from the DG.

Nick Nicholson had disappeared the day after he'd agreed to do an interview with another newspaper in London which had revealed his name. Scotty, ignoring the high security arrangements at the camp had slipped down town for a drink. He barely missed being hit by a car when he came out of the pub, which raced off into the night.

The Israeli's had sent a Kidon, an assassin to the U.K. to avenge Wyborski.

CHAPTER 50.

Dianna returned late that evening, weary from her trip and the days work at Rochester. She remarked on the amazing change in both Kieran and Jennifer who were outside pounding each other in the barn.

"Kieran was down in the dumps last night hardly talking to anyone and now he's bouncing around the place! What on earth did you do to him Danny…. ah Brad?" she exclaimed.

"Oh I just introduced him to some possibilities if he's ever attacked again. Even now he'd be a big surprise to anyone who tries to have a go at him. He's actually taken to it like a duck to water. Could turn out to be an on-going interest for him as a matter of fact."

"Hmm…. and what have you done to my sister then? She's more enthusiastic than I've ever seen her, even when she was throwing the javelin in college and doing her track and field."

She looked skeptically at him.

"That wasn't our agreement was it, turning Jennifer into superwoman?"

"Well no I agree. It just happened that I needed an extra body to bring your son up to speed, and lo and behold she turned out to be a natural. Helped me make great progress with Kieran today."

He scratched his head and remarked.

"Strange in a way. It's almost as if she needed an interest of some type. Like she was almost bored with her routines around the place. She just came alive out there when we were practicing and Kieran loved her being involved too. It sure helped us cover a lot of ground."

She stretched her back, her face creased with fatigue.

"Whatever you say Danny, as long as we achieve the desired result."

She reached down to her brief case on the floor and snapped it open. Taking out an envelope she handed it to him.

"Something for you. Open it" she prompted.

Looking surprised, he did so and took out a series of photos. They were of a specific building he had never seen before, taken from various angles. He threw her a questioning look.

"My route today by-passed Buffalo. It was a short diversion to go down town. They're some shots of the Empire Security Services building in the city. It's right on the water that looks straight across at the Canadian town of Fort Erie, so I couldn't get any shots of that side of their building. Sorry."

He looked at her in amazement.

"Good God Dianna. No wonder you look bushed, doing this photo shoot on top of everything else. That's fantastic!"

He examined the photos closely and as an after thought looked up at her again.

"No chance anyone saw you doing this?" he asked tentatively.

She looked slightly miffed at his question.

"Give me a break Danny. I was doing this stuff in the company for years prior to going into profiling. Don't worry, no one spotted me" she assured him.

He held one of the photos up to the light.

"It's four storeys. Quite an impressive piece of property. Did you by any chance notice if they've rented out any of the floors, or are they occupying the whole building?"

"I did stroll past once, walking beside an older woman and coincidentally on purpose, speaking with her, and looking sideways at her face. As I did so, and I happened to notice that there were no other business plates attached to the front entrance. I'd say it's a safe bet that they occupy the whole building, don't you?"

He smiled.

"I can just see you doing it too. Strolling past and chatting with an old lady. You're a charmer all right Dianna."

He examined the other pictures again.

"This certainly gives me something to go on. Now I have to decide how to proceed from here."

She reached across and gripped his arm.

"Danny these are very capable people with all sorts of resources at their disposal. They're actually in the security business, so that building is probably harder to get into than Fort Knox. You're completely on your own without your SAS troopers, and on strange territory. As I said, one slip up and the police will put you away forever, that is if the Empire people don't nail you first. You only need to be pulled over by a New York police trooper on the way up the highway, 90 East, carrying a load of weapons, and it's curtains for you. Look, why don't you let me slip the word to Langley about their involvement in some black operation in Iraq, and they can get the FBI to start sniffing around?"

He looked at her thoughtfully.

"Thanks Dianna but I'm not forgetting the mission I came over on. You're right on one thing. I need help with this one. How difficult would it be to track down a member of a Delta team, or an ex Delta team member at that? There's someone who still owes me a favor. His name is Rory Hanlon."

She looked at him in astonishment.

"Oh no Danny. No you don't! I'm not chasing up any more of my old contacts for you. Look you're leaving footprints a mile wide on this already for crying out loud! Even the local police are looking sideways at you."

She threw her eyes up to the heavens.

"A financial planner, says he. Some flaming legend is all I can say! You look anything but a financial planner, let me tell you Danny" she finished in disgust.

He raised his hands helplessly.

"But the fact is Dianna, I am a financial planner. Okay, in the U.K. and under a different name, but......."

She stood up, too tired to take it any further.

"Look I'm off to bed and I'd suggest you get your two charges out there in the barn to do the same. They'll be wrecked in the morning."

With that she hauled herself tiredly across the kitchen and headed upstairs. Danny stayed sitting at the table looking at the pictures. He wished like hell that he could just pick up the phone and call in an air strike on the building. Military targets were much simpler.

CHAPTER 51.

They moved to the barn the following day to continue their practice. He was amazed at how fast their reactions had become. Their block, strike, block, strike routines had developed into a fast moving process, and they now needed their protective gear, especially against kicks. He spent another hour building on their techniques and perfecting the hand and foot strikes to be more explosive and precise. Kieran's best blow was in the snappy use of his elbow, which seemed to come naturally to him. The head-gear protected Jennifer a number of times when he slammed the elbow at her jaw. Danny swapped places with her and pushed him harder, showing him how to still keep his vulnerable areas protected while throwing punches and edge-of-the-hand strikes. Finally he stopped and went through the same exercise with Jennifer. She loved the snappy kick to the shin bone followed by an upward knee strike to the face as her opponent hopefully bent forward with the pain of the kick.

They stopped for a break. Then Danny showed them in more detail how to use the side of the foot to block kicks. The idea was to turn slightly sideways as their opponent threw a kick, and snap a side-kick at his shin bone thereby blocking it, and at the same time inflicting an extremely sharp pain. They also worked on an additional blocking technique to counter kicks - snapping down with crossed arms on the kicking leg, causing pain to the attacker's shin-bone. A follow through was to grip the leg as you blocked it and heave upwards, delivering a return kick to their supporting leg or their crotch area.

They discussed the challenge of fighting two or three people who were coming at you at the same time, but that was getting beyond their skill level.

Danny realized that two or three days practice on the basics could not turn them into the type of fighters who could take on multiple attackers. He satisfied himself by showing them how to do a back knuckle strike to the nose of someone coming at them from the side. It was imperative that they maintain eye contact with their primary opponent, and use their peripheral vision to strike their second assailant, ideally to their nose, which caused extreme pain and bleeding. He stopped short of showing them any techniques that could seriously harm an individual, bearing in mind that Kieran would only be involved in a school fight. Hopefully, it wouldn't come to a fight at all, if Billy Joe's father had warned his son about potential police charges for any further assaults.

They continued sparring until Dianna came out and called them to lunch.

When they finished she said she wanted to talk to him before he went back outside again.

Kieran and Jennifer took advantage of that to hurry back to the barn to water the animals and continue their training. As they disappeared Dianna shook her head.

"Those two! I haven't seen such enthusiasm and energy in a long time. They really have taken to this haven't they Danny?"

He nodded.

"Very keen both of them, and really quite good at it already. I have to say I'm very impressed. They've made amazing progress since we started yesterday" he remarked.

"I'm not telling you your job Danny, but I hope you're not teaching Kieran anything really dangerous. I've heard about you SAS people. You have a reputation for not taking any prisoners."

He chuckled.

"Don't worry, you won't have a budding Rambo in the house, or two of them for that matter. I'm just teaching him enough to make him more confident and defend himself if he's called upon to do so. Remember, he could have been seriously hurt at school a few days ago when he ended up getting kicked on the ground. I've warned him to play it cool and not go showing off to other kids or to ever instigate a fight. He's a good kid Dianna and he's got an excellent attitude to what we're doing and why. I wouldn't worry about him if I was you."

She looked relieved.

"Well thank God for that. Now I've been doing some work for you while you were out in the barn this morning. Your friend Rory Hanlon is no longer in the military. He got out two years ago and is working in Detroit."

It wasn't easy to surprise Danny, but his jaw dropped.

"Rory is in Detroit and out of the military? That really shocks me Dianna! I was sure he was a lifer. Hell he loved the military, especially being part of a Delta team!"

He thought for a moment.

"Detroit isn't too far away is it?"

She shrugged.

"Well you could fly out of Buffalo, but I generally drive. You could make it in five hours if you drove straight through, but hadn't you better check with your friend Hanlon first? Things look different I'm sure when you're out of the military. If he's working he can't just swan off on some operation with you. He could be married as well, and that changes things a lot you know, responsibilities and all that"

He looked reflectively at her.

"Now that you mention it, I do recall how different things were for me when I got out. I think I'll call him later on today and I'd have a better chance of talking with him after he finishes work."

"Your choice Danny. If he's in Detroit he may work for the car company and that means shift work. You might just find him at home right now. Oh I've got his home phone number too" she added, passing him a slip of paper.

CHAPTER 52.

The phone rang several times before it was picked up.

"Hello."

The voice sounded dull and listless. Danny didn't think it belonged to his old Delta colleague.

"I'm looking for Rory Hanlon" he said.

There was a moment's silence at the other end.

"This is Rory.... who's that?"

Danny was surprised at the tired-sounding voice and wondered whether he'd just woke him up

"Ah Rory.... it's Danny Quigley. You're old 'Sass' buddy" he answered.

There was a stunned silence at the other end.

"Danny Quigley? Not THE Danny Quigley from Afghanistan?"

The voice sounded incredulous.

Danny laughed.

"The very same, old son. Did I wake you up?" he asked.

"Wake me up? No of course not! Why do you ask?"

"You sound tired. I thought you might have been on the night shift at the car company. Sorry if that's the case."

Rory laughed cynically.

"You're a little behind the times on your information Danny. I got laid off a month ago. The bail out or stimulus money didn't help me! You know, downsizing. The short timers like me were out first. It's no big deal today. Par for the course."

Danny knew from his voice that it was a big deal. He thought for a moment and pressed on.

"Rory I heard you got out of the military and that surprised the hell out of me. I thought you were in for the duration. You know, the old pension and all that."

"Yeah, I thought I was too Danny. However crap happens. My eldest brother was supposed to be looking after my mother but he met some girl and they headed off to the west coast over a year ago after sticking her in some home. A neighbor visited. She found her in an awful state and wrote to me about it. It wasn't possible to arrange anything satisfactory while I was in the Forces so I got out and found a decent home for her, which I have to pay extra for but she's happy there. She's made some friends and the staff are quite caring. I bought a house near her and got a job as civvies do, but now that I've been laid off I can't see how I can manage to keep her on there or pay for the house for that matter."

Danny thought it was a good time to interrupt gently.

"Look Rory, I need to come and see you about something. I need your help. I'm in the U.S. right now over in the Erie direction. I could head over tomorrow if that suited."

"I couldn't help anyone right now the shape I'm in Danny. I've let things go the last few months. Anyway what sort of help are you talking about?"

"Can't say too much on the phone Rory but it could help your situation somewhat. I'll tell you more when I see you. Let me have your current address and directions and I'll head over tomorrow. Look, even if you can't help out, it will still be great to talk to you mate."

The conversation carried on for a couple more minutes and he heard some animation coming into Rory's voice. It was arranged that they would meet the following afternoon.

Dianna was busy in her small study when he finished so he headed back outside to resume the training. Kieran and Jennifer were busy sparring in the barn and he noticed their increased sharpness and speed in carrying out the offensive and defensive moves. He watched them for a while, not interrupting until they both broke away and sat down breathless on the floor in front of him. He nodded approvingly.

"You're both doing absolutely fantastic! I can't believe that we only started this yesterday and now just look at the pair of you! I can tell you this, even I would have to watch myself sparring with either of you right now."

Big grins broke out on their faces.

"Here's the thing. I have to go to Detroit tomorrow, back the following day. I'm going to spend the next few hours showing you some pretty cool wrist-locks and how to break choke holds from a front or back position. I believe that at the end of today Kieran, you'll be one hundred percent ready to handle anything that might come at you in the school. I'd suggest you both spend tomorrow going over and over what you've learned until it's second nature to you. How d'you feel about that?" he asked, appraising them closely.

Kieran sprang to his feet, his face excited.

"Hey that's awesome Danny! I know I'm ready." He pointed to Jennifer. "She can hardly lay a glove on me now!" he shouted, throwing some mock punches at her.

She jumped to her feet and they both started sparring round again. After a couple of minutes he broke them up, laughing at their enthusiasm. They removed the protective gear for the next session on breaking chokeholds and applying wristlocks and basic takedowns. The time flew by and despite the focus on the techniques, Danny found his mind drifting to his meeting with Rory the following day.

He hadn't sounded like the old efficient Delta team member that Danny had once known. He wondered what he would discover when he visited Detroit.

CHAPTER 53.

He left early the next morning and got back on 90 West keeping a close eye on the speed limits. The traffic was moving at a consistent rate and he gradually ate up the miles. He found driving on U.S. highways boring and had to concentrate to stay alert. Three hours later he turned off and stopped for a satisfying American style breakfast at a diner. Then he hit the road again and was on the outskirts of Detroit within two hours. Rory's directions and suggestions for a short cut were invaluable, otherwise he would have been wandering all over the city trying to locate his address. Mentally tired after the trip he finally pulled into the driveway of Rory's home. There was no vehicle in the driveway.

As he was getting out of the car, the door of the house opened and Rory emerged grinning and hurried to meet him. His hair was long and he sported a short beard. While he still looked reasonably fit, he had gained about 20 lbs since Afghanistan, and his eyes had lost their luster. However there was no mistaking his delight in seeing Danny again.

He gave him a massive hug and stood back to look at him.

"My God Danny, you look obscenely fit buddy! Still in the 'Sass'?"

"No, got out nearly two years ago. Working in financial services in the U.K. now."

Rory looked at him askance.

"Financial services? Come on, pull the other one Danny! " he snorted.

"Well Rory, you look like one of those Peaceniks in the 60s, out protesting the war. Anyway I'm not here to throw rocks mate."

Rory thumped him on the shoulder.

"Let's go inside, shall we? "I haven't forgotten that I owe you one from our one and only mission together."

Danny slapped him on the back as they went inside.

"Yeah and I'm here to collect as well. However I may just be able to sort out some of your problems for a quid pro quo, using some of your old Delta skills. Is that coffee you got brewing over there Rory?"

The American looked appraisingly at him as he poured them both a coffee and they sat down.

"Okay Danny let's have it. I hope like hell you don't want me to help you rob a bank or something. Though in fairness I'm desperate enough for anything right now."

Danny looked at him over the rim of the cup.

"I'll brief you in a minute Rory, but first give me the bottom line on your situation that you hinted at when we talked yesterday. No excuses or complaints about civvy street. I went through all that myself. Just the bottom line for now. I'm sorry to be so blunt but I want to know first if I can help you before I involve you in this. Okay?"

Rory looked away avoiding his eyes. Finally he sighed heavily and looked directly at him.

"Fair enough Danny. Okay I have a mortgage of a hundred and sixty thousand on this house, which will be repossessed by the bank within six weeks if I can't pay arrears of three thousand dollars and give some commitment to recommence and maintain mortgage payments. I also have credit card debts of seven thousand and no job at present. Oh, and my car has been repossessed. Is that blunt enough for you?"

Danny ran the figures around in his head and nodded.

"Thanks for leveling with me Rory. I do believe I can help you out there. How about this, I deposit one hundred and fifty thousand in your bank account over the next fifteen months? I have to investigate a way of doing it without attracting IRS interest under the money laundering banking rules. The money will be there, but the delivery method has yet to be defined to keep you under the IRS radar or indeed those organizations tracing unusual transactions. I understand I can send you just under ten grand immediately without any disclosure involved. On completion of the operation, a further fifty thousand. We can discuss the method of payment of the fifty K later. Perhaps you could nip across the border into Canada and open an account there.

Oh, and I also have an idea for you to get some regular income coming in here. How does that sound?"

Rory's jaw dropped, his eyes widening with amazement and shock. He reached forward and grabbed Danny's hand.

"You're not shitting me here Danny are you? Please don't say you are" he pleaded.

Danny shook his head.

"I wouldn't do that to you old friend. I respect you far too much to mess with your mind right now. No, this is for real. I just need your help and I'm hoping you can deliver."

He looked meaningfully at the man's shape.

Rory flushed.

"Yeah, I've slipped a bit I'll admit that, but the old embedded skills, you never forget. You know that, but tell me, just what the hell is this operation that you can help me out to that extent? It's got to be as illegal as hell!"

"The good news is that I'm not going to rob a bank but I am dispensing justice. Refill this cup and let me tell you a story."

Two hours later they were looking at the pictures of the Empire Security building and brainstorming strategy. Rory was in and Danny was delighted to have a second trained set of eyes taking a hard look at the challenge. He had already been percolating various ideas around in his head for the past few days and shared them with Rory who checked them out by attacking them from a number of sides. Finally they sat back and Rory looked at him.

"God I suddenly feel alive again Danny! I can see that's what was missing in my life. I've got a purpose for a change!"

"Well I can see a dramatic change in you since you dragged your ass out to meet me a couple of hours ago." He shook his head sadly. "You know I can't believe the government would neglect someone like you who's given so much for his country. Such a waste of all those expensive skills they taught you too. Now since we met a couple of hours ago Rory I've decided to alter the arrangement somewhat."

Rory's face fell.

"Please don't tell me you've changed your mind Danny."

He waved his hand.

"No nothing like that. However I've decided that even if you feel any doubts about this operation I'll still deposit the one hundred and fifty thousand in your account. After all you're really trying to provide a good home for your mother and I gather that you're all she's got right now. It's not as if you're free to go racing off half-assed chasing the bad guys, especially without the massive resources you used to have behind you. I'm giving you another chance right now to pull out and I won't think any the worse of you."

Rory sat there shaking his head.

"You're something else Danny Quigley. Try keeping me out at this stage you son of a gun. No way man!"

Danny looked relieved.

"Okay, here's the drill. I have to fly down to the Caymen Islands to sort the money side of things out. Depending on flights, that could mean two, three days before I'm back. I need details of your bank account and I'll email you just as soon as the first deposit is transferred. Drive me to the airport in my car, hang on to it, and pick me up when I return. We'll head up to the farm directly from there. Will you have to explain your absence to anyone?"

Rory grinned widely

"Just to a neighbor who'll keep up the visits to my mother. I'll tell her that I'm going on a job interview, which is actually partly true when you think about it."

"Yeah, you're right! Now one more thing Rory. I'm not looking for miracles from you in two days, but get a shave and a hair cut and start gearing your mind into going back into action again. I won't kid you mate, there's considerable risk involved here. By the way, say nothing to anyone about this operation. You know the drill."

Rory's eyes took on a steely look.

"I gotcha Danny. To be totally honest I'd sooner be on your side than sitting up there in Buffalo. Those bastards don't know what's coming after them. There's a hundred and sixty Taliban and Al Qaeda who wish they'd avoided running into you, and they're all dead. I'll be ready and waiting at the airport when you get back."

CHAPTER 54.

Jennifer drove Kieran to school that morning and promised to pick him up in the afternoon. Dianna had been collected by a police team from nearby Erie to do a presentation for a seminar they were running for regional police forces.

Kieran didn't need a crystal ball to know something was brewing on his first day back after the assault on him. One girl he'd hung around with in the past whispered to him as he was getting a coke from the machine.

"Watch out, Billy Joe's going to get you after school."

She turned and dashed off. Kieran felt butterflies in his stomach but was otherwise calm with even a sense of anticipation. At one time prior to a class starting, Billy Joe had brushed past him where he was seated, and caught him solidly with his shoulder. Kieran just smiled and continued chatting with a friend sitting opposite. His friend looked furtively after Billy Joe.

"He's coming after you when school's out. He's mad 'cos you sent the cops round to his house."

Then all conversation stopped as the teacher came into the room and the class started.

At 3:30 when the bell went, there was a mad dash outside. The kids being collected jumped into their parents' vehicles and departed. A larger number of kids than usual hung around outside the gate. Billy Joe stood off to one side with his own group talking loudly together and watching the gate. Finally Kieran emerged and walked straight over to Billy Joe's group. They all stopped talking and watched him approach. He stopped directly in front of Billy Joe and stared up at him.

"I understand you're going to get me today. Well, here I am" he said almost flippantly.

Billy Joe looked uncertainly at his friends, then shouted "get him" and grabbed for his collar.

Three things happened almost simultaneously. As Kieran was aware of the group reaching for him, he delivered a sharp back knuckle strike to the boy on his right who screamed and fell back clutching his nose as it spouted blood.

Jennifer who had arrived to drive him home, now slipped up quietly behind the group and kicked at the back of the knee of a second boy who had drawn his fist back to strike Kieran, sending him sprawling backwards way to the ground. The rest of the group drew back. Kieran grasped Billy Joe's hand, which had fastened on his collar, in a firm wristlock and spun sideways, leveraging down, exerting painful pressure on the wrist. The bully dropped straight to his knees, howling in pain. Kieran could have left it there if he'd wanted to but he didn't think Billy Joe had learned his lesson yet so he casually put his foot on the boy's shoulder and pushed him almost casually backwards, letting the wrist go at the same time. He went sprawling on his rear end. Some of the kids who had hung further back and were not involved in the attack, started laughing and catcalling.

"Not so big now Billy Joe, sitting on your butt!"

"Come on Kieran, give him some more!"

"Don't like being on the receiving end Billy Joe, do you?" taunted another.

Billy Joe jumped to his feet, his face suffused with rage.

"I'll kill you!" he screamed, hurling himself at Kieran.

That afternoon Billy Joe was given a lesson in fighting. It was almost a blueprint of the work Kieran had done back in the barn. Block, block, strike. Block, block, strike. Block, block, strike. Billy Joe kept hurling himself at Kieran, punching and kicking, but he never landed even one as the boy circled around totally in control, blocking and punching back at will. Kieran finally decided to finish it. By now Billy Joe's face was bruised and streaming blood from a cut eyebrow. He charged Kieran again, his arms flailing. Kieran blocked both blows and stepped in close bringing his right fist up into the gut of Billy Joe's stomach, sending him sinking to his knees. He weakly held up his hand.

"I've had enough. Don't hit me again please!" he pleaded, as he sank to the ground.

Just then there was a loud bellow and a big man started to rush up to the group - Puck McGlebe.

"What the hell have you done to my boy?" he shouted, pushing through the people who were starting to gather round. The man looked at his son on the ground and turned to Kieran grabbing his arm with one hand and bringing his massive fist back to strike him.

"I'll teach you to hit a McGlebe" he snarled.

A voice rang out sharply.

"No!"

It was Jennifer's.

She stepped forward and snapped a solid kick with the point of her shoe to McGlebe's shinbone. He screamed, letting go of Kieran and bending forward with the pain. Kieran brought his elbow round in an awesome scything blow, catching him on the side of the jaw. He dropped pole-axed to the ground. A huge cheer went up from the gathered kids.

Both McGlebes were down, lying almost parallel to each other. Then there was a frozen silence as Kieran and Jennifer turned and stared mutely at each other.

Kieran screamed.

"You just spoke Jennifer! My God you spoke!"

She nodded dumbly reaching up and touching her lips. Nodding she moved her lips.

"No" she whispered again.

With that they fell into each other's arms, the two inert forms on the ground forgotten. They broke the embrace and gave each other a high five and another cheer went up from the kids at the gate. There was the sound of car doors slamming and the policeman Tim and his buddy suddenly materialized beside them. They looked in amazement at the sprawled figures.

"How the hell did you to learn to do that? We were staked out in the car over there hoping to stop any trouble today. Jesus, I can't believe what I've just seen!"

Kieran looked questioningly at him.

"Waited long enough didn't you?"

The two cops looked at each other. Tim looked back at him.

"It's not often we see justice actually get done in this job Kieran. Didn't like to stop it before it took its natural course, and alleluia it sure did today! Now let's get this sorted out and get you on your way. At least I don't have to apologize to your mother again."

He looked at Jennifer.

"Did I just hear something about you speaking?"

Kieran jumped in excitedly.

"She did Tim, she did! Said 'no' loudly and clearly and whispered it again just now. It's amazing!"

Tim turned to her.

"Well I never thought the McGlebes would be good for anything but it looks like they may have been responsible for you speaking. How about that?"

He waved a finger at her.

"And just where did superwoman come from? I gotta find out where you two learned this? Probably from that financial planner," he finished disgustedly.

CHAPTER 55.

Danny's trip to the Cayman Islands was uneventful. He was glad about that. He had felt some nervousness about actually walking into a strange bank and claiming two million dollars. He'd taken his Danny Quigley passport with him when he traveled out as Brad Kincaid. No one queried his claim. That's what the Cayman Islands were all about - easy access to hidden money.

Quickly he arranged a meeting with a manager and completed his business. The money went speeding off to Rory Hanlon's account and he used the bank's email to confirm it to him. They discussed a method that would enable Rory to receive the balance of the funds on a regular basis, without alerting any authority. Danny would form a shell company in the Cayman Islands and pay the funds through it. It required two directors so the manager brought in one of his staff to sign as the second director. Rory would have to register a company in Detroit, get a letterhead and forward periodic invoices for irregular amounts to Danny's company in the Cayman Islands. The invoice would detail training and consultancy services. He would declare it as income to the IRS and pay taxes on it.

Danny didn't like the balance of the funds sitting in a current account earning no interest, so on the manager's recommendation he transferred one and a half million over to an interest bearing mixed currency fund. The balance was set up in such a way that Danny could access it from abroad and didn't have to return to the Cayman Islands. He also drew a check for the fifty thousand dollars that he'd promised Rory on completion of the operation. He intended that it would be available for Rory's mother's on- going care if he was killed or injured in the action. He had some ideas on how Rory could access the amount without raising any bells with the authorities.

Danny stayed overnight and managed to get an early flight back via New York the following morning, where he made a fast connection to Detroit. Rory picked him up, his face flushed with excitement. His beard was shaved off, he'd had a haircut and was wearing some new chinos and a t- shirt. He looked completely transformed.

"Danny you won't believe the afternoon I've just had! After I got your email I went down to the bank and sorted out the mortgage and my credit cards. Can you imagine that? I'm just cooking on gas right now buddy."

Danny grinned at his enthusiasm.

"Seriously Rory you had a break coming to you after all you've done for your country, putting you life and limb at risk. Speaking of which…."

He proceeded to outline the method that had been set up to process the funds on an ongoing basis, then reached into his inside pocket and withdrew an envelope with the extra check in it.

"Here, have a look at this" he instructed.

Rory fumbled with the envelope and withdrew the check.

He gasped. "But this ……."

"Yeah I know Rory. If you don't come back from this operation, or if you get hurt I want your mother to have access to it. Counter sign it and stick it in an envelope at the farm with your mother's location and Dianna will make sure she gets it. It's only fair buddy. We've seen too much action to kid ourselves about coming out in one piece."

Rory looked at him tentatively.

"Are you sure about this Danny? You could always hang onto it until we've done the job."

"Look, if I don't come out of it, I want your mother to have this, no ifs ands or buts. Believe me, you're going to earn it! Now when you do survive as I hope and expect you will, just cross over into Canada with your new company registration and open a corporate banking account. You can deposit the fifty thousand in it as seed capital for future expansion."

They headed straight for the highway leading back to Erie. Rory drove and Danny slept for about two hours, after which they pulled off the road and went into a diner. They both went for the western sandwich with lots of coffee. Danny normally drank tea but wasn't impressed with American methods of brewing it. Having finished, Rory looked across at him.

"Danny you've already brought a miracle into my life so I should be satisfied. However something you said when you first came to the house kinda stuck with me."

"What was that?"

"That you had an idea of how I could earn a living after this. I gather you had something definite in mind?"

Danny sat forward his face lighting up.

"Have I ever my friend! Now let me fill you in on how I stumbled onto this. Dianna, who I've already mentioned, has a sixteen year old son who got beat up recently at school by some bully and his pals. She agreed to tap her old CIA contacts to find out where you were as I needed help and I thought of you. She did it with one condition: that I teach her son Kieran how to defend himself."

"Well, I'm flattered you thought of me. I hope you won't regret it."

Danny shook his head.

"No way old son. I can feel the good vibes already about us doing this op together. Now, to get back to this idea I had. I just spent two days working with her young son and his aunt who's about 26 years of age. She was dead keen and really got stuck into the training. I taught them all the bog basic stuff, you know, blocking punches and striking back. I threw in some wristlocks and had them practice on each other, and they've really blown my mind how much they improved in two days. Just two days, imagine that!"

Rory looked impressed.

"Two days? Man that's something all right. Where do I come in?" he queried.

"Simply this Rory. There are loads of parents who'd like a fast track course in self-defense to stop their kids from being bullied. Lots of women as well. They don't want to go back and forth into smelly gyms for the next few years to learn how to do it. What's to stop you starting up something like that in Detroit? Use the same company you're going to register as an umbrella for this as well. Just rent a room from some health club to start with and take it from there. I figure you could call it Delta Defense and let the word out that you're an ex Delta team member. Hell they'd be knocking your door down for God's sake!"

"Delta Defense" Rory said reverently. "I can't believe something so simple could work just like that, but you know what? I really like the sound of it and the idea that I would have my own business and not have to run the risk of being laid off again in some redundancy or downsizing scheme. Wow!"

Danny glanced across at him.

"I have to tell you, it's the simple ideas that work. In my first year as a financial planner I came across all sorts of businesses that were started up on a shoe-string and worked because they provided a service or solution to people's problems. You've got the skills in self defense and find someone to do the admin work, initially on a part-time basis."

Rory nodded eagerly.

"You know what Danny, you may just be onto something here.... Delta Defense" he scratched his ear. " Hmm.... working at something I enjoy and my future security in my own hands for a change. My God Danny, this is exciting!"

Danny chuckled.

"Just wait till you see those two going at it in the barn after only two days! As I say, it totally blew my mind and you would be an absolute winner in teaching self defense."

He stood up.

"I'm going to use the washroom and then we'll gas up and hit the road. We should be at the farm by late afternoon Oh, and I'm known as Brad at the farm...Brad Kincaid."

CHAPTER 56.

What a welcome they ran into! Kieran and Jennifer met them at the front of the house with Kieran's words tumbling out so fast Danny couldn't even understand what he was trying to say. Dianna emerged smiling a moment later.

"What he's trying to tell you is that Jennifer spoke her first word today, isn't that incredible .... ah.... Brad! And if that isn't enough for one day, Billy Joe McGlebe went for him after school and Kieran thumped him all over the school yard" she said proudly.

Danny looked across at him.

"Wow isn't that something?" he said, grabbing him and lifting him off the ground. "Hey I knew you were a winner buddy as soon as I started training you."

When Kieran's feet touched the ground again he struggled back out of Danny's embrace.

"And there's more," he said pointing to Jennifer who was standing there her face shining.

"Jennifer and I dropped Puck McGlebe when he came up after I'd thumped Billy Joe. She kicked his shinbone and I dropped him with an elbow smash. Boy did he go down! That's when she spoke her first word. It was awesome!"

Danny's jaw dropped as he looked from one to the other. He'd only been training Kieran to handle himself in a schoolyard scuffle, but he and Jennifer had really lifted the bar taking on an burly ex athlete and stopping him cold. Seeing the pride in Jennifer's face and eyes he gave her a high five. Dianna came across and hugged him.

"I guess I owe you one Danny. Thanks for what you did for Kieran, and obviously Jennifer was an avid pupil too from what we've heard."

Turning to Rory she asked with a smile.

"So who's this you've brought us, not another financial planner I hope?"

Rory stuck his hand out.

"Rory Hanlon, Ma'am. An old acquaintance of Dan…. Brad, and I'm just here to help him out over the next few days. Hope you can put me up as well. I guess we should have called you first."

"Not a problem Rory. Nothing surprises me any more where Brad's concerned. Now let me introduce you formally to my son Kieran and my sister Jennifer. As you just heard they have had quite a dramatic afternoon and I suspect that Kieran may want to tell you both in great detail, blow by blow, what actually transpired. Let's all go inside and get some supper as he does that, shall we?"

Rory cast a shy glance at Jennifer.

"Gosh, you're beautiful!" he exclaimed.

Jennifer's eyes widened in amazement and amusement and her lips moved as if she wanted to say something. That set the tone for the evening with Danny and Dianna teasing him about his remark.

It was hours later that both men finally manage to crash out. The next day they were to start their training for the move against Empire Security in Buffalo.

CHAPTER 57.

As pre-arranged, Danny and Rory were up early and went for a run around the local roads. On the way they passed a number of Amish buggies going in both directions. They waved as they ran past and some of the drivers waved back while others stared stonily ahead, ignoring them. When they returned they found the farm deserted, but enjoyed the breakfast that was laid out for them on the kitchen table. Then they went outside and managed to make up mats for falling on out of a number of old mattresses that they found stacked against the wall of the hay barn. They pegged some tarpaulin down over the top and soon had a makeshift dojo for practicing hip and shoulder throws and leg sweeps.

Both of them had come from different schools of unarmed combat but there was a common thread in the tactics of the Special Forces. To kill or hurt the enemy as fast, as efficiently, and as silently as possible.

There were limits to what one could do in practice without hurting each other, but they worked through an agreed sequence of throws and blocks against a would-be attacker using his hands, feet or a variety of weapons. Rory was extraordinarily adept with his feet and hip throws, and created opportunities to slip under Danny's guard and slam him to the ground. Danny had incredible hand speed and a powerful upper body which he used to maximum effect, and his leg sweeps caught Rory time and time again.

When they stopped after two hours they heard clapping from the side and saw both Kieran and Jennifer sitting on some bales of hay. So engrossed had they been in their practice that they hadn't noticed them. Kieran's eyes were flashing with excitement.

"Gosh, both of you are absolutely amazing! Brad can you teach us some of this stuff please?"

He made a face.

"Unfortunately not on this trip Kieran 'cos I'll be leaving soon. However Rory may be starting up his own training school in Detroit shortly. Perhaps your Mum might run you across for a weekend seminar with him. I'm sure he'd go easy on the fees, wouldn't you Rory?"

"Sure Kieran, we'd love to have you, and there'd be no fees for either of you."

He walked over until he was standing directly in front of Jennifer.

"Would you like that?" he asked her.

"Yes' she answered, clearly and distinctly.

There was a moment's silence and they all whooped at once. Rory grabbed her and swept her off the ground, swinging her around and around. Kieran raced off in high excitement to tell his Mum.

That finished the training for the time being but later Danny donned some padding and they worked through a solid punching and kicking session, exchanging gear and carrying on for a further hour. Finally they shed the gear and sat back on one of the bales of hay, the perspiration pouring from them. Rory tapped him on the shoulder breathing heavily.

"I'm out of shape but I'm glad I made you work, you bastard. You're still pretty sharp Danny. I'd say you haven't lost much since you left the 'Sass'."

Danny groaned.

"I work on a variety of martial arts back home, but God I had no idea how much I'd slipped back on this contact stuff. You came on well though Rory. You still have the tactics down pat and your kicks are as fast as a striking snake. That was a super workout. Okay, I don't expect that the operation will involve much unarmed combat but it'll start to sharpen up our reactions for the other stuff. Unless I'm mistaken, we'll settle this with Empire Security using weapons."

Rory looked pleased.

"Thanks for the vote of confidence Danny. Yeah, I could feel the old skills surfacing again. Hell they had to, or I would've had my ass kicked for sure. Your hand speed is incredible and those leg sweeps - man, you caught me every time! I've got to master those. I can see where they can get you out of trouble."

Danny stood up stretching himself.

"Yeah, good session. Now lets go have a shower and a coffee. I want us to look over the weapons this afternoon and discuss the plan. Obviously we need to shed those two keen young people as I suspect Dianna has kept that hoard to herself."

CHAPTER 58.

She had, and had arranged for Jennifer to take Kieran off to the bike shop in her car that afternoon to have the wheel fixed that Billy Joe had put his foot through. She then insisted on taking both men out to lunch instead of preparing something herself. Danny suspected she had other thoughts on her mind as well.

They traveled in Danny's car with Dianna driving and cut through various back roads until they popped out onto a main highway again. A few miles further on she pulled into a diner with half a dozen cars parked outside. She glanced across at them.

"It's quiet, but they serve the best all-day breakfast you've ever tasted. I'm not saying you can't get a decent lunch as well, but it's the breakfast I come for guys."

She jumped out of the car and was half way to the diner before both men caught up with her. Some of the customers glanced up and gave a friendly nod to the newcomers then went back to their coffee.

Dianna headed to a booth at the far corner and eased into her seat. Danny sat beside her and Rory slipped in across the table from them. In a moment a pleasant faced middle-aged lady with a gray pony tail came across and smiled at them.

"I don't need to ask what you want love" she said glancing at Dianna "but what about your friends?" she asked, raising her eyebrows.

Danny looked up at her.

"Dianna praised your all-day breakfast so highly, I wouldn't dream of ordering anything else."

The woman looked closer at him.

"You're British. Can't hide that accent. My mother came from Birmingham after the war with her GI. People tell me I still say the odd word like her."

They chatted for a few minutes before she left with their orders. They had all asked for the same. Dianna was looking slightly embarrassed.

"Hey guys I didn't mean to push you into going for the breakfast, especially Danny, oh shit Brad! Hell I don't know what to call you any more."

Danny reached across and patted her hand.

"If you're buying Dianna, we'll eat whatever you tell us to, so there."

She looked uncertainly at both of them and they burst out laughing. She thumped Danny on the shoulder.

"Oh you two. I never know what to make of you. Trained killers the both of you, yet you act like a couple of kids."

They were still chuckling when the waitress came back and slapped down three large mugs of coffee. Danny took a swallow and, glancing around covertly to make sure no one could overhear them and nudged Dianna.

"Tell Rory your reasons for having built up such a large cache of weapons back there. I must confess I was fascinated myself."

Her face changed expression and she struggled to marshal her thoughts. Finally she sighed.

"Okay, it sounds cuckoo when you look around and see everything normal, like here for example."

She pointed to a group laughing and chatting across the room.

"My father warned me on his death bed that a bad time was coming on America. Just something in his spirit. He was part First Nations on his father's side and he remembered having visions in the sweat lodge about a terrible chastisement coming on the world. That's the word he used - chastisement for man's abuse of the planet and the corruption of his ways. With his last breath he sat up in bed and clutched at my arm. "It's close!" he rasped. "the chastisement is close!"

She stopped, looking away, her eyes moist. Danny reached over and rested his hand on hers but she gently disengaged his grip.

"I'm okay really. It's just that every day when I turn on CNN I can see that day almost upon us. Tent cities going up across the country. Over in Ohio the police department is down to one squad car and they don't investigate property crimes any more. They switch the lights off in streets to cut costs. Some counties are breaking up paved roads that they can't afford to fix and going back to gravel. Think of all the pissed off people who have lost their jobs and homes. The mad scramble by ordinary citizens to buy weapons. The militias up in the mountains who are talking revolution and civil war. Look at the squabbling government parties, too polarized to do what's right for the country, because they're too busy trying to win the next election. This country is a time bomb just waiting to go off. Just listen to the hate pouring out of the radio shows about President Obama and having a black president. Apart from that, America now has many enemies who want to destroy us. It wouldn't take much: a cyber attack on our satellites and computer systems; a single nuke from Iran, North Korea or Russia would do it. Oh yeah, Putin can't wait to get revenge on us for bringing down the old Soviet regime. He's just quietly waiting in the eaves for us to falter. The country's broke right now after Iraq and Afghanistan and bailing out the collapsing banking system. The Gulf coast has no illusions about being bailed out long term from the BP oil spill after the debacle of Katrina."

The story was interrupted by the waitress bringing their meals and fussing around them with a coffee top-up. Dianna suddenly looked very self conscious and started eating. The two men did the same and made noises of appreciation as they attacked the stack of food in front of them. Finally she stopped with half the food left on her plate. She wiped her lips and sat back, a look of resolve on her face.

"Look guys, I hope I'm not coming across as some cookie in the backwoods storing up survival food and weapons waiting for U.N. Forces to take over America. You see the farm and my herd are part of my plan to survive this bad time my father warned me about. It's survival food on the hoof as it were. And bet your boots when times get rough around here, the Government will want to take what I've got and spread it around to keep the population from looting and rioting."

She took a couple of deep breaths and looked seriously at them.

"So you can see why I want you to brief me on your plan. I need to be fully informed as to what you intend to do and to see if I can help you. I'm going to be fighting this government sooner or later and I might as well get some practice in early. Let's get these coffee cups topped up and start working on a plan."

CHAPTER 59.

Dianna, first out of the diner, skidded to a stop. The others bumped into her still form. Looking over her head Danny could see a black suburban vehicle with tinted windows, slewed across the nose of his rental car, blocking it. Standing in front of the suburban were three men dressed in almost identical blue suits, white shirts and ties. The older man was a lean middle aged six-footer with steel gray hair and an alert stance. He had a square jaw and prominent tanned face and he now watched them approach with an almost detached interest. The other two were younger blockier versions, wearing light raincoats and they kept their hands in their pockets. They each had the look of the weight trainer come marathon runner about them, and their eyes were narrowed and focused as the two men and Dianna walked up to them.

She said nothing but looked at their blocked vehicle and the older man questioningly. He tilted his head back looking over them appraisingly and his gaze came back to Dianna.

"Your old friend from the company said to say hello Dianna. He hopes you're keeping your nose clean. Oh, I'm Brett Zeitner by the way" he said slowly articulating each word.

He didn't offer to shake hands. Dianna's face lost color as her gaze flicked across the group.

"I knew you people traveled in packs Zeitner, if that's your real name, but isn't the CIA's brief outside the United States or has 9/11 changed that as well as everything else?" she said insolently.

The two young men in suits tensed and one of them took a step forward.

"Keep a civil tongue in your head Ma'am or we may have to do more than just block off your vehicle" he snapped.

Dianna never took her eyes off Brett Zeitner.

"Where did you recruit these apes from Zeitner? From some bloody high school basketball team? I've heard better dialogue in a B movie!" she rasped, her eyes flashing.

The two suits stiffened and glanced at their boss expectantly. He waved a casual arm at them and shook his head chuckling.

"I was warned that you were a feisty one Dianna. Yeah you're right, it is hard to get good help these days" he said glancing sideways at the two men who were now glaring angrily at her. "Especially two that can't read the signs. They don't realize that even with their Glock's, those two blood hounds of yours would have them face down on the ground, probably with some broken bones, within five seconds of any trouble starting. No, if I wanted to hassle you I'd be here with a back-up SWAT team from the FBI and you'd all be trussed up by now heading for an interrogation center."

Danny spoke for the first time.

"So what do you want.... ah Zeitner" he asked.

The man cocked his head appraising him.

"I want to talk to you.... Quigley," he nodded back into the parking lot, "alone" he added.

He gestured to the two suits and they reluctantly climbed into the suburban, after one last hostile glance at Dianna. Danny strolled back into the parking lot with Zeitner, his mind spinning. This man knew who he was. He now wanted to speak to him alone and without witnesses. He hadn't brought any police backup with him or they would already be cuffed and out of the game. What was going on?

Zeitner stopped and turned, facing him.

"You're probably wondering how we picked you up. Well when Dianna's name was flagged up after an enquiry from an intelligence source in the U.K., of course we started watching her. Lo and behold, along comes a Mr. Brad Kincaid who comes to the notice of the local cops quite quickly. You're obviously a soldier and not a spook or you wouldn't last five minutes in this business. We got a shot of you right away and ran it as a priority, through facial identification. Who pops up? Danny Quigley! We do some more research and what do we discover?"

Danny looked away.

"Yeah, I can imagine" he muttered, disgusted at himself for being picked up so easily.

"Right! The same Danny Quigley that created mayhem with the Taliban and Al Qaeda in Afghanistan and received a private decoration in London from our the Vice President there. So I ask myself, what exactly is he doing here in the U.S.A.? It so happens that I was involved in finding out what became of an old friend of mine Charles Percival Saunders of MI6 in London. He disappeared and no trace of him was found until a crematorium was located that, in the last few days turned up his DNA, along with some others. Now my goal is to find out who burned him up. I discover that MI5 had been following a person of interest to that crematorium in a place called High Wycombe. D'you know what I did next?" he asked.

"I can't imagine. Anyway, what has this to do with me?" Danny asked impatiently.

"All in good time. All in good time. Now I contact MI5, a very helpful lady called Rebecca Fullerton-Smythe. She tells me that the man they followed to that crematorium was someone called Basil Sinclair, our CIA man in London. Apparently up to other skullduggery as well using a variety of names, and who has now disappeared. He's suspected of fleeing the country completely. She tells me that he was connected with an outfit called Empire Security in the U.K. whose head office is based in Buffalo New York State. I discover, on quizzing her further, that the entire Empire Security team in the U.K. just disappeared overnight. No trace of them showing up anywhere in the world. This, despite Scotland Yard being in possession of their IDs from a previous raid on their offices in Southampton. Imagine that! A whole bunch of people disappear without a trace. Can you shed any light on it Danny?"

Danny shrugged.

"As I said, what has this to do with me Zeitner?"

The CIA man chuckled.

"Danny, Danny, the job of intelligence is one where you gradually over the years work out an accommodation with other alliances and share information. If you like, you worm your way into the very fiber of their organization, either through friendship, money, blackmail or whatever. Take it from me that I know your full involvement. The missing troopers, your under the radar assistance to MI5, your personal vendetta in seeking revenge for the death of two of them, your success in carrying it out in Southampton."

Danny was both shocked and puzzled at the same time. He moved back a few steps and looked him directly in the face.

"So what exactly do you want with me, Zeitner?" he asked.

"Quite simply to work with you on this Danny" he replied.

"To work with me? Shit you have the whole of the resources at Langley, the FBI and other police forces to work with!" Danny retorted, still not sure what the CIA man was implying.

"There's two things I want Danny - to find this man Sinclair and take care of him for my old friend Percy Saunders. Hell, he was up for a knighthood shortly and I was invited over to London for the occasion."

"And the other thing?"

"To have a chat with him first, before I kill him that is. I want to find out how a CIA agent got involved in bringing a nuclear weapon into Iraq and I want to find the location of it."

Danny felt his stomach tighten. The American appeared to have access to a whole slew of information already. He shook his head.

"If there ever was a bomb to begin with" he said quietly.

Zeitner looked sharply at him.

"What do you mean?"

Danny went on, "Well I talked to the SAS Major who had the task of collecting the crate off the plane and taking it into Iraq. He believed that it was a CIA plane by the way. Now obviously he didn't know what was in the crate at the time. However it never left their sight all the way to the meeting place in Iraq where the case was opened and it contained nothing but rocks. I don't think there ever was a bomb in the first place. That's just my theory."

Danny suddenly had the flash of an idea and carried on.

"You know I wondered if it really was a plot to kill some of the players involved. The SAS troop helped fight off a raid when they got to their camp which might have been planned to eliminate General O'Donnell and his team from Empire Security. Were they lured into Iraq to finish them off for whatever reason? Oh, and there was a Colonel Minter in Kuwait, U.S. Marine Corps, and a ranger, who was the facilitator there and vanished when the 'Sass' team managed to get back. Now he could explain a lot if you could locate him" he offered lamely.

Danny was deliberately misleading Zeitner at this stage, who was now looking at him doubtfully.

"Hmm…. not so sure about that one Quigley. There's got to be more to it than that."

Danny made a face.

"What I don't understand is why you need me at all. It appears that you're in possession of most of the facts as it is. I know the CIA brief is outside the U.S. but why not use your vast resources and liaise with the FBI and chase those people down?"

Zeitner smiled.

"Good question Danny. Tell you why. If I make it official, sooner or later it gets out believe me. That's the CIA today - everybody covering their asses. The secret of today ends up a leak to some congressional oversight committee and the company gets slaughtered, especially on funding. You demonstrated that you could take care of things in the U.K. and carry out a clean sweep. I want to bury this whole thing and I'm prepared to use you to get rid of that rat's nest, Empire Security up in Buffalo. It didn't take a genius to figure out why you were sitting down the road an hour and a half from Buffalo and have just picked up an ex Delta colleague. By the way, we know of your trip to the Cayman Islands and the money transfer. Don't worry, we'll make sure the IRS will never show an interest in your friend Hanlon. As stated I want Sinclair alive for interrogation, but he won't be long for this world once he falls into our hands."

Danny was conscious that he was walking through a minefield. Zeitner held all the cards while himself, Dianna and Rory would simply be picked up and possibly held indefinitely or disappear completely, if he didn't go along with him. As his mind raced, he debated if he could actually turn the situation to his benefit. He pursed his lips thoughtfully.

"Okay. We'll work with you along the lines you mentioned. You get a whack at Sinclair, however."

He raised his finger.

"You know what combat is like I presume. You're probably ex military anyway so I can't guarantee when the action is over that your

CIA friend Sinclair will be standing there without a scratch and waiting to sing like a canary for you Zeitner."

The CIA man's eyes were icy cold.

"That's your problem Quigley. However you play it, I want to have a chat with the bastard first. I don't mind if he has a few holes in him when you deliver him to me. By the way it was the Marines, Force Recon, that I was in."

Danny looked impressed despite himself. Force Reconnaissance was the Marine Corp's Special Forces and had done some impressive missions in Vietnam.

"A tough outfit. At the 'Sass' we copied some of your methods. Now, what help can you give us in terms of assets... ah Brett?"

"Personnel.... none.... you only have to look at those two specimens over there in my vehicle to see why. As mentioned, confidentiality would be difficult if I involve any of my people. Equipment-wise I could help to a limited degree. What did you have in mind Quigley?"

Danny pursed his lips thoughtfully.

"I want Hanlon wired up for an informational gathering visit to the Empire Security in Buffalo. He'll be there looking for a contract and as an ex Delta Force team member, he should get a good welcome. Bearing in mind that these people are in security and will probably do a good job checking him for such a device, what have you got that they wouldn't pick up on? Oh it would also be helpful too if it could be utilized as a bug to keep track of his movements when he's in a car for example."

"No problem there. We have stuff that's not even on the street yet and certainly not known by security firms. Where would you track him from, your rental? Those Canadian plates stand out quite a bit."

Danny had considered the problem before but wanted to see if the CIA man could offer any solution. He cocked his head looking at him.

"Any ideas from your side?" he asked.

"That's easy. We can drop a van off at the farm for you. Something the DEA confiscated recently and it won't show up on any police bulletins. Dump it in Buffalo when you're finished with it" he laughed cynically. "Hell, it'll be re-sprayed and on sale up in Toronto within the month!"

He continued to stare at Danny as if trying to read his mind.

Finally he sighed.

"Okay what else do you need Quigley - weapons, communications equipment?" he asked.

Danny considered this.

"We could use three walkie-talkies and a cell phone for each of us pre-programmed directly to yourself. We don't need weapons."

As soon as he said that he cursed silently. Zeitner looked at him, a dangerous glint in his eyes.

"Got a store already have we? Dianna's name has come up under another flag recently. She's become a real rabble-rouser recently, writing in to the various farmer's journals about lack of government support. Not a CIA problem but you can tell her from me that she has some trouble coming down the spout at her. Tell her to keep a very low profile from now on. Her old company contacts couldn't help her if she becomes obstructive to the U.S. Government in any violent way. To get down to basics, the van will have the other equipment you asked for. Now when do you intend to start your operation against Empire Security?"

"Tomorrow Hanlon walks into Empire Security looking for a job. He doesn't need a legend as such because his real situation is ideal and will be easy for them to check - ex Delta team member, who has just lost his job in Detroit. His objective will be to gather information as to who's presently there and he has descriptions of Sinclair, General O'Donnell, Tom Bradley and Colonel Minter, who was in Kuwait. If he gets a job with them fine, we run with it and see where it takes us. It's unlikely that those people are all there right now sitting in one room and just waiting for us to walk in and shoot them."

Zeitner nodded grudgingly.

"Okay, sounds like a plan. I'll have the van and equipment dropped off at the farm during the night. Don't wait up for us. Now one last thing, I want Sinclair alive, understood?"

"Fine by me and.... ah.... thanks. I guess we could be over in that prison in Angola if you really wanted to be nasty. I hear it's not a nice place to be!"

Zeitner's face hardened.

"If you screw up on this, Angola won't be an option Quigley. You and your two buddies will just disappear into thin air like you did to that crew down in Southampton, capice?"

Nothing more was said as they turned back and walked over to the two vehicles. Dianna and Rory were already sitting in his rental.

When Zeitner got to the suburban, as if by arrangement a hand came out the window holding a leather attaché case which he handed to Danny.

"A present Danny, for you." he said stepping back.

Danny gazed down at it wondering if he was holding a bomb that would go off once they got into their vehicle. The CIA man chuckled.

"God, you're a suspicious one, especially after all the relationship building I just finished with you."

He reached and snapped the two catches on the attaché case and lifted the lid. Danny gasped. Inside was a beautiful revolver, a make that he had never seen before, nestling in a bed of foam, with some boxes of shells slotted in beside it.

Zeitner looked at it proudly.

"It's called the Taurus Judge because of the number of judges who carry the new Taurus model .45/.410 into the courtroom. It fires both .410, 3 inch Magnum or 2.5 shotshell and .45 colt ammunition. It's becoming the prestige weapon out on the street now with gangsters and drug smugglers. Like it?"

Danny lifted the weapon out and hefted it. Like all Special Forces he loved guns and always planned to have the very best available when going into combat. Gun manufacturers stayed in close contact with Special Forces to determine their changing needs and to use them as sounding boards for new models.

"Wow, it's beautiful! A pistol that uses shotgun shells! A small shell admittedly, but what a weapon!"

He looked at Zeitner.

"Why give it to me?" he enquired.

The CIA man's face was somber for a moment.

" I had it specially packaged by the company Taurus to present to Sir Percy when he went to collect his knighthood at Buckingham Palace. Of course I wasn't going to give it to him at the Palace. After all it would be illegal to own now in the U.K. We had arranged for it to be sent across the Atlantic in the diplomatic pouch. Now he'll never see it. Because it's called the Judge, I wanted you to have it, going after these bastards."

Danny hefted it dubiously.

"You know if I use this on Sinclair before handing him over to you for interrogation, there won't be very much of him left for you to work on."

Zeitner said nothing. He gave Danny a long hard look before jumping into the front seat of the suburban which backed up from the front of their vehicle, turned and quietly drove out of the parking lot.

Danny got into his rental car and both passengers looked enquiringly at him.

"Let's get back to the farm. We now have a sleeping partner for the operation…. the CIA. Have I ever got a lot to tell you guys!"

They tore out of the parking lot.

CHAPTER 60.

Zeitner's unexpected visit raised a lot of concerns with the group. When they got back to the farm they spent the following hour debating whether it heralded a plus or a minus in the operation. Danny, who had the experience of a face-to-face meeting with the agency man was more inclined to welcome the CIA's involvement. In terms of the actual operation, it was supplying some badly needed equipment. His only reservation was having to capture Sinclair alive and deliver him to the CIA. What would happen to them if he failed to carry that out? Dianna, as an ex agent, didn't trust the agency at all and wondered if there was some sort of double game going on. They had a reputation for cleaning up after operations and she worried that they might be part of the clean up. Why would Zeitner, she speculated, who was so concerned about leaks, leave them around as potential witnesses? She couldn't figure out what his game was but was very shocked that he had given her a warning about her involvement in anti government rhetoric. She had great reservations also, that Zeitner now knew that they had a weapons cache available. Rory, who had no reason to distrust the U.S. government, welcomed it's unofficial backing, and especially the vehicle and communication material which he couldn't wait to get his hands on.

On balance they decided that the CIA's involvement was in their favor while they were carrying out the operation, but that they would have to watch their backs when it was completed. None of them were impressed with Brett Zeitner's two colleagues. If they got involved, they could mess things up and possibly compromise the mission. They discussed various possibilities that might occur once Rory walked into the Empire Security building the following day.

What if they turned him down and he had to walk back out again?

What if they took him off to some other location to meet other members of their team or to question him further?

What if the unobtrusive wire supplied by the CIA didn't work properly and they lost contact with Rory?

What if he was asked if he'd heard of Danny Quigley while on his tour in Afghanistan?

What was their specific outcome or outcomes for the mission and how could they all extract themselves from the area afterwards?

Their exit strategy in other words.

What about the rest of the security organization personnel? What if they got in the way? Who were the bad guys in other words?

Did they assume that everyone at Empire Security was disposable or were they specifically targeting General O'Donnell, and his buddy from the desert Tom Bradley?

What about Colonel Minter from Kuwait who organized the handover? What about the van and equipment afterwards, especially the weapons?

What was the worst case scenario and if they were in dire need, could they call in assistance through the CIA to the FBI or local police?

What about communication between them when they split up?

Danny brought up the topic of the boat he had arranged to pick up and he filled them in as to how he envisaged using it.

The discussion on weapons moved them back outside into their secret location where individually, they selected those that they felt suited the operation. Dianna's choice surprised both the men. The German Heckler and Koch 7.62-mm PSGI Sniper's Rifle with a five round magazine, and a day and night telescopic sight. The weapon had a comfortable wooden pistol grip. Danny knew the weapon quite well. She took half a dozen extra magazines with her too.

Seeing the surprise in Danny's face she said

"Forget where we met first Danny? On that marine's sniping course. I'm comfortable with this weapon and have used it in a real life situation, so don't start going macho on me."

He raised his hands.

"Hey I'm not saying anything. I need all the back-up I can get girl."

Rory chose the Heckler and Koch 0.45 in MK 23 (SOCOM) U.S. Special Forces command pistol, specially designed for them. It had ended up in it's subsequent development, as a combination of a H&K pistol with COLTS Knight's sound/flash suppressor. Known as the SOCOM pistol it used a 12 round box magazine, and with the bullets being sub-sonic, it avoided the characteristic crack of super-sonic bullets. It had a (LAM) Lazer Aiming Module too, which put a red dot on the target.

He also selected the U.S. 5.56 -mm M16A1 Assault rifle, 30 round magazine, fitted with a 40-mm M203 grenade launcher which had a plastic stock and pistol grip.

Danny was taken aback.

"Looks like you're going to war man. That's heavy stuff you got there...take the whole damn building down" he exclaimed.

Rory's face slanted up at him.

"I never underestimate the enemy Danny. Saw some of my friends die because of that. Prepare for the worst, that's my motto. Remember the old war truism, plans only last until the first contact with the enemy"

Danny looked at him in amazement.

"Your choice buddy. You know you can't go in for your interview carrying this stuff" he kidded.

Dianna thumped his arm.

"You two! It's like you're going on a bloody picnic. Come on let's move it before Kieran comes back and starts looking for us" she said tersely.

Danny chose a few small items first - six sets of plastic cuffs, a U.S. knuckle duster trench knife with a skull crusher, a set of Dutch night vision goggles with head harness, a British Simrad day and night vision binocular telescope, a dozen magnesium-based stun grenades. He then carefully selected the weapons. He hadn't forgotten the Taurus Judge he'd already received from Brett Zeitner, however he had his own favorites too.

He chose the U.S. Ingram, 9-mm Mac 10, 32 round sub machine gun with silencer, which had a folding stock and a sliding stock rail. He removed this along with the hand strap for more compact use. Like

Rory he wanted to take along some extra firepower just in case and his final choice stopped both Rory and Dianna in their tracks. A Soviet Parachutists RPG rocket-propelled grenade launcher and PG-7 rocket-propelled grenades with collapsible stabilizing fins.

Dianna gasped.

"You give out to Rory about starting a war! These are the kind of weapons you see those hoary bearded mountain men in Afghanistan carrying all the time, with the rockets sticking out the end, or Hamas in the Gaza strip! My God, you're upping the ante here aren't you Danny?"

He nodded.

"Yeah, you're dead right, but these Empire Security guys go into some tough places and probably have the best. You know as well as I do Dianna, that here in the U.S. you can buy anything on the roadside at those gun shows. As Rory says, better to be safe than sorry."

Rory blinked.

"I said that?"

"You sure did mate. Now I think we're just about there. Don't forget to load some grenades for that launcher of yours. We'll stack this inside by the door and load it directly into the van in the morning."

Dianna brushed her hair back wearily.

"I've had it right now. Let's get some food and an early night. I'll talk Jennifer into cooking something for us."

She looked at the weapons stacked by the doorway.

"After tomorrow, nothing's going to be quite the same again round here. The rehearsal and role-play are over. Oh, I've already sighted in the sniper rifle by the way. Now I guess it's time to kick ass."

Before they turned in, Danny called the fisherman in Fort Erie and arranged a time for pick up of the boat on the following day.

CHAPTER 61.

Danny wasn't sure what woke him. Still half asleep it had sounded like a car door slamming shut out in the farmyard. He sat up to listen and heard a vehicle drive away. He glanced at his luminous wristwatch. It was 2 am. He decided to investigate and slipped out of bed. He reached under the bed, pulled out the case with the Judge Taurus pistol in it, and crept silently to the door. He cracked the door an inch and listened.

Nothing.

Opening it he eased out onto the landing and stood still for five minutes as he listened for any signs of visitors.

Still nothing.

He moved swiftly to both ends of the corridor and checked through the side windows. Everything was still outside.

The weapon dropped to his side as he started back towards his room.

He paused outside Dianna's room, and after a moment's reflection, gently tapped on the door.

No sound from within.

He turned the handle and stepped through, closing the door behind him.

Just then he felt what he assumed was the barrel of a gun pressed into the side of his neck.

"Dangerous creeping into a ladies room without an invitation Danny, and carrying a weapon. What exactly are your intentions my man?"

Oh shit, he thought. He'd just blown it. He felt the gun lowered as she moved to his front pressing herself up against him. He felt a jolt when he realized that she wore nothing under the thin nightie. Her head came close to his ear.

"Cat got your tongue?" she whispered.

"Ah.... I thought I heard something... thought I'd check it out. Just wanted to make sure you were okay Dianna."

"Hmm.... I could be better now that you mention it. Having trouble sleeping actually. Got any ideas? You're supposed to be a resourceful man Danny. In any event it's opportune that you're here because I wanted to thank you."

"Thank me.... for what?"

"Kieran and Jennifer of course. What you've done for them since you got here".

"You don't have to thank me Dianna."

She started pulling away.

"Oh well, if that's the case...."

His arms fastened around her tightly.

"On second thoughts it would be nice to be thanked." he teased.

She kissed him.

"This for starters" she murmured.

There was silence for a long moment as he savored the taste of her before gently disengaging his lips.

"What else did you have in mind Dianna?" he asked.

She gently reached down and removed the Judge Taurus from his hand, placing it on the floor. Then she caught his arm and led him across to her bed which they both collapsed into. Dianna's nightgown and Danny's shorts were instantly discarded as they molded their bodies to each other, their breathing increasing as their demands grew. They both knew that they didn't need any more foreplay and Dianna initiated their coming together when she swiftly climbed on top of him. That drove him almost crazy with pleasure and he drove upward into her as she responded with almost primal ferocity. They both knew that they were doing this for their own physical and emotional needs and the knowledge that the future might never offer this opportunity again. Finally she shuddered and collapsed down against his chest at the same time as he felt the life flow out of him.

She lay on top of him for several moments and finally slid down beside him where he held her tightly, kissing her forehead gently. After a while he felt himself stirring again and started kissing her with an increasing urgency. Dianna came alive again kissing and touching him as he started to move his mouth over and down her body. She gasped as his lips started teasing her inner thighs and moved between them.

He prolonged this until she was clawing at his back and finally moved on top of her. This time they were doing it for each other rather than selfishly possessing each other's bodies. An hour later they were bathed in perspiration and lying exhausted together.

"You're insatiable, you know that don't you?" he said hoarsely.

She chuckled throatily.

"I've waited three years for that. I just had some catching up to do."

"Well I hope it was worth waiting for and that you don't wait as long next time Dianna."

"Yes to the first. It sure was worth it. Fantastic! In fact I didn't know it could be soooo good! As for waiting, I'm not sure just how the next few days will pan out. We'll see. You've given me a whole new perspective on myself and how I've been burying myself away here on the farm and missing out on so much."

"Does that mean that Tim the policeman will be dragged into the hay loft next time he puts in an appearance round here?" he asked.

She thumped his chest none too gently.

"You sure know how to ruin a good thing Danny, bringing another man's name into our lovemaking. Just for that you're going to have to spend the rest of the night alone with your lustful thoughts. So back you go to your own room, and I hope those thoughts keep you awake!"

He reluctantly slipped out of bed and quietly left the room collecting the Judge Taurus as he went.

He lay there listening to his heart rate slow down and mentally going over the last incredible hour in Dianna's room before drifting off to sleep.

When the first light of dawn was leaking in the window he sat cross-legged on the floor and re-orientated his mind into battle mode. He focused on the mission and the people he was up against. He stiffened his resolve to carry through on avenging his murdered mates and re-lived in his mind all the battles he had carried out successfully in the past. He saw himself as an almost indestructible figure - rock-like, moving inexorably against his foe like a warrior, and overcoming them with power and crushing force. Finally he stood up and worked his way through a series of calisthenics and exercises which incorporated strikes, punches and kicks, until he felt the sharpness hum through his veins and muscles.

He was ready.

CHAPTER 62.

When they looked out in the morning, the van promised by Brett Zeitner was parked in the farmyard. It was a GMC vehicle, slate gray in color, and when they tested the motor, found it had obviously been souped up by the previous owners.

As soon as Jennifer had taken Kieran to school, they loaded up, stored the weapons and covered them with hay. On top of the hay they placed some animal cages, which Dianna sometimes used to transport young lambs and goats. One of the main items they had to check out was the wire that Rory would wear into his interview. This turned out to be a regular looking belt and they assumed that the bug was embedded in the buckle. It was either an old belt or had been scuffed up to give the impression of age. Surprisingly it was Rory's waist size, so it looked quite natural on him. They set up the listening device in the van and found that it gave a really clear sound from a hundred yards away. They were all supremely impressed with the CIA's new technology.

Also in the van was the tracking device, which would enable them to follow Rory to other locations when he moved. It also worked off the specially designed belt, which had a dual purpose. Rory was the expert in that area and had it running smoothly in no time. He explained how it worked to Dianna, who had previous knowledge of surveillance techniques.

Then they set out.

Danny drove his rental car and Rory took the van with Dianna as a passenger. On reaching highway 90 East and collecting their toll tickets, they both kept under the speed limit and were glad they had when they passed two New York police cruisers parked on the meridian. Danny spotted a large wooden statue of an Indian on the opposite side and assumed it signaled some reservation owned by the Six Nations. Eventually they passed through the tolls at the other end and Rory took highway 190 North leading into central Buffalo.

Danny split off following the exit 53 Canadian border signs. He crossed back over the Peace Bridge half an hour later with only a couple of cursory questions from the Canadian border guard. There was no U.S. post to cross through. He did have to pay three dollars at a kiosk further along and within minutes turned off the QEW into the Canadian city of Fort Erie. He drove back down alongside the Niagara river. From there he looked directly across at the city of Buffalo and found that he could see the target building belonging to Empire Security directly across the water.

Parking the car, he made contact with the boat owner who spent twenty minutes familiarizing him with the craft. Danny casually explained that he was taking some Buffalo business executives out fishing, after which he would come back across and return the boat. Then he intended to make a dash back up to Hamilton airport for his flight. In that way he could avoid getting stuck in a queue at the Peace Bridge.

His actual plan was to fly out of Pearson Airport in Toronto, but Danny was laying a false trail in case an alert went out for him after the operation.

He pushed away from the bank and was shortly making steady progress across the river heading for the small boat marina close to the target building on the Buffalo side.

In the meantime Dianna had driven to the bus station to verify the times in from Detroit that morning to confirm Rory's story of having just arrived in Buffalo. They had to make sure the times matched his story in case it was checked. It turned out that a bus had come in at 7 am so he would have to account for, if asked, how he had spent the time since he had arrived. While they were waiting for Danny to cross over in the boat, they found a small medium-priced hotel for Rory and he dumped his rucksack in the room then dashed back out to the van. Dianna managed to get a small motel a short walk away for Danny and herself.

They turned back along the route and eventually eased down to where boat owners at the marina parked their vehicles. A number of different sized boats were already tied up with owners and fishermen creating a hive of activity. Rory got the glasses and surveyed the stretch of water on the Niagara river between themselves and Fort Erie.

Finally he stiffened and pointed.

"There he is" he said excitedly, handing her the glasses.

"Yep, that's our Danny, always on time" she said.

He smiled slyly at her.

"Do I sense a double meaning there Dianna? Danny did look a bit tired this morning I thought. You're not calling him Brad any more either I see."

She thumped him but didn't reply.

He did notice however, a small smile touch her lips.

A short while later Danny had managed to tie up at a vacant spot well down from the target building, and they moved alongside it. Danny went off and talked to some fishermen about paying for a temporary berth while waiting for his guests to arrive later, then they all climbed on board the craft. It was bigger than they expected and had a good-sized stateroom and wheelhouse. They put some coffee on and re-capped their operational plans. Danny wanted to move some of the weapons from the van into the boat but decided to wait until it was dark. Rory had one question.

"Is there not some sort of watch on this side by immigration or border patrol agents? Surely it's not this easy to just run across from Canada?"

Danny nodded.

"Good question. When I was back in Fort Erie I was in conversation with an old guy fishing on the bank and I casually slipped in the same question. For starters it's the RCMP who patrol the Canadian section of the river, and the coastguard on the U.S. side. They have responsibility for watching for people, smugglers and others, who would be tempted to cross here. They patrol up and down the Niagara River quite frequently. He said that the two cities had been living side by side for hundreds of years. They even fought each other a couple of hundred years ago and have a regular re-enaction of the battles. All in good spirits of course. They join in each others festivals and special events and have close economic ties as well. A Canadian fisherman out on the Niagara River just pulls across to the Buffalo side to buy a carton of cigarettes or a pack of beer and the Americans might go across to the Canadian side for a meal out in the evening. They rent out boats on both side to tourists like myself. Any smuggling of people would be spotted quickly enough and you'd better believe it, the coastguard and RCMP would get a fast call. Seriously though, smugglers and terrorists would pick a more deserted place to enter the U.S., possibly farther up the St Lawrence River, so we're okay. Especially as I produced a Canadian ID and paid a large deposit."

Rory was looking a bit on edge and Danny knew it was time for the next stage. Dianna tapped him gently on the arm.

"Just a thought Rory, before we bring you up there. Remember that you are an ex Delta team member who has seen lots of action. When the CIA used to put a spook in a similar position they would have to take on board a complete new identity. They called it a legend. They would memorize it so that they couldn't be tripped up even by trained interrogators. You had to be a bit of an actor to carry it off particularly over a long period of time. In your case you don't have to do that. You are who you claim you are. In this case I'm suggesting that you walk in there as a 'kick-ass' ex Delta team member and don't take any crap. You're not going hat in hand begging for a job or a contract. You listen to what they have to offer and you decide if you want to work for them. You have other options, and one could be that you re-enlist back into the military now that your mother is sorted and the civvy job has fallen through. Does that help you?"

His eyes thoughtfully considered her as he nodded.

"Yeah, that's good Dianna. I was torn between not letting Danny down and how much I wanted to be accepted in there, but what you say is right. I need to play the hard-ass role to avert any suspicion that I have some other agenda going on. Yes, that's quite useful. Thanks."

Danny nodded his approval.

"Good advice Dianna. Now Rory, you have the descriptions of our three targets and if you can repeat the names of any of those without sounding like a parrot, please do it. You know 'General O'Donnell, pleased to meet you' kind of reaction, or just 'General'. Make sense? Now this sounds like take-off instruction in a civilian aircraft, but in the unlikely event that they cop on to you and the balloon goes up, I'll be straight down and through that front door wreaking fucking havoc as I go, and your job will be to survive as best you can until I get there. Oh, and if someone is accompanying you up on an elevator it would help if you casually asked 'what floor are we going to?' so I'll know where to locate you. Hope I don't have to come barging in, 'cos then it means we've lost the plot. And one more thing ..."

He reached into his jacket pocket and removed an object which he placed around Rory's neck.

"Here's the Indian necklace that you gave me in Afghanistan prior to action. I believe it's now time to hand it back to you. May it guide and protect you my friend".

Rory reached up and touched it reverently.

"Wow! I couldn't have asked for a better or more timely gift. Thanks Danny."

Dianna nudged Danny's arm.

"No more advice or trinkets at this late stage Danny. He's going to be fine. Come on let's do it."

The three left the boat, climbed into the van and eased back onto the main road. The Empire Security building was just three hundred yards from the boat, on the right hand side of 190 North, with the front façade of the building facing the road, and the rear, the Niagara River. Higher up behind the building and looking down on it, was a small side road where they intended to stop and monitor Rory's attempt to infiltrate the organization. She took an exit and drove Rory as close to the Empire Security building as possible without any risk of being spotted. As she stopped the van behind some cars at a medical clinic, he climbed out and, without a glance at either of them, started walking towards the building.

Dianna turned, darting smoothly across some side roads and stop signs until she was overlooking the target building and stopped. Both of them climbed into the back and switched on the listening device. It was the beginning of the end of the operation.

CHAPTER 63.

When Rory pushed through the front door, he was confronted by a security guard sitting behind a desk. The man was large and overweight. He flicked a condescending smirk at the smaller man then stuck an officious jaw out.

"What can I do for you?" he asked, running his eyes up and down Hanlon.

Rory gave him a hard look.

"I want to speak to one of the Empire Security managers about a position here."

"Have you an appointment?" the guard enquired, looking like he was enjoying his blocking role.

"No I don't, but I believe they'll want to talk to me" Rory responded confidently.

The guard eyed him up and down again.

"Oh, what makes you think that?" he asked with a hint of derision in his voice.

Rory leaned forward.

"Because I'm an ex-Delta team member, you tub of lard, and if you turn me away you'll probably be looking for a new job yourself tomorrow. Now get me someone in authority on the phone before I really get pissed off" he snarled.

The security guard's expression froze and he stepped back from the counter, blinking with surprise at the sudden aggressive change in the man confronting him. Without really thinking about it he turned and fumbled with the switchboard then mumbled into it. He pointed to the elevators and squeaked.

"Someone's coming down" he said looking warily at Rory.

Without a word Rory strode over to the elevator and watched it descend. When it opened a tall, smartly dressed woman of about thirty five stepped out and looked at him. She had long black hair held back in a pony tail shaping an intelligent oval face, and a pair of shrewd blue eyes which she concentrated on him.

"I'm Cindy Hawthorn, PA to Tom Bradley. I understand you're looking for a job with us in security. I don't know what you said to Horace over there, he was practically incoherent on the switch board."

Rory scowled.

"Nice to meet you Ms. Hawthorn, I'm Rory Hanlon. As for the guard, he appears to have injected himself with an overdose of his own self- importance. I just pricked his balloon a little. As I mentioned to him, I'm an ex Delta Force team member and I'm here checking out contract opportunities with Empire Security. Now who do I have to see for that, Ms. Hawthorn?"

"Be that as it may Mr. Hanlon, we have ways of doing things around here and normal practice is to phone up for an application form, which you complete and send in. We check it out and if we like it we call you in for an appointment and take it from there. Now......"

Rory cut in.

"Look Ms. Hawthorn, I'm only in Buffalo for today and I'm heading off to Rochester tomorrow where I have some definite job contract offers to follow up on. The reason I stopped off in Buffalo was because your company's name was mentioned when I was overseas, as a place where professionals like me were appreciated and welcomed with open arms. Now can you arrange for me to see your boss, Bradley did you say, or I'm heading out of here? While you're at it, you can tell him I earned two purple hearts in Iraq and a third in Afghanistan."

She looked uncertainly at him for a moment then turning, pushed the elevator button. In a chilly voice she said "follow me please" as she stepped into the elevator.

Rory followed her and asked "what floor are we going to?"

"The fourth" she said stiffly.

"The fourth" he repeated. "I like starting at the top."

She ignored his attempt at levity. When the elevator stopped she stepped out quickly, marched over to her desk and spoke into a telephone. She turned to him.

"Mr. Bradley will see you in a moment. However as a security precaution, all visitors to the fourth floor have to be screened."

She smiled for the first time as she looked at two large men who had just edged through a doorway off to the side. Both sported brush cuts and wore short sleeve shirts, which showed off their weight-trained muscles. They moved confidently in unison across to Rory, stopped and looked down at him at his smaller form. The largest of the two men chuckled.

"Doesn't look much like Delta Force to me Jim. What do you think?" he asked his colleague.

"Naw, those guys are animals Chuck. This fellow looks like a pussy cat to me" he said stepping around Rory and starting to run his hands roughly down his back. His bigger colleague pushed Rory forward with his elbow and attempted to kick his feet apart into the spread position.

Rory would have been quite prepared to accept a professional frisking similar to what one had to go through at an airport, but this was an attempt to humiliate him and he wouldn't normally have accepted being treated like this. He could have reasoned with them but he'd met types like these before, working as bouncers at nightclubs and glorying in their ability to bench press huge amounts, or raise dust from a punching bag.

He moved suddenly, stamping down savagely on the instep of the man behind him and striking back into his groin with the clenched back of his fist. While he was screaming and dropping to the floor, Rory snapped two incredibly fast kicks to the shin and stomach of the large man in front, and as he crumpled forward, brought his knee up smashing it into his face, then chopped the side of his neck.

He collapsed onto the floor moaning as blood spurted from his broken nose. The other man was writhing on the floor clutching his groin. Ms. Hawthorn stood mesmerized at her desk, her jaw practically on her chest.

An authoritative voice rang across from behind Rory.

"Enough of this! I think you've made your point Hanlon."

Rory turned to see a tall gray haired man with military bearing, standing in an open doorway. He knew from Danny's description that he was looking at Tom Bradley who had been in the Iraq desert, waiting to receive the delivery from the SAS troop. There was a frosty look to his gaze, but at the same time Rory sensed an appreciative glint when his eyes flicked to the two groaning men on the floor.

Bradley gestured to him.

"You've got your appointment. Come on in" he said briskly.

Rory walked across and passed Bradley, walking into what he assumed was his office. When the door slammed shut behind him he turned to face the gray haired man who cocked his head and looked at him.

"If you don't mind I'd like to do a very quick frisk on your person, just to make sure that you're not carrying a weapon or wired up for whatever reason."

Rory shrugged and raised his arms sideways.

"I've no problem with that. Your two goons started to rough me up, otherwise we could have been having this chat without that unpleasantness out there. I'd say they were weekend warriors who run round with rifles and play soldiers, but I'm not putting down all the fine national guards I've met overseas who do an excellent job."

Bradley finished his search and stepped back looking at him.

"Did you have to be so rough on them? They'll probably be off for a month recovering, and I may very well not take them back considering that you could have come in here with a more deadly purpose."

Rory returned his look, his face bleak.

"When I go for someone there's no half-way measures I'm afraid. I could just as easily have killed them both, but I wouldn't get any more medals for that would I?"

Bradley relaxed, a smile starting to play round his lined features.

"When you put it like that, I'll tell them later just how lucky they were. Now sit down and tell me why you're here."

Over the next half hour Rory laid out his story and Bradley took notes. Occasionally he interrupted and asked questions. Eventually he stopped Rory and made a brief phone call. A moment later a young man came into the room, took the details that Bradley had written down and left without a word. Rory took advantage of the break to ask some questions himself. He looked around appraisingly.

"Fine looking building. Does Empire Security own it or rent it?" he asked.

"We never rent. We like to own our property.... keeps out nosy landlords."

"I'm impressed. What do you use the four floors for? That's a lot of space for a security organization?"

"Well we have several world wide areas of operations to deal with and we split these on each floor. Providing security for VIP's in trouble spots like Iraq and Afghanistan, Kossovo, Darfur, and Lebanon is a major part of our business, as is providing security cover for U.S. construction workers. Add in visits by foreign diplomats, pop stars or Arabian Princes on a shopping trip, and you're just getting a sniff of some of the things we're involved in. We also get pulled in by the U.S. government on more sensitive missions occasionally, and they like to know that we can provide ex Delta Team members like yourself. One of the reasons I still agreed to see you, after you disabled my two so called protectors. Now let's get on with the interview, shall we?"

Twenty minutes later the young man came back in, laid a bunch of paperwork down in front of him, then whispered in his ear for a moment before leaving. Rory stopped talking as Bradley worked his way through the papers.

Finally he looked up.

"We are a security organization and of course we have to check people out all the time in the work we do. That makes sense doesn't it? For that we have access to enormous amounts of information, and what we don't have, we hack into. That young man who left is a computer geek and he can find out everything about anyone in the U.S.A. and elsewhere if we need it. I can tell you that in the post 9/11 world there's no hiding place for anyone. It was a great boon to security companies like ourselves, and Uncle Sam has been an enormous help to us, devouring every list and any pieces of information they can get their hands on. We could even tell you how many fillings you have in your teeth if it was relevant. Now I've found out that you are who you claim to be, Rory Hanlon, and you did get honorably discharged from the U.S. military approximately one year ago at Fort Bragg. You do have the decorations you claim, in fact several others that you didn't mention to Ms. Hawthorn. I'm impressed! We also have photo identification of you from the military. It's a younger picture but most definitely you, and we have confirmed by telephone with the car company that you worked for them and that you have been let go recently, after working there since you took your discharge. My young computer geek also checked out the nursing home that your mother's presently living in, so we can now start to have a real conversation about some work with our organization. You might just be a gift from the Gods at this particular time Hanlon. Where are you staying in town?"

Rory told him.

Bradley snorted.

"We'll have to get you something better than that tomorrow. That's not suitable for someone working for our organization and I'm assuming right now that you will be. Don't worry I can assure you that the rewards and benefits will exceed even your wildest dreams. Now this evening I want to pick you up from there and take you to meet some of my colleagues. They're going to be very impressed with you my friend, I can tell you!"

CHAPTER 64.

Danny and Dianna gave each other a hug after Rory's penetration of the security organization. They waited and eventually saw a cab pull up and Rory emerged from the building, get into it and drove off. They watched to see if he was followed, but failing to spot anything, they pulled in several cars behind the cab. It was unlikely that the security company would follow Rory as they already knew which hotel he was staying in. They also assumed that his cover story had been accepted and that he wouldn't be under suspicion or surveillance. The cab stopped at the hotel and Rory strolled casually inside.

They parked three blocks down in a small strip mall which had a take-out pizza place, a convenience store and a health clinic. Danny dashed in for a large pizza while Dianna used the binoculars to keep Rory's hotel in view. Just as he came out again and started walking, Danny jumped back into the car with a box of pizza and some cans of 7-Up. They cruised slowly behind him from a distance keeping him under view with the glasses. They spotted no surveillance but realized that a massive operation involving multiple units would be hard to spot in any event. It was unlikely that the security company could launch such a plan at short notice so they moved to the next step.

As Rory made a right turn onto another street, they were already parked with the side door open and he scrambled in slamming the door behind him. Dianna took off and made the first turn she came to, then fifty yards on took the next left, pulling into an alley-way twenty yards further up and stopped. Danny was peering out the back window of the van since they had picked Rory up. Now he turned and sat down on the floor of the vehicle.

"Clear back here folks. Can't spot a thing" he said cheerily, then gave Rory a big high five and handed him the box of pizza and a can of drink.

"You did real good in there…. haven't lost anything Rory! You sure kicked ass! For a moment I thought you'd gone too far. We could only hear the action but we had a good idea of what was going on."

Dianna chipped in.

"From the sounds we heard you sure took those two security types out fast. They hadn't a clue what they were bringing down on themselves. God I'd have loved to have been a fly on the wall right then!"

Rory grinned.

"Yeah, the old reactions kicked in when I needed them. Apart from that, those two heavies were ready to be taken down and it was a pleasure to do it. Impressed the hell out of Bradley, I can tell you!"

Danny chuckled.

"I actually loved the way you handled the security guard when you went inside. We could hear his voice literally change to a squeak after you tore a strip off him. A tub of lard you called him. You sure know how to win friends and influence people Rory!"

Dianna nearly choked on her 7-Up.

"Oh I loved that part! I could just see that typical overweight officious guard before you took the wind out of his sails. Wow! And Bradley seemed to buy into you for sure. How do you see this visit tonight Rory?" she asked, glancing back at him.

He took another bite of pizza followed by a drink while he was considering her question.

Finally, "I don't really know Dianna. It sounds straight up. Bradley has bought in to me and wants to run me past some of his colleagues. What more could it be right now? I'm hoping that I get to meet some of the other players in the game, you know General O'Donnell or that Colonel from Kuwait. What are your thoughts Danny?"

Danny screwed his face up thoughtfully.

"You know something has been niggling at me since Bradley talked to you about how he can access anything about you, including the fillings in your teeth. I mean he's absolutely right. Today the government can find out what books you took out of the library, your health records, who you call on the telephone, where you shop and so on. Presumably Bradley has hacked into all those areas, or as a security company doing business with the U.S. government has been handed all that information already. It wouldn't surprise me. It's what he didn't check you out on, or worse still neglected to tell you about, that worries me - your financial situation for instance. He could have hit your bank account as easy as pie and for someone as thorough as he appears to be, that's pretty sloppy."

"Which would have told him what exactly?" Dianna prompted.

Danny glanced at Rory who shrugged.

"Danny transferred just under10K into my account a few days ago to help me out. Sorry, we didn't see any reason to pass this on to you Dianna" Rory said almost apologetically.

She stopped eating for a moment, glancing at Danny.

" O-kay" she said slowly. "Well, it's none of my business anyway. Doesn't change anything with me really guys, but what's your point Danny?"

He leaned forward.

"Don't you see? If he did check his bank account, which I bet he did, because it would re-enforce his imminent need for a job, he would have asked him where the 10K came from. It would have been a natural question to ask. It wouldn't have been severance or redundancy pay with just a year on the job."

"So why didn't he ask me?" Rory asked, shifting around to make himself more comfortable.

Dianna's face paled.

"Shit, they're onto us! They probably didn't ask him because it would have broken that loop of acceptance they were creating to make him out to be the greatest thing since sliced bread, and they wanted him on the team. Yeah sure! Probably been expecting us for fuck's sake! But how? Tell me that Danny?"

His face stilled as he considered the situation.

"There are three possibilities as I see it. Who knows about this operation apart from us? MI5 in London and that information, as far as we know is limited to Rebecca Fullerton-Smythe and Jack McAllister. The other is Brett Zeitner and presumably his two colleagues, who didn't exactly take to us."

"What's the third?" Rory pressed impatiently.

"Empire Security were wiped out in Southampton by us, but some of the prime players are still on the loose. They simply came up with the quite plausible answer that we would come after their Buffalo operation. After all the U.S. address was clearly marked on their letterheads that were seized by the police when they raided their office in Southampton."

Dianna looked from one to the other.

"Are you saying we're blown" she whispered, "before we're even out of the gate?"

Rory butted in.

"Which of the three possibilities do you favor Danny? Was it a leak or just very shrewd thinking on their part?"

"Wheels within wheels guys. Let me just talk around it for a moment before answering. Brett Zeitner knew everything about our operation in the U.K. when I talked to him the other day. Now who else apart from Rebecca was privy to that information?"

"McAllister was involved all the way along from what you've told me." Dianna answered.

Danny nodded.

"Exactly, and I now believe he's been Zeitner's little song bird, not just recently, but over the years for whatever reason. Why? Who knows, sex, money, the thrill of it, the promise of a future with the CIA. Here's the thing though. I don't think he blew our cover, nor did Zeitner. He has his own reasons for wanting us to succeed. Hell he even got involved in equipping the operation."

"Then who Danny? Stop messing with our heads here" Dianna snapped.

"Okay, here's what I think. It was more than likely the two morons we met outside the diner with Zeitner. He told me how cut-throat the organization has become and this just might have been their little way of getting Zeitner put out to pasture. There's probably a puppeteer behind those two back in Washington who has his or her own agenda."

She grunted assent.

"Yeah, it's a bitch of an organization to work for anymore. One of the reasons I bailed out when I did. So you lay responsibility at their feet then, assuming that we haven't been blown in the first place Danny?"

"On balance I'd say yes and Empire were just sitting there waiting for us to approach them. Hell as I recall, I even mentioned to Zeitner how we planned to initiate the approach. Shit!"

Rory had been sitting there considering his thought process and now coughed.

"I can't figure out what their goal is. Why didn't they call the cops and have me charged with assault on those two guards? Lots of witnesses. I'd have probably spent the next ten years in prison."

Danny knew the answer but waited for them to arrive at the same conclusion. It was Dianna who spoke first.

"They want the rest of us don't they? Probably specifically you Danny, as the person who wiped out their organization in the south of England. Sinclair was there and knows you were the prime mover. He may also have had friends in the team you disposed of and wants revenge. Perhaps his pride is involved. After all you killed his career and any potential future he might have had in Intelligence. From what we heard from Rory's visit, they have a far flung organization and they want to be seen as one that looks after it's own. The word ripples out, and what happened in Southampton has probably filtered out already. We have a problem don't we?" she concluded.

Danny was about to answer but suddenly sat up rigidly, his face alarmed. He reached for one of the cell phones and thrust it into Rory's hand.

"They know where your mother is for Gods sake. Get onto that nursing home right away and warn them that some people may be landing up on their doorstep at any minute, probably dressed in nurses uniforms with a doctor in charge and with a signed authorization from you for the transfer of your mother to another facility. If that happens tell them to call the cops right away and not let them in the building. Have them warn the whole staff and if needs be hire some additional security for the complex and agree to pay for it."

Rory sat there stunned. Then he grabbed the phone and started dialing. .

Dianna stared at Danny.

"Why would they go to those lengths? They're picking up Rory later this evening and will have him in their hands for Gods sake!"

"Leverage. I could be wrong and I hope I am but imagine the effect on Rory at the crucial moment this evening, before they take him down, when they tell him that they have his mother. It would cut the legs from under him Dianna."

"Good God Danny! If this is the military thinking you're talking about I think it's sick! I wouldn't have anything to do with it."

He looked at her levelly.

"You're right, it is sick. Now while we're at it, and I don't think this is as likely a danger, but it might be a good idea for Jennifer to call that friendly cop Tim over to the farm until this is over. She can't leave the farm with the animals needing tending, but Zeitner's two morons know where you live as well, and that you're involved."

Her eyes widened.

"You can't be serious Danny! They wouldn't go as far as to go after a young boy and a woman who can't speak surely?" she protested.

At the same time she reached for the other cell phone and slid rapidly out of the van to avoid cutting across Rory's conversation.

Danny sat there thinking, his mind racing over the situation and how it was starting to evolve. After a short while Rory finished his call.

Danny looked at him.

"Is your mother still okay?" he asked.

"Yes, thank God! I talked directly to the lady in charge at the nursing home and shocked the hell out of her. Oh, they've had relatives in the past coming and trying to move a family member to somewhere else, ostensibly to improve their situation, but generally it's to gain more control and influence over them. In other words, to change their will. So they have pretty strict guidelines in place but nothing as formidable as the force I suggested might roll up to their door step. Christ Danny, you scared the shit out of me back there!"

Danny nodded grimly.

"The game has begun my friend and the stakes are high. There are no rules, just to win at all costs. I've told Dianna to take some precautions back at the farm as well. Get that cop Tim over, the one who fancies Dianna, just in case until this is over."

Rory looked shocked again.

"Hell, we never thought........" he started to say.

"We didn't know we were lumbered before we even left the farm or we might have put some contingency plans in place. As it is, we're reacting to their moves at this stage and we have to break the cycle."

"But how….?" he started to ask.

Dianna, who slid back into her seat overheard him and repeated Rory's question.

"Yes, exactly how Danny?"

Danny held up his finger, silencing them both and slipped out of the van taking the cell phone with him. He was back in his seat within five minutes and there was a look of satisfaction on his face. He now leaned sideways and spoke to both of them slowly and deliberately.

"I've always been a student of past battles and the leaders involved in them, sometimes against the most overwhelming odds. Two of those leaders operated in the latter part of the last century: General Patton and Moise Dyanne of Israel. Now can either of you remember their philosophy in battle?"

Rory's face lit up.

"Absolutely! Their only philosophy was, when in doubt attack. Most often they were proved right and won the day."

"Spot on Rory…. attack. We're going to take Empire Security down tonight. Not a prolonged operation as we thought, where Rory infiltrates their organization and winkles out where the targets are. I've just made a phone call and started the ball rolling. I've told Zeitner that we're going to break into the Empire Security building later tonight."

"You did what?" Dianna gasped.

Rory looked perplexed.

"Jesus Danny……" he started.

Danny chuckled.

"Don't worry guys, we won't be there, at least not in the way they think anyway. The net result will be to suck a big piece of their manpower away from Rory's meeting place where they no doubt have a nice reception planned for him. That's where we're going to hit them and hit them hard. We need to do it in a way that gives Rory every chance of surviving it. Here's what I propose. Let's get back to the boat and do some serious planning. Now who's for taking the initiative and bringing the fight to the enemy?"

Rory and Dianna looked briefly at each other and back to Danny. She spoke for both of them.

"Let's get the bastards Danny" she said fiercely.

CHAPTER 65.

It was getting dark when a silver Mercedes pulled up outside Rory's hotel and a driver got out. He proceeded inside the hotel and emerged moments later with Rory strolling alongside. As he opened the passenger door and looked inside the vehicle, Rory scratched his right ear.

Signal. The driver was alone.

They dropped in behind, several cars back with Danny monitoring the tracking device. They saw the vehicle ahead pull onto highway 190 North and followed behind some other cars. He was also watching for any vehicle behind that might be tracking the lead car and watching for anyone showing an interest, a difficult task with drivers now using headlights. After several minutes he figured they were clear of watchers, none-the-less they were able to keep well back with the tracking device working smoothly. Traffic on 190 North moved at a fast pace and cars were exiting and coming on to the highway aggressively and confidently. After twenty minutes Danny noticed a repositioning and slowing down in the vehicle ahead.

"It's getting off Dianna. Probably the next exit. The sign said Riverside Park"

"Roger that. I'll get off but keep close watch for directions after the ramp. Some of these Buffalo roads make it difficult to just turn around if I take the wrong turn" she replied calmly.

He sat forward watching closely.

"It's a right…………" he called out. Then a while later "Now a left turn…. going straight ahead!"

Out of the corner of his eye, he saw Dianna follow his directions and as she made the left turn, he saw that they had come into a residential area, which appeared to run alongside the park.

"Slow right down here Dianna and keep back. We're too easy to spot with so few other cars around. Just ease right back."

He watched the monitor

"Hold it, they've stopped. Let me out here" he instructed.

Danny jumped out. He was clad in a black tracksuit, with a runner's head band and started jogging up the road in the direction of the Mercedes. On his right were a number of well designed residences with lots of space and well trimmed hedges and gardens. On the left hand side was an extensive park which ran straight ahead. The street looked like an up market area with two open carports for each house and some double garages. Two hundred yards up he spotted the car, which had pulled into a car port. He stopped short of running past and stepped sideways behind some foliage sticking out from the fence of the next-door neighbor's house.

His first reaction was surprise that Bradley, if this was his house, didn't have some sort of gated residence with a manned entrance gate. The place looked too easy to attack. He started to wonder if he had got it all totally wrong and that the organization had accepted Rory for what he claimed to be, an ex Delta team member looking for a job. Then he realized that Bradley, living in Buffalo, was not in a situation where he needed protection from any hostile force and even if he did, properties like that were difficult to find close to the city. He may have only moved house fairly recently and just wanted to fit in like any normal citizen, albeit a highly successful one to be able to afford a property like this. Or it belonged to a colleague and they chose it to make Rory relax his guard as it looked like he was visiting a normal house in the suburbs.

He noticed three parked cars pulled off on a grass verge to the left of the driveway and nosed into some trees. Another was parked alongside the Mercedes in the carport. Three more were parked directly on the roadway outside. That made eight cars in total.

A lot of guests!

The house was a bungalow with a front deck, and a door leading inside. From his vantage point he saw that it had an impressive frontage but that it was also extensive and ran back a considerable way into the site. He saw no hydro poles so knew that it would have taken more time than he had to locate the connection and sever it. That eliminated blacking out the residence prior to any attack. The park, which was directly across from the house offered some possibilities.

He pushed further in through various bushes and ferns to the neighbor's white picket fence. The neighbor's residence was a sprawled bungalow with lights on in various rooms. The fence that ran between the bungalow and the target house was fairly well in the shadow from a number of small overgrown bushes. It offered some possibility of scouting out the rear of the house next door. Danny hoped they didn't have a dog.

Debating the wisdom of creeping back there right then, he immediately dismissed the thought. He wasn't armed if he ran into any trouble and he hadn't completed his reconnaissance. It was imperative that he get back to the van and check what was going on inside with Rory, but first he decided to take a chance.

He pushed his way out of the bushes and started jogging towards the house, needing to know if the cars parked on the street had watchers in them. He kept his eyes straight forward as he came abreast of them. From his peripheral vision he could see that the first two cars were empty. The third had tinted windows and he knew it would be difficult to see anyone inside. He was just going past it when he spotted a shifting in the light and shadow inside the vehicle. There were spotters inside!

He kept going, feeling extremely exposed knowing that if they came after him to check him out he was unarmed and vulnerable.

There were no sounds of a vehicle starting up or of doors slamming. He started to breathe easier but his heart was pounding for another reason.

The game was on!

This was more than a simple invitation to Rory to meet with colleagues, when they had watchers sitting outside waiting. Waiting for what?

He jogged all the way down to the end of the road and around the corner, then dashed across into the park. There was a perimeter track running around the inside of the park and he made his way back along it, staying in the shadows. He passed the house and the manned vehicle outside and studied it for a moment. Then he trotted back along the perimeter road until he came to an entrance leading into the park with a locked barrier across it. He examined the lock and grunted in satisfaction. Within minutes he scuttled back across the road and slipped into the back of the vehicle. Dianna started.

"God you gave me a shock! The last I saw you were disappearing off up that road. What's the story?"

He told her.

Before starting out he had unhooked the parking light that comes on automatically when starting up North American vehicles, as well as the interior lights in the van. When he'd finished the report he asked what was happening with Rory.

"Okay so far. Sounds like he's met three people, one of them Bradley and the other the General and someone else. So there's two of your targets there. No sign of Sinclair and that Colonel from Kuwait, Minter. When they offered him a drink, which you advised him not to take in case they'd slipped something into it, he apparently grabbed a bottle of water instead. He signaled some other information as well"

"What was the signal?" he asked impatiently.

"Oh, he just commented, I'm disappointed I'm not going to be meeting with your family, Tom. I hope they didn't all leave when they heard I was coming. So there's no women there as far as we know. Otherwise we would have had to be real careful when we hit the place."

They listened to some small talk on the receiver and Danny finally stirred. He grabbed a pair of metal cutters and sprinted across the road twenty yards back from where she was parked and chopped the lock off the barrier. Dianna slowly reversed the van, stopped and turned the vehicle across the road into the park. Danny put the barrier back up before throwing some camouflage netting across the windscreen and front of the van to reduce reflection that might be spotted by the watchers. He proceeded to guide her slowly back down the perimeter road. When she reached a spot where she was able to ease the van into some bushes without being seen from the road, she stopped and switched off the engine. From there she had an excellent view of the house and the cars parked out front. He studied the road for a few moments.

"No traffic, that's good. Now here's what I intend to do."

CHAPTER 66.

Danny ran back down the perimeter road inside the park and came out where he had previously entered it and where he had disappeared from the watchers view. He started jogging in the direction of the vehicle with the watchers in it. As he came closer Dianna appeared, walking briskly from the opposite direction like someone out for some aerobic exercise. They were both trying to judge the decreasing distance between them so that they met at the front door of the car. As Dianna came abreast of it Danny stopped, reached across and grabbed her.

"Hey" he said. "I've seen you before out here. We're practically friends. How about we go across to the park and get better acquainted?"

She shrank back from him, a muted cry of fright coming from her as she pushed his arm away.

"Leave me alone!" she shouted, looking around desperately.

He grabbed her again.

"Now that's not the way to treat a friendly neighbor. I'll bet you'll like me when you get to know me. Come on, just for a few minutes" he said nodding towards the park. "I promise I won't hurt you honey."

A growl of anger started to edge into his voice.

She pushed him back again.

"I told you......" she began.

Just then the front car door opened and a large bald-headed man emerged and reached for Danny.

"Look you slimy perp, the woman said......"

Those were the last words he spoke. Danny struck him straight into the heart with the trench knife. As the man was collapsing on the ground he pulled him off to one side and Dianna filled the doorway instantly with Rory's silenced SOCOM pistol, placing the red dot on two startled faces in the back seat. Two shots were all it took. Danny heaved the body of the man on the sidewalk into the front seat and slammed the door shut. Dianna ran back across the road to the park, scrambled over the fence and into the van. Danny ducked down and cut the tires on all three cars. He crawled over to the brick wall directly in front of the target house and observed the windows for a few minutes. There appeared to be no sign of movement or life in the front room.

He scuttled over to the three cars nosed into the trees and used the trench knife on them too. Six cars out of operation. Two more to go. He wanted to reduce the possibility that Rory could be driven away at a moments notice.

With another long glance at the windows he darted across the front of the house to the two cars in the carport and quickly sliced through their front tires. Pausing for a moment he rose, then ran back across the road and over the fence into the park.

At the back of the van Dianna was waiting for him and passed the equipment he'd asked her to get ready. The first was a satchel to carry some of his gear in. He chose the silenced 9-mm US Ingram, 32 round sub machine gun in the hope that they could make a silent killing and get away before an alarm went off and roadblocks went up. From past experience he knew it to be a powerful, reliable and effective weapon. He stuck an extra magazine in his side pocket along with the six sets of plastic cuffs. As a sop to Zeitner he took the Judge Taurus revolver and loaded shotgun shells into it. He didn't think he would use it because of the noise factor alone. For Rory, when he got inside he took along the silenced SOCOM pistol and as additional firepower for himself, he took the MI 30 round assault rifle with fitted M203 grenade launcher already loaded.

The night goggles, he wasn't sure about because of the amount of street lighting out front but he took them anyway as he didn't know what it was like round the back of the house. Lastly he took the walkie-talkie to stay in contact with Dianna as to the status of Rory and the situation inside. They had a signal arranged, two presses on her button, which he would acknowledge with two in return, before she sent a message to him. That was to avoid him giving away his position if he was close to the enemy contact. Equally he would hit his button twice to request an update.

Dianna was set up with the Simrad day and night vision binoculars and a sniper rifle covering the front door. Now that the watchers in the car were neutralized she took off the camouflage material and turned the truck around in the direction of the park exit. Danny nipped back to the park entrance and lifted the barrier off, hoping no one would notice late at night. He gave her a thumbs-up and disappeared over the fence.

She watched him as he went across the road, pushed his way into the foliage of the next-door neighbors house and climbed over the fence. The bungalow was in plain view, and he could see signs of a TV in one of the rooms and shadows of people behind the kitchen curtains. Still no signs of a dog.

Cautiously, he started working his way down along the fence between the two properties. With his dark clothing he was pretty much invisible but he moved slowly, knowing that a slip up now endangered the whole operation. At any moment someone might come out to the car to relieve the watchers or bring them refreshments. Having come to the end of the fence, he paused and took stock of his position. He was well down the bungalow garden in the darker section. The fence was about seven feet high between the two gardens. He could scramble over it SAS style but if there were sentries posted round the back they could easily detect the noise. He found an empty knothole in the wood and tried to peer through but all he could see was darkness on the other side. Swiveling his head, he looked back at the rear of the house and saw two metal garbage cans standing there. Creeping back he chose the more solid one and brought it back to his position. He slipped the satchel and weapons off and placed them down on the ground before slipping on the Dutch night vision goggles harness. It took a moment for his eyes to adjust. When they did he caught the top of the fence and carefully bracing his right leg on the garbage can, eased himself upwards until he was peering into the rear garden of the target house.

He stood there for ten minutes without moving.

Finally he spotted the guard at the top end of an empty rectangular swimming pool. He was sitting on a poolside chair with his back to the house. Danny only spotted him because of the cigarette he'd just lit up, the only light being a slight glow from the paint in the empty pool.

With the night goggles Danny could see that his chances of getting over the fence and crawling thirty yards up through a garden with no cover whatsoever, and taking this guy out had zero chance of success. Not from where he stood at least.

Climbing down he moved the garbage can and the equipment back to where he estimated he was slightly behind the seated man at the pool. He silently stood up on the garbage can and peered over again. Not quite the right position. He moved it another six feet and looked again. It was spot on.

Reaching down he picked up the H&K SOCOM pistol with the silencer and laser aiming device, which put a red dot on the target. Standing up and still wearing the night vision goggles he propped his arm on top of the fence and placed the red dot squarely on the back of his target, directly opposite his heart. He breathed in, and as he exhaled, squeezed off two rapid shots.

There was the sound of a chair falling over, a moment's silence and a further dull thud as the man disappeared into the empty swimming pool. Then silence.

He waited a second to see if there might have been a second guard somewhere in the vicinity, or in case someone inside came out to check the noise. Nothing.

Danny leaned forward, grasped the satchel and the rest of his kit and scaled the wall in one smooth movement. Once on the inside he paused, crept over to the edge of the pool and looked down. He could see the outline of the man's body lying still on the bottom. There was no doubt in his mind that he was dead. Satisfied, he turned to assess the rear of the house and the garden. At the back of the garden stood a small shed which he assumed was for the storing of lawnmowers, garden chairs and other pool equipment. He dismissed it immediately. The residence ran back almost to the pool and appeared to be sectioned into an extensive ground floor level with basement quarters.

The curtains were drawn in the ground level rooms and he could hear voices came from inside. He moved closer to the window and listened for a moment, but the double-glazing reduced the sound to a distant murmur. He prayed that Rory was still okay inside.

Moving back along the wall of the house towards the carport he spotted a small window almost at grass level and cautiously knelt down to peer inside. He was glad he did. He was looking into a converted basement.

Four large, tough-looking men were busily engaged in playing a game of snooker. All had their coats off revealing holsters, two of which had weapons lodged in them. Two of the others had set their weapons off on a side table, probably to facilitate playing the game. He noted the outlay of the room and where a flight of steps emerged from upstairs.

He crept back to what appeared to be the back of the carport and checked a door which seemed to lead into it. It was locked but the key was on his side. He unlocked it, and opening the door, found himself looking directly into the area where he had previously disabled the two cars. Another door led directly into the house from the carport and he tested it. It was unlocked, which surprised him. Then he figured that the three men on duty on the outside road probably used this entrance to use the toilet or grab some refreshments.

He decided to check in with Dianna and clicked the walkie-talkie twice. He wanted to know what was going on inside with Rory.

CHAPTER 67.

Rory was surprised at the reception he received at the house. He was escorted inside by the driver where three men were waiting to greet him. He recognized two of them from the descriptions given to him via Danny from Major Wainwright.

General O'Donnell was a squat, bald-headed individual who tonight was in civilian clothes, but he exuded the air of a military-honed man in his stance and deportment. He grasped Rory's hand strongly and used the advantage that larger men sometimes take advantage of to pull him slightly forward and off balance. Balance was one thing Rory was well versed in from his combat training and he stood solid and in control, while staying alert and aware. Many a man had been caught off guard by someone clamping one of his hands while a second dropped a garotte over his neck. O'Donnell's voice was brittle and obviously used to command.

"Heard about you Hanlon. You look in good shape for someone out of the system for a year. Was in myself you know.... reached a one star. Got out to make some money while I was still young enough to enjoy it. Worked with Delta a number of times. Excellent warriors, first class."

Rory tried to look impressed.

"So, do we still call you General? That's fine by me. You obviously earned it. Glad you mentioned the money - that's why I'm here I guess."

"General's fine Hanlon and we'll talk about money later. Now let me introduce our CEO, Cole Watson. He's responsible for world-wide operations, the recruiting, training and provision of effective teams in trouble spots, which is why he was keen to meet you this evening. He's going to be your main point of contact until he allocates you to a unit. He'll also talk to you about the opportunities that exist at Empire right now. The world is full of trouble spots and that means more business for our services. Cole, meet Rory Hanlon the ex Delta guy."

Rory felt a coldness come over him as he reached forward and shook the man's hand. It was damp with perspiration and his handshake brief and slack, but it was his dark gray, nearly black eyes that disturbed Rory. There was almost a feline calculation and hatred shining in them. He wasn't a large man, but there was a tautness and strength in the way he held himself that told Rory he was facing an extremely dangerous individual, also an enemy. No pretence here. This man knew the purpose of the evening and couldn't wait for the action to get started.

They both mumbled something to each other but the words slipped past Rory as the warning bells continued to go off.

The General nodded to Tom Bradley.

"You met Tom earlier today and I must say you impressed him to no end with your method of getting an interview. Tom is CEO and general manager of the Buffalo office and mainland U.S. operations. I'm not sure he'd want you around his office for too long. The staff turnover and injuries would make his job far too difficult!

Now let's get you a drink Hanlon. What will you have?"

"Oh one of those bottles of water is fine" he said turning round and casually reaching for a capped bottle on the table behind him. As he unscrewed it he looked around in apparent surprise.

"I don't see any of the ladies around. I thought I would have the pleasure of meeting some of your women folk to-night."

Bradley blinked.

"Oh you mean our wives? Well they have their regular monthly meeting this evening and I did throw this little meeting together at a moments notice when we met earlier today. However not to worry, the chauffeur whom you met earlier, doubles as a chef when required. I'm sure you won't be disappointed. Isn't that right Cole?"

"Yeah, he's good" Watson responded woodenly, never taking his eyes off Rory.

After some more conversation dominated by the General, they went into the next room which was obviously the dining room, with a table laid out for four people.

Rory took advantage of the usual hesitation of people hovering around to slip over to a corner seat where he had a better command of the room. Watson flicked his eyes across at O'Donnell, in what seemed to Rory to be a warning.

They all settled down and the chef almost immediately brought in a massive roast beef on a platter, followed by additional plates of vegetables. He also went round the table filling wine glasses.

Rory declined, as did Watson. The meal proceeded without incident.

The conversation, initiated by the General was focused on things military. Rory was starting to relax and enjoy the meal when suddenly the General looked across at him.

"You mentioned one or two operations that you were involved in over in Afghanistan. Ever hear of an S.A.S. chap called Danny Quigley while you were there?" he asked.

The conversation stilled around the table.

Rory touched his chin thoughtfully.

"Quigley? Danny Quigley? Can't say that I have, and yet it seems to ring a bell somehow."

Watson cut in.

"It should ring a bell. He killed a whole bundle of Taliban and Al Qaeda while out on a Delta operation. I would have thought that's the sort of thing you guys talk up when you sit around shooting the shit."

Rory slapped the table.

"Danny Quigley. Of course! How could I forget? He was out with one of our other teams when it happened. He's now a bloody legend in the SAS as I understand."

Watson regarded him stonily.

"Strange you should forget a story like that so easily Hanlon. A legend at that."

Rory laughed and looked across at O'Donnell.

"I'll bet the General doesn't remember every action he was involved in or heard about second hand. The ones that stay with you are the ones where you managed to get back out without getting shot to pieces."

O'Donnell nodded enthusiastically.

"Well said. Watson there wouldn't know anything about that. Tried to enlist and was rejected. The psychologists didn't like something about you isn't that right Cole?"

Watson squirmed.

"The way you say it General sounds like I was a complete reject. It was just…"

The General snorted.

"They turned you down for fuck sake. Just accept it!"

Rory wondered why the General was needling Watson. There was obviously some history between the two of them. He wondered if he could use it if trouble started. Then he mentally turned the 'if' to a 'when'. No doubt there was imminent action on the menu tonight.

CHAPTER 68.

Danny checked in with Dianna on the walkie-talkie and got back a terse message from her about the conversation inside. He wondered what they were waiting for but he didn't intend to wait as the initiative was still on his side. However his demolition of the outside security personnel could be discovered at any moment. He had informed Dianna that he was going inside, leaving the walkie-talkie and the other material under the front bumper of one of the cars in the carport.

She told him to be careful.

He discarded the night vision goggles, and the heavier MI assault rifle with the fitted M203 grenade launcher. He took with him the Taurus Judge tucked in under his track suit in his belt.

He carried the silenced US 9-mm Ingram. His knuckle duster trench knife was tucked into his boot.

Rory's SOCOM pistol was in the satchel along with the plastic cuffs. He pulled on a black balaclava, useful for shock purposes, then, opening the side door, slipped carefully inside.

Dianna had warned him about the driver/chef who was somewhere in the house, so he was on high alert as he edged along the corridor he had stepped directly into.

The first thing he came to was a short staircase leading down to the basement. It presumably led down to the snooker room and the four heavies. He checked the Ingram once again to ensure the safety was off and ready for action before moving quietly downstairs. Near the bottom he could hear the raucous laughter and comments of the men at the pool table.

Danny well knew the advantage that surprise gave an attacker, especially when he was outnumbered. He peered round the corner and measured the distance between himself the pool table and the individual positions of the men, then waited until the attention of all four was on the far side of the table. He strolled casually towards them. It surprised him how close he actually got before one of the men looked around and saw him.

Danny said.

"Hi guys."

The man gasped out.

"Oh shit!" and grabbed for his holstered weapon.

Danny shot him directly in the forehead and kept moving as the second man with a gun in his holster reached for it. He took him down with a double tap directly over the heart, slamming him back across the table. The other two men who had been frozen during the explosive action, now started to move towards their weapons on the side table.

Danny dived over behind them.

"Freeze you bastards or you're both dead meat" he hissed.

They hesitated momentarily, glancing at each other.

"On the floor now or I blow your fucking heads off" Danny snarled, leaning forward and pressing the Ingram against the first man's ear.

"Your choice buddy! On the floor now or you join your friends. Down!" he snarled.

Beaten, they both dropped to their knees.

Danny reached back and pulled some plastic cuffs out of his satchel, dropping them in front of one of the men.

"Cuff him now. Get on with it!" he grated.

The man, still on his knees, glared at him but crawled sideways and cuffed his colleague. Then Danny had him roll on to his front putting his hands behind him. He felt the tension in the man's body as he assessed whether to have a go at Danny who had to use both his hands to fasten the cuffs. Instead Danny slammed the metal skull crusher pommel on the knife against the back of his head and he slumped to the ground. Then he cuffed him.

He stood up and surveyed the scene. Two more dead and two prisoners. He took a waist belt off each man and secured their legs thoroughly. So far so good. He couldn't immediately find anything to gag the men with but sliced the laces on their boots, pulled them off and their socks as well.

Looking around he grabbed two of the cue balls and stuck one in the mouth of the man who was still unconscious and used two socks tied together to gag him.

The second man refused to open his mouth until Danny held the blade of his knife against his throat. Finally he opened it and Danny secured him in the same way as his colleague. Then he leaned forward, pulled the conscious man's head around and whispered

"If you make a sound, any sound at all, I'll come back down and finish you both off. Two more doesn't make any difference to me buddy. Understood?"

The man shuddered and nodded vigorously. Danny stared into his eyes for a moment before turning away. It was time for the next stage of the plan.

CHAPTER 69.

Upstairs the coffee had been served and while that was normally a time for people to relax, Rory felt a tangible notch up in the tension around the table. Watson finally pushed his chair back and spoke angrily to the General.

"Oh for Christ sake get on with it General! I'm sick and tired of sitting here playing games with this bastard. Come on, stop mucking around and let's give him a reality check."

Rory pushed his chair back and stood up. The General smiled at him.

"Standing up won't help you at this stage Hanlon. As my friend Cole says, let's give you a reality check. For starters, by now we have taken your mother from that nursing home, so any resistance on your part will be instrumental in her death. Also I should say that your friends will have quite a welcome when they break into our building this evening. We have a team waiting for them and I can tell you there won't be any arrests."

He slid his chair back a few paces and stamped his foot down strongly on the hardwood floor. Rory interpreted it as a signal, either to people in the nearby room or down below. Watson glared at him, hatred clearly visible in his gaze.

"You talk a good fight Hanlon. Let's see how clever you are when the odds aren't so favorable."

They all glanced at the doorway and Rory realized that this was where the danger was coming from. The General looked across with irritation at Bradley and stamped his foot even stronger on the floor. A look of relief flashed across his face as the door started to open, then alarm as a tall muscular man wearing a balaclava stepped into the room carrying a weapon and with a satchel slung around his shoulder.

Danny said distinctly to the shocked group.

"Did somebody call? Oh I'm sorry to disappoint you. You see they got tied up. Hard to get good help these days General, isn't it?"

Rory shook his head.

"Your timing is spot on Danny. They were just about to offer me dessert."

The General looked shocked.

"Quigley! It's that fucking Danny Quigley?" he burst out, tottering to his feet.

It was Watson who moved suddenly. Jumping up he threw his left arm around Rory's neck and shoved a steak knife that he'd taken from the table, against his throat.

"Drop that gun Quigley or your buddy gets his neck sliced!" he screamed

The General's jaw dropped.

"You, Watson? I'd never have believed it! Good man."

He started to move as if to come towards Danny.

Danny's voice cut through the rising babble of voices.

"Nobody move without my say so. Now sit down General while you still can."

He swung the Ingram around until the red dot was squarely on the forehead of Watson.

"One squeeze of this trigger my friend and you'll have drawn your last breath on this earth. Now put that knife down before I'm tempted."

Watson pulled Rory further back and tried to hide behind him, at the same time tightening his grip.

"Go ahead Quigley, do your macho stuff, but I'll take this bastard Hanlon with me," he hissed, his eyes venomous.

It was a stalemate, but not for Rory who had practiced hundreds of escapes from similar holds over the years. Admittedly it wasn't a practice and the stakes were high but the technique was always the same. He exploded into action clamping the back of the knife hand and the elbow with his two hands then ducked, bringing Watson crashing down on the wooden floor. As he landed Rory dropped straight down on the back of his neck with his knee, cracking it. The General and Bradley stared at the prostate figure.

"My God you killed him" he stuttered.

As Rory climbed back onto his feet Danny threw him the SOCOM pistol from the satchel and moved over behind the General.

"Yeah, he's dead alright General. Surprised at your reaction though. Could all those ribbons you wore in the desert in Iraq have been earned from behind a desk, with the occasional cautious trip into trouble spots?"

He pressed the Ingram against the back of his neck.

"Now General, tell me about the bomb. Whose idea was it and what were you going to do with it once it was delivered to you?"

The General shrank away from the feel of the weapon.

"I don't know what you're talking about Quigley" he blustered.

Danny sighed.

"I haven't time to hang around here."

He moved the red dot over onto Bradley's face and squeezed the trigger. The man and his chair crashed backwards. The General blanched and started trembling, raising his arms as if to ward off the next shot. Danny put the tip of the barrel against his neck.

"Three seconds, so start talking."

"Okay, all right. I'll tell you."

Those were the last words he spoke before his head exploded and debris splattered across the white tablecloth. At the same time the door behind Danny that led into the kitchen opened and the chauffeur from Rory's car jumped in pressing a revolver into Danny's back. Hearing the sounds of imminent action coming from inside the room, Danny had momentarily forgotten Dianna's warning about the chauffer.

Simultaneously the other door that Danny had entered by was thrown open and the barrels of two assault rifles were thrust through. A familiar voice came floating into the room.... Sinclair's.

"I believe it's checkmate Quigley. Put your weapon down and tell your friend to do the same."

There was a tense silence in the room. Finally Danny shrugged.

"Let's put our weapons down Rory. Sinclair has us dead to rights."

They both carefully reached forward and placed their weapons on the table. The chauffeur pushed Danny along the edge of the table until he was beside Rory and then stepped back a pace covering them both.

It was then that Sinclair stuck his head into the room, following a slim wiry individual built like a jockey. He appeared to have Indian blood reflected in his taut, bony face and handled the assault weapon as if he were used to it. Sinclair stepped fully into the room, solid and authoritative, and looking very pleased with himself.

"Well, well, cat got your tongue Quigley? Last time I saw you, you were chasing me out of the compound in Southampton. Now here you are, totally under my control. How life changes things. I owe you a lot my friend but I haven't the time nor the equipment here to make you suffer the way I intend to, for screwing up my career and my retirement plan with Empire Security. Too bad about the General and Bradley. Still we may resurrect the company again with less people to share profits with. You and your friend are coming with me for a short trip."

He turned and whispered to the short wiry man beside him who dashed off out of sight. They all stood there and waited. Within five minutes he was back with one of the men Danny had left tied up in the basement. When he saw Danny he rushed across and slammed his fist into his face, knocking him to the ground where he proceeded to kick him.

"Bastard killed my buddies" he gasped as he continued kicking. "The one he knocked on the head died too, right in front of me."

Rory was measuring if the intrusion offered any chance to fight back but he had three weapons aimed at him. Sinclair chuckled at the sight.

"That's enough for the moment Karl. You'll have another opportunity to work on him and his pal shortly. Back off for now."

Karl gave Danny another savage kick to the stomach leaving him lying there. Rory leaned forward and tried to help him to his feet but it took all his strength before he managed to lift him up. Danny moaned and sagged forward on the table.

"Something hurts inside.... broken rib I think.... oh shit.... the pain!"

He clutched at the table heaving as he partially threw up on it.

Sinclair looked disgusted.

"Don't like it when it's coming back at you Quigley do you? This is just the warm up you bastard! Now let's get out of here. We'll take two cars. The one I just arrived in and one from the carport. Put Quigley and his mate in the trunk of each to avoid them trying any of their little combat stuff on us, though Quigley is out of playing any of his little games for sure."

He pointed to the chauffeur.

"Take that satchel off Quigley and gather up those weapons. Let's go!"

Rory caught hold of Danny and put his arm around him to help him as he hobbled around the table and out through the door. He got a shock when he did so because he felt the outline of a weapon tucked down the back of Danny's track suit and covered by his sweater. He couldn't believe that no one had searched Danny for a second weapon after he'd put the Ingram down on the table. That was really slip-shod, but he wondered if he would have a chance to use it, with three men covering them.

It looked like Danny was out of it with some sort of internal injury. It was now up to him.

They all stepped into the carport and the wiry one bent and stared at the tire. He straightened up, spat on the ground and looked at Sinclair.

"Tires are shredded boss. The ones on the road are probably done too."

Sinclair's eyes darted back and forth. Finally he pointed to Karl.

"Finish them off right here."

Rory tensed, ready to fight for his life, though he knew it was pretty futile. As Karl raised the assault rifle, almost magically, he developed a second nostril, delivered by a very efficient sniper rifle from across the road.

Rory hurled himself at the chauffeur as he started to raise his pistol and they both crashed to the ground. Danny jumped sideways grabbing the assault rifle in the hands of the short wiry Indian. He hadn't been as hurt as he'd made out, but he was shocked by the incredible strength of the small man as they crashed back against the carport. The man tried to club him with the stock of the rifle and Danny blocked it with his elbow, kicking out at one of his knees. He heard the man grunt and tried for a leg sweep which the man blocked and lashed back at him with a boot. Rory was struggling with the chauffeur in the far corner and Danny became aware that Sinclair was running to the car.

He was about to escape again.

He increased his leverage against the small man spinning him and the rifle until he was standing behind him. He snapped the rifle across the front of his throat and using it like a stranglehold, dropped straight down, hearing the neck break.

Sinclair's car had backed up onto the street and was starting to take off.

Danny grabbed the MI rifle with grenade launcher and, ignoring Rory struggling in the corner, raced back out the driveway to the road. Sinclair's car was thirty feet away when he got there. He lifted the weapon, braced himself and sighted carefully. Then he squeezed the trigger of the grenade launcher.For a moment he thought he'd missed but the car exploded and was lifted into the air, crashing sideways into the brick wall of the garden next door.

Danny turned and ran back up the driveway in time to meet Rory staggering out. The chauffeur was lying still on the ground. He snatched up the satchel with the weapons stowed in it, and the gear he'd placed under the car earlier. He shouted to Rory.

"Go straight over the wall there. Dianna has the van. Tell her to meet me at the park gate. Go for Christ sake!" He shoved the satchel and weapons into his hands.

Rory looked uncertainly at him for a second, then turned and started running. Danny was on his heels but veered left towards the burning car. He wanted to make sure that Sinclair was dead.

Dashing up towards the car he spotted a couple emerging from the bungalow next door and gaping at the burning vehicle. Danny came as close as he could with the heat but he could clearly see a body inside with the head jerking, the mouth open and screaming. He pulled the Judge Taurus out and fired two quick shots into the figure, watching him slump back with the impact.

Sinclair was dead.

CHAPTER 70.

Danny kept running down the road, and on reaching the park gate found the van emerging. Thankfully it was out of sight of the couple at the bungalow and he hoped no one else had seen him. He even lifted the barrier back up on the park gate before jumping in. The van sped off.

Dianna's concerned face looked back at him in the mirror as she reversed the route out onto the highway, making sure to head south on route 190.

"That was too close Danny. God I thought I'd lost both of you when you came out with all those guns trained on you!"

He thumped her shoulder.

"Your shot was beautiful and the timing perfect. Now the cell phone" he demanded.

Rory tossed it back and he hit the pre-programmed number for Zeitner.

His voice answered.

"Yeah, Zeitner."

"Quigley here. Sinclair is dead. Sorry about that but I used the judge on him if that's any consolation. Your two goons informed Empire Security that we were coming. I think they have some other agenda to put you down. Better start covering your ass 'cos someone is out to get you. We're off. Cheers."

He fired the cell phone back to Rory.

"Check the nursing home and see if anything's happened."

Rory fumbled around for a few minutes as he got the number out and got a torch to key it in. He spoke for a couple of minutes before switching off, then looked across at both of them.

"You're not going to believe this. After my call earlier the nursing home director got very worried and called the cops. Two police cars responded and waited round the back. Guess what? A private ambulance rolled up with a doctor, one female nurse and two male nurses. The cop cars swung immediately into action and blocked them off. The two male nurses made a run for it and they were obviously armed because there was a shoot out in the grounds. One's dead and the other wounded. The doctor, so called, is in custody and the female nurse is apparently singing like a canary. Thanks for warning me Danny. When they sprang it on me inside I felt my heart melt. I wondered if they'd actually managed to kidnap her."

Dianna's face looked concerned.

"Rory, quick, call the farm."

She rattled off the number. In a moment he was speaking to someone and after a few minutes he switched it off.

"Guess what? Tim the cop went round to baby-sit and some people came to the door. He'd been watching the front, expecting trouble and spotted that they were carrying weapons. He fired straight through the door and heard someone scream. Next thing he heard the car take off and when he opened the door the steps were splashed with blood. So there's an APB out and the hospitals are being checked."

Dianna was shaking her head.

"What an evening! God, when I saw the car pull up and those men go inside I thought you were both goners. I had the sniper rifle set up to take as many as I could when they came back out."

"One hell of a shot!" Danny commented. "Now what are your plans, both of you?"

Dianna answered.

"We shoot through 190 South onto 90 West and get off at Eden, then go over to 62 South just to get off the highway. I don't think a full blocking alarm will go out in time to snare us. The cops will have their work cut out trying to get a handle on this one. You were probably seen finishing off Sinclair but I doubt that the van was spotted. I'm going to take it to the farm, re-spray it and keep it. What about you Danny?"

He'd been thinking about that.

"Okay drop me on the road by the marina. You'll save time not driving in there. I'll take the weapons with me and dump them overboard in the river, then dash in and take off on the boat, and Bob's your uncle. I'm off up to Pearson Airport and away."

She glanced at him in the mirror.

"That sniper rifle is a sweet weapon Danny. Hate to just get rid of it like that....... difficult to replace it. Can I not take it back to the farm with me?" she asked.

"No discussion here Dianna. I take it with me. All you need is one State Trooper who decides to search you and it's curtains."

"Guess you're right. However, I'm not sure about you Danny. You've got that gleam in your eye that I don't trust."

He grinned, saying nothing.

Outside the marina he jumped out and reached back for the bundle of wrapped weapons and the satchel. He then slipped around to Dianna's door. She wound the window down and looked at him.

"Will I see you again Danny?" she asked, her eyes softening.

"Count on it." He gave her a brief kiss.

She held his arm.

"If I ever need you, will you come? We have trouble that's building up over here in this country. It's going to come to a head soon Danny."

He gazed directly into her beseeching eyes.

"You only have to call" he said.

He reached across and grabbed Rory's hand.

"Thanks old friend. I'll be in touch." Then he disappeared into the marina.

Within ten minutes he had cast off and with the motor purring quietly, made his way around the horseshoe structure of the man-made harbor. Once out in the open water he swung back against the current and headed upstream parallel to the 190 highway on his left. He spotted the building within five minutes. The Empire Security building.

Danny suspected that a team of heavily armed men were crouched inside waiting for a break-in that wasn't going to happen. Something else was going to happen though.

He slowed the motor down and tied the steering wheel loosely with a piece of rope. Then he lifted the RPG rocket launcher up to his shoulder with the grenade already inserted and straightened the tail fin. He took aim at the building and squeezed the trigger. Nothing happened. Placing the second grenade in, he took careful aim and fired again. In what seemed like seconds, the center of the building exploded and collapsed downwards dragging the whole structure with it. The rocket had hit something inside the building, perhaps ammunition or a gas outlet. With one last lingering look at the building now in flames, he released the wheel, turned up the speed and swung towards the far shore at Fort Erie.

Halfway across in the stronger current, he threw the satchel, the bundle of weapons and the rocket launcher over the side, and lastly the Judge Taurus. The strong tide required his full attention then as he focused on coming ashore on the Canadian side, where he had parked his rental. The trip was uneventful and he tied up within ten minutes.

He spent a few minutes wiping off areas that he and the others might have touched just in case an investigation led to the craft. The deposit he'd paid caused him some concern. A normal fisherman would make a point of going back to the owner's house and collecting it. He scribbled a brief note saying he was running late for his flight from Hamilton airport and to keep the down payment towards the education of that clever young son that he had mentioned to him.

Danny was flying out of Pearson Airport near Toronto, not Hamilton Airport, but he was trying to lay a false trail just in case. An hour and a half later he turned in the rental car. He then had to make a decision. Did he book a flight in the name of Brad Kincaid or Danny Quigley?

If the CIA agent Zeitner dropped the dime on him, he knew both his names. He'd flown in under the Kincaid name and had filled in a landing card under that name. The name Danny Quigley might create some attention as well. He wouldn't know until it was too late, waiting to board or sitting in his seat. Perhaps nothing might happen until he landed at the other side.

He gritted his teeth and decided to go with the Kincaid name.

He got a flight out within forty minutes and was rushed through immigration and security. He landed in Amsterdam in the Netherlands eight hours later and in a new time zone six hours ahead. Then he had to wait for four hours before he could catch a connection to Tel Aviv.

Meanwhile he called Rebecca in London. She woke up irritated.

"Yes, I know it's nearly morning but this better be good!" she said stiffly.

"What, had a late night Rebecca? Danny here, just checking in" he said lightly.

He could hear the alertness come back into her voice.

"Danny, is everything okay?" Her voice was anxious.

"Yeah, just wanted you to know that I took care of that little job."

"I watch CNN Danny. Some little job" she said dryly.

"Oh good. Now two things. It looks like McAllister's been in the CIA's pocket for quite a long time. I think Brett Zeitner of the CIA runs him. He knew the whole thing about our op in the U.K. Stuff only McAllister could know. Check him out - you know, his bank accounts, the usual stuff. It could be something else though apart from money."

"Shit! McAllister! Are you sure Danny?"

"Looks that way.... over to you. Is Scotty still okay?" he enquired.

"Still fine. He's under close guard but he can't spend the rest of his life like this Danny."

"That's my second point. I'm off to Israel to talk to the Mossad. I want that contract cancelled Rebecca."

She gasped.

"For Pete's sake Danny, they'll have your balls for book ends! They play rough my friend! What do you want from me? I gather that's why you called."

"I want some insurance in case they're tempted to make me disappear. If I tell them that you are involved and fully informed and incidentally highly pissed off that an assassination team is operating in the U.K., will that be okay?"

"Will that be okay?" she mimicked. "Danny if this becomes public knowledge that I'm involved in blackmailing the Israelis, the Home Secretary will hang me out to dry, not to mention MI6 for meddling in areas I'm not authorized to and that will bring in the Foreign Secretary for crying out loud! Danny you're asking for my very soul here."

Danny chuckled.

"I knew I could count on you Rebecca. Bye!"

He hung up.

Next stop Tel Aviv.

CHAPTER 71.

Danny was pretty wrecked when he finally landed in Tel Aviv. The trip and the landing were uneventful and his new passport raised no eyebrows. With only his carry-on pack he was out in the blasting heat within half an hour of landing and was relieved to get a taxi right away. Relieved too to settle back in the air-conditioned interior. The driver, a chunky, dark skinned middle-aged man, shot him a look over his shoulder.

"Where to?" he asked briskly.

"The Hadar Dafna building on King Saul Boulevard" he answered.

The man's eyes opened wide and he looked closely at him. The fact that this was the HQ of Mossad was open knowledge in the city, though the building housed other businesses as well. It was a sure-fire way to kill a conversation, and the rest of the journey was carried out in silence, which suited Danny.

The building turned out to be a gray, multi storied concrete structure which, from his observation was quite a common design in the city. When he alighted from the taxi and walked towards it he was surprised to find no guards outside. Once he'd gone inside he was confronted by two armed security personnel who asked him his business, briefly frisked him and checked his pack. Their main concern seemed to be making sure that he wasn't wearing an explosive vest. He looked around the main lobby, uncertain where to go next. He stopped a young man going past, towards the door he'd just come in.

"I'm looking for the Mossad office" he said tentatively, aware that his request sounded strange even to his own ears.

The reaction in the young man was to smile easily and point across the lobby.

"Yes, they don't publicize themselves very well do they? It's that door with the security sign on it."

Danny was expecting something much more impressive for Mossad headquarters. He muttered his thanks, went over to the door and knocked on it. Not receiving any reply he opened the door partly and stuck his head in. A woman was walking towards him, obviously hurrying to respond to his knock. She was young and slim with shiny black hair pulled up in a bun on top of her head. She looked almost exactly how he envisaged a young Israeli woman would look. Her brown eyes examined him closely and dropped to the pack he was carrying.

"Sorry I took so long answering the door. I was in the next office. How can I help you?" she asked.

Danny had stepped in and closed the door behind him.

"I need to talk to someone who can arrange a meeting with the head of Mossad, preferably today" he replied, realizing how innocuous his request sounded.

Her eyes widened slightly and at the same time a small smile played around her lips. He wondered whether they had many kooks coming in asking to join Mossad and become a spy.

"You want to talk to the head of Mossad? May I ask what your business is… ah Mr…. ?"

"My name is Danny Quigley and look, I know how weird this sounds. I appreciate your top man isn't sitting up there hoping some dizzy Brit will wander in here wanting to talk to him. Israel is at war and I appreciate that he's a busy man. I just flew in from Canada via Amsterdam, with some vital information that will benefit the State of Israel and I believe he will talk to me. Can you please start the process for me to meet with him Miss?"

Her demeanor changed and she hesitated, observing him closely. Without another word she went and picked up a sheet of paper from a nearby desk and came back to him.

"Will you spell your name for me please?" she asked.

"Danny Q-U-I-G-L-E-Y."

"Fine Mr. Quigley. Now if you'll follow me back here, we have a small interview room where you can wait. I'll get someone higher up to talk to you."

She didn't say for him not to build up his hopes about meeting with the Mossad head, but he could read the sceptical look on her face as she went out of the room.

It was over an hour before the door opened again. This time it was a tough fortyish man who abruptly strode in, pulled a chair back and sat down, regarding him. Being ex-military Danny could tell he was dealing with a soldier and someone who'd been in action. He had a white gash running down his neck and his left arm hung at his side as if he had limited use of it.

"Tell me why you're here" the man asked briskly.

"Okay, I didn't think this was going to be easy, coming in here and asking to see the head of Mossad. I don't know if you have weirdos here in Israel like they do in London, who come in regularly wanting to become spies like James Bond and save the world. Quite simply I have information that, as I mentioned to the girl outside, will be beneficial to the Israeli Government and particularly the Mossad."

"Tell me what the information is?" the Israeli asked impatiently.

Danny sighed.

"I can't do that I'm afraid. It's highly confidential stuff and with all due respect to yourself, should be told directly to your boss."

"Not good enough Quigley I'm afraid. You won't get to see him on the basis of some vague hint that you have information that will benefit the State of Israel. Credit me with some intelligence. I need to hear more at this stage or you're out of here."

Danny hesitated, trying to formulate his thoughts.

The man cut in again.

"Look, I wouldn't even be seeing you if we hadn't run a check on you and discovered that our Special Forces have been using your Afghan experience for their escape and evasion training, so I know you're the real deal Quigley and not some kook as you say. On that basis they cut through the red tape and came straight up to myself because I work directly for the man. However I need to know more and right now" he concluded, impatience creeping into his voice.

Danny studied him for a long moment. The silence built up in the room.

"Okay, all I'm prepared to say is that it's about a bomb."

"A bomb!' The Israeli looked perplexed.

"Yes. A missing Israeli bomb."

"Missing from where? What kind of bomb?" he demanded, sitting forward, his face inches from Danny's.

Danny let the silence build up again.

"Nuclear!" he said quietly.

The Israeli leaned back and stared at him, shock clearly reflected on his face.

Danny's eyes narrowed.

"You knew nothing about this, I can see."

The man stood up and looked down at Danny.

"Good God, if this is true..." he exclaimed.

"Believe me it's true, and I just happen to know where it is."

The man stood there shaking his head.

"If I didn't know your record Quigley, I'd be chasing your ass right out of here and on to the first flight. As it is, I have no option but to take this further. My boss is not here right now but I could haul him out of an important meeting with the Prime Minister and his staff and have him here within three hours. I'd suggest you head back into the city, we'll get you a taxi, and come back here later."

Their meeting ended.

CHAPTER 72.

Danny spent the next three hours wandering around downtown Tel Aviv. He stopped to have the first decent meal he'd had in four days and longed for a shower. He was impressed but not surprised at the level of security in the streets and entrances to bars and restaurants. He felt sorry for the numerous Arabs who were being stopped and searched, but he also appreciated that it was this vigilance that was preventing more slaughter of civilians. The Mossad organization, he knew wouldn't let him wander off into the city without surveillance, especially after the message he'd just left with them. It was there but despite trying to spot it, he couldn't. The Israelis were the best in the world at it.

He was surprised at how much he enjoyed his wander round the shops and all too soon he was being dropped by a taxi at the Mossad headquarters again. Inside the door he was met by the same Israeli, who this time introduced himself.

"Caleb Kishlon. The old man was willing to meet with you. Eager in fact, so something is going down that, as you suspected, I haven't been told about. He's on the eleventh floor and I suggest you just call him Kemuel. He wants me to sit in with him on this Quigley."

Nothing more was said until they got off the elevator, turned right down a corridor and stopped at a solid-looking office door. They stepped inside.

The office had a monastic look to it with sparse solid furniture, four straight-backed chairs, and a counter with a coffee maker.

There wasn't a computer in sight.

Immediately a tall, slim individual in his mid 60s stood up and came towards them. He had a lean bony head that was completely bald and a pair of startling blue eyes that now regarded him with interest.

"Danny Quigley I believe. I've heard about you prior to today, but never expected to have the pleasure of meeting with you. What you did in Afghanistan was utterly unbelievable! You would make a real Israeli warrior, the way you fight.... attack.... attack. That's what I like. If only the modern Israeli army had the same spirit. Look how poorly they did in Lebanon last time. Now let's sit down. I believe you have some information for me. I have had to apologize to Caleb for keeping him in the dark, but mainly because all I had was rumors and I'm not a believer in spreading rumors. However, I have been connecting the dots and your timely approach this morning has started bells ringing. So to business. What have you got for us?"

Danny sat down and the two men did the same.

He had been rehearsing his approach during his flights but now became acutely aware of his situation, sitting in front of the head of Mossad and preparing to make demands on them. An organization that could make him disappear forever with a nod or a phone call.

He took a deep breath.

"Okay Kemeul, while I'm pro Israel and all that you guys stand for, I'm here to negotiate a deal with you. I'm not giving you information out of the goodness of my heart. I want that understood from the start."

Kemeul's eyes narrowed to slits.

"You want money?" he asked harshly.

Danny waved dismissively.

"Absolutely not."

"What then?" Caleb interjected.

"One of your Katsas as you call them, Reuben Wyborski by name, was killed in the U.K. recently. The shot was fired by a friend of mine Scotty McGregor using a weapon that belonged to someone called Nicholson. You've placed an assassination team, a Kidon over there with an order to kill McGregor. I want that order rescinded."

The Mossad head jerked back as if struck in the face.

"Who says we have an assassination team in the U.K.? We have an agreement not to operate in any of the base countries. That would put our present relationships with the U.K. authorities at risk Quigley."

Danny leaned forward.

"Nicholson went to the papers and talked pretty openly. You guys picked him up and of course he talked and fingered Scotty. I'm saying that you have had your revenge. It was Nicholson who threw the weapon across to him and he saved my life by shooting Wyborski."

Caleb looked at his boss.

"Is this true? Why wasn't I told about this? A kidon team in the U.K.?"

The Mossad head looked angry.

"That's all speculation on Quigley's part. Anyway what if he is right? We always chase down the killers of our people, no matter how long it takes."

Danny chuckled.

"I wonder if you sent the request for the assassination to your Prime Minister as you're supposed to, and who then no doubt referred it to the special judicial committee who would then try my friend Scotty in abstensia and give the go-ahead for the assassination?"

Caleb saw the shock on his boss's face.

"Shit Kemuel, you actually did this didn't you? Without proper authorization! Good God!"

The Mossad boss avoided his gaze and appraised Danny.

"Who else knows about this? Your ass is pretty exposed here right now!"

Danny yawned. He pointed to the phone.

"Call Rebecca Fullerton-Smythe at MI5 and ask her. I'm not so stupid that I'd walk into the lions den without some backing"

The man's face paled.

"She knows about this? How come we haven't heard even a whisper? I talk to her all the time" he exclaimed in astonishment.

Caleb looked at Danny's face and back to his boss.

"He might be bluffing you know. Call her."

Kemuel reached for the phone muttering.

"He's not bluffing."

For the next ten minutes Danny and Caleb sat there as an unseen lady tore strips off the head of Mossad. All they could hear was his side of the conversation which was short disclaimers, followed by profuse apologies. Finally he hung up and sat there wiping his brow.

He looked disparagingly at Caleb.

"Bluffing was he? In your fucking dreams! Now that is one pissed off lady I can tell you. She even said that if we didn't pull out our assassination team she would send Quigley after them and that would end in only one way. Even more embarrassment for Israel."

He turned to Danny.

"Okay, I'm willing to deal. I'll call off the hit team but I want the location of that fucking bomb before it explodes on the Government. First tell me what you know Quigley."

"I haven't got the whole story but what I know is this. Somehow the CIA station head in London, a man called Sinclair, got together with your chap Wyborski and obviously some other contacts here in Israel, and decided to build or steal a nuclear bomb and transport it to Iraq. Sinclair, posing as a U.K. Government official tricked the SAS into doing the transport of the bomb from Kuwait into Iraq. There it would be discovered and take the U.S. Government off the hook on weapons of mass destruction. It was a black operation all the way. Obama's people knew nothing about it. Rumor has it that Saddam Hussein's daughters were going to bring charges against certain members of the Bush administration in the international criminal court for murder of her family and a host of other charges. An illegal war for starters. Blair's testimony in London and his book, showed that the invasion was totally without any legality. So to pre-empt this, a black operation was put together to slip a nuclear weapon into Iraq, which would be discovered and diffuse the charges before the final withdrawal of U.S. Forces. That would be good for Israel too, with the problem of Iran looming, but not if it was discovered that the bomb was made in Israel and transported down there by CIA civilian aircraft. It was supposed to be delivered to a General O'Donnell and a Tom Bradley from a U.S. security firm. The bomb never arrived."

The Mossad man nodded.

"You have pretty well put it together. We got wind of it when one of the scientists involved at our nuclear facility failed a regular lie detector test. We checked his financial background and discovered that one hundred thousand dollars was deposited in a bank account in the Isle of Man recently. There were another eight people involved as well."

"But how could they make a bomb that wouldn't have the Israeli imprint on it?" Caleb interjected, "and why wasn't I informed? I'm your 2IC for God's sake!" he demanded.

The Mossad man looked at the floor.

"They designed the outside material of the bomb from some of those unexploded Iranian rockets that Hamas keep firing into Israel. The plan was to blame it on the Iranians. Perhaps it would have provided the new team in the White House with the excuse to hit the Iranian nuclear facility. Who knows."

He glanced at Caleb.

"Sorry Caleb, I wanted you to be able to completely deny that we had any involvement in this, which we didn't officially, if it wasn't for Wyborski's stupidity. I'm actually glad he is dead, so you can take it from me that the Kidon will be pulled out of the U.K. Now those two people you mentioned, O'Donnell and Bradley. What about them Quigley?"

"Dead, two days ago in Buffalo."

Caleb's eyes widened.

"You killed them?"

"Mmm… plus a few others that got in the way. Oh, there was a Colonel Minter in Kuwait who made the transfer of the bomb from the CIA aircraft to the SAS team. I've no idea where he is."

Both men were staring at him as if he had suddenly become a pariah. Finally the Mossad man stirred.

"So where is the bomb right now?" he asked quietly.

He told them.

They both made some notes.

Danny stood up, knowing their business was finished.

"We have a deal then? Scotty McGregor can come out of hiding?"

The Mossad man stood up and shook his hand.

"Yes we have a deal, on one condition, you come with us to recover the bomb. It's still a dangerous place, Iraq, and you have a reputation that would reassure me if you came along with us. Caleb will head up the mission. Good luck."

CHAPTER 73.

It was ten days later that Danny flew back into Heathrow Airport in London. He hadn't called anyone that he was arriving but a man in a chauffeur's uniform held a sign up with the name Quigley written in large print. He eased over to the side and then recognized that it was Rebecca's driver, the same man who had collected him when he flew in from Ireland for the start of the mission.

He followed him out of the airport and saw her car twenty yards down the road. Jumping in he was surprised to be enveloped in a long hug by Rebecca.

The car moved out from the curb.

"Danny Quigley as I live and breathe, back from the desert of Iraq and brown as a piece of leather. You scared the shit out of me when I heard you were going out there with the Israelis. Don't ever do that to me again" she said hoarsely.

"Rebecca, I didn't know you cared," pleased despite himself at her greeting. "Now tell me about the situation here. You know, Scotty and the McAllister development?" he asked impatiently.

She lifted her hands off her lap as if marshalling her thoughts.

"Okay, Scotty first. He's out of the security quarantine and back downtown in Hereford bothering the barmaids. We think we spotted part of the Israeli assassination team leaving the country, so we've marked them for future attention. McAllister isn't a happy ending I'm afraid. We got a search warrant for his residence and grabbed his computer which had all sorts of compromising material" she hesitated, then went on, "including loads of filthy child porn."

"Ah, so that's the hook." Danny guessed. "Somehow I wouldn't have suspected Jack of kiddie porn. I guess you never can tell."

"Zeitner must have caught on to his perversion and used it to get him on side."

Danny looked puzzled.

"So where's the problem?" he asked impatiently.

"McAllister threatened to go to the media and drop us all in it regarding MI5 authorizing a team to kill a bunch of civilians in Southampton and disposing of them. He wanted full pension benefits, plus an honorable discharge from MI5. He's got a position lined up with Zeitner in the U.S."

"Hell, this is blackmail Rebecca! What's to stop him coming back for more goodies in the future?"

She smiled sweetly.

"I used your name Danny. It seems he has an enormous respect for your ability to make people disappear. I told him if he ever raised his head in this country again or started shooting his mouth off, I'd send you after him, despite any stories he might try to circulate to the media."

"Oh thanks a bunch for that. Remind me to pass on my public relations portfolio to you. I'm sure it would really do things for my business, which I must definitely get back to. Anything else before you drop me?"

She pursed her lips thoughtfully.

"Let's see. A Colonel Minter disappeared from a U.S. base in Heidelberg. No signs of him since."

"The Israelis! God, that was fast!" he breathed.

"Probably. There's been no connection to you coming out of Buffalo. Pretty shitty investigation when you think about it. They tied the attacks in Britain and the U.S. together as being some terrorist initiative to scare off civilian security firms from working in Iraq and Afghanistan. The Southampton police have made no progress with the disappearance of those security personnel but the Israelis have stopped harassing them about finding the killer of their man Wyborski. That's about it really."

She tapped her forehead.

"I nearly forgot. I contacted your ex-wife and did some PR on your behalf. I took the blame for the screw-up that day with your daughter. She said to tell you that you can recommence your weekend visitation rights as soon as you get back."

"Wow, that's fantastic Rebecca. Thanks a lot!" he said, a huge grin on his face.

"Oh, and there's more. Your friend Jacky said she'd be home this evening, when I called her and told her you were coming back today. She sounded really excited Danny."

He grabbed her and gave her a massive hug. The driver's eyebrows shot up and the car wobbled for a few yards. Then Danny sat back and scrutinized her face.

"Any word of Jamila?" he asked.

"You and your flipping women Danny! You'll soon need a PA just to keep track of them. Okay I was wondering whether I should mention it or not."

"Mention what?"

"She returned to Afghanistan last week.... permanently as I understand it."

"Oh shit!' he exclaimed "I've screwed up her dream of becoming a doctor. Son of a bitch!"

He slammed his fist into his palm.

She reached over and caught his forearm.

"She has two years medical training behind her Danny, thanks to you, and that will be of tremendous help to her people. Who knows, she may come back and complete the rest of the training at a later date. Don't take on the burdens of the world my friend. It's tough enough just sorting out the ones that come at us personally."

She hesitated, looking across at him speculatively.

He swiveled round.

"What? What aren't you telling me Rebecca?"

She sighed, looking down pensively.

"You left your mobile phone with that journalist Jacky, when you left for Canada."

"Yes, yes, go on. What's happened for God's sake?"

"A text message came in on it yesterday. All it said was 'Help me. Indians' and the name on it was C.C."

He felt the breath go out of him.

"He's alive! Courtney is alive!"

THE END.

379

16805429R00204

Made in the USA
Charleston, SC
11 January 2013